HOOK ME UP

THE LOVE ONLINE TRILOGY BOOK ONE

TIFFANY SNOW

The characters and events portrayed in this book are fictitious. Any similarity to real persons, living or dead, is coincidental and not intended by the author.

Published by Tiffany Snow, LLC
ISBN 978-0-9853742-6-6
www.tiffany-snow.com

Cover design by Letitia Hasser of RBA Designs: Romantic Book Affairs
Printed in the United States of America.

ALSO BY TIFFANY SNOW

acknowledgments

A HUGE THANK YOU to Tara Hathaway, for reading (twice) and providing invaluable feedback that made this manuscript better. You've been a faithful reader of mine for a decade and I appreciate you so much.

Thank you to my sweet daughter, Erica, who still believes in me even when I don't.

And lastly, thank you to my readers who follow me and my work, even when there's been a large gap as I've gone through personal trauma over the past few years. I hope you enjoy this start to a new series.

For Roman

chapter one

TWENTY DOLLARS FOR a salad? It's lettuce, for crying out loud. And it's an additional five dollars to add chicken?" I glanced up from my menu. "Why can't we go to our usual place?"

"Because our usual place got closed for health violations." Bridget's matter-of-fact reminder made me sigh.

"Besides," Carly added, taking a sip of her wine, "we're a little above burgers and tater tots, don't you think?"

"I like tater tots," I groused, looking over the menu again.

"Yeah, well, my ass doesn't," Carly shot back.

"Exactly," Bridget added. "Welcome to your thirties, ladies."

Bridget and Carly were my best friends. We'd all met at Purdue and been in the same sorority. Though all three of us were in different fields—Carly was in marketing, Bridget was an engineer, and I was a lawyer—we'd bonded over too much tequila, holding each other's hair, exes, and the growing pains of adulting. We'd all settled in Indianapolis and met at least once a week for lunch, no matter how busy we were.

"They say the thirties are the new twenties," Carly insisted. "And the forties are the new thirties." Endless optimism immediately countered by Bridget.

"Which is just a way to fool you into thinking you're *not* getting old."

"Well, aren't you two just a pocket full of sunshine," I interjected. I'd get the overpriced salad—with the chicken—because the scale had inched up three pounds in the past month. A chardonnay habit and a fondness for tater tots did that to a girl.

The waiter came by and we ordered—all of us getting low-cal options, I noted. Yes, my twenties were officially over. Well, they'd officially been over two years ago, but why rush things? Every girl was allowed to turn twenty-nine twice—okay, maybe three times.

"So let's discuss the next social event hanging over our heads," Bridget said. "Clarice's wedding."

Carly and I let out a collective groan. Clarice was a good friend of ours who worked in a big law firm here in town as secretary to a very powerful attorney—someone I definitely would never want to go up against.

"The wedding's in a month," Bridget said, ignoring them. "What are you two going to do about dates?"

"Says the woman with a steady boyfriend," Carly groused.

"Green isn't your color," Bridget said mildly.

"There's no law that says you have to bring a date to a wedding," I said. "Carly and I will just go together. Maybe there'll be a single groomsman or two."

"Emmy, how long has it been since your last date?

Or better yet, the last time you slept with someone?" Bridget's blunt question wasn't out of character. She wasn't a beat-around-the-bush kind of person.

"I had a date a few weeks ago," I protested. "I tried that app you told me about. You know, the one where the woman has to message first? Met a guy and we had a cocktail." I took a sip of my wine, fruitlessly hoping Bridget would let it go at that.

"And?"

I sighed. "He was a retired grain farmer from Iowa," I mumbled, toying with my silverware so I wouldn't have to meet my friends' gazes. "Boring as hell."

Carly made sympathetic noises.

"Why would you go out with a retired farmer?" Bridget asked, exasperated. "You're thirty-two, not sixty-two!"

I shrugged. "He seemed nice online. Respectful and, you know, kind of manly."

"Sweetheart, if you spend the rest of your life trying to find a duplicate of Chad, you'll end up alone."

Bridget's reference to my dead husband made me wince. Even after six years, it was still hard to talk about him.

"Bridget!" Carly's sharp rebuke cut through the air.

"What? It's true," Bridget said. "I'm just saying what you're thinking. Both of us want her to be happy."

"Yeah, but you have the subtlety of a sledgehammer."

"Well, excuse me—"

"Stop," I interrupted. "It's okay. Bridget's right." And so was Carly, but I thought that would be better left unsaid. "Yeah, I don't want to be alone. But dating…finding someone…starting all over again. Just the thought of it exhausts me." And considering the few men I'd met over the years, the dating pool was shallow, indeed.

"What about sex?" Bridget persisted. "Did you sleep with the farmer?"

"Of course not!" There hadn't been a thing about him that I'd found attractive once we'd met in person. A receding hairline, a voice that droned on and on, and a lack of conversational skills about anything not pertaining to himself all combined to be a distinct turnoff.

"You say that like I'm asking if you drowned a kitten." Bridget rolled my eyes. "A casual hookup may be just what you need."

I was already shaking my head. "No. No way. Random sex with a guy I've just met isn't my thing."

"How do you know unless you've tried?"

"Because it's too intimate. Getting naked and vulnerable with someone whose last name you don't even know…" It was beyond my way of thinking about sex. I'd been a virgin when Chad and I had met in high school. He was the only man I'd ever been with. To hook up with some man for a one-night stand seemed to…cheapen it.

The waitress came by and dropped off our salads.

"Bridget has a point," Carly said, carefully poking the lettuce leaves with her fork and avoiding looking at us.

"No," Bridget gasped, my eyes widening. "You? Seriously? When did this happen?"

Carly's cheeks reddened, but she answered. "It was a couple of weeks ago. It was a Friday night and, as usual, I was home alone. Sooooo…I got on Tinder and started swiping." Finally, she glanced up. "His name is Troy, he works construction and…" she grinned. "And he's twenty-four."

"Holy shit!" Bridget crowed. "Look at you, robbing the cradle."

I was fascinated. I'd heard Tinder was just a hookup site but had never known anyone who'd actually done it. Leaning forward, I asked, "So? How was it?"

"Let's just say I was walking funny the next day, and I didn't mind a bit." Carly's eyes twinkled with mischief.

"Have you heard from him since?"

She shook her head. "No, and I don't really want to. We didn't have anything in common except wanting to have sex. In that department, we turned out to be a good match. A *really* good match." Her grin would've put the Cheshire to shame.

"See?" Bridget said, turning back to me. "It doesn't have to be romance and flowers and your soulmate. It could just be a good time on a Saturday night. Like scratching an itch."

My brows rose. "You're likening casual sex with scratching an itch?"

"Everybody needs sex," Carly said. "So long as you feel comfortable and are safe, it can definitely help your self-esteem and health. Endorphins are good for your mental well-being."

"It sounds like you're doing some rationalizing," I said, my tone wry.

"And it sounds like you're doing some judging," Carly shot back.

No one spoke for a moment, all of us concentrating very hard on our salads, the silence awkward.

"I'm sorry," I said at last. "You trusted me to tell me and yes, I was being a bit judgy." I hadn't realized—not really. I'd just been so surprised. "If you had a good time, then I'm glad for you."

Carly grinned, her brown eyes twinkling again. She never could hold a grudge, thank goodness. It just wasn't in her. "No worries. I know I probably shocked you."

"I'm just saying, maybe that would be a way to get back in the dating waters," Bridget said. "Rather than dipping a toe, just jump in. You've been taking it slow for years and look how that's turned out."

"Even if I do 'jump in,' as you call it, it's not going to give me a date to the wedding."

"You never know," Carly said. "Troy mentioned going out to dinner or something, but I turned him down."

"Even if you don't have anything in common, a friend with benefits is useful," Bridget said. "Why turn him down?"

"Because a one-night stand is *not* how to begin a relationship," Carly said, fully confident. "It's doomed to failure. If you meet someone you actually like, *that's* when you hold off on sleeping with them." She shrugged. "Everybody knows that."

I shook my head. "There's too many rules. I've been out of the game too long. I deleted that app anyway."

"Don't worry. There's about a dozen others you can try. I'll text them to you."

Carly whipped out her phone and I stifled a sigh. It's not that I didn't appreciate my friends wanting me to find someone, I just doubted the possibility.

After splitting a dessert and the check, we each went our separate ways with a promise of brunch on Sunday. I headed back to my law office downtown near the courthouse. I was a junior partner at a local firm and specialized in family law, which meant I'd seen just about everything.

My afternoon was full of paperwork and meetings, replying to emails and fielding phone calls. I loved my job and it kept me very busy. Too busy to worry about trying to find a date to Clarice's wedding or trolling for a hookup on one of the dozen apps Carly had texted.

So it wasn't until I parked inside my garage and went inside my dark house that I was reminded of being alone.

I didn't mind being alone, not usually. I loved my home, a Tudor-style brick in Meridian Hills, north of downtown Indy. It was warm and homey and my two dogs greeted me with slavish adoration. Twin yorkiepoos I'd adopted from the same litter. One was a chocolate brown girl and the other was a blond boy. They both had the same adorable brown eyes that could turn me into a pile of mush. I'd named them Donny and Marie. What could I say? My mom had been a diehard Osmonds fan. They were just lucky there were two and I couldn't exactly name them both Elvis.

"Hi, my babies," I crooned, crouching down to pet them. They scrambled all over each other, trying to get to me. I laughed, my mood immediately lighter. When I'd gotten them, I'd worried about having to train two puppies at once, but it had been the right decision. They kept each other company during the day while I was at work. "Did you have a good day? Any piddling on the floor?"

The potty-training thing only worked about sixty percent of the time. Even though I had a doggy door installed, if the mood struck, they'd just go in the house. Luckily, their piddles were about a tablespoon and the doodles were the size of Tootsie Rolls. Hardwood floors helped, too.

After feeding the twins, I went upstairs to my bedroom to change. Nylons, heels, bra, skirt…all of it felt so good to come off. Pulling out my favorite faded pair of lounge pants and a T-shirt, I grabbed a pair of fuzzy socks and went back downstairs.

Since I liked to cook but lacked the time, I used a meal delivery service. Dinners for two, all ingredients included and ready to cook, delivered to my door once a week. Though I rarely cooked for two people, extras meant leftovers for lunch the next day.

I set all the ingredients on the granite island next to the cutting board, then poured myself a glass of wine. I'd turned on the stereo and the relaxing strains of smooth jazz filtered through the room.

As I chopped Kalamata olives and artichoke hearts— occasionally glancing at the recipe card for "harissa chicken with olive tapenade and seared romaine"—I thought about the conversation at lunch. It wasn't that I disagreed with Bridget and Carly—it would be nice to have a date occasionally—it just required so much effort to go about finding someone. I wasn't twenty-two anymore. I was pickier now, though I didn't think I was shooting for the moon in wanting a reasonably attractive man (not looking for a Ryan Reynolds lookalike, though that would be nice), who had a successful career (not looking for a millionaire, but again, that would be nice), was funny, quick-witted, and could carry on a conversation that wasn't ninety-nine percent about himself.

So sometimes I was lonely. Wasn't everyone? Better to be lonely alone than lonely with the wrong person. Though a man's touch *would* be nice. It had been way too long since I'd had actual sex with a real person. My vibrator and a bottle of wine took care of the basics, but making love…that required a person.

Which was how I found myself downloading Tinder after dinner that night. I uploaded a handful of selfies I had to scrounge for (I wasn't one to take loads of them), then considered what to write on my profile. In the end, I decided bluntness was the best way to go.

Single, successful woman looking for a man who can make me laugh, be charming, who has more than one topic of conversation. If your photos include your car/truck, you holding a dead fish, wearing a baseball cap backwards, your kids, or if you have a beard, please swipe left.

There, I thought, that should weed out most of them. I was baffled at the number of men who put pictures of their kids on a dating app. If their intelligence was that lackluster, I didn't want to bother. And the current beard craze was incredibly annoying. Women were supposed to be essentially hairless from the neck down, but men couldn't be bothered to shave their face once a day? Whatever.

I closed the app, put my phone in do-not-disturb mode, and went to bed.

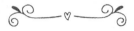

"I'm sorry, but we just don't have any positions available right now."

The woman was apologetic, but that didn't help me any. I needed a job, not sympathy.

As if sensing my frustration, she helpfully added, "But we'll keep your application on file."

I forced a smile that was more of a grimace. "Thanks," and headed out the door.

That had been the sixth security firm to turn me down, and the last one in Indianapolis. The answers were all the same.

"Yes, as an Army veteran, you're extremely qualified. But we're just not hiring at the moment."

One of them had even suggested I look into personal security. "You mean a bodyguard?" I'd asked. "There's a market for bodyguards in Indianapolis?"

She hadn't seemed very sure of the answer to that second question, which made her suggestion pointless.

I'd been back from Afghanistan for two months and was no closer to finding a decent job. And not only was finding a job imperative—after all, I was rather partial to having a roof over my head and food in my belly—I had lawyer fees to pay. That's what happens when you step off the plane from your fourth tour in Afghanistan and your wife had divorce papers served to you as a welcome home present. I hadn't even gotten my duffel off the carousel.

The damn lawyers were bleeding me dry and not doing much to help me. I'd had to beg Lisa—my soon to be ex—just to be able to see my daughter.

Speaking of which—I glanced at my watch—I was supposed to pick her up from school today, then I got to have Amber for approximately three hours before I'd have to return her.

My truck was old, but it still ran. Which was good because I damn well couldn't afford a new one. I fired up the engine and pulled out of the lot.

Amber's preschool was a private—and expensive— Montessori place that Lisa's parents had insisted she attend. They'd also decided to foot the bill, which they could well afford. It was a sprawling red brick building with an expansive fenced-in playground. As I parked, I could see kids out playing on the equipment. The sound of children's laughter and their jubilant voices rang through the heated summer afternoon air.

I scanned the playground and caught sight of Amber. She was on a swing, carefully trying to work her legs correctly to get it to move. She'd only just learned how to pump the swing herself. I had taught her last week and she'd been excited not to have to ask someone for a push anymore.

I headed over to where the fence ended. Two female teachers stood there, chatting, each with a whistle on a string looped around their neck. When they saw me, they stopped talking.

"Hi," I said with what I hoped was a friendly smile. "I'm here to pick up Amber Mackenzie."

"And you are?" one of them asked.

"Her father."

The one who'd spoken rifled through the clip-board she held. "What's your name, please?"

"Callan Mackenzie."

She stopped at one page and looked over it. "I'm not seeing your name here for approved pickups of Amber. Have you ever picked up before?"

I gritted my teeth. "No, this is the first time." I should've known Lisa would do something like this.

"I'm sorry," the teacher said. "But we can't let her leave school property with someone not on the list."

"Who can add me to the list?"

"Amber's mom will have to."

My temper spiked in frustration, my fist clench-ing. I glanced over toward the swings just as Amber looked up and saw me. She grinned.

"Daddy!" Hopping off the swing, she sprinted toward me, her twin ponytail braids bouncing as she ran. I caught her up in my arms.

"How's my snuggle bunny?" I squeezed her tight and pecked a kiss to her soft cheek.

"Did you see me swinging?" she asked. "I've been practicing."

"I did see you. You're doing a great job."

"I'm sorry, sir," the teacher interrupted. "Recess is over and Amber needs to come in now."

Reluctantly, I set Amber down.

"You're not taking me home?" Amber asked, con-fused.

"I need to wait until your mom gets here," I explained, which I knew wouldn't be for another forty-five minutes. I'd be cooling my heels waiting in my truck. Fantastic.

"Oh. Okay." She accepted my explanation without qualm.

"Come, Amber," the teacher said, holding out her hand. "It's time for a snack."

That got her attention. Amber had a sweet tooth, which made her a bit rounder than other four-year-olds. Not that I minded. She had an incredibly sunny disposition for a child, and if three cookies instead of just two made her smile wider, that was fine with me. Life was too short for just two cookies.

I leaned against the fence with a sigh as the teachers rounded up the kids and led them inside. This was just another little trick Lisa was using to cut back on my time with Amber. She'd made no secret of the fact that she wanted Amber to see me as little as possible.

"She barely remembers you," Lisa had said the first time I'd called after returning from deployment.

The words had cut like knives, robbing me of breath. "I know it's been a while, but she's my daughter. I have a right to see her."

"You should've thought of that before re-enlisting."

And that was it. The bone of contention. Lisa had vehemently argued against my last re-enlistment. I'd been torn, but in the end, hadn't been able to leave my men over there without me.

"We've had this argument," I said. "I know you're still angry, but that doesn't mean you should take it out on our daughter."

"We weren't enough for you," she argued. "You bet I was angry. Angry and hurt. But not anymore. I've moved on, Cal. You know I'm with someone else now."

I ignored the pain those words produced inside. There was nothing I could say that would erase the past or make things right. Not now. Time enough for regrets later. "I want to see Amber."

It had taken arguing and threats and cajoling, but finally she'd acceded. One night a week and every other Saturday. It wasn't much, but I'd take what I could get for now. The lawyer was supposed to be working on better arrangements and fifty/fifty custody.

I waited in my truck, occupying myself with searching for jobs online. There were a few sales opportunities, but with no degree or experience, I wasn't holding my breath that I'd hear anything back from my applications.

At four-thirty, the lot began getting more traffic as people stopped to pick up their kids. I watched until I saw Amber come outside, clutching not Lisa's hand, but Sharon's, Lisa's mom. I got out of the truck and intercepted them on the way to her car.

"Hello, Callan," Sharon said coolly. She was a beautiful woman who'd aged well but was very thin. She kept an iron grip on her weight but needed about twenty pounds to help fill in the hollows age had left in her face and frame. She'd look younger but would never allow herself to gain that much weight. Without it, she looked her age and then some, and her expression of chilly disdain didn't help.

"I was supposed to pick up Amber today," I said.

"So you're late then?"

"No. I'm not on the list. They wouldn't let me take her," I explained, reaching for Amber's hand. "Please ask Lisa to fix that. I'll have Amber back in a few hours. Say goodbye to Grandma, sweetie."

"Bye, Grandma," Amber echoed. She was carrying a white sheet of paper with a watercolor painting on it, which she handed over. "Will you keep this for me? It's not dry yet."

Sharon's eyes warmed as she took the painting. "Of course. Be good, dear." She glanced back at me. "Have her home by six."

"I'm supposed to get three hours with her," I argued, lowering my voice so Amber wouldn't catch on.

"She's supposed to be home by six. No later." She lowered her voice as well. "I know Larry doesn't want to have to notify the police."

"Don't threaten me," I gritted out.

"Then we'll see you at six."

She walked past me to her Cadillac and got in.

"Daddy, you're hurting me."

Amber's protest made me immediately loosen my grip on her hand. I hadn't even realized.

"I'm sorry, sweetie. C'mon, let's go. Are you hungry?"

"Not really," she said, obediently walking with me to my truck. "We had a snack."

"How about the park?"

She glanced up hopefully. "The dog park?"

Amber loved dogs, but there was no way Larry and Sharon were going to let a dog into their pristine home. Lisa had moved them back into her parents' shortly after my return and put our house up for sale.

"Absolutely."

I ordered another beer and watched as the Cubs went another inning without a base hit against the Cardinals. I'd dropped off Amber an hour ago after a trip to the dog park to "play with the puppies" and a drive through Dairy Queen for ice cream cones. She'd arrived home a little sticky and her clothes littered with dog hair, but she'd been smiling.

Every time I had to leave her it felt as though part of my soul died.

So I'd come to my local watering hole, a neighborhood joint that was far enough away from the center of downtown to have reasonably priced beer and plenty of televisions. My buddy Shane had just texted me, too, and was going to stop by for a drink. We'd done two tours together, but Shane had gotten out nearly a year before me.

Shane rolled in about twenty minutes later and bellied up to the bar next to me.

"Hey, man, how's it going?" He motioned to the bartender and ordered a Guinness.

"Same shit, different day." I took a long pull from my bottle.

"Any luck with the job scene?"

"Nope. And if something doesn't change soon, I'll have to switch to the cheap beer."

"Fuck that shit," Shane commiserated. "How about the wife? She still giving you problems about seeing your kid?"

"Her and her parents, yeah. It sucks. And the lawyer

is bleeding me dry and getting nowhere. I'd do just as good by farting in the wind." I took another drink.

"Is that their plan? Cost you every dime until you can't fight back, then they get whatever they want?"

It was a hard thing to realize, but, "Yeah. I think that's exactly what the plan is. And the way it's going, it'll work." It wasn't fair. I deserved to have half custody of Amber. But you needed lawyers to fight for you and for lawyers, you needed money.

"Listen, Cal," Shane said, lowering his voice. "You need to do what I do. I make two grand a week. You should see what I've got socked away. I figure a few more years and I'll be able to fucking retire."

I stared, open-mouthed. "What the fuck do you do?" I couldn't imagine that kind of money.

Shane glanced around, then leaned closer. "I'm an escort."

I couldn't have heard that right. "You're a what?"

"An escort. You know," he glanced around again before continuing. "Women pay me to go to lunch, carry their shopping bags…and have sex with them."

At first, I thought Shane was pulling my leg, but his face was dead serious.

"Man, it's not something I go around giving out business cards or puttin' up signs," he continued. "I wasn't even going to tell you, but…well…you know."

Yeah, I knew. I was flat broke and was going to lose my kid. I took another long pull of beer, thinking. Did I want to know the details? *Two thousand a week.* Yeah, I wanted to know.

"Tell me," I said. And he did.

Wealthy women, usually over forty, sometimes married. Looking for a younger man, in shape, who could go all night long and still leave them feeling like a lady and not a whore. Sometimes the husbands knew but turned a blind eye. The single ones were usually career-focused, but had needs, just like anyone else. Some were divorced with no interest in getting married again. But a date on Saturday night—with someone who was good-looking, could converse intelligently, and had no relationship expectations—was welcome.

"And they love ex-military," he continued. "Gets them all hot. And once you're in it and get a few regulars, it's not a bad job." He shrugged. "The women appreciate you more than the twenty-somethings. And they're good in bed. They're interesting to talk to, because they've lived some, and there's no strings attached. I'm telling you, I fucking love it."

"And it doesn't make you feel…" My voice trailed off. I didn't want to insult Shane, but I couldn't stop from asking the question.

"I know, right? You'd think it'd make me feel cheap or some shit. But like I said, they treat me real good. I've only had a couple who didn't, so I just didn't go back."

I thought about it while Shane signaled the bartender for another round. By the time he'd brought over two more beers, I had decided I wanted to know more. Not that I'd decided to jump right onto that kind of career path, but it'd be nice to know it was an option.

"How?" I asked.

Shane showed me the ropes, what dating apps to use and what to look for in profiles to find women who were looking for what I could offer—they just didn't know it yet.

"So what do you do when you find someone?" I asked.

"I text a little, see if they are interested. Try and get them on the phone to chat. Maybe go in for a hookup, if they're looking for that. Then, afterwards, if they want to see me again, I tell them what I do. They're usually shocked. I tell them that it wasn't like that this time. They're different—special—and I wanted to stay for free. But if they want to see me again, I have to charge them. I go easy and tell them it's the logical thing to do, this day and age. You get what you pay for. That I'm worth it."

I thought his "routine" was kind of shitty but wasn't going to say that. Not when he was talking as though he was giving away state secrets. I listened, but mentally filed the information away. I wasn't that kind of guy, even if they wanted to pay for it. I'd just have to figure something out. And soon.

chapter two

E IGHTEEN HUNDRED AND sixty-five dollars. I stared at the invoice on my phone which my attorney's office had so helpfully emailed me. There was a bunch of line-items with descriptions of writing emails and filing with the court and telephone conversations with opposing counsel. All those hours and I was still only getting to see Amber a fraction of the time I'd been promised.

"Hey, Mackenzie! Get off your phone. You're not getting paid to text your girlfriend."

The foreman's yell could be heard over the sound of the machinery and forklifts in the sweltering warehouse. I'd finally gotten a day job that required brawn and no brains—unpacking huge containers of feed for livestock. The bags were fifty pounds each, which wasn't a big deal. But I handled hundreds of bags each day. It was back-breaking work, but between that and the six-mile run I did to and from the warehouse each day, it meant I didn't have to spend time—or money—going to the gym. My workout was free of charge.

Pocketing my phone, I got back to work, the foreman still watching me. He wasn't a bad guy, but he
ran a tight ship. It was only ten in the morning and I
was already pouring sweat. It was going to be another
hot and humid July day.

The job paid decent, but not enough to keep
covering nearly two grand in lawyer fees every few
weeks. Shane had been right. They were playing the
waiting game, trying to bleed me dry, all while still
coming up with lame excuses to keep Amber away
from me. It'd been ten days since I'd last gotten to see
her, which felt like an eternity.

I'd talked to my mom just last night but hadn't let
on how tight things were. She'd insist on trying to
give me money, which I knew she couldn't afford.
She lived on my dad's police pension and her social
security—which was enough to keep her comfortable so long as she budgeted carefully, but definitely
wasn't enough to throw away on my lawyers.

I spent the rest of the day turning over ideas in my
head. No, I couldn't borrow the money. That was just
robbing Peter to pay Paul. Not to mention that I had
no one to borrow money *from*. I had three younger
sisters, but no way was their big brother going to beg
them for money. I still had my pride. For now.

I thought of Shane and his whole idea of an escort.
It had grown in the back of my mind like mold, dank
and dark, and stubbornly refusing to go away. Trying
things Shane's way would get me out of a bind but
would leave a nasty aftertaste.

It's just for a little while. Not a permanent way of life.

The voice was seductive, as was the promise of a
large "paycheck."

At the end of the day, I changed from my jeans into running shorts and stuffed the denim into my backpack. I left on my white tank. It was already covered in sweat and dirt. The early evening heat was oppressive, but I wasn't going to go running shirtless. I wasn't That Guy.

Six miles later, I was unlocking the door into my apartment. It was hotter inside than out, since I wasn't paying for air conditioning, and the slight breeze from the open windows wasn't enough to cool the place down. I flipped on the cheap flat screen TV and grabbed a bottle of water from the fridge, chugging it down.

My evening was the same every day. Shower, frozen dinner microwaved, then job searching on my phone with the TV on in the background. Tonight, in an acknowledgment of it being a Friday night, I grabbed a bottle of beer from the fridge. So far, I hadn't caved to buying the cheap beer, but I did limit my intake.

The couch was one I'd picked up for fifty bucks at a secondhand used furniture store. That, plus the card table and two folding chairs, was the extent of my furniture. Lisa had sold most of our furniture, then used the money to pay off the credit card debt she'd incurred while I was deployed. She'd said shopping was her "therapy." Real therapy would've been cheaper.

Now she lived rent-free with her parents, who were more than happy to have their only child back under their roof, no doubt older and wiser after her brief stint of rebellion, i.e., marrying me. They doted on Amber the way they'd doted on Lisa. She'd said she was already seeing someone else. They probably introduced her to one of their rich friends' single, successful sons. Some douche who wore a tie every day to work, played golf in patterned slacks on the weekends, and had a wine cellar.

One good thing about working in the heat all day: it acclimated me to not using air conditioning. Shirtless, wearing a pair of jeans, the apartment wasn't too bad at night with all the windows open. And the futon was a better bed than my bunk in Afghanistan had been.

The news was on and I turned up the volume to catch the sports highlights. I didn't have cable, but it was amazing the number of channels I got with just an antenna.

I was procrastinating. I'd already decided to try Shane's plan but was putting it off. Which fooled no one and didn't help pay the bills.

With a sigh, I unlocked my phone and scrolled until I found the Tinder app. I'd made a profile on it a week ago—during another spell when desperation struck—and hadn't looked at it since. I didn't take a lot of selfies, so I'd uploaded only two photos. One of me in my fatigues that a buddy had taken, the other a selfie I'd snapped right then.

So many of the women's profiles were obvious fakes, or designed to lure you in, give you a phone number to call, which then you had to pay to speak to them. Nice scam. And there must be fools who fell for it.

"One born every minute," I muttered to himself, swiping left again.

Too young. *Swipe.* Too many kids. *Swipe.* Too many filters. *Swipe.*

Swipe. Swipe. Swipe. Swi—hold up, what's this?

A redheaded bombshell with green eyes and a shy smile.

Fake? I read the profile.

Single, successful woman looking for a man who can make me laugh, be charming, who has more than one topic of conversation. If your photos include your car/truck, you holding a dead fish, wearing a baseball cap backwards, your kids, or if you have a beard, please swipe left.

I chuckled. Now I knew what kind of shitty pics men put on here.

She looked young, but over twenty-five. Single and successful must translate into career woman. Why was she on here? Maybe too busy to date the old-fashioned way?

I swiped right, hoping she'd seen me, too. But if she had, she hadn't swiped right. No match. I sighed again and kept going. The night was still young. She might yet be up and on Tinder.

Thursday and Friday were incredibly busy for me. I had a trial Friday which included having to stand in front of the judge—on behalf of my gum-smacking, leopard-leggings-wearing, teased-hair-dyed-red client—and demand the "bag of dicks" she'd left in her soon-to-be-ex-husband's apartment.

I thought the judge was going to choke, trying not to laugh. He cleared his throat once, twice, made a "hmmm"ing noise, then said, "A bag of…what?"

Ugh. I was never going to live this down. Ronnie, the bailiff, was red-faced, his lips pressed tight together. The court reporter was studiously avoiding looking at anyone.

"My client maintains it's a 'bag of dicks,' Your Honor," I repeated. "She asserts they have monetary and sentimental value to her and the defendant has thus far refused to relinquish her property."

This was even worse than the time me and the opposing counsel had been on our hands and knees in the middle of the courtroom, gamely separating a huge pile of Beanie Babies into two equal halves. I'd scrambled for that Princess Diana one. Yes, four years of college and three of law school and it came down to Beanie Babies and bags of dicks.

"I burned them, you bitch!" The husband had jumped to his feet even as his lawyer tried to tug him back down.

"You bastard! I wouldn't have had to buy them in the first place if you could get your limp dick to work!"

"If I'd worn a blindfold, that might've done the trick!"

The judge was calling for order and pounding his gavel. It took a few minutes to get everyone quiet and seated again. By the time the trial was over, my head was aching, and I'd had about all the "bag of dicks" jokes I could handle.

The court reporter—a thin, reedy man with wire-rimmed glasses—approached me while I was packing up my things.

"Um, excuse me, Miss Grace," he began. "Can I ask you something?" He shifted nervously from one foot to the other, his hands in his pockets.

I was surprised. I'd never actually had a conversation with him before, even though he was a constant presence in court, and I struggled to remember his name.

"Of course. It's Kenny, right?"

He stood up straighter, pulling back his thin shoulders. "Ken, actually," he corrected me. "I go by Ken now."

Ken-not-Kenny looked to be in his mid-twenties. His skin was sallow and bore acne scars. His hair was dark brown, the cut simple and not very flattering. He'd begun working here almost a year ago and was a very diligent worker, but also seemed very shy. I'd never seen him palling around with anyone in the halls or in court.

"What can I do for you, Ken?" Surely, he wouldn't ask me something about the bag of dicks.

"I, well, I was just wondering..." He stopped and shifted his weight again, glancing at the floor before blurting, "Would you like to go to dinner sometime?" His ears were bright red.

Oh. Oh no. My stomach sank. He'd worked up the courage to ask me out and I'd have to turn him down. I hated doing that. I searched for an excuse other than *"No, I'm really not interested."*

"I'm seeing someone," I lied. His face fell in disappointment. I tried to make it better. "But that was very nice of you to ask me. Thank you." I smiled, but he didn't smile back.

"Um, yeah, okay." He turned and walked out of the courtroom, passing Ronnie, who'd watched the exchange. I watched him go, feeling like a heel.

I finished packing up with a sigh and headed for the door as well.

"I think you might've crushed poor Kenny's heart, Emmy," Ronnie teased.

"He's a nice kid, but no." I shook my head. "Just no."

Ronnie chuckled. "Maybe all that talk about bags of dicks got him all hot and bothered."

I groaned. "I'm going to be known as the 'bag of dicks' lawyer for all eternity." Awesome.

Ronnie shrugged, still grinning. "There are worse things to be called."

Maybe, but for the life of me I couldn't think of anything else right now.

Carly called while I was driving home.

"What're you doing tonight?" she asked.

I sighed. "I'm thinking pizza, wine, and a long, hot bath." I told her the bag of dicks story. Carly laughed until she snorted.

"So, he actually burned them?" she finally got out.

"I guess so, who knows? But I think I've hit a new low in my career."

"Hell, I'm thinking I've been too cheap in buying my toys. I only have two, not a whole bag full. I might have to go shopping."

That made me laugh, which felt good after the day I'd had. "You're probably right. And I just have one. Obviously, we're woefully undersupplied. What are your plans tonight? Other than shopping?"

"Oh, I'm supposed to be meeting this guy for drinks, then maybe dinner, if I like him enough," Carly said.

"A new guy? Where'd you meet him?"

"Bumble. He's thirty-five, supposedly six feet tall and is a VP at Angi's."

"Still haven't heard anything from Troy?"

Carly hesitated. "He texted a couple of times, but I didn't reply. I need a grown up."

Hmm. "Okay, well good luck. Text me and let me know if you need the emergency get-me-out-of-here call."

"Will do. Talk to you later, hon."

"Bye."

At least Carly had a date. I hadn't heard from Bridget, but I assumed she was going out tonight with her boyfriend, Rick.

Another Friday night, home alone with Donny and Marie.

That pang of loneliness struck again, along with that empty feeling when you feel as though everyone else is having a good time except you. Happens most often on Friday nights, New Year's Eve, and Valentine's Day.

At times like this, I really missed my husband. Losing him had been the most excruciating experience of my life. His deployment had been so close to being over, just weeks away. He'd joined so that he could pay for college. In the end, his death had paid for *my* college and law school. And I'd give it all up in a second to spend one more day with him. Life was grossly unfair.

My heart ached, but my eyes were dry. Time helped ease the pain, but it never truly healed. Scar tissue and memories remained.

The fur babies were as excited to see me as ever, fumbling all over themselves to get kisses and hugs. I went through the usual routine, changing my clothes and opening a bottle of merlot. I ordered a pizza and settled in to catch up on episodes of *Stranger Things*. I was woefully behind in my Netflix queue.

Three hours, half a pizza, and most of the bottle of wine later, I was well into the swing of my pity party, guestlist of one. Thumbing aimlessly through my phone, I saw the Tinder app I'd installed. Feeling reckless and tipsy, I opened it.

A man's face appeared on the screen. Now what? I'd seen enough about it on social media to know swiping right was if you liked someone, swiping left was a no, and swiping up meant you *really* liked them. With a sigh, I began swiping.

Beard...no. *Swipe left.*

Baseball hat, sunglasses, *and* a beard. No.

Fuzzy photo from ten feet away that looked five years old. No.

This one looked cute. Clean shaven, nice smile. Hmm.

I scrolled down to read his profile. *Word hard. Play hard. Sleep hard.* Wow. A man of few words, and a poet. Rolling my eyes, I swiped left.

Thirty minutes later, I'd only swiped right on three men. Two who were attractive and actually had interesting profiles. The third was a shot in the dark because he was *way* out of my league. Dark hair, deep set brown eyes, a prominent jaw blessedly free of a beard, and an aw-shucks smile that said *I'm the man that'll rub your feet and tell you how pretty you are.* The bulging muscles in his chest and arms didn't hurt either. The app said his name was Cal and that he was twenty-nine. A little on the younger side since thirty was my cut-off, but it wasn't as though he was an option. Not really.

Shopping for men. What an odd century to be alive. What would dating be like a hundred years from now? DNA matches for those who would be most suitable partners? Wait. They probably already had that.

Closing the app, I shifted Donny and Marie from where they were asleep, cuddled in the crook of my knees as I lay on the couch.

"Time for bed, you two." I glanced at the clock. Ten-thirty. What a gripping life I led.

I was brushing my teeth when my phone buzzed. Glancing down, I saw the notification.

You have a new Tinder message.

Finishing up, I washed my face and toweled dry before opening the app. One of the three men I'd liked had sent me a message, but which one?

Ah. The "Specialty Product Project Director," whatever that entailed.

Hi.

Really? That was it? Didn't he read the part where I said I wanted someone who could carry on a conversation?

Hi, I typed.

I climbed into bed, both dogs jumping up and getting settled, too. It was a full ten minutes before he responded.

Hey. How are you?

Nice. Leave it to the woman to have to prove how interesting I was. No doubt he was messaging a handful of other women at the same time. It felt like a contest. Gee, would I be worthy of more than a "Hey, how are you?"

Irritation made my respond.

How am I? Well, I'm sad that I've finished watching all the seasons of Supernatural. Twice. And I'm rather worried about the Ukraine situation. I'm also irritated at my dogs because they refuse to be potty-trained and although they don't doodle a lot, they doodle on my floor and it's the principal of the matter. Also, I'm feeling a little bitchy today. How are you?

There. That ought to teach him to ask some ridiculous, open-ended question. Unsurprisingly, several minutes went by with no response.

Good riddance, I thought. Though I'd wasted—a quick glance at the clock—thirty minutes on a man who couldn't be bothered to say more than "Hey."

Just as I was about to switch my phone to Do Not Disturb, another notification popped up. Maybe Project Director had messaged me back after all. Yippee. But to my pleasant surprise, it wasn't him, but the hot, younger guy. Cal.

Love your photos. And I consider myself both witty and charming. What about you?

Hmm. Not great, but certainly better than "How are you?"

Men are charming. Women are mysterious. Haven't you heard of the Feminine Mystique?

I like a mystery. And a challenge.

Interesting. I snuggled deeper under the covers. It was July, but I couldn't sleep if I was hot. I had to have the weight of blankets on top of me. Consequently, my electric bill in the summer was huge. The cost of keeping the house at a chilly sixty-eight degrees at night. Even the dogs snuggled under the blankets. Marie was already snoring. Ironically, Donny never did.

He sent another message before I could reply.

What are you doing on Tinder on a Friday night? Dare I hope you're looking for a date?

Well *that* was certainly straightforward.

That's what this app is for, right? I sent back.

Depends on what you're looking for. Are you looking for a date? A relationship? Or an amazing night you'll never forget?

My heart-rate sped up. He was flirting with me. As in, possibly proposing a one-night stand hookup. What Carly and Bridget had said flashed through my mind. Sex without strings might be a good thing. Good for health and endorphins and all that crap. I was rationalizing, but let's not get technical. Leave that to the professionals.

I guess that depends on what you're offering. You could be a psycho for all I know.

I waited for his reply, realizing that I was nervous. What if he wanted to come over? What if he was an ax murderer? What if he wasn't?

Let's talk. Here's my number. Call me.

Okay, well at least his number would be on my phone, should they find my dead and mutilated body.

I dialed *67 to block my number, then input his. It rang once before he answered.

"This is Cal."

Oh my. His voice. Deep and smooth. No trace of an accent. It fit his photo perfectly.

"Hi," I said. "I-it's Emmy." I spoke to judges and other attorneys on a daily basis, but a hot stranger on Tinder was making me tongue-tied.

"Nice to speak to you, Emmy," he said. "I'm glad you called."

"Why is that?"

"Because it's damn near a crime that you're alone on a Friday night. You deserve someone to warm your bed. Someone to warm *you*."

The way he spoke, slow and sultry, sent a spiral of warmth through me. His voice in my ear was strangely intimate, perhaps all the more so for being a stranger.

"Is that an offer?" I managed.

"It would be my pleasure," he said. "I think you and I would get along very well. I'm looking at your pictures now. You have gorgeous eyes. And that hair is begging for my fingers to run through it. It's a river of fire. Like a maple in the autumn, red-gold that looks kissed by the sun."

I had never liked my hair color and could only thank the stars that it was straight and not frizzy curls on top of being red, but never had a man referred to it as "a river of fire." I'd been right. He was charming. Which begged the question...

"With a silver tongue like that, what are *you* doing on Tinder on a Friday night?"

"That's easy. I was looking for you. I just didn't know it."

Wow, he was good.

"So, what do you think, Emmy? Can I come over? Get to know you better?"

I hesitated. It would be such a stupid thing to do. Completely illogical and irresponsible, two words that *never* described me.

Which maybe was part of the reason why, six years after Chad's death, I was still alone.

"Yes," I said, abruptly deciding. "Yes, I think I'd like that."

"I guarantee you will. What's your address?"

A whisper of caution. "I tell you what, how about I send an Uber for you?"

"An Uber? Why?"

"Because then I'll have your address and a record of you coming over here, in case you're an ax murderer." Attorney instincts died hard.

He let out a low laugh. "I like your style. And you're smart. An underrated quality."

"Is that a yes?" I asked.

His voice was a warm, soft current of promise. "Yes. We'll do it your way. Order the Uber in case you want to send the cops after me later."

"Will I need to send the cops after you?"

His chuckle made me break out in goosebumps. The good kind, not the heebie-jeebie kind.

"Only if I can't make you come at least four times."

Well, damn. I was going to do it. I was actually going to send an Uber to pick up a booty-call. Holy Mary, Mother of Pearl.

"Send me your address."

chapter three

I WAITED OUTSIDE FOR the Uber. The woman, Emmy, said she'd ordered it ten minutes ago. It should be here any minute.

I still couldn't believe I was doing this. I'd tossed on a T-shirt and ran my fingers through my hair, then brushed my teeth. I'd shaved after my shower because I didn't like to bother with it in the morning. Why clean up when you're hauling sacks of feed in hundred degree heat all day? While I was getting ready, I'd argued with myself to call it off—yet I'd still gotten dressed and came outside.

The Uber pulled up before I could change my mind, and I got in the front seat with the driver, a young guy who looked like he took classes at the University, judging by the decal around the car's plate. He was swigging a Red Bull.

We exchanged a few pleasantries, and not much else. I wasn't in the mood to chit chat. I was thinking through what I'd do when I got there. I remembered what Shane had said.

"It has to be handled delicately. Most women are shocked

at first and have to grow accustomed to the idea, persuaded
gently into realizing that there was nothing wrong with
paying for a product they need. Like buying makeup. They
pay a higher price for the good stuff, but it lasted longer and
did a better job. Just like an escort."

The Uber dropped me off outside a house in Meridian Hills, though "house" was doing it an injustice. It was a Tudor-style near-mansion, with lots of ivy and at least an acre of lawn. The neighborhood held other homes that looked even more palatial, including one with columns and a half-circle drive. This was how the Other Half lived, just like my in-laws.

I rang the doorbell. The porch light wasn't on, but I wasn't surprised. Women like Emmy who lived in neighborhoods like this didn't have late night visitors. At least, none that they wanted the neighbors to know about.

She answered right away, which meant she was nervous. I couldn't blame her. I doubted this was something she made a habit of, or perhaps had ever done before. I braced myself, clamping down on my own nerves and misgivings. It was too late to back out now.

The soft glow of a lamp lit her from behind, casting her face into shadow. It lit her hair, though, making it look like a halo of fire that caressed her shoulders. She wore a satin dressing gown of deep green, belted around a narrow waist.

She was smaller than I thought she'd be, the top of her head barely brushing my shoulder. Her feet were bare and I caught a whiff of scent. Her perfume. It was more exotic than I thought she'd wear—she looked like a floral kind of woman—but the spicy scent suited her.

I smiled, an easy smile that hopefully didn't betray my nerves. "Emmy?"

Her smile was tentative. "You must be Cal."

"I certainly hope so," I said. "Unless you hedged your bets and are waiting for Option B to show up?" I asked it lightly, teasingly. A laugh always eased the tension, right?

Her smile widened. "He's in the closet."

"So long as he's not trying on your shoes."

"I'll keep that in mind."

A silence.

"May I come in?"

She stepped back and I followed her inside, closing the front door behind me.

The foyer was massive, with hardwood floors of deep mahogany and a wrought iron chandelier hanging above. A picture window above the door would showcase the chandelier from outside when lit. There was a large, round oriental rug underfoot and beyond Emmy, I could see a great room on the left and French doors on the right, currently closed.

I followed her into the great room where a fire was lit in the fireplace. It was a silent fire, though. Not real wood. One of those you turned on with the flip of a switch. The furniture was a mix of a leather sofa and armchair, plus two cloth accent chairs. It felt homier than it should have for the size of room.

"Can I get you a drink?" she asked. "I have liquor or wine. No beer, though."

Alcohol should probably be avoided at this point. It impaired judgment and...other things.

"Some water would be great."

She reached down and I saw a small beverage refrigerator with bottles of water. She handed me one, asking me, "Do you mind if I have a drink?"

"By all means. Feel free."

She poured from an open bottle of red and I took the opportunity to get a closer look at her now that the lighting was better.

The hem of the robe stopped right above her knees, and her legs were bare. She was very fair—probably due to the red hair—and had a smattering of light freckles. When she turned around, I could see that though she was petite, her breasts were full and larger than what her slight frame would imply.

She was even more gorgeous than her photos. If I'd seen her in a bar, I'd have bought her a drink and prayed she was single. There was an energy to her—a charisma—that belied the size of the package containing it.

I had a flash of regret that we were meeting under these circumstances.

"Have a seat," she invited, being perfectly poised and polite despite the fact that her crimson-painted toes were curling into the carpet, betraying her nervousness. It made me feel better. At least we were on the same page in fighting nerves.

I wished I could have a glass of wine, too. Nerves weren't the only thing eating at me. Guilt was also gnawing at my conscience. I was lying to her in an incredibly personal way, which basically meant I was a dick.

Amber. I had to remember why I was doing this. She was the only thing worth prostituting myself.

She sat on one end of the sofa. I took the middle seat, angling my body so I was facing her. She'd curled her legs underneath her and used both hands to hold the stem of her wineglass.

Her fingers were thin and delicate. The nails French manicured, but not overly long. A sensible length for someone who typed a lot. Red toes and conservative nails. A dichotomy.

"So what do you do for a living?" I asked. Something well-paying, obviously. That or she'd inherited money.

"I'm an attorney. I've been practicing for a while now."

Ugh. A lawyer. I was disappointed. Lawyers were currently my least favorite people. A necessary evil that cost a fucking fortune. I felt slightly less shitty about this now. Not much, but a little.

She took a sip of her wine. Her lips were a soft pink and full. Her tongue darted out to swipe her lower lip and she glanced up at me. Her eyes were a soft mossy green, luminous and fringed with lashes the same color as her hair and brows.

Despite the current circumstances—a one-night stand with a Tinder stranger—it was clear Emmy was a lady, despite her unfortunate career choice. Hopefully, she was a lonely lady who would pay well.

"Where'd you grow up?" I asked, taking a swig of my water.

"Carmel." A very affluent town north of Indy. "You?"

"North of here, too. A tiny town called Cicero. Barely five thousand people."

"I've heard of it."

There was a slightly awkward silence between us before I spoke again.

"Can I ask your story?" It would be easier to figure out the best approach if I knew about the divorce or the breakup or whatever the current ex-situation was. And less likely that she'd call me a sick bastard and throw me out on my ass.

She shrugged, causing the satin V of her robe to part a bit more. Her cleavage was amazing. I tried not to stare.

"I work a lot. I've been very...driven...the past few years."

"Because...?"

Her eyes met mine. "I'm a widow."

I frowned, getting a bad feeling about this. "You're awfully young to be a widow."

"Yeah, well, Chad was young when he died." She looked down at her wine. "He was in the Army."

Oh, fuck.

"He was just two months away from coming home when it happened," she continued. "One of the Iraqi soldiers they'd been training. Turned on them and killed a half a dozen soldiers before they got him. Chad was one of them."

Fucking hell. Not only a widow, but a gold star widow.

That turned my plans straight to shit.

Some things were sacred and you didn't fuck with them or try to fuck them over. Single moms. Women with a terminal illness. And widows of my brothers.

It took me a moment to recover and regroup. And I didn't lie to myself. I was relieved. I didn't have to go through with it. Wouldn't have to see the interest in her eyes morph into loathing, or worse.

"I'm sorry to hear that, Emmy. That's really tough." Inadequate words. But what was there to say?

"Thank you." She took another fortifying swallow of wine, then managed a smile. "So, Cal. What do you do?"

"I'm in between jobs right now," I lied. No way was I telling her the truth. *"Yeah, I'm an ex-soldier who's looking to charge for sex because I can't find a job that pays me enough to keep up with the lawyer bills. During the day, I sling livestock feed for a living. Sexy, right?"*

"That's hard. Are you staying with family while you look for work?"

"They don't live around here." More lies. They did live around here, but I couldn't shove in on my mom or my sister. But enough about me. The last thing I needed was her feeling sorry for me. Pathetic was so not sexy. "What made you get on a dating site?"

"My friends convinced me to give it a try."

"Looking for love?"

She shook her head. "I'm not ready for a relationship. But…a friend would be nice."

Her cheeks flushed in embarrassment. Wow. She really *was* new at this.

Emmy wanted to get laid. And by someone she could trust. Not looking for something permanent. Just friends with benefits. Damn. I would've been a perfect candidate. It wasn't as though I was in any position for a relationship either. And it had been a really long time since I'd had sex with something other than my right hand. Eleven months, to be exact.

But poaching a fellow soldier's widow in a moment of weakness just Wasn't Done.

"You're a beautiful woman," I began, then paused, trying to come up with the right words.

She frowned. "I hear a 'but' coming."

"But you're a widow. And you're lonely. And you deserve more than a one-night stand with a stranger." All of which was true. She was breathtaking, and one part of my brain—the one connected to my dick—was berating me for turning down her invitation.

Warmth faded from her eyes and she took another sip of wine. "Then why did you come? Seems like a waste of your time to come here looking to get laid and then have an attack of scruples. If I give you some other story, will that be the 'right' reason to have a one-night stand? I didn't realize you had specific criteria."

I flinched at the chill in her voice. Here I was trying to do the right thing and she was going to hate me anyway *without* even knowing I'd been planning to try and charge her for it.

She set aside her wine and got to her feet, briskly tightening the belt of her robe. "I'll see you out. You can call your own Uber. Or walk. I don't care."

Fuck. She was pissed, and probably hurt. I shouldn't care, but I did.

I jumped up and followed her. She was already in the foyer.

"Emmy, it's not you—"

"Oh my god," she spun around, cutting me off. "If you even finish that sentence." Her hands were on her hips and fire flashed in her eyes.

I scrubbed a hand over my face. I wanted to fix this, somehow. "Listen, Emmy, I'm a soldier, okay? There are certain rules we abide by, and one of them is not to fuck with another soldier's wife, or in this case, widow. I'm not judging and it's not that you're not incredibly sexy—you are. I'm doing the honorable thing here. Or at least trying to."

She looked dumbfounded, but at least she'd stopped yelling at me.

"I finally get the courage for a hookup and I had to get a guy with a conscience."

I couldn't tell if that was chagrin or resignation in her voice.

She stepped toward me, reached up, and lightly rested her hands on my shoulders. The scent of her perfume drifted in the air. Her satin-clad body pressed against mine, her breasts against my chest. I stiffened, in more ways than one.

"What are you doing, Emmy?" My hands wanted to rest on her waist and feel the curves of her hips, but I kept them fisted at my sides.

"I'd think it was obvious," she said, pressing her lips to the underside of my jaw. "I'm seducing you."

Moving slowly, I cupped her cheek. Her skin was soft against my calloused hand, roughened from too many years working in the dirt and sand of the Middle East. Her lips parted slightly, my gaze dropping to her mouth. The hand on her thigh slid up to her waist, taking the robe with it as our lips met.

I deepened the kiss, sliding my tongue against hers, and she made a little sound. A sound of desire and want. A sound which seemed to say that it had been much, much too long.

My hand was on her thigh, smooth and warm to the touch. She didn't flinch away. Instead, she moved closer, twining her arms more tightly around my neck.

My cock was already hard. She was pliant and responsive. Shit. I may come in my fucking jeans. Grasping her waist, I lifted her and set her on the closest surface, which happened to be some kind of fancy table people with money put in their foyers. It brought our heads to the same height and the tie of her robe within reach.

She let out a surprised little gasp, then began kissing me again in earnest, making more of those little sounds that were slowly driving me insane.

The tie of her robe was easily undone, and I parted the sides. Pulling back so I could see her.

She'd gone to some effort. Matching bra and panties in a deep green with black lace. Her breasts were full, the pale flesh spilling over the demi cups with a kiss of freckles inside her cleavage.

It felt like my birthday and Christmas rolled into one. Out of all the shitty things in my life right now, somehow I'd hit the jackpot tonight.

Her waist was narrow and stomach flat, save for a small pocket of flesh right below her navel. I'd had always loved that part on a woman, though I'd yet to find one who didn't complain about it. It was a distinctly feminine feature, the softness there, and sexier than a six-pack.

She let me look at her, not trying to hide or cover up. The only betrayal to her poise were the spots of color in her cheeks. Her eyes had turned a brighter green and her lips were wet and red from our kisses. She looked like a woman I'd give a limb for to have in my bed.

I paused for a moment, just long enough to tug off my shirt and toss it aside. She murmured something under her breath that I didn't catch, but since she went right back to kissing me, I assumed it wasn't something bad. Her hands wandered, exploring the muscles of my shoulders and chest. The sacks of feed had done their job.

As nice as the couch was, a bed would be better. A pause would be good, too, and give me a chance to regain control. If I was going to do this—and it appeared that I was—I wanted this to last.

I stood, my arms supporting underneath her thighs and keeping her with me. She tightened her legs around my waist.

"Bedroom?" I asked.

"Upstairs. Door at the end of the hall."

The stairs were hardwood but didn't creak. I took my time. She was kissing my jaw, then settled her head against my shoulder as I carried her. It unsettled me slightly. I didn't want to hug or cuddle. The last thing I needed was my thinking this would turn into anything more than a one-night stand. An emotional entanglement wasn't something I needed right now.

Her bedroom was softly lit by a lamp on a table next to the bed. The sheets were turned down, a muted pattern of tiny leaves and a green blanket that reminded me of my fatigues. I set Her down on the bed, then went about the business of stripping off the rest of my clothes, shoes first. Hopping around on one foot with your jeans around your ankles because you forgot to take the shoes off first was *not* sexy.

She watched me, her eyes widening slightly when I unzipped my pants and my erection sprang free.

I wasn't some ten-inch porn star, but neither was I sporting a nub.

When I approached her, she moved forward, her gaze locked on my cock. She touched me, softly at first, then with more sureness. I made an approving noise and she glanced up at me. Still watching, she leaned over, taking me in her mouth.

It was highly erotic, and I sucked in a breath at the touch of her tongue. And while I'd like nothing more than to let her continue, tonight wasn't about me. It was about caring for the widow of one of my brothers. She had needs, and I could meet them. Hopefully, in a way that would leave her pleased and satisfied.

I gently pushed her back until she was lying down. I tugged her panties down her legs and off, before kneeling on the floor and positioning her sweet spot within easy reach of my tongue.

She tasted sweet, her body exquisitely responsive, and I gave her two orgasms that left her weak, wet, and pliant beneath me.

I turned aside to put on a condom and saw her slip out of her bra. The sight of her bare breasts made my fingers itch to touch them, squeeze them, caress the rosy nipples. I braced myself above her, the green of her eyes brighter than before, her breath still coming in pants.

"You're very good at that," she said.

"I enjoy doing it," I replied. "And when you're doing something you love, you tend to be pretty good at it." I kissed her, a deep, slow, wet kiss. The head of my cock nudged her entrance and she lifted her hips.

"I'm hoping you really enjoy this part, too," she murmured.

Her fingernails lightly traced up my back, her breasts pressed against my chest. I did actually love sex. Some men just liked getting off. I liked it all. The feel of a soft body beneath me, smooth legs wrapped around me, warm feminine sighs in my ear. Giving and receiving pleasure in the most intimate way was a natural high.

She was small—petite and no kids yet—so I took it slow and easy at first. Despite the disparity of our sizes, we fit well together, and things turned heated. Urging me on with her hands on my ass, I moved faster and deeper. Then she kissed me.

It wasn't just the kiss that bothered me. It was that now she was holding my face, a palm on each side, cupping my jaw.

Layers of intimacy. Kissing. Hand to hand. Hand to head. Hand to face. More emotion was required to stroke someone's face than fucking, in my opinion. It was something Shane had urged me to avoid with my clients, to be very clear from the outset that their relationship was a friendly business arrangement. Nothing more.

Of course, Emmy didn't know that.

I felt her tightening beneath me and stilled, riding out the wave of her orgasm. It felt fantastic, her wet heat gripping my cock. She gasped and cried out, which was good because she was no longer kissing me.

"Turn over," I said, helping her onto her front. Not my favorite position, but it worked to depersonalize things a bit.

She rested her head on the pillow, her back curved in that enticing way that made her waist look tiny. I could see the delicate bones of her shoulder blades and indentation of her spine. Her hair streamed down her back, a waterfall of deep red.

I entered her, watching my cock slide inside her pussy. Utterly erotic. I didn't think I could get harder, but I did. I pumped in and out, watching and listening to her sighs and moans, holding her hips. I moved deeper and faster. She was so wet and tight. Incredible. Best fuck I'd had in years.

But it was the freckles that did it. I was depersonalized right up until my gaze wandered and I saw the cluster of freckles just above her right ass cheek. They looked like I could connect-the-dots and create a star.

I ground out a curse as I came, the orgasm washing over me more intense than I'd expected. It robbed me of breath, then I was panting, my bones turned to jelly. I stayed inside her as I bent over, pressing soft kisses to her shoulders and back. My skin was damp with sweat.

Finally, I eased out of her. Turning aside, I disposed of the condom in a tissue from a box by the bed. I'd toss it later.

I lay back against the pillows, my arms folded behind my head. Closing my eyes, I breathed. After a moment, I felt Emmy curl into my side.

My instinct was to get up and leave right away, but that would be a dick move. Instead, I shifted her so my shoulder was her pillow, then I tugged the sheet up over us. I wasn't cold, but she probably was. Little things like her always got cold. She let out a soft sigh and nestled closer.

I longed for a cigarette. I swore I'd give it up once I was discharged, and I hadn't had one in months. Even after sex, I'd lost the urge. It was only when stress hit that the craving came back. And I had good reason to be stressed. I needed a client. Maybe more than one. Soon. Weekends were supposedly the best for finding them, and I'd just wasted a Friday night.

"You want some water or something?" Emmy asked, sidetracking my thoughts.

"Sure. Water would be great."

She squirmed away from me, shrugging back into her robe, then disappeared down the hallway. Her bare feet padded softly on the floor and in a few moments, she was back, carrying two bottles of water. She handed me one before discarding the robe and climbing back into bed. She pulled the blanket up over the sheet, shivering slightly.

Like I said, always cold.

A few gulps of water later and the urge to smoke drifted away. I'd have to spend tomorrow on my phone, trolling through profiles and texting. It would suck hours of my time, but there was no way around it. The bill from my lawyer was burning a hole in my phone.

"You seem lost in thought," she said, setting aside my own bottle of water. "Everything okay?"

"Yeah. Everything's fine." I smiled. "Just relaxing."

She smiled back, then resumed nestling against me. Absently, my fingers trailed down her side as I studied the ceiling.

"So what kind of job are you looking for?" she asked. "I know a lot of people. Maybe I can put you in touch with someone who's hiring."

"I have no degree," I said wryly. "Just an honorable discharge, which means I'm basically unemployable."

"There's still other things you can do, I'm sure," I said. "If you go into the business field, you can work your way up somewhere. I have a friend who's an HR manager at Angi's. They always seem to be hiring."

It sounded good, but my pride was already taking a beating with her knowing I was a down-on-my-luck ex-soldier.

"That's okay."

"Are you sure? I could—"

"Thanks, but I'll be fine."

She dropped it then, seemingly content to caress my chest. I didn't wax, though I kept things under control. No woman wanted a walking carpet or to spend time braiding a man's chest hair in bed. But I drew the line at waxing. It itched like a sonofabitch when it grew back in.

We lay in companionable silence. After a few minutes, she spoke. "If you want to stay, I make a really incredible western omelet." Her voice was tentative, and I could hear the fear of rejection in her voice. Again, I cursed that fucking app and the false positive on Emmy.

"Sorry," I said. "I have an early interview tomorrow." Sort of true.

Her body tensed, but she nodded. "Okay. Yeah, you don't want to miss that." I couldn't tell if she believed

me or not. Not that I should care if she believed me
or if I hurt her feelings. After tonight, we'd never see
each other again.

I took a deep breath and snuggled closer to Cal,
forcing my body to relax. If I closed my eyes, I could
pretend it was Chad—rather than a stranger—in my
bed. A bit pathetic…but no one had to know but me.

Cal seemed like a nice guy. Definitely hot. And fantastic in bed. My first orgasms since Chad had died
that weren't self-inflicted. I sighed. It had been a long
time. Cal obviously had just needed an itch to scratch
tonight, which was fine. I imagined he'd probably
make an excuse and leave soon, which was too bad.

Was I ready for a new relationship? Time didn't
heal wounds. It just made them more bearable. Dating, as a general rule, was awful. The most ineffective
and worst waste of time ever created for the purposes
of finding a mate. Apps were supposed to make it
easier but were even more a waste of precious time.
Though tonight was an exception.

I inhaled the scent of him. A spicy cologne that was
heavenly, tinged with the aroma of our sweat. Not a
bad smell at all. And he was warm and muscled in all
the right places. The slow stroke of his fingers up and
down my back was soothing.

I drifted in and out of sleep, waking when I felt
him shift me onto the pillow so he could slide out
of bed. Feigning sleep, I watched him dress through
slitted eyes. I hadn't gotten to see him from the back

earlier, which was a crime, considering his ass was as perfectly muscled as the rest of him.

He had a tattoo on his bicep that I'd missed earlier, but it was too dim in the room for me to make out what it was. The thin line of a scar stretched from his side around his back and up. It looked like an old surgery scar. I wondered why he'd needed surgery.

Cal turned toward me and I closed my eyes, waiting. Soft footsteps crept closer, but rather than head out the door and into the hallway, he paused by the bed.

A soft touch to my hair, fingers gently combing through the strands. Then the faintest brush of a touch against my cheek. I barely breathed, not daring to open my eyes. I hadn't expected this and had no idea what to think.

In the next moment, he'd stepped away, and I didn't open my eyes until I heard the front door open and close downstairs. He was gone.

chapter four

CARLY AND BRIDGET had already ordered by the time I arrived, breathless and late for brunch.

"Sorry," I said, dropping into an empty chair. "My mom called and I couldn't get off the phone." She'd been really persistent lately about wanting grandchildren before she was "too old to enjoy them." Not for the first time did I wish I wasn't an only child.

"We ordered a mimosa for you," Bridget said as the waiter came by with our drinks.

"Good call."

We chatted for a while about our respective weekends while we went through two rounds of mimosas. Bridget and her boyfriend, Rick, had just moved in together a couple of months ago.

"It's been a bit difficult," she said. "I like my space and my routine. I don't know if I was ready for a man messing with all of that. But I know it's best to try-before-you-buy, right?"

"Living together tests the waters before you get hitched," Carly confirmed, taking a bite of her egg white omelet. "Unless you're not wanting to marry him. Then I think it's rather pointless."

"Of course, I want to get married. What's the whole point of dating if you don't want to get married?"

"But maybe not to Rick," I suggested, wiping some syrup off my chin.

Bridget shrugged, picking morosely at her eggs benedict. "I don't know. Every time I think he's the one, he does something stupid."

Carly and I murmured our agreement. We'd heard the stories.

"Well, I had an interesting weekend," I said, deciding to change the subject.

"Oh? Do tell." Carly motioned the waiter for another round.

"I took your advice." I took a deep breath. "I hooked up with a guy off Tinder."

They both stared, open-mouthed. Carly found her tongue first.

"Seriously?"

I nodded. "He was really nice. Good looking." An understatement. "Gorgeous body. We had a good time." Another understatement.

"Did you meet at a hotel?" Bridget asked.

"No. He came over." I explained how we'd texted and why I had him Uber over. "He left in the middle of the night."

"Wow," Bridget said. "I'm impressed. I mean, I know we told you to loosen up and have some fun. I just didn't expect you to jump right in."

"I'm not getting any younger, as you two so helpfully pointed out."

"Hey, if your friends can't tell you to dust the cob-webs off your vagina, then who can?"

I laughed. I had spent yesterday cleaning house—including washing the sheets—and processing Friday night. It wasn't something I felt the need to do again, but it had made me feel like a woman again, and not some aging spinster whose next stop on the Highway of Life was comfortable shoes and an eighteen-hour bra.

"I'm happy to report that said vagina was given a thorough examination and found to be in good working order."

"You're sure it was just a one-night stand?" Carly asked. "I mean, if you liked him, why not text him?"

"You're the one who swears that nothing can come from a one-night stand," I reminded her.

"That's *my* philosophy, but you never know."

"I don't know," I said. "Is that how it works? I mean, is it okay to text him?" Maybe he'd want to get din-ner or something. I might like that. We hadn't talked much Friday night, but he'd seemed nice, intelligent, and funny. Not to mention sexy as hell.

"It's not like there are rules," Carly said.

"Exactly," Bridget added. "If you like him and you had a good time, what do you have to lose by texting him? The worst that can happen is he'll say no."

I grimaced. "Ugh. Rejection. My fragile ego might not survive."

"Fragile ego, my ass. You're one of the best family law attorneys in this city, and on top of that, look like a mini-Emma Stone. You're successful and beautiful. Any man would be lucky to have you."

"Are you my best friend or my mom?" I teased.

"Your mom would've told you to put a hole in the condom."

I laughed. Both Bridget and Carly knew about my mom's obsession with grandkids. "True."

After brunch, the idea of texting Cal was still floating in the back of my mind. Donny and Marie were terribly excited to see me, especially since I had left-over bacon.

I held out until that night, debating the pros and cons. The pros were that I might end up in a relationship in which even casual dating would be welcome, plus regular sex. The con was merely my dignity. And by eight o'clock, my dignity was taking a back seat to my libido.

Hi Cal, my text began. *How'd the job interview go?*

If he'd even had one. Who interviews on Saturdays? But hey, I didn't want to automatically assume he'd lied to me.

It took about ten minutes for a reply.

It went good. Thanks for asking.

Hmm. Well, not exactly inviting conversation. But maybe he was busy. Or a bad texter.

Time to shed a bit more of that overrated dignity.

Glad to hear it. I was wondering if maybe you'd like to get together this week. Maybe for a drink or dinner?

I stared at my phone, watching as the three little dots indicated he was typing a response.

Sorry. I'm pretty busy. Thanks for asking though.

Ouch. I hadn't been as prepared as I thought I was for the rejection. Still, it was better to be rejected via text than in person, though that wasn't saying much. Okay then. They'd had a nice time, but he wasn't looking for more. *C'est la vie.*

"Looks like it's just you and me, guys," I said to Donny and Marie, neither of whom looked particularly surprised by this pronouncement. They were cuddled on the couch with me, one on each side, Marie softly snoring.

Back to square one with the dating scene. I sighed. I thought when Chad and I got married, that I'd never have to do the dating thing. Of course, I didn't think I'd be a widow at thirty-two, either.

Tears didn't come for once, though the sadness and feeling of loss persisted. It was duller now, no longer the sharp stab of pain that would steal my breath. The anger was gone, too. Anger at him for leaving me alone, for not being the happily-ever-after I'd thought we'd be.

It had taken four long years to get to the point where I thought I could move on. *Really* move on. Which meant searching once more for that elusive thing called love. Though the thought of being that vulnerable again was terrifying. I'd questioned whether the happiness I'd had with Chad was worth the agony of losing him.

Sometimes I still questioned it.

chapter five

MY PHONE BUZZED in the pocket of my jeans. I paused in hefting the bags of feed and pulled off my gloves to answer, running my forearm across my brow to swipe away the sweat. When I saw the caller ID, my stomach knotted.

"Yeah," I answered, my voice guarded.

"Callan, it's Larry," my soon-to-be ex-father-in-law said. "I don't think it's going to work out for you to see Amber this evening."

My hand fisted and I tried to get a grip on my anger and disappointment.

"Why not? We agreed I could see her one night a week—"

"Yes, but she was invited to a birthday party and she'd like to attend."

"She's four, Larry. She'll forget about the birthday party."

"I'm sorry, Cal. We'll see you next week."

"I have a right to see my daughter—"

"Goodbye."

The call ended.

It took every ounce of willpower I had not to throw my phone against the wall. But that would be dumb because I certainly couldn't afford a new one.

Deep breath. Deep breath.

Ten minutes later, I was on the phone to my lawyer.

"They won't let me see her," I said, relating what Larry had told me. "The birthday party was just another excuse. I've only gotten to see her six times since I've been back."

"Take it easy," my lawyer said, in an infuriatingly patronizing tone. "You don't know they weren't telling you the truth."

"Bullshit," I snapped. "You were supposed to be helping me at least get visitation while the divorce is proceeding. So far, you've gotten me squat."

"I'm doing my best," retorted the empty-suit lawyer. "But your in-laws are formidable in this town and the lawyers they hired know how to stonewall. Not to mention, half of them with any political ambitions at all know they need the support of Larry Atwell. Pissing him off by taking the opposite side of a custody battle over his granddaughter isn't the smart choice. You're lucky I even took this case."

"There's no reason why I shouldn't get fifty/fifty custody."

"Your wife is arguing otherwise, that you were an absent father and wanted nothing to do with Amber."

"I was *deployed*. It wasn't like I was gone because I wanted to be."

"They disagree."

The last straw snapped. "That's it. You're done. I shouldn't have to explain all this to you. You're supposed to be on *my* side. You're fired."

"Fine. Have a good day."

I ended the call, the phone's case creaking slightly in my viselike grip. I'd fired my lawyer. Supposedly, one of the best attorneys in Indy. If he had been the best, God help the poor bastards who had the worst.

Now what? How was I going to find a new one, much less one who would take on my father-in-law?

"Hey! Can we get some help over here?"

I was yanked from my thoughts by the yell. I looked over to see one of the forklift drivers had misjudged the weight of the pallet, which was currently on the verge of crashing down, taking the forklift and driver with it.

I ran toward it, as did several other of the warehouse workers, but I got there first. The driver was struggling to get out of the forklift as it was slowly tipping. The tall pallet was off-kilter as well, and sliding forward, about to bury the forklift and driver.

Grabbing the driver's arm, I hauled him out of the seat and pushed him to safety. The lift shifted, even more unbalanced with my weight on one side, and everything that had happened in slow motion previously now moved at a dizzying speed.

The crash of wood and grind of metal screeching against concrete was deafening. I leapt off the forklift, but something hit me, causing a rending pain in my upper arm. A huge weight hit me across the back, knocking the breath out of me, but also throwing me clear of the deadly collapsing tower.

Dust filled the place, obscuring my vision and making me cough when I could finally draw a breath. Picking himself up off the floor, I glanced around. Men were yelling, coordinating stabilizing the nearby pallets, but no one appeared hurt. The forklift driver was pale as a ghost but seemed fine.

"Fucking A, dude, that was close." Another worker—a big guy who went by the nickname Bud—said. "Looks like it got ya." He nodded toward my arm.

A long, jagged cut ranged from the top of my arm, down my bicep, ending right above the elbow. Rivulets of blood were smeared across my skin and more blood was pouring out.

"Shit, that's gonna need stitches," Bud said, digging in his back pocket and handing over a long, grimy rag.

"Thanks," I said, wrapping it around my arm. Bud tied it in a knot for me. "Just what I fucking needed today."

"Least you ain't gotta pay for it yourself," Bud said. "And it coulda been worse. The way you jumped it there, you saved his life. A fucking hero, man."

"Yeah. I guess." The cut hadn't been a clean slice, but had torn the skin. There'd be a scar even with stitches. Just one more to add to the collection. At least it hadn't been the other arm. That might've fucked up my tattoo, which would've sucked.

"Tell Wilson I'm going to the ER," I said. "I'll try to get back after, if it's not too late." And get a tetanus shot, probably. I hated waiting in an ER. It took forever. Guess it wasn't a bad thing about Amber. I'd have had to cancel anyway.

"Want me to drive you?" Bud asked.

"Nah. I got it." I'd been hurt worse. This was just a fucking nuisance. "Thanks."

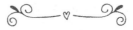

Monday was as hectic as usual for me. Meetings, a deposition, and a last-minute court filing meant I was eating a late lunch at my desk. Well, trying to eat. In between phone calls and answering emails.

It was in the middle of stuffing another forkful of kale in my mouth and wishing it was a quarter pounder when I heard yelling. A man was in the hallway, yelling something. Then I heard my name.

"Where is she? Emerson Grace is his name and I know he's here. His name's on the door. I want to see that son of a bitch right fucking now!"

Oh shit.

The voice was getting closer and now I could hear Karen, the receptionist, threatening to call the police.

The law office was in an older building that had been turned into office space. The result was a maze-like hallway that led to a handful of large offices, all with heavy, wooden doors. The hallway and reception area were lawyerly in décor with heavy furniture and dark colors.

I had gone for a lighter feel in my office, with plush, off-white carpet and walls, comfortable chairs, and lots of feel-good knickknacks. I even had a wooden sign that said *It's Never Too Late For Happily Ever After.* Being a divorce attorney meant I often saw people at the lowest times in their lives. When they stepped into my office, I wanted them to feel a bit of hope.

Unfortunately, the décor and color scheme did nothing for the angry man who burst into my office.

He looked momentarily taken aback, then recovered.

"You," he said, glaring at me. "I thought you were a man, but I should've known you'd be a fucking woman."

I swallowed the lump of kale in my mouth. I had no clue who this guy was, but he was big and mad. At least six feet tall and over two hundred pounds, he wore a rumpled suit with no tie.

"You're the reason I can't see my fucking kids."

He made two steps toward me before I scrambled out of my chair and backed up.

Karen was at the door. "I'm calling 911." Her cell was in her hand but I knew from experience that she'd have to go back to the lobby to get reception. Karen looked as panicked as I felt.

"Please, Mister…?" I'd hoped he'd fill in the blank, but instead, he just looked more pissed off.

"You don't even know my fucking name," he spat. "You ruined my life and can't be bothered to remember me?" He advanced toward me again.

"I'm sorry," I said, trying to keep my voice calm. "I handle a lot of cases—"

"You mean you ruin a lot of fucking lives." With one arm, he swept everything off my desk. My computer monitor fell with a crash that made me jump, along with picture frames, my coffee mug, filing basket, and stacks of paper. Even landing on carpet, I could hear the crunch of stuff breaking.

"This isn't going to help your case," I said, scrambling backward. The problem was, I was running out of room to retreat. "Going to jail for threatening an officer of the court won't look good."

"Who said anything about threats?" he retorted.

"You're right. If I'm going to get arrested, it better be worth it."

He came at me. I screamed, throwing my hands up to ward him off, but then he had me by the throat, cutting off my cry. He slammed me against the wall, knocking the breath from my lungs and banging my head. I saw stars, then just his face, mottled with rage. He reeked of alcohol and his eyes were bloodshot.

I couldn't breathe. He was gripping my throat and had pulled me up, so my toes were barely touching the floor. I clawed at his hand, but it was like trying to move stone.

Suddenly, he was off me. I choked, gulping in air, and began coughing.

Lee and Ash, two other attorneys, had pulled the guy off me. Ash was an average-sized guy, but Lee was six-five and proud of the size of his biceps. Between the two of them, they each had one of the man's arms, holding him back from me.

"You fucking whore! I'm going to fuck you up!"

Lee and Ash dragged him out, struggling and shouting obscenities the entire time. Sirens were outside the building and a moment later, Karen hurried back with the cavalry.

My legs were shaking. Everything was shaking. I collapsed into my chair, fighting back the tears that really wanted to come. I would not be That Girl.

But I really, really wanted to be.

"Are you okay?" Karen asked anxiously. She'd crouched down beside my chair.

I nodded, not trusting myself to speak without bursting into tears.

"That was Peter Winston," Rosie said. "Shelly Winston's ex."

Ah. Now it made sense. A particularly difficult case that had gone to trial three months ago. After two DUIs, being fired from his job, and an arrest for public intoxication, full custody of the two children had been awarded to Shelly. It didn't look as though Peter was handling it very well.

"Can I have some water?" My voice was rough and my throat felt raw. Karen jumped up and left, returning a moment later with a plastic cup of water. It helped and I took several long gulps.

An EMT wanted to speak to me and Karen moved out of the way. A few questions and a few vital signs later, he pronounced my neck severely bruised.

"And you have a bump on the back of your head," he said. "We should take you in for an MRI, just to be safe."

Which meant the entire afternoon was now blown to smithereens. I had a case to prep for, too.

"Are you sure?" I asked, hoping maybe he'd give me a pass. "I'm so busy and have appointments to keep."

"A subdural hematoma could kill you," he said bluntly. "That would definitely stop you from keeping your appointments."

Well, okay then.

I felt ridiculous, riding in the back of the ambulance, which they insisted on. The only good thing to come of it was that the second EMT who rode in the back of the ambulance with me was absolutely adorable. About a decade too young for me, but it didn't hurt to look.

Since the incident happened at work, there was more paperwork to fill out because the firm's insurance would have to pay, which would take more of my time that I already couldn't afford to lose. The wait for the MRI felt like an eternity, and I felt conflicted when the results came back that all was well with my brain.

"That's good news," I said to the doctor with a sigh, "but also means I've wasted the entire afternoon."

"Better to be safe than sorry," he said with a placid smile, handing me a form. "Just give this to the desk at the front for your discharge. Drink warm fluids the next few days and a heating pad or warm compress around your throat should help with any pain or discomfort."

I slung my purse strap over my shoulder and pushed back the curtain to my little exam area of the ER. A man sitting in the area directly across from me glanced up. His curtain wasn't drawn and our eyes met.

A shock of recognition went through me. It was him. Cal.

An instant after I remembered him, I saw the blood. His grimy white tank was stained with it, as was his arm and jeans. He had on heavy workboots and sported a day's growth of whiskers. A makeshift tourniquet was wrapped around his upper arm and was red with blood.

I was walking toward him before I even thought about it and he stood at my approach.

"Odd place for a second date," he quipped, one corner of his lips twitching upward in a half-smile.

"What happened?" I asked.

Despite the blood, he looked sexy as hell. The tank fit him like a second threadbare skin, leaving his muscled arms beautifully bare. He had those muscles that stretched from his neck outward, making the line of his shoulders an arc instead of a slope. It was incredibly sexy. He looked even better in the daylight than he had in the semidarkness of my bedroom.

He shrugged those muscled shoulders. "Just an accident at work with a forklift. I need a couple stitches."

"More than a couple, I'd say," the doctor said as he walked in the area. It was the same doctor who'd treated me and sent me in for that MRI. A nurse followed, tugging the curtain halfway shut behind me. "You two know each other?"

"Um, yes," I said. "We're…" I faltered.

"Friends," Cal supplied. "We're friends."

"Well, she's welcome to stay, if you'd like," the doctor said, pulling up a rolling stool and taking a seat. The nurse was busy getting a tray of instruments and bandaging ready.

"What do you say?" Cal asked with a grin. "Want to stay and hold my hand?"

If *I* was getting stitches, I'd absolutely want someone to hold my hand. So I nodded. "Sure."

Cal sat back down and took my hand, pulling me close to his side while the doctor and nurse donned latex gloves and busied themselves cutting off the tourniquet. His hand swallowed mine, warm and dry, and calloused from hard work.

"Sorry for the dirt," he said in an undertone.

I didn't reply, just squeezed his hand. The tourniquet was gently pulled off the wound and I gasped.

Not a squeamish person by nature, I nonetheless

felt my head swim at the sight of the jagged skin ripped apart. Fresh blood oozed from the cut that had to be a good six inches long. The doctor began cleaning the cut, saying, "This may sting."

Sting? It had to hurt like hell, but Cal wasn't even paying attention to what they were doing. He was looking at me. Specifically, my neck.

"What happened to you?" he asked.

I shook my head. "It's nothing." And compared to the raw skin I was seeing, he was in more pain than I was.

"We're going to give you a shot to numb you first," the doctor said, switching Cal's attention away from me, "which will take a few minutes to take effect—"

"Can we just skip that?" Cal asked. "I need to get out of here sooner rather than later and back to work."

"Are you sure? I'm going to need to put in probably at least twenty stitches, some will be internal. I really recommend numbing the area."

"I'm good, doc. Let's just get this show on the road. Besides," he glanced back at me, "I've got someone to hold my hand." He winked at me.

I was appalled, even as the doctor shrugged and set aside the syringe.

"You can't be serious? Let them numb you."

His brows rose in disbelief. "For this? It's a scratch, babe."

I heard the endearment with some surprise but filed it away to dwell on later. "It's not just a scratch," I argued. "It's a deep wound."

Cal scoffed. "Please. I've *had* deep wounds. This," I tipped my head toward where the doctor was preparing to start the first stitch, "is a scratch." The needle went in and Cal didn't even flinch. "So are you going to tell me what happened or what?" His gaze went back to my neck. "Who did that to you?"

I cursed Crazy Pete—as I'd now decided to call him. His damn fingers had left marks that could really be mistaken for nothing else. I'd have to wear a scarf around my neck for the rest of the week.

I glanced at the nurse and doctor, both studiously paying attention to the stitching and supposedly not our conversation.

"We can talk about it later," I muttered.

Cal seemed to catch my drift and nodded. Letting go of my hand, he reached up and moved aside my hair to get a better look at my neck.

"Stop that," I admonished, leaning away from his touch. He was getting awfully nosey after one night together and refusing my attempts at an actual date. Which I *should* be mad about, not here holding his hand for comfort he obviously didn't need while getting stitches.

The doctor was working steadily, now on an area that was a bit deeper. I watched, my vision growing darker at the sight of the needle digging into skin and muscle. How could Cal not be hurting?

"Hey," he said sharply. "Look at me."

Oh god. He's pulling the skin, tugging it back together—

"Emmy."

Cal grabbed my arm, jerking my attention away from the doctor.

"You're white as a sheet," he said. "Sit down before you pass out."

Pass out? I did feel a bit lightheaded…

"I think I'll just sit for a second," I murmured as my knees folded. I sank heavily to the floor next to Cal's chair, landing on my ass a bit too hard for comfort.

"Put your head between your knees."

I didn't have time to obey, he was already pushing my head forward. The nurse abandonded the doctor and crouched down by me.

"Close your eyes and take deep, slow breaths."

Breathe in. Breathe out. Breathe in. Breathe out. Not so difficult now, and I didn't feel so dizzy anymore. My forehead pressed against my bent knees, held in place by Cal's palm at the back of my head. He'd managed to hit the sore spot from Crazy Pete and I flinched.

"I'm okay," I managed, slowly sitting upright. He released his grip and I rested back against the wall, taking another deep breath. Now that the spell had passed, I was mortified. "I'm so sorry. I've never passed out in my life."

"It happens," the nurse said. "Good thing he saw the signs." She stood and got me a cup of water. "Here you go. This will help."

"Yes, you certainly don't need *another* head injury," the doctor added, still focused on my work. I kept my gaze far away from what he was doing.

"Head injury."

Cal's flat statement had an undertone that made me flinch, but I avoided his eyes. Again, none of his business.

My butt was numb and with my skirt, I was probably flashing everyone who walked by. I got to my feet, smoothing the wrinkled fabric and dusting off my rear.

"You okay?" Cal asked, reaching for my hand. His

palms weren't even sweaty as the doctor stitched him up.

"I'm fine. Guess I can rule out my backup career as surgeon."

"That's not what I meant."

"I know." So nosey.

Another nurse stepped into the alcove, dressed in peach scrubs. She was a brunette of average height. Pretty, but her eyes were hard, and she was unsmiling.

"Cal. They said you were here. What happened?"

"Lisa? What are you doing here?"

Cal seemed shocked. And who the heck was Lisa?

"Duh. I work here," she replied. "What happened to your arm?" She was peering over the doctor's shoulder and glanced at the nurse assisting him. "Hey, Tracy."

"Hi," Tracy replied. "He had a nasty cut, but the doc is fixing him up."

I was starting to feel decidedly awkward in the overcrowded space. Then Lisa's gaze landed on me.

"Who are you?" she asked, and not in a friendly way. "And why are you holding my husband's hand?"

Mystery solved.

I dropped Cal's hand like it burned, my anger warring with my embarrassment. He was married. Hadn't mentioned *that* little tidbit now, had he.

Pasting a fake smile on my face, I said, "Merely an acquaintance. I was just leaving."

Grabbing my purse, I bypassed them all and kept going, despite the last-minute "Emmy, wait," that Cal offered. It even *sounded* half-hearted.

No wonder he didn't want a date. He probably

would've had a hard time explaining Date Night to his wife.

I'd been wrong about him. I was too damn naïve for my own good. A hookup wasn't supposed to make you hurt inside, which I was pretty darn sure was what I was feeling.

Screw Cal. I'd delete him from my phone and that would be the end of it. And my Tinder profile was going in the dustbin, too.

I watched Emmy storm out, completely ignoring me. Not that I blamed her. What was I supposed to say?

"By the way, I'm married. Sorry I forgot to mention that. But hey, we're getting a divorce, so technically…yes, adultery, but you know, not really…"

Yeah, that would've gone over just dandy. Now she thought not only was I a jerk for not wanting to go on a date with her, but I was also a cheating husband. For a follow-up, I could always kick a puppy. That oughtta do it.

Fuck.

"Who was she?" Lisa persisted. "Already dating, Cal? Nice. Does Amber call her mommy?"

The bitch factor was off-the-charts.

"Hey, doc," I said. "I'll take the numbing now. Stick it in my ears, would you?"

"Ha ha, you're so funny. Here I was worried when they said you were in the ER and I come down to find some other woman with you."

"Why'd you even come see me if you're just going to yell?" I asked. "Aren't you supposed to be in the other wing?"

"I figured if you were dead, I'd still get the life insurance, so I'd better come check."

The pain from the remark hurt more than anything the doctor was doing to me. Even the nurse Tracy seemed taken aback by the venomous words, carefully keeping her eyes averted from us both. The doctor just kept stitching.

Lisa seemed to remember we had an audience, and backtracked. "I-I didn't mean that. I'm sorry."

She actually did seem remorseful, but I couldn't tell if it was because of what she'd said, or who'd heard her.

"I'm alive," I said. "Sorry to disappoint."

"All finished," the doctor said, thankfully interrupting. "Tracy will get you finished up and I'll give you a script to prevent infection. Do you want one for the pain, too?"

The pain I felt couldn't be fixed with a pill.

"Nah. I'm good."

The doctor left and though I wished she would go, too, Lisa remained. Thankfully, I held my silence while Tracy bandaged me up.

"The stitches will dissolve," she said, "so there's no need to make an appointment to get them removed. You should change the bandage at least twice a day and try to keep the area from getting wet." She gave Lisa a nod as she left, but didn't seem nearly as friendly as she had before towards her.

"Your dad is making sure—yet again—that I don't get to see Amber," I said. "He cancelled tonight."

Lisa crossed her arms over her chest and glanced away from me. "Sorry. He didn't mention it to me."

"I want to see my daughter."

"We already agreed on a schedule—"

"Yes, but if your parents fuck up the schedule, then I should get another day. I want to see her tomorrow night."

"I can't. My parents are taking her to Disney World tomorrow for two weeks."

I stared in disbelief. "Are you kidding me? Since when? And why are you just now telling me this?"

"It's a surprise for Amber. Are you going to tell me that my parents can't take her to Disney World?"

Her hands were on her hips now as she challenged me, and she was right, damn it. They'd backed me into a corner. If I put up a fight, I'd end up looking like the bad guy.

But someone else was taking *my* daughter to Disney World for the first time.

My stomach was in a knot and I swallowed hard. "It just would've been nice if her parents had been the ones to take her," I said at last. The anger was gone. Now my voice was full of the sadness that consumed me.

Lisa heard it and her eyes softened, though her words were stiff. "We don't always get the things we want, or what we expect. I know I didn't."

The same argument, and not one I cared to repeat.

"I've got to go," I said. "Thanks for coming down."

I passed by her and glanced at my watch. Too late to get back to work in time, not that I was in the mood for it. The news that I wasn't going to see Amber for another two weeks had sucker-punched me. Lisa left without a word.

"Just a second," I heard behind me, and paused. It was the nurse Tracy, who glanced around before approaching me.

"I wanted to give you this," she said, handing me a slip of paper. There was a name and phone number.

"What's this?"

"I couldn't help overhearing," she said.

"No kidding. Sorry about that."

"It's fine. But I had a friend who went through a nasty divorce and custody battle. She had a really great lawyer." she shrugged. "I texted and got the name and number. Thought you might be able to use it."

Considering I'd just fired my attorney, her timing was impeccable.

"Thanks," I said, pocketing the information. "Really. Thanks a lot."

She gave me a smile. "Good luck."

I called the minute I got in my truck and got a four o'clock appointment for the next day. The boss wasn't happy when I asked off early, but considering I'd saved them a much worse worker's compensation claim, he couldn't complain too much.

I worked until three then drove to my apartment to get ready. After showering, I dressed carefully for the appointment. I didn't own a suit, but I wore black slacks, a white shirt, and a crimson tie. If there was one habit the Army had taught me, it was ironing. My shirt was crisp with starch and flawlessly pressed. A buddy had given me a set of cufflinks made from bullet casings—souvenirs from an ambush we survived. The other side hadn't been so lucky, but that's what happened when you took shots at U.S. service-men. It might be the last thing you ever did.

My shoes were shined like ebony mirrors as I gave my name to the receptionist and was directed to take a seat. The law office was in an older building, rich with dark wood, thick books on shelves, and heavy, leather furniture in the waiting room. There was even an old brick fireplace, currently cold and dark in the summer weather.

I rested one ankle on the opposite knee, taking a deep breath to calm my nerves. I had no idea why lawyers made me nervous. Probably because my daughter was at stake. I had to make a good impres-sion—try to get him on my side—against a powerful, wealthy opponent. It was an uphill battle.

"Mr. Mackenzie."

I stood at the sound of my name behind me, spo-ken by a woman. Probably another secretary.

I turned, and promptly felt my stomach drop to my feet.

chapter six

I HADN'T EXPECTED TO see Cal ever again. Yet there he was. Fate must think she's really funny, throwing us together like this.

Apparently, "Cal" was short for "Callan Mackenzie." I had no idea why he was here. Had he tracked me down? What did he want to do? Try to explain why he'd slept with me when he was married?

Years in front of juries enabled me to keep my surprise from showing on my face. Unlike him, who looked shell-shocked, with his jaw agape. I smiled a welcoming, impersonal smile.

"It's nice to meet you, Mr. Mackenzie," I said, holding out my hand, which he shook, seemingly on autopilot. I didn't think he'd even blinked yet. "Please, follow me to my office. We'll talk there." I didn't need gossip getting around if he decided to make a public display.

I turned, but his hand on my elbow stopped me.

"Wait. *You're* Emerson Grace?"

Ah. Well, that explained a lot. He hadn't been looking for Emmy, the hookup, but Emerson, the lawyer.

"I am. Are you looking for an attorney?" Maybe he'd 'fessed up to cheating on his wife and now she was dumping him. Smart woman.

"Yeah. I mean, yes."

"Did you still want a consultation with me?" Some men didn't want a female lawyer, and he'd obviously thought I would be a man. A common mistake, but "Emmy" was too girly to put on a business card that had "Attorney at Law" following it.

"Um, yeah, I guess so."

Such a vote of confidence. Since my back was turned, I indulged in an eye roll as I led him through the labyrinthian hallway.

His eyes widened when he saw my office and I motioned him to a seat as I rounded the desk to my chair.

"This…isn't what I expected," he said, settling in the chair.

"Which part? Me? Or the office?"

"Both."

At least he was honest. "You're here for a consult, Mr. Mackenzie. Did you want to discuss your case?"

"Can I apologize first? For yesterday?"

"I prefer to keep things professional," I said.

He hesitated. "Then isn't this a conflict of interest or something? Since we've…" His voice trailed away.

"If we had an ongoing romantic relationship, yes. One-night stands don't count." He flinched ever so slightly, then it was gone.

He looked good. Really good. Slacks and a white dress shirt with creases so sharp, it looked like it could cut paper. His tie was neatly knotted and he even wore cufflinks. He crossed his legs, resting one ankle on the opposite knee, and I caught a glimpse of shoes shined to military perfection.

"How's the arm?" I asked. I could barely see the bandage through his white shirt.

"It's fine. Like I said, just a scratch." He focused on me. "What about you?"

"I'm fine, thank you." I'd worn a scarf around my neck today, and I still couldn't believe he'd had stitches without medication. Crazy.

Cal exuded a maleness that was impossible to ignore. Whether he was in jeans or a tie, his presence was palpable. He was one of those people that had a natural born presence which couldn't be learned. I wondered what rank he'd attained. I'd bet the bag of mini-Reese's hidden in my bottom desk drawer that he'd led men. He had that air of command about him that he wore as naturally as he wore the tie.

"How can I help you?" I asked.

"It's about my wife…and daughter."

My stomach sank, but I kept my expression neutral. So he was not only married, he had a child. Why in the world had he been on Tinder? It just didn't seem to fit with the rest of him.

"When I came back from my last tour a few months ago," he continued, "she served me divorce papers."

Knowing his wife had filed months ago made me feel a little better about the hookup with me. At least he hadn't went from my bed straight back to his wife's.

"I'm sorry for what you're going through. I know it's rough."

There was a pause as he regrouped. "Yeah, well, it is what it is."

I picked up my pen and began making notes. "Your wife is Lisa, correct?"

"Yes."

"And your daughter?"

"Amber. She's four."

"So you're looking for a divorce attorney, correct?"

"I had one, but fired him."

That caught my attention. "Why did you fire him?"

He took a deep breath. "Because of who my in-laws are."

I waited.

"Lisa is Lisa Atwell. Only daughter of Larry and Sharon Atwell."

Ah. I sat back in my chair. "Are your in-laws involved in the divorce?"

"Very much so. Lisa and Amber live with them and they're helping Lisa financially. She wants full custody of Amber."

I frowned. "That's unusual. It's very rare that a judge is going to not split custody between the mother and father."

"We're not exactly having an amicable divorce," he said. "She'll do anything she can to hurt me."

"Not surprising," I said, taking more notes. "Do you know why she wants the divorce?"

"It was difficult for her, when I was away. She's said she met someone else."

Divorce was hard, no matter the circumstances, and I felt for him even though he was speaking matter-of-factly.

"And your previous attorney was…?"

"Lewis Freeman."

I paused. I knew him and worked with him often.

He'd always been upfront with me in the cases we'd worked from opposite sides, and I'd never heard of him giving up a case he'd already agreed to take. Something didn't add up.

"What was the specific reason you fired him?"

"He didn't have the balls to take on my father-in-law."

"And you think I do?"

The tips of his ears turned pink. "I meant that figuratively. And yes, I heard you're a pretty damn good lawyer." He paused. "So? Will you take my case? Or are you afraid of Larry Atwell, too?"

His tone was slightly belligerent, as though daring me to say no. I half-expected him to "triple dog dare" me. Maybe it had been a conflict of personalities, which given his current agitated state, I could understand.

My professional judgment was to pass on this case. Yes, I'd said our prior history wasn't a concern, but I also wasn't so self-unaware as to think it wouldn't affect me—positively or negatively. I felt for his situation—which was completely unfair and sucked—but there were lots of family attorneys in the city.

"While I don't have any qualms about Mr. Atwell, I think I'm going to have to decline your case. My case load is full. However," I started writing, "I can recommend several other attorneys who are very good—"

"So that's it? You're supposed to be the best. But I mention Atwell and suddenly your 'case load is full?' I think you're full of shit."

I stiffened. A flash of Crazy Pete coming at me went through my head. Cal was a big guy—bigger than Pete—and he was upset. And here I was again, alone and vulnerable, in my office. I really needed to get some kind of panic button installed.

"You're entitled to think what you'd like," I said, tearing off the sheet of paper and thrusting it at him with hands that shook only slightly, but I still managed to knock over one of the photo frames on my desk. It clattered to the floor.

Cal bent down to get it, glancing at the picture. He froze, his brow furrowed.

"Who's this?"

I was taken aback at the rude question. I snatched the frame from him. "It's my husband, obviously." A candid wedding photo—me in bridal white and him in dress uniform—as we smiled into each other's eyes. I carefully set it back into position on my desk.

"I knew him."

My gaze jerked to Cal's. His expression was grim.

"What?" I managed to choke out.

"I knew him. Third Battalion, Fifth Marines, right?"

I nodded, my voice no longer working.

"We were in the Battle of Fallujah. The second one, anyway. We were briefly holed up in a house together. I remember him. Chad. But everybody called him Ch—"

"Chopper," I finished. I glanced down at my desktop and blinked several times to clear the tears from my eyes.

"Yeah, Chopper. I let him bum a smoke off me. Said he was trying to quit. That his wife would kick his ass if he came back home smelling like an ashtray."

The blinking wasn't working and a tear spilled down my cheek. I hastily brushed it away and cleared my throat. Cal maintained a respectful silence as I regained my composure. This changed things. Damn it all to hell.

It was as if Chad's ghost had materialized between me and Cal, binding us together. I knew how Chad had felt about his fellow soldiers. They were his brothers. Pure and simple. If one of his brothers needed help, he'd go through hell and high water to provide it. And he'd want me to do the same.

"My services don't come cheap," I said at last, grateful that my voice was steady, despite my quivering emotions. Money and payment were always delicate subjects, but I didn't work for free. "My hourly rate is two seventy-five, billed in quarter hour increments. A three-thousand-dollar retainer is required at all times."

Reaching into my desk, I withdrew the "welcome packet" reserved for new clients. I handed it to him.

"You'll find information in there about the firm as well as what you can expect as the proceedings move forward. I'll need to prepare some paperwork to transfer the case from your previous attorney."

Cal glanced at the folder, then back at me. "I can pay."

His tone was slightly defensive. Since he'd gotten injured at work then he obviously had a job now and was offended I'd think he didn't have money. Men and their egos...

"Great," I said brusquely, once again all business as I handed him a pen. "Then just sign the contract and I'll walk you to see Karen. She'll take care of payment."

He stood and placed the contract on my desk, leaning over it to sign with strong, bold strokes of the pen.

Taking the papers, I stood as well. "You'll want to get started on the paperwork. I'll email you electronic copies as well. And I'll let you know once the case is transferred—"

"May I ask you a question?"

His interruption startled me and I glanced up at him. "Of course."

"Are you going to tell me what happened to your throat?" He nodded to where I had the scarf knotted around my neck.

I forced a thin smile. "You're obviously not going to let this go, so fine, I will tell you. It was an unexpected visit from an irate ex-spouse of a client. He was...upset."

"He just forced his way into your office? Or did he ambush you outside?" His gaze narrowed.

"He got past Reception, but I believe they're looking into additional security now, because of the incident."

Cal's eyebrows lifted. "'The incident?'" He echoed. "He could've had a weapon. The *incident* could've been a homicide."

A shiver ran down my back. The same thought had occurred to me, but I hadn't voiced it the way Cal had just done.

"Thankfully, it wasn't," I said.

"Is he in jail?"

I shook my head. "I filed a restraining order but didn't press charges."

"Why the hell not?"

I was under no obligation to explain myself to him, yet I found herself doing so anyway. I sighed.

"Divorce is hard, Mr. Mackenzie. I don't think I have to tell you that. For most people, it's the most difficult, heartbreaking thing they've ever gone through. I've had clients tell me that the death of a parent was easier to endure than a divorce. No one gets married thinking that one day it will end in a pile of paperwork and exchanges of That's Mine/ This Is Yours. The man was upset. The case involves his children, which is any parent's number one issue, as I'm sure you can relate.

"I'm giving him the benefit of the doubt. A bit of grace, if you will. That he regrets—*profoundly* regrets—what he did and that he'll start to get his life together and move on with his new reality. In short, I'm giving him the chance to be human and make mistakes."

Cal didn't answer, just seemed to mull over what I'd said, and I couldn't tell if he thought I was being kind or being a fool. Either way, it didn't matter and I shouldn't care.

"Now, if you'll follow me."

I could almost feel his eyes boring a hole into my back as I led him. My skirt was pencil and form-fitting. Would he stare at my ass? A completely unprofessional thought, and yet, it took an act of will to walk normally. I prayed my heels wouldn't slip on the linoleum.

Luckily, I arrived at Reception without mishap and delivered him to Karen. I held out my hand.

"It was good to meet you, Mr. Mackenzie."

"Please call me Cal."

He smiled and my heart skipped a beat. Damn, but he was hot. Wow. In uniform, he had to be devastating.

"Of course. Cal. I'll be in touch."

His hand enveloped mine, warm and work-roughened, and as dry as it had been yesterday. Our eyes met and for a moment, a waterfall of memories washed over me. His lips on mine, his body—naked and warm—pressed against me. The hard length of him inside me, making me gasp.

I was frozen, holding on a bit too long. My face flushed with heat as I abruptly jerked my hand away. His lips gave a barely perceptible twitch.

"I look forward to hearing from you."

I gave a curt nod and thin smile, hurriedly retreating to my office and leaving him in Karen's capable hands.

Sitting back at my desk, I could set aside Emerson Grace, the attorney, and let Emmy emerge. I picked up the photograph of me and Chad, staring at it. We'd been so happy. The happiest day of my life.

Lightly caressing the picture through the glass, I was lost in memories. Good memories. Chad had been the first boy to pull my pigtails in fourth grade, and my first kiss in eighth. He'd made me laugh. Infuriated me. And been the boy I'd obsessed over and shared all my secrets with for years.

He'd proposed when we were eighteen. We'd been in bed together—my prom dress a pile of satin on the floor, the pieces of his tux scattered in a trail towards the bed. The aftermath of making love had left us both bathed in a warm afterglow, wrapped in each other's arms.

"Graduation is only a month away," he'd said.

My heart had seized, as it always did when the future was mentioned. Chad had joined the Marines. He left for boot camp in eight weeks. Each day that passed was another day ticking toward when we'd have to part. We hadn't been apart for more than a couple of weeks since we were nine years old.

"Is this a news flash?" I'd teased, deliberately keeping my tone light. I'd shed enough tears in private over his decision to enlist. He came from a long line of service in his family, all the way back to the Civil War. It had never occurred to him *not* to enlist.

"No, but I want to ask you something." He'd readjusted our positions so he lay on top of me and pressed a kiss to my forehead, then my chest, then scooted further down to press a kiss right above my navel.

I combed my fingers through his hair, relishing its length, which would soon be buzzed down to military regulation requirements. He propped his chin on my stomach and looked up at me. His eyes were serious and a wave of apprehension washed over me.

"What is it?" I asked. "What's wrong?"

"I love you, Emmy," he said.

My breath eased and I smiled. "I love you, too."

"I want you to marry me," he said. "Before I leave. I know it's asking a lot, marrying a soldier, but—"

I pressed my fingers against his lips, my eyes filling with tears. My smile was watery. "Yes. Yes, I'll marry you."

The ring had been small, but I hadn't minded. The wedding was likewise, and though our parents had misgivings because of our age, no one objected.

Chad and I had been inseparable for so long, we'd even been voted the Forever Couple by our graduating class.

We'd moved when he'd been assigned to the 5th Marines and he deployed while I attended college and got my prelaw degree, then continued into law school with a brief break in between to take a breath. Years of sporadic visits home, Skyping, and emails. Years of endless worrying, fear a constant companion. He'd surprised me at my law school graduation, somehow getting a pass home for four days. It had been one of the most ecstatic moments of my life, seeing him walk across the stage as I accepted my degree. He'd been in full uniform. I'd ran to him, crying, and he'd caught me up in my arms. The crowd had gone nuts.

Three months later, he was dead.

And Cal had known him.

Carefully, I set the frame back on my desk, angling it so the light didn't reflect and obscure the photo.

What would Chad think if he knew I'd slept with another man? A stranger, at that?

I knew what he'd say. First, he'd want to know why in the hell it had taken me so long. Chad would've wanted me to move on more quickly than I had. To not let my youth pass me by, mourning his death.

But it hadn't been only his death I'd been mourning.

A while later, the alarm on my phone dinged, reminding me that it was time to go. I'd developed a bad habit of losing track of time when I worked and not leaving until eight or nine o'clock at night. Donny and Marie took out their displeasure at this habit on my carpet. After cleaning up one too many spots on the floor, I had set an alarm for six o'clock. Any work not done by then would either wait until tomorrow, or go home with me.

Sliding my work tablet into my satchel, I added a few files that needed to be read over tonight. I had a trial Thursday that I needed to prep for. After grabbing my purse, blowing out the *Fresh Cut Roses* scented candle, and locking the door, I headed out.

I always parked in the back lot behind the building, letting clients have the spaces in front, and the evening shadows had already progressed as I crossed to my car. As I got closer, I noticed that it looked weird, as though it was sitting at an odd angle. I was right on top of it before I figured out the problem.

Two flat tires.

"You have got to be kidding me," I muttered, stopping in my tracks.

Both the driver's side front and rear wheels were flat as pancakes. Rounding the car I checked...the other two were fine.

Setting my stuff on the ground, I crouched down to examine the wheels more closely. Had someone done this? But it was too shadowed in the unlit lot to tell, which was when I realized that if someone *had* done it deliberately...they were probably waiting to ambush me. Just like Cal had said.

"Hey—"

The sudden voice behind my made my yelp. In my scramble to stand and turn around, my body couldn't decide which to do first. Which meant I ended up slipping sideways onto my ass with my back against the car. A dark figure loomed over me.

"It's okay. It's me," Cal said, crouching down.

My breath released in a *whoosh* of relief when I recognized him. My heart was pounding and I was lightheaded from blood rushing to my limbs in the *flight* part of *fight or flight*.

"You scared me half to death," I snapped, my relief warring with embarrassment. He offered his hand, which I reluctantly took as he helped me to my feet. I was glad of the shadows, sure that my face was beet red by now. To disguise my embarrassment, I brushed at the gravel dust now covering my backside. I'd just had this skirt dry-cleaned, too.

"Sorry about that," he said. "It looked like you were having trouble with your car. I thought you might need help."

"Why are you still here?" I asked, ignoring his comment. "You over an hour ago." A client lying in wait for me in the parking lot wasn't at *all* creepy.

He hesitated before answering, then his jaw hardened, as though resolved. "I didn't like the angry client story. There's not enough lighting in this parking lot and you're the last to leave. You're a fucking sitting duck out here and obviously your partners don't give a shit."

The cold anger in his voice surprised me, and I was momentarily at a loss for words.

"Two flat tires?" he continued. "Not a coincidence." He bent down to examine them. "Slashed. And not even a damn security camera recording the parking lot."

I blanched at the revelation that my tires had been slashed. That…wasn't good.

"Um, are you sure?" I asked. He just looked at me. "Did you see anything?"

He shook his head. "I left for a while, then it just kept bothering me, so I came back to check on you."

Hmm. "Okay, well, then I guess I'll just call a tow truck."

I was a capable woman. I'd been taking care of myself and my problems all by myself for years now. If there was one thing I'd learned, it was that there wasn't anything that a Google search and a phone call couldn't handle. Sure enough, within two minutes, I'd hired a tow truck that promised to be there within thirty minutes.

Cal had watched all this transpire with an expression I couldn't read. He was leaning against my car, arms folded across his chest and one ankle resting on the other. I deliberately kept my gaze from wandering. That pose tightened the fabric of his shirt over his shoulders and biceps, which appeared more formidable than when he'd been sitting across from my desk. He'd rolled back the shirt sleeves, lost the tie, and undone the top buttons of his shirt, exposing his throat.

So much for not letting my gaze wander.

"Um, well, thanks for sticking around," I said, feeling as awkward as a teenager suddenly left alone with the high school's requisite Bad Boy. "The truck should be here soon." Should I tell him to leave? That would be rude. Probably. But standing here in the lot for the next thirty minutes, trying to make small talk, sounded excruciating. I opted for rude.

"You can go," I blurted. "I'm sure I'll be fine. I'll

just wait inside my car." The engine worked so I'd have air conditioning.

"You can wait wherever you'd like, but I'm not leaving."

My mouth fell open. I closed it with a snap. "Listen, I appreciate the whole...bodyguard thing you're doing, but it's unnecessary. I can take care of myself."

His lips twitched, which was infuriating. And sexy. Damn it.

"Whoever slashed your tires obviously has a knife. Do you have a weapon on you?"

I pressed my lips together. My silence was obvious.

"Didn't think so."

His gaze was disconcertingly direct. And fringed in the longest, lushest lashes I'd ever seen on a man.

And now I'm sounding like a romance novel.

"How do I know that *you're* not the one who slashed my tires?" I asked, the thought suddenly occurring to me.

"What possible motive would I have for doing that, counselor?"

Thinly veiled amusement in his voice made me grit my teeth. "I don't know. Crazy people do crazy things. Maybe so you'd be out here, pretending to be a...a knight in shining armor and I'd be indebted to you? Who knows?"

"Can't someone be nice without wanting something in return?"

"Not in my experience, no." My bluntness seemed to sober him, the slight smile fading from his lips.

"I'm not opposed to you being indebted to me," he said, and the undercurrent beneath my words made inappropriate images spring to my mind. "However, I was honestly just looking out for you."

"But...why?" Yes, we'd slept together once, but he'd made it clear he wasn't interested in a relation-ship. And now as my client, I was the one who should be looking out for him, not the other way around.

His gaze held mine. "Because you need it, and I'm capable of giving it."

If that wasn't a double entendre, I would eat my law license.

This was not my area of expertise. Flirting. The dat-ing dance. Mating ritual. Whatever. I'd married my high school sweetheart. The last time I'd flirted had been when I'd made a mix-tape for Chad in eighth grade.

Not that I should be doing *any* of those things with Cal. He was my client now. That's it. I stiffened my spine.

"While I appreciate your...chivalry," my tone said *chivalry* in his case might be overrated, "I don't 'need' it. What I do need, is for our relationship to be a pro-fessional one. I hope you understand and accept that."

"I wasn't suggesting it wasn't." He gave a careless shrug, as if my mild rebuke was unnecessary. "Call it me being a good guy. There are some of us still left, you know."

Okay, now I felt embarrassment creep up. Had I misread his words? Maybe he really was just being a nice guy, and I'd thought he was flirting with me. Maybe he was secretly laughing at my jumping to conclusions. Lord, when did this get to be so hard?

I was saved from answering by the arrival of the tow truck. I gave the guy the keys and puttered nearby, watching, and generally trying to avoid Cal, who persisted in sticking around. Finally, the car was loaded up and the driver gave me a clipboard with paperwork to sign.

"Where am I taking it?" he asked. The name *Rich* was embroidered on his left chest. Rich was a short, stocky guy with a thick moustache. Polite, but he obviously wanted to be done with his shift for the day.

The question momentarily stumped me. I hadn't gotten around to Googling a tire shop.

"Um, a tire place, I guess." *Could I sound any more like a girl right now?*

"Take it to Randy's, over off Ohio and Wabash," Cal said to Rich, then turned to me. "I know him. He's a buddy of mine. He won't screw you."

"Oh my god, could you please stop with the sex talk?!" I felt like snapping at him, but bit my tongue instead, nodding. "Sure. Sounds good."

Rich didn't seem to care one way or the other what I thought and was jotting it down. "Got it. You need a ride, lady?"

"I've got her," Cal said before I could respond, which was good enough for Rich, who was already climbing into the cab of his truck. With a snort of diesel smoke and groan of metal, he pulled out.

Which left me with Cal.

I dug for my phone. "I'll just get an Uber home. Thanks for staying." Ah, manners. The things we lie about in the name of being polite.

"I can give you a lift. I'm headed that direction anyway."

Someone please send a bolt of lightning, right now. I

wasn't sure if I wanted the bolt to hit Cal or me, but either one would work.

"It's really not necessary," I tried again.

"Please," he said, giving me a disarming smile. Damn. There was that one dimple again. "Allow me to give my new lawyer a ride home."

There was legit no way out of this, and though my better judgment said I should avoid any more time than was necessary with him, I nodded, giving in with a sigh.

"Okay, then. I accept."

chapter seven

I HELD THE DOOR open for her, wishing I had a nicer car than a decades-plus old Ford pickup that had seen better days. At least the seat was clean, and I'd just run it through a car wash.

Emmy didn't get in. I glanced at the height of the cab, then down at her. I realized the issue a moment later.

"Here," I said, taking her purse and satchel from her with one hand, while offering my other to assist. Between the heels and pencil skirt, she wasn't exactly dressed for climbing into a truck. She hesitated for a split second before taking my hand.

The bones of her fingers felt too delicate in my grip, her palm soft and smooth. Her manicured nails lightly scraped against my skin, evoking memories of those same nails against my back.

Fuck. Instant hard on. *Nice. Now she's going to think you're a total jackass.*

Since I was "already there," so to speak, I enjoyed the view. The pencil skirt clung to her nicely rounded ass and her legs were the perfect curve from calf down to slender ankle. Which only brought back memories of those legs wrapped around me—

I cleared my throat and tore my gaze from her ankles up to her face. She was perched in the seat now and gave the purse I still held a pointed look.

"Oh. Oh, yeah. Sorry." I handed the purse and satchel over, then shut the door, wincing at the creak and slam it made.

Okay, I had to get my shit together. She was my lawyer now, and not someone I should be fantasizing about and ogling like I was a teenager.

I slid behind the wheel, glad I'd decided to come back after our meeting. Once I'd gotten over my surprise at seeing who exactly "Emerson" was, that is. And the sticker shock of her retainer. My bank account was now dangerously low, but what else was new?

The parking lot was a stalker's dream, with poor lighting and no foot traffic to speak of. The tires couuld've been slashed by anyone with a single witness. Speaking of which…

"Does your insurance cover vandalism?" I asked. My insurance was strictly liability—the cheapest—but I bet she had the full package deal.

"Um, yeah, I think so." She shrugged. "I'll call my agent in the morning."

"Do you own a gun?"

The look she gave me was startled. "Of course not."

"Why 'of course not'?" I asked. "You're a woman, living alone, with a job that obviously makes enemies. You should own a gun for your own protection."

"I have my dogs," she said, a note of defensiveness in her voice.

I laughed outright. "Tweedledee and Tweedledum? Yeah, they're vicious predators."

"They're Donny and Marie," she corrected me, crossing her arms over her chest. "And they serve as more of an...early warning system."

"So you can what? Grab a rolling pin?"

"Or run away," she retorted.

"On those legs? You'd only escape if your home invader was a midget."

Those emerald eyes of hers narrowed and I could practically feel the spark of anger I'd lit in her. It was the red hair. Fiery in bed. Fiery out of bed. I bet that in a courtroom, she was something to see. She probably had juries eating out of her hand.

"Little people," she said, turning to look out the windshield.

"What?"

"The proper term is little people, not midgets."

I grinned. "Are you going to sue me?"

"It's not against the law to be ignorant."

Ouch. Man, she had a mouth on her. My grin widened. I liked it. I liked a woman who gave as good as she got. Dumb got boring pretty damn quick. Not that I should care about how much fun she was to tease, or whether or not she owned a firearm.

"Tell me about your daughter," she said, abruptly changing the subject.

The windows were down because I had no air conditioning in the truck, which I didn't mind, but I doubted she was used to it. She didn't say anything about it though, just tucked some flyaway hair behind her ear.

I sobered. This was business. The most important

business I'd ever had. "Her name's Amber. She just turned four. You know that part. She's a sweet kid. At the moment, she won't go anywhere without wearing her sparkly pink tutu. Even the playground. It's getting pretty beat up. She goes to a pricey pre-school Lisa's parents pay for, but she loves it there."

"Has she and her mom always lived with her parents?"

I shook my head. "No. We had our own place when we first got married. Then she got pregnant and I was on my second tour. There were problems with the pregnancy and Lisa was put on bed rest. That's when she moved in with her parents. She never left. Sold a lot of our furniture and put the house on the market."

By now, Emmy had taken out a legal pad from her satchel and was taking notes.

"Have you currently come to an agreement on visitation while the divorce proceedings go through?"

"I thought we had," I replied. "But they keep changing things. On days I'm supposed to see her, she'll have a birthday party to go to. Or they say she doesn't feel good. It's always something." I tried and failed to keep the frustration out of my voice. "Lisa just told me yesterday that her parents took her to Disney World today. For two weeks."

"Without consulting you?"

"Yes. She's never been before." The pain hit again, but I ignored it.

"And how did you take Lisa wanting a divorce?" Emmy asked, seeming to zero-in on that something in my voice I'd tried to conceal.

I pressed my lips together, remembering my anticipation on the flight home. I couldn't wait to have my little girl in my arms again. Lisa, too, but things had been rough between us. I'd had hopes of repairing our relationship, now that my final tour was through, even though she'd said she was seeing someone else. I was the father of her child. Surely that counted for something.

"You know how you see those videos on Facebook," I said, "of servicemen and women being met at the airport by crying family members waving American flags and handwritten signs?"

"Yes."

"There was a man holding a sign with my name on it. Instead of seeing my little girl run towards me calling me Daddy, I was served with divorce papers."

Emmy was silent for a moment, and when I chanced a glance toward her, I saw sympathy in her gaze. My lips twisted in a humorless smile.

"I bet you hear a lot of sob stories," I said.

"I do," I agreed. "Some are worse than others, though. That one is pretty bad. Were you and your wife experiencing problems?"

I gave a harsh laugh. "Being halfway around the planet for months on end with limited communication tends to be a bit rough on relationships."

"I'm sorry to hear that."

Another glance at her. She seemed sincere. Our gazes caught and held for a moment, then she turned back to her pad, scribbling something.

"I've tried reasoning with her," I continued. "But she won't do anything about it. The last thing she said about it was that her mom would be handling the exchange of Amber on the days she was to visit me. I'm always to drop her off at their house, with anywhere with just Lisa."

"So when was the last time you saw Amber?"

I did a mental calculation. "Twelve days." I turned into her neighborhood. She hadn't given me directions, but I hadn't needed them either. Neither of us mentioned it.

"Well, the first thing I'm going to do after filing your change of attorney with the court is establish visitation. If this is going to drag out, there's no reason why they should be keeping your daughter from you. And judges aren't stupid. It's not as though your in-laws are the first to come up with myriad excuses to get out of visitation."

"That's good to know. I miss my little girl." Pulling into her driveway, I put the truck in Park and turned off the engine.

"Thanks for the ride," Emmy said, already stuffing the notepad into her satchel. "But you don't have to get out."

"I thought I might check your house," I said, creaking open my door. "Just in case." By the time I was out and had rounded the truck, she had slid down from the seat and was gathering her things.

"It was probably a random vandal," she said, not looking at me. "Those things happen."

"Sure. You bet. I'm sure it's a complete coincidence that the victim happens to be a beautiful, single woman leaving work alone." My sarcasm was thick, but I was getting irritated. For a smart woman, she was acting dumb.

Her gaze shot to me, her eyes wide.

"It's obvious you don't do *criminal* law," I groused. "You'd never make it."

Emmy didn't argue the point, instead leading the way to her front door. When her key scratched the lock, the dogs started going crazy inside. She shot me a smug look over her shoulder.

"See? They sound vicious. A more useful—and safer—deterrent than owning a gun."

"Until they get inside and find out the attack dogs just want to cuddle."

Her smug look soured. Pushing open the door, two fluffy bundles bounded out. No longer barking, but swarming Emmy's legs before noticing me and rushing to give me the same welcome.

"Their tags should say 'Welcoming Committee,'" I joked, reaching down to scratch one behind the ears. The dog promptly flipped onto it's back for a tummy rub.

"No, don't!" Emmy shoved me out of the way. "Donny! No!'"

I jerked back in surprise. "What?"

"You can't pet his tummy when he's just met you." Weird. "Why? Too personal?"

She glared at me. "No. It's because if he gets too excited, he piddles."

"He what?"

"You know." She wiggled her finger. "He piddles. Sprays potty."

Oh. "Charming."

"It's not his fault he has bladder control issues." The dog flopped back over and gazed up adoringly as I patted his head.

"Where did you put them the night I was here?" They'd just kind of disappeared.

"They were in a separate room," she said. "Usually, they sleep with me, but…you know." She shrugged, her cheeks turning pink.

I grimaced. "Yeah. I don't much care for an audience either."

She burst out laughing. I grinned, too, realizing I hadn't heard her laugh yet, though it was worth the wait. It was the kind of laugh that made you want to laugh along with her. It lit up her face and made her eyes twinkle like they described in books.

"Exactly," she said, leaning closer and lowering her voice. "I don't want to shock my dogs. They'd never look at me the same."

We shared another laugh, and suddenly I was more comfortable with her than I'd been before. Even when I'd been in her bed.

Sex was easy. You didn't even have to *like* someone to have sex. But I liked Emmy. I liked her a lot. Damn it.

"Okay, well, I think the house is clear but if it'll make you happy, help yourself." She gave a wave toward the foyer and I preceded her into the house.

It was just as I remembered. Spacious, expensively decorated, yet still homey. I wondered if she'd done her own decorating or hired it done.

Honestly, I didn't think anyone had broken in, but the tires hadn't been some random coincidence. I'd bet my left nut on that. Whether it had been someone who'd wanted to ambush her, or just cost her money and frustration, I didn't know. So while no one was probably under her bed or in the closet, I could get a look at the security and locks she had on the house. Maybe recommend improvements, if they weren't good enough. Something to make myself useful... and avoid going "home" to my empty apartment.

Damn, I hated my apartment with a passion. The place smelled, there was never enough hot water, and the people above me walked around like a herd of elephants. It wasn't "home." It was just a place to crash. My home was gone.

I left Emmy downstairs, still greeting the furballs, and headed up.

The hallway was shadowed. The long carpet runner over the hardwood cushioned my steps. Two other bedrooms up here, other than the master, and both were void of any strange visitors. The windows were solid and there wasn't any way someone could get to them from the ground. While the back yard had plenty of full-grown trees, no branches that were close looked sturdy enough to hold a person's weight.

The master bedroom...smelled like her. I took a deep breath, remembering. It wasn't just her perfume, but *her*. And I realized why the house seemed like a home. It was her. *She* smelled like home.

I shook my head. I was seriously losing it. I'd been with this woman one time. Granted, she'd been the first in an eleven-month drought, but still. If I was going to afford her fee, I'd need to take Shane's advice. And going gooey-eyed over a woman I'd slept with once wasn't going to help pay the bills.

And she couldn't know about any of that. If Emmy found out why I'd come that night—or what I was going to have to do to make the serious kind of money her firm charged—she'd fire me as a client and despise me. Probably in that order. I wasn't dumb enough to know that if anyone found out about my "occupation," I'd lose any chance of getting Amber back. But I was desperate, and if a few lonely house-wives could help me pay the bills until then…well, sometimes you had to swallow your pride and do what you had to do.

When I returned downstairs, she'd let the dogs out into the yard and kicked off her heels. I found her in the kitchen, leaning into the open fridge. Her sleeve-less blouse was untucked as well.

"You know, it doesn't help to say I'm going to check the house if you don't stay in one location," I chastised her.

She stood, holding a wine bottle in one hand and a package of raw chicken in the other. With one hip, she nudged the refrigerator door closed.

"Like I said, my noise machines would've let me know if someone was here," she said, setting the wine and chicken on the granite island in the center of the kitchen.

The "noise machines" were currently scratching at the sliding glass door. Her kitchen had an adjacent sitting room that looked out over the back yard. I walked through to let in the dogs. One of them trot-ted in while the other launched herself inside as if on a springboard. There was a large deck on the back of the house, which held a set of wicker patio furniture and a gas grill.

The evening had settled in and the shadows were getting deep. I closed and locked the door, then flipped on a lamp next to the leather loveseat. This appeared to be a room Emmy used quite a bit. There was an open book lying face down on the coffee table and plush blanket folded over the arm of the couch. A brick fireplace was built into the corner with a bookcase next to it, its shelves full.

I perused the titles, expecting...I didn't know what exactly. But what I *didn't* expect was that the majority of the books would be romances. I picked one at random. *The Duke Finds His Lady*. A woman in a gown was on the cover, her hair flowing over her shoulders. *Hmm*. I tried another one. *How to Marry a Marquis*. Similar cover. I began to read the summary on the back.

"What are you doing?" Emmy snatched the book from me, replacing it on the shelf. "You shouldn't snoop."

"I wasn't snooping. They're books on a shelf. That's not snooping. Now, if I looked in your medicine cabinet, *that's* snooping."

"Whatever." She crossed her arms over her chest and glared at me. "You going to make fun now?"

"Hey, I don't care what you read." I shrugged. "A little surprised that English aristocracy is your thing, that's all. If you're interested, I hear Prince Harry is available."

She didn't smile at my teasing.

I held up my hands in a gesture of surrender. "No more cracks. Promise."

She relented, uncrossing her arms. "Good. I deal with enough broken hearts and marriages at work. I like to read about happy endings when I need an escape."

"To each their vice of choice," I said. "I prefer *Playboy*, myself. You know, for the articles." I winked and she rolled her eyes, passing me to head back into the kitchen.

"Actually, he's not available," she said as I followed her.

"Who isn't?"

"Prince Harry." She dug around some more in the fridge, removing some vegetables and adding them to the growing stack on the island. "He's married now. How could you not know that?"

"I must have missed my British Royalty Update memo."

She did smile a little at that crack and I felt a thrill of satisfaction. Making her laugh was harder than making her come.

I watched her for a moment as she began prepping the vegetables. Her knife block held some serious stuff and she was handling the massive chef's blade like she knew what she was doing.

Another pang of sadness struck me. I couldn't cook worth a shit and couldn't remember the last time I'd had a decent home-cooked meal. Food lately was either fast food, sandwiches, or microwaved frozen meals. Lisa had been a pretty decent cook, when she'd had the time.

Divorce sucked.

"You're quiet," Emmy said, raising an eyebrow at me while she sliced a zucchini. "Still considering your lack of current knowledge as to the marital state of the Windsor family?"

Since she wasn't kicking me out—yet—I perched on one of the four bar stools on the opposite side of the island, watching her.

"Just thinking how much divorce sucks," I said

bluntly. "Little things wives do that you don't really appreciate until they're not there anymore. A lit candle that makes the place smell like cookies. Never running out of toothpaste. Pictures on the walls and too many throw pillows. Plants scattered around. Stuff that makes a house into a home, I guess."

"I take it things between you and Lisa weren't always bad, then."

"Of course not. We were your stereotypical in-love, blissful couple for a year. Bought a small house together, a starter home. She decorated it. I mowed the grass and built her a flower bed. We grilled out on Friday, had date night on Saturday, and friends over to watch the game on Sunday."

"So what happened? If you don't mind my asking?" She moved on to chopping a red bell pepper.

"Short story is I got laid off. Money got tight. I joined the Army."

"That must've been a hard decision to make, deciding to enlist," she said with a frown. "How did she take it?"

"She wasn't happy, but we looked at what we needed to do for her to stay in school. Becoming a nurse was very important to her. Her parents never approved of her marrying a guy from the wrong side of the tracks. Guess in the end she figured they were right. She's seeing some doctor now." Of course she was. I should've seen that coming a mile away.

"How long were you in the service? Four years?"

I hesitated. "A little over eight, actually."

My brows rose. "You re-enlisted."

"Turned out, I was pretty good at what I did."

"Which was?" She dumped all the chopped vegetables into a mixing bowl and reached for a bottle of olive oil.

"Infantry. Nothing special. I led a squad for a while, got promoted until I'd be promoted to a non-combat position next, then I got out."

She went still, her eyes wide. "Really? Wow. That sounds...incredibly dangerous." She drizzled the oil over the vegetables, not even having to measure.

"Shooting bad guys who don't look like your typical bad guys isn't a safe occupation. You have to do some things that civilians couldn't imagine. But you do what has to be done, no matter what." The thought I'd just had upstairs. Funny how I was equating the two occupations in my mind.

Emmy went to her pantry and took out a box of something and a jar of what looked like spaghetti sauce.

"So, what are you making?" I asked, wanting to change the subject.

"A lighter version of chicken parmesan. Served over sautéed veggies in marinara, rather than pasta."

I watched her get out a mallet and plastic film, spreading the film onto the counter before opening the chicken and placing the raw meat on it. There were two chicken breasts.

"Are you through checking the house then?" she asked, raising her voice to be heard over her pounding the breasts flat.

"Um, yeah. Sure," I said, sliding off the stool. That must be my cue. "The locks you have are pretty good, though I'm surprised you don't have an actual security system. The dogs don't count," I added, cutting her off before she could say it.

I eyed the chicken as she began dipping them into flour, then a mixture of egg and milk, then bread crumbs. Chicken parm sounded amazing, even if it wasn't with noodles. I didn't need the carbs anyway, not with the crap I'd been eating lately. Good thing I ran to and from work, it helped with all the slices of frozen pizza I'd consumed.

My stomach growled and she must've heard it because her lips curved.

"Since you did give me a ride home, I guess I should invite you to stay for dinner, if you—"

"Awesome, thanks!" I sank back onto the stool. "Anything I can do to help?" A home-cooked meal. My mouth was already watering.

"You can open the wine." She handed me the bottle and corkscrew.

"That I can do." I worked the corkscrew while she got two glasses from the cupboard and set them in front of me.

"Do you cook much?" she asked, removing a large skillet from a cabinet and setting it on the gas stove behind her.

"My culinary skills extend to whatever can be microwaved or delivered."

She laughed again at that. "To be honest, I love to cook, but there's not quite as much satisfaction in cooking for one." Still smiling, she added. "There's no one to make yummy noises and tell me how good it is."

I poured the wine. "No problem. I can make yummy noises all night long." It was out of my mouth before I had thought that through and I winced. She just snorted.

"Men always oversell themselves."

I chuckled, delighted that she'd made a joke. She seemed much more relaxed and like the woman I'd first met, rather than the formal professional she'd been in her office. Well, she'd probably wondered at first why the hell I was there.

"So did you think I was some crazy stalker or something, showing up in your office today?"

She turned on the stove burner and adjusted the flame. "I was a bit taken aback at first."

"Must've been fate." I winked.

She rolled her eyes. "I don't believe in fate. It was an unlikely coincidence."

"You don't think you have a grand plan in the universe?"

She shook her head, her expression turning grim. "If fate exists and there's some grand plan, then I must've pissed somebody off in a past lifetime."

I was confused for a minute, then remembered. Chopper. Dead. Of course. No wonder she was cynical about life. What had she said that night? Only two months from coming home...

"A guaranteed death sentence," I mused.

"Excuse me?"

I glanced up at her. "Soldiers are a superstitious bunch. Crazily so. In a firefight, you never stand next to someone who's under the Soldier's Curse."

She frowned, adding the chicken to the hot skillet. The filets sizzled in the hot oil. "What's the Soldier's Curse?"

"It's a trifecta that you don't do," I said, counting on my fingers. "One. Never get engaged or married right before you're deployed. Two. No getting your girl pregnant before you're deployed. And three, the eight-week countdown. Knowing it's almost time to go home makes you relax, more careless. Any of those things is just tempting fate. The Soldier's Curse."

She didn't say anything, just turned away and fiddled with the chicken cooking in the pan. I winced at my own insensitivity. Just because I could be matter-of-fact about that shit didn't mean she'd take her husband's death with the same stoicism.

Emmy had stopped messing with the chicken and just stood there, her back to me. Her spine was rigid, then I heard a sniff.

Shit.

I slid off the stool and rounded the island to stand next to her. I tentatively laid a hand on her shoulder, felt the warmth of her skin through the thin satin of the blouse.

"Hey, I'm sorry. That was a shitty thing to say. I can be a total dick sometimes. I didn't mean anything by it. It's just superstition."

She glanced up at me, and I was horrified to see tears shining in her eyes, turning them an even more brilliant green. Fuck. Women crying. My Achilles Heel.

Raised with my three sisters, I'd always had the burning need to fix whatever it was that was making one of them cry. Whether it was a bully at school, a nasty fall from a bike, or a breakup with their latest boyfriend, their big brother would take care of it.

And now not only was this woman crying, *I* had been the one to cause it. *Asshole dick fucking douchebag idiot.* But calling myself every name I could think of wouldn't help Emmy.

"It's just a dumb superstition," I said helplessly. "Please don't cry. Let's talk about something else." Should I hug her? She probably wouldn't want that, since I was a client now, not a lover or even a hookup.

She took a deep breath and blinked away the tears before turning her attention back to the pan. "It's almost ready. You should go wash up."

That was my cue to give her some privacy to collect herself. I gave her shoulder a squeeze—not too hard. The bones I could feel seemed as delicate as those in her hands.

"I should just go," I said gently.

"No, no, it's okay. Really. I'm fine." She gave me a wan smile. "Besides, I've made too much food for just me, and you promised to make yummy noises."

I hesitated, not wanting to overstay my welcome. But the smell in the kitchen was making my stomach growl again. And I knew from experience that if I left now while she was down, she'd likely be down all evening. I'd made her cry. Now I should sit my ass down and make her laugh again.

"You're sure?"

She nodded. "Absolutely."

"Okay then. I will go…wash up." I smiled, then realized I was still touching her shoulder, and snatched my hand back. Which was so Not Smooth. To cover my embarrassment, I hurried away. I'd seen a bathroom down the hall toward the foyer.

I watched Cal go for a second, then turned back to get the chicken from the pan before it burned. The marinara and veggies went in, then chicken, then cheese, and all into the oven for a few minutes.

Then I stood there, letting the wave of remembered grief wash over me.

It didn't come as often anymore, and sometimes there were whole days when I didn't think about Chad and the life we'd almost had. I hadn't been mentally prepared for what Cal had told me. It had come straight out of left field.

Significant dates, certain songs, particular odors… those were things I knew about ahead of time and could handle. But now, knowing that I myself might've contributed to the awful tragedy fate had dealt Chad…

I couldn't think like that. At least, not right now. Cal was going to be back any second and didn't need to find his attorney a weeping mess. Besides, I didn't believe in fate. Or superstitions.

By the time Cal came back, I'd gotten out two place settings and silverware, and was removing the skillet from the oven. The cheese had melted and turned a nice golden color. I plated the food and set one in front of me, the other in front of the stool to my right.

"This looks amazing," he said, taking a seat, his eyes glued to the piled high plate. He waited until I'd sat, too, before picking up his fork and diving in.

I watched with some amusement at the enthusiasm with which he ate. There was nothing quite like the satisfaction of having a meal you'd cooked be devoured by a man who appreciated it. I ate more slowly and was only half done by the time he'd all but licked his plate clean.

"That was fantastic," he said, sitting back with a satisfied sigh. "Literally, the best dinner I've had in years."

I laughed. "That can't possibly be true, but I appreciate the compliment."

He shook his head. "No, I'm serious. Thank you for the meal."

He did indeed sound sincere, so I smiled. "You're welcome. Thanks for the ride home."

I took the two plates to the sink and set them down. Donny and Marie dutifully trotted after me, waiting for a bit of scraps that I'd begun spoiling them with years ago. It was an impossible habit to break once started. I gave them each a couple bites of chicken, Marie carefully sniffing it first, just in case this was the one time it could be poisonous. Donny didn't even chew, but just swallowed it whole.

Now it was time for my new client to leave, which was too bad. It had been nice not to eat dinner alone. When I glanced up, I found him watching me intently. Our gazes caught and my breath froze in my chest. I felt that same tingling awareness that night when I'd let him inside my house and he'd looked me over from head to toe. He'd devoured my dinner, and now it looked like he wanted to devour me.

Cal was so…manly, for lack of a better term. He was big and muscled, with deep set eyes, gorgeous cheekbones, a square jaw, and strong brow. One look at him and you knew: military. He'd let his hair grow out, though, which had been a good decision. He had great, thick hair. His hands were large and strong, the nails very short, and he carried himself with an assured confidence that didn't lean over into arrogance.

He'd been a passionate lover, in control, and intuitive. I'd relived the encounter in my mind several times since, even after he'd blown me off. I'd expected to have pangs of guilt afterwards, but it seemed I really had moved on from Chad. At least, in some ways.

"Well," I said, forcing a smile and breaking the suddenly tense silence. "I guess I'll be in touch as soon as I have some news."

He slid off the stool as I rounded the island to show him out. I had another flash of memory and briefly regretted circumstances were such that a relationship with Cal was impossible.

"Thanks again for taking my case," he said, pausing in the doorway. "And remember to lock your doors. If you decide you want to buy a gun, I can help you."

I shook my head. "I appreciate that, but I wouldn't feel comfortable. Thanks for the offer, though."

He said nothing, just smiled as though he'd already known what I was going to say before I'd said it.

"Goodnight, Cal."

"Goodnight."

I watched him walk to his truck and fire it up. It was the kind of truck I'd imagined him driving. Not flashy or new, but something that had seen hard work and hard times and wore its age well. Kind of like Cal.

I cleaned up the dishes and let the dogs out for their before-bedtime potty break. I prepped the coffee pot for in the morning and made my lunch. More lettuce and vinaigrette. Keeping weight off was a bitch, especially when you were short. *Petite,* I mentally corrected.

Yeah. Whatever.

"Donny! Marie! Come!" I huddled in the doorway, the night having turned unseasonably chilly. Donny bounded up the steps, always eager to leave nature behind for the comfort of the Great Indoors.

"Marie," I called. As usual, Marie was taking her time, her dark coat blending in with the shadows. "Come get a treat!" Marie pretended deafness unless food was involved.

I expected to hear her collar jangling, but there was nothing.

Slightly uneasy, I stepped onto the deck, scanning the yard. "Marie, come!" The wood of the deck was warm against my bare feet and a light breeze filtered through the thin silk of my blouse.

A slight yelp made me twist to the right. My heart stopped, then sped into overtime. I ran to the side of the deck.

"Marie! Come to mommy! Come get a treat!" My feet thumped down the stairs and I saw the shadow of something streak away across the lawn. "Marie!"

The jangling of metal against metal made me breathe a sigh of relief as Marie trotted up the stairs. I scooped her into my arms.

"You scared me to death," I chastised, cuddling the dog close. Marie apparently felt the same, because she squirmed, frantically licking my face. "What was that? A mean squirrel? Bunny rabbit?" Marie was notoriously timid, but she also was protective of "her" territory. Maybe she'd decided to take on an animal.

There was a prickling on the back of my neck and I paused outside the door, looking back over my shoulder. But the shadows were still and silent, except now they seemed menacing instead of peaceful. Between the tires and Cal's warnings, my paranoia was in overdrive.

I shuddered, hurrying inside before carefully bolting the door and drawing the blinds. Maybe I should take Cal's advice and see about getting an alarm system. It hadn't been a bad idea.

Making a mental note and still carrying Marie, I headed upstairs, Donny trotting behind in our wake.

chapter eight

I SETTLED INTO A corner booth of the bar, keeping an eye on the door. I ordered a Glenfiddich, neat. I was a few minutes early, which was preferable to being late.

My mind wandered as I waited. Last night had been nice. Too nice. I liked Emmy. Liked her in a way that I shouldn't even consider. Not only because she was my lawyer now, but because she was a fellow soldier's widow. It was bad enough that I'd slept with her. Call that weakness and lack of judgment—*and* I'd thought I'd never see her again.

She was gorgeous and sexy, smart as hell, and could cook like a dream. The whole package—that was completely off-limits. Even if she wasn't my lawyer, you didn't go poaching a brother's widow. It just wasn't done, no matter what Nicholas Sparks said. And it wasn't as if I had a lot to offer a woman like her. Getting divorced, broke, and a dead-end job. Every woman's dream. Not.

The door opened, the small bell clanging against the glass and distracting me from my thoughts. Two guys, about mid-twenties entered. Not who I was looking for.

A few sips of my drink and a handful of minutes later, the door opened again. An older woman entered, perhaps mid-to-late fifties. She wore black slacks and sensible heels, with a deep wine-colored wraparound shirt. It tied at her hip and matched the color of the purse she carried. Her hair was a striking mix of black streaked with silver and brushed her shoulders.

It had to be her. Time to forget about Emmy and get my mind back on how I was going to pay her. Amber was worth whatever needed to be done, and Emmy was my best bet at getting her back.

I slid from the booth and stood, drawing the woman's eye. She hesitated, then headed toward me, her stride purposeful.

"Mr. Mackenzie?" she asked once she got closer.

"Cal, please," I said, gesturing to the booth. "Have a seat."

She obeyed and I slid in opposite her. She fussed with her purse for a moment and I took the opportunity to study her.

On closer inspection, she looked older than I'd initially thought. Fine lines marred her skin and there were dark circles under her eyes that couldn't be concealed with makeup. She looked weary, but still held signs of classic beauty and poise that age couldn't diminish.

"You must be Donna," I said, holding out my hand. "It's a pleasure to meet you."

Her fingers were chilled, but her grip was steady and firm. "Likewise."

"May I get you a drink?" Easiest way to break the ice, plus give them both something to do with their hands.

"That would be lovely, thank you."

I signaled the waitress. Donna ordered a chardonnay and I waited for it to be served before saying, "Thank you for meeting me."

"I'm happy to," she replied. "Shane said you and I might get along rather well."

Yeah, Shane had been happy to pass along the name and number of a new potential "client." Apparently, he was fully booked nowadays.

"Well, I'm glad you came. I'm sure we can come to an arrangement." I smiled, hoping to put her more at ease. I'd lay odds she'd never done this before, judging by how she'd yet to look me fully in the eye for more than two seconds. That made two of them.

She fiddled with her glass stem before finally meeting my gaze. "How does this work exactly? I've never done this before."

"Um, well, we can have a couple of cocktails, if you'd like. Maybe grab dinner." I parroted what Shane had told me to say. "Then maybe go back to your place for a while." The *bow chicka wow-wow* was implied.

"Is your hourly rate the same as Shane's?"

Four hundred an hour. "Yes," I answered, waiting for her to laugh in my face. I couldn't imagine anyone paying that kind of money for the dubious privilege of being screwed by me.

"And you're...what's the word? Clean?"

"Yes, though I still use protection." No way was I going to do this bareback. I was starting to get a knot in my gut. Being interviewed to be someone's Boy Toy wasn't ever on my Bucket List. Humiliating didn't even begin to cover it. Though Donna seemed nice, it was still demoralizing.

"How do I know that it'll be…" Hery voice trailed away and she waved my hand as if I knew what she was going to say.

"That it'll be…what?" I asked. "Confidential?"

"No. That it'll be satisfying. For me," she clarified.

Ah. She was asking if I was good in bed. How to answer that? I'd thought I was probably rusty, but Emmy had seemed to have a good time. She could've been faking, but I didn't think so.

"Multiple orgasms or your money back?" I offered.

She laughed. "That'll work."

My smile was tight. I noticed a wedding ring on her finger but decided not to ask. Maybe she was a widow.

The next hour was spent making conversation while Donna had a couple glasses of wine. I made my one drink last, sure that Donna wouldn't want to pay for a date who'd had too much liquor that impaired my ability to perform. And it wasn't as though I had Viagra in my back pocket.

By the time she'd finished her second glass, she had switched sides to my booth so we sat side by side, scooting close to me. She was flirting now and smelled good.

"I should get to inspect the merchandise first," she said in my ear just as her hand landed on my crotch. I jumped about a foot.

Okay, guess Donna wasn't shy and nervous anymore.

"Um, we can leave, if you want," I said, grasping her hand and moving it away from where she was trying to feel the outline of my dick through my jeans. If she was looking for an erection, she was going to be disappointed. It wasn't that she was unattractive—it was the whole paying-for-it thing. Though if I was going to do something worth paying for, I'd better get over that.

"You're awfully skittish for a man of this occupation," she said with a huff. "But yes, we can go."

I paid the tab and we left. Donna ordered us an Uber and attacked me the minute we slid into the back seat.

"Um, let's wait until we're alone," I said, turning my head away from her questing lips. She hadn't put on a seatbelt and was half-straddling my thighs.

I liked a woman who made the first move as much as the next guy, but this was a bit much, even considering my long draught. And it certainly wasn't helping the erection issue.

"He's not paying any attention," she replied, referring to the driver. She started kissing and licking my neck. "Mmmm, you smell wonderful."

"Thanks."

She was unbuttoning my shirt now and slipped a hand inside, despite my attempts to move her off my lap.

I bit back my irritation. I wanted to shove her off me, but that would be bad for business, right?

"I'm paying you," she said, clearly getting angry. "You can at least pretend, for God's sake. You're as bad as my husband."

Fuck. "You're married?"

"What does it matter?" In a huff, she finally climbed off me.

Suddenly, it did matter. It mattered a hell of a lot. No way was I climbing into some other man's bed with another man's wife. Not even for four hundred bucks an hour.

"This isn't going to work," I said, my voice flat.

"Are you kidding me? The male escort is getting judgy?" Now she was pissed.

"I'm not judging you, I just can't do that. Sorry." Thank God, we were pulling into a neighborhood. "Give Shane a call."

"I'll do that. I bet he can at least get it up."

Ouch.

We stopped in a driveway in front of an elaborate two-story and she got out, slamming the door behind her.

"Wow," the driver said.

"Dude, take me *anywhere* else and I'll give you twenty bucks."

"No problem."

I fell back against the seat, heaving a sigh. That was not how this was supposed to go. Obviously, I wasn't cut out to be a male escort, which still left me with a cash flow problem. I had to come up with something, and fast, before my in-laws bled me dry and I lost Amber by default. I had to think outside the box.

I turned up the volume on my phone and glanced down to see how much more time I had to go on the treadmill-from-hell. Twelve more minutes. The platform eased the incline up another inch and my thighs screamed in protest.

"That's what you get for storing every crumb of bread I eat," I muttered. Out of breath and sweating, working out was second only to getting a root canal on my list of Things I Hated Doing. And honestly, if the dentist was cute...

Keisha, P!nk, Taylor, and a smattering of Maroon 5 got me through the next twelve-minutes-that-felt-like-thirty. I gave the benign-looking torture machine a glare when I finally climbed off, tugging out my AirPods.

"Hey, you keep that up and it'll burst into flames."

I jumped, startled, and whipped around to see a man grinning at me. He was tall—but everyone was tall in comparison to me—with dirty blond hair, brown eyes, and a blindingly white smile. "Um, what?"

He nodded toward the treadmill. "The look you were giving it. As though calling down the wrath of the gods."

I laughed. "Yeah, well, they could use that thing at the CIA for interrogating prisoners."

"That's where they bought them from, actually. I hear they got a new model for the CIA. It plays Taylor Swift and Ed Sheeran continuously."

"Hey! I like them!"

"Oh, yeah, me, too," he said, mock surprise and innocence on his face. "I have the lyrics memorized."

"To which song?" I asked.

"Why, to all of them, of course."

"I bet you couldn't name a single Taylor Swift tune," I challenged him.

"I could," he protested. "There was that one. They

played it on the radio. Constantly." He grimaced and I laughed.

"I'm Paul," he said holding out my hand.

"Emmy." His grip was firm but gentle, his palm soft.

"Pleased to meet you, Emmy." He smiled the mega-wattage again. He was clean-shaven with delicious cheekbones.

"You, too." He even seemed age-appropriate, perhaps mid-thirties.

"I don't usually hit on women at the gym," he said, "but I was wondering if maybe you might want to get a drink sometime?"

I hesitated. I was new to this gym. My old one had closed to relocate, so I'd found one closer. I'd never been crazy about men coming up to my while I was working out, but how else to meet people? The online thing wasn't going anywhere. And this guy was hot, funny, and didn't appear to be a psycho. Usually you only got two out of three and it was a crapshoot as to which two.

"Sure," I said. "I'd like that. I'm going to my locker to get my things. I can give you one of my cards."

"I'll definitely be waiting."

I was a little excited as I headed to the women's locker room. I had a date. Maybe even this coming weekend. What a change that would be from sitting at home binge-watching *Real Housewives of Wherever* with Donny and Marie.

"Excuse me," said a woman entering the locker room behind me.

"Yes?" I asked, surprised.

"That man you were talking to? Paul?"

I was starting to get a bad feeling about this. "What about him?"

"He's married."

My jaw dropped. "But-but…he wasn't wearing a ring." And being married certainly wasn't something he'd mentioned.

"He takes it off when he comes in," the woman said. "He's got a kid in my daughter's dance class. Most of the women around here know about him, but you're new, right?"

I nodded, still dumbfounded.

"I mean, it's up to you, but I thought you should know."

"Um, yeah, thanks."

The woman passed me and headed for the showers. I just stood there for a moment.

Well.

I was embarrassed, naïve, and dumb. He must've spotted me coming a mile away. With all that *"I don't usually hit on women at the gym"* bullshit.

I grabbed my things and slammed the locker door. Now I was pissed.

As Paul said, he was waiting for me in the lobby area.

"Here's my card," I said, handing it to him. "I'm a divorce attorney, so be sure to give it to your wife. She may need to hire me at some point." I smiled sweetly and left him standing there as I headed for my car.

Men sucked, I thought as I drove home. Well, not all men. Cal was a nice guy, fighting for his daughter.

Chad would've done the same, if given the opportunity.

I'd forced myself not to think of my last conversation with him, but now I couldn't help but remember.

"Two more months, babe, then I'll be home for good."

I was smiling so hard, my face hurt. "I can't wait. I miss you like crazy."

"I miss you, too. How's the new job going?"

"Great. Busy. But it's good. Keeps me from dwelling and worrying."

"Don't worry. I'm fine. Promise."

I sighed. "I know but telling me not to worry is pointless." I hesitated. "Especially now."

"Why 'especially now?' You know something I don't?"

I smiled at his teasing. "Actually, I do. Chad, I'm pregnant."

There was a stunned silence on the other end of the line, then, "Are you sure?"

"One hundred percent. Looks like you were home the perfect weekend." Almost exactly three months ago.

Suddenly, he was whooping and hollering and I pulled the phone away from my ear with a laugh. I could hear him shouting.

"Hey! I'm going to be a dad! Ya'll hear that? How 'bout them apples!"

I laughed again, delighted that he was so thrilled.

"How you feeling? Have you been sick?"

"I'm okay. A little nausea, but not bad." A slight understatement, but he didn't need to know. He'd just worry.

"Aw, babe, damn. I wish I was there."

"You will be. Just a few more weeks."

"I love you."

"What a coincidence, because I love you, too."

That had been the last time we'd spoken. He'd been killed the very next day, but not before he'd ordered me a dozen roses. They'd arrived the day after, when I was still in shock and paralyzed with grief.

All my love, to my greatest love. Forever.

—*Chad, xoxo*

I'd stared at the card for hours. A week later, I'd miscarried.

The next six months were a blur of grief and despair and anger, my emotions ricocheting between the three like a ball in a pinball machine. It had taken my family, friends, and time in order to heal, along with throwing myself into my work.

And now I knew it could've been my fault that Chad had died, telling him about the baby when he was so close to coming home. Had he been reckless? Too careful? Done things differently than he would have if he hadn't known? I'd been tempting fate, telling him, I just hadn't known. My excitement at being pregnant had overtaken any thought of *not* telling him, and it hadn't occurred to me that I shouldn't.

I swiped at the tears on my cheeks, then turned into my driveway. Hindsight was twenty-twenty. And regret would only bog me back down in the dark pit of grief that I'd worked so hard to climb out of. I knew what Chad would say. He'd say I was being ridiculous, and that superstitions didn't kill people. He'd chide me for abandoning logic in favor of black cats and walking underneath ladders. He'd make me laugh.

I gave a deep sigh as I got out of the car and closed the garage door. Sometimes, I missed him so acutely, it was a physical pain inside my chest. Time had dulled the pain to an ache, but I knew it would always stay with me. I should be glad Paul had been a creep. If I met someone and fell in love again, there was always the chance of losing them. I'd barely made it through the pain of losing the man I loved and our baby the first time. I'd never survive it twice.

Donny and Marie were as excited to see me as ever and I paused to give them each some attention before letting them out the back door to relieve their bladders. They were back inside in no time, anxious for treats.

I was sweaty from the gym and needed to clean up before I made dinner, not that I particularly felt like making dinner, but no way was I eating more lettuce or kale. I shuddered at the thought as I climbed the stairs.

Stripping off my sweaty tank as I walked, I set my AirPods on my dressing table and toed off my shoes. Turning toward the bed, I froze.

There was a Barbie doll placed in the perfect center of the bed.

It took a split second longer than it should for my brain to process what I was seeing.

Someone was in the house.

My veins flooded with the cold rush of adrenaline. I snatched up my cell, but my fingers were shaking so badly, it wouldn't unlock. Frustration mounted as I tried again. My fingers slid across the screen and I pressed *Emergency* and dialed 911.

"911, what's your emergency?"

"I think someone's in my house." My voice shook as I whispered. Were they still here? Had they gone?

"Are you alone, ma'am?"

"Yes." Should I try to get out? What if I ran into them?

"What's your address?

I gave it to her, barely breathing.

"Okay. Stay on the phone with me. I'm dispatching the police now."

"Please hurry." Glancing around, I saw nothing I could use as a weapon. My conversation with Cal echoed inside my head. I didn't even own a bat.

My dogs.

I rushed down the stairs, my heart pounding. My panic over my dogs overruled any sense of self-preservation. "Donny! Marie!" I called out.

"Ma'am, are you all right? Ma'am?"

Sirens in the distance. The police were on their way.

"Donny! Marie!" Dashing into the kitchen, I grabbed a knife from the knife block. A jingle behind me. I spun around, my heart in my throat.

It was Marie, looking bemusedly up at me, Donny trotting up behind her, still licking his chops from the treat. Relief flooded through me.

"Ma'am, the officers are at your door. Are you able to answer the door?"

"Yeah." Fighting back tears, I hurried to the door, knife still in my hand.

The police were waiting on the front porch. Donny and Marie greeted them enthusiastically.

There were two officers—a man and a woman— and they looked like they meant business. I was immediately relieved.

"I just got home," I said. "There's a...barbie doll... on my bed upstairs. It's not mine."

The officer, his badge said *L. Davis*, nodded. "Okay. We'll take a look." He nodded at the woman and headed upstairs. She turned to me.

"Can you stay here while I search this floor?'

I nodded, my knees folding under me as I sank onto the couch. Donny and Marie hopped up next to me, nudging each other aside for who'd get the prime real estate on my lap.

A few minutes later, she was back.

"No one's here," she said. "I took a look at your windows and doors. There doesn't appear to be any signs of a forced entry."

Officer Davis descended the stairs. "All clear," he said. "Does anyone else have a key to the house?"

I nodded. "I have two best friends. They each have a key, just in case."

"And neither of them would do this as a joke? A prank?"

I shook my head. "No way. We're all single. They wouldn't try to freak me out as a joke."

The cops glanced at each other and I could tell they didn't believe me.

"I didn't make this up," I protested. "Someone was in here. I don't own any Barbie dolls. Someone left it for me to find."

"May I ask what you do for a living?" the female officer asked.

"I'm an attorney. Family law."

"Are there any clients who might know your home address and have access?"

"No. None." The face of the guy who'd tried to choke me to death flashed through my mind.

They glanced at each other again. I felt angry frustration rise inside. No one in my entire life had ever not believed something I said. Not since I was seven and lied about breaking mom's vase in the front room.

My jaw hardened. "Okay, well, I guess we can just forget about it. Thank you for your time." I stood, the dogs jumping down to follow wherever I decided to go.

"We'll file a report, but that's all we can do," the female officer said. I noticed her tag said *M. Lorrie.* "We just don't see any signs of an intrusion."

"Other than the property that wasn't mine left in the middle of my bed."

She winced a bit at that, but I was over it. I wanted a shower, dinner, and an alarm system. Not necessarily in that order.

A few minutes later, they had gone, and I sat down at the kitchen table, staring at my phone.

I was unnerved. And anxious. And scared. None of which I was accustomed to feeling. But too much had happened too quickly. First the attack from the angry ex, then my tires, now this. Whatever was happening felt like it was escalating.

Feeling like I was making a mistake, I still picked up the phone and dialed. The call rang twice, then was answered.

"Hey, Cal. It's Emmy. I was wondering if you were busy?"

chapter nine

IT TOOK TWENTY minutes to drive to Emmy's house. I made it in ten.

Her words on the phone kept repeating inside my head.

"I think someone broke into my house. They left a Barbie doll on my bed. The cops came and no one's here but...I was just wondering if you could come and check it out."

The tires and now this. Someone was obviously stalking her. But to get inside her house was taking it to the next level. My gut churned. What if she'd walked in on them?

I'd only taken enough time to throw on a T-shirt with my jeans and grabbed my gun before taking off.

I parked my truck in her driveway, hoping it wouldn't leak oil on the pristine pavement, and hurried to the door. She answered within seconds.

"Thanks so much for coming," she said with a wan smile. She was holding one dog—I didn't know which—and the other sat at her feet, looking up at me. "I'm so sorry to bother you. I just didn't know who else to call. It was obvious the police didn't believe me that it wasn't some kind of joke or prank."

"Hey, no problem at all. Happy to help." I walked in and she shut and locked the door behind me.

She was wearing workout clothes—tight leggings, a half shirt sports bra thing that bared her stomach, and a ponytail. She looked about nineteen and smelled like perfume tinged with skin and sweat and woman. I forced my gaze away.

"The police checked all the doors and windows?" I asked. She nodded. "Okay, well, I'm going to check them again. That okay?"

She nodded again, the line of her shoulders relaxing. "Yes, please. Um…do you mind…I really want to take a shower. I just didn't feel…"

The sentence hung in the air and I could tell what she'd meant in the shifting of her eyes. It was no small thing when someone came uninvited into your personal space. It was an incredible invasion of privacy. I wouldn't have wanted to be behind an opaque shower curtain after something like that either.

"Sure thing," I said. "I'll keep watch. No one's going to get in while I'm here."

Her eyes met mine for a moment, and she nodded. "Thank you."

I started my tour of the doors and windows. Nothing looked out of place or tampered with, until I searched the basement. There was one small window at the top of the concrete wall, right at ground level to the outside. It was too high to reach, but there was a big, square plastic cooler parked right underneath it.

Well, well, what do we have here?

Taking the phone out of my pocket, I turned on the flashlight and stepped closer. The naked overhead bulb did okay, but with the flashlight, I could see the slight smear of dirt on top of the cooler's lid. The cooler looked sturdy. Let's see how sturdy.

Grasping the top of the wall, I stood on top of the lid, which held my weight. Good brand. And now that I could see the window, I saw it was also unlatched. It wasn't big enough for someone my size to get through, but someone smaller, like Emmy's size, could probably squeeze through.

I locked it and climbed down, thinking. Someone who entered the house this way meant to come back the same way. Leaving the doll was a message, but was it just to show that Emmy's space wasn't secure? Or was it a message about Emmy herself?

By the time I got back upstairs, Emmy had returned. She wore loose, black pants—I think they were called yoga pants though no one seemed to do yoga in them—and a fitted Indiana Colts T-shirt. Her hair was wet and draped down her back and her feet were bare.

"Did you find anything?" she asked, crossing her arms over her chest.

"Yes, which is both good and bad."

"Why is that?"

"Good to know how they got in, bad that we can confirm it wasn't a random prank."

"So how did they get in and why didn't the police find it?"

I walked her downstairs and showed her. "They either missed it or didn't bother checking the window."

Emmy looked decidedly put out. "Nice to know the police can't be bothered," she groused.

I shrugged. "People make mistakes, and I locked the window for you. If you got an alarm system, they could wire that window for you."

"Oh, trust me, that's the first call I'm making in the morning."

We headed back upstairs. "Do you have the doll?"

She nodded, went into the kitchen, and came back with a Barbie. After handing it to me, she sat on the couch, folding one leg beneath her. I took the chair opposite and examined the doll.

It looked like any other Barbie. Long blonde hair, makeup, vacuous smile. She wore a pantsuit complete with a set of rubber high heels. Like a girl had asked for a toy to commemorate Take Your Daughter to Work Day. I began removing the clothes and paused.

"What?" Emmy asked, watching me.

"There's writing."

I removed the clothes and looked at the doll, the heat of anger rolling through my veins.

It was covered in slurs, from *bitch* to *whore* and everything in between. The place between her thighs had been cut deep and the breasts had been removed. I turned it over. There was a different message on its back.

I'm coming for you.

"Let me see," Emmy demanded. I handed it to her and watched her face drain of color. She swallowed hard. "Have you found a job yet?"

Okay, I think I got whiplash from that change of subject.

"Um, no…but I don't see what that has to do—"

"I want to hire you," she said firmly. "We can exchange services. I'll handle the divorce. You find out who's doing this and why. I can have your deposit refunded."

I picked up my jaw. "Why would you want to do that?"

"You have experience. The police are obviously not going to do anything until something happens to me, which by then it will most certainly be too late."

I was still too surprised to do more than stare at her.

She frowned. "Is it not enough? I mean I suppose I can pay you, as well, but—"

"No," I hurriedly interrupted. "That's a great idea. I'd be glad to help."

The relief on Emmy's face was palpable and her shoulders relaxed. She smiled. "Perfect. It looks as though you walking in to my office was rather fortuitous."

"So it would seem."

"Um, do you mind...I mean can you stay tonight until I can get an alarm company out here?"

"You bet." Air-conditioning I didn't have to pay for? Yes, please.

"Well," she stood with a forced smile, "I think I've had enough excitement for one day. I'm heading to bed. I can show you to the guest room."

"I'd rather sleep on the couch, if that's okay. Rather be on the first floor, just in case."

"Okay. Let me just get you some bedding then."

She was gone before I could tell her that wasn't necessary—I'd slept on a lot worse things than a couch—and returned with an armful of sheets, blankets, and a pillow. I took them from her before she could start making up the couch for me.

"I got it. Thanks."

Emmy gave me a tentative smile. "Well, thank you very much, Cal. And goodnight."

"Goodnight." I watched her walk upstairs, thinking about the night I got to follow her up. I wondered what would have happened if I'd asked her out after that night…and regretting that I hadn't.

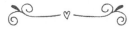

I changed into my pajamas, did my skincare routine and all the other things, then climbed into bed. Donny and Marie settled, one on each side, pressed against me. It made me feel better. Maybe they sensed how upset I was. They say dogs are in sync with their owner's moods.

At least I felt better than I had before Cal had come. He was taking this seriously and I'd be lying if I didn't say that having him downstairs was probably the only reason why I'd be able to sleep tonight. I had surprised myself by asking him to stay, but the moment the words had left my mouth, I'd hoped he'd say yes.

It had struck me as a brilliant idea: I needed a cop. He needed a lawyer. Quid pro quo. Although it sucked to say it, I was a little afraid of going to work. At least tomorrow was Saturday, though the relief that brought me was frustrating. I realized that I hated feeling afraid.

You'd feel much better if Cal was sleeping beside you rather than on the couch.

No. Nononono. Don't start thinking that way, Emmy. You're just lonely, that's all.

Yeah, the amazing sex had nothing to do with it.

It had been pretty darn amazing. My mind drifted… Cal's body was slabbed with muscle, his shoulders carved and his stomach hard. And that ass… I sighed, then shook my head.

I had to get my head back in the game and quit mooning over Cal. Besides, a man who was literally still married was a walking, talking red flag. I had a case to prepare for but would just have to work over the weekend. It's not like I had anything else going on. Oh wait, other than a creepy stalker. I sighed again and flipped over.

It took a while to fall asleep. My tossing and turning caused more than one irritated grunt from my bedtime companions. Finally, I fell into a fitful sleep.

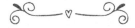

I woke up and instantly knew something was wrong. It was still dark. The dogs were gone. It was just me in bed.

My heart began to pound and cold rush of adrenaline flooded me. There was a shadow in the room, deeper than the others.

"Cal?" My voice shook. I wanted to pull the covers up over my head and pretend I was safe, like a little kid. "Cal?" I repeated.

The shadow lunged.

I sat straight up in bed and Donny woofed, startled. The nightmare had seemed so real. I was drenched in sweat and breathing like I'd just run a half-marathon.

Not a whole marathon because, come on, who are we kidding?

Marie snored, oblivious.

Okay, this wasn't going to work. I couldn't just turn over and go back to sleep. I needed a drink of water. Or a shot of whisky.

I had to maneuver around the two lumps to get out of bed. They obviously were not feeling the doggie devotion at, I glanced at the clock, two-thirtyish in the morning. If I snuck downstairs, I could probably keep from waking Cal, get my—whatever I decided to drink—and come back up. I knew where all the squeaks were and could navigate in the dark.

Thinking sneaky thoughts, I crept down the stairs, sticking to the wall and avoiding one stair entirely. It was too dark to see Cal on the sofa, so I padded by on silent feet into the kitchen. The hardwood was chilly under my toes. I thought I remembered a half a bottle of chardonnay in the fridge—

Suddenly, I was shoved to the floor and a weight landed on my back. The breath left me in a whoosh.

"Don't move."

The voice was solid and menacing and I was certainly disinclined to move, especially when I felt the hard metal of a gun barrel against the back of my neck.

It was Cal. Shit. I had almost peed myself. I tried to breathe, to tell him it was me, but my lungs wouldn't expand.

I felt him move slightly and the weight on my back disappeared. I drew a deep, ragged breath.

"Em? Oh shit I'm so sorry."

He hauled me to my feet with such speed and

strength, my toes briefly left the floor. Then the room was flooded with light.

"Nightmare," I explained, still gasping. Fewer words were better at the moment. "Needed wine. Don't wake you."

"Ah." He eyed me. "Are you okay? Did I hurt you?" I took a deep breath. "Just need a minute. I'm okay." I tugged on the hem of my oversize Bon Jovi T-shirt that I slept in. It came to mid-thigh and covered the important parts, but I was suddenly self-conscious.

"I'll get you that wine," he said, shoving the gun in the back of his jeans. I noticed then he'd taken his shirt off.

Lord have mercy. I was abruptly grateful for my nightmare. Maybe I couldn't touch, but I could certainly look. Yes please, and thank you.

Cal grabbed the bottle of wine off the shelf in the fridge, dumped half of what was left over into a glass, and handed it to me.

"Thanks." I took a sip while he watched. Okay, this wasn't uncomfortable at all. "Can we go sit for a minute? I need to chill after that."

"Yeah, of course," he said, leading me into the living room. He turned on a lamp. It was cozy and felt like we were the only ones awake in the whole wide world.

Cal sat on his makeshift bed on the couch. I took the armchair opposite, curling my legs underneath me, and took another sip of wine.

Silence reigned. Another sip. Cal was trying not to stare at me. I watched him underneath my lashes.

"What was the nightmare about?" he asked, breaking the silence.

Ugh. I didn't want to think about it, but I answered him anyway. "There was someone in my room. The dogs were gone. I thought it was you, but you didn't answer me. Then he came at me." I shuddered at the memory. It was still too soon, too real.

"I'm sorry."

I shrugged. "Not your fault. Probably would've been worse if you hadn't been here. At least I had the comfort of your presence once I woke up enough to be logical."

Cal didn't say anything, so I glanced and met his eyes. His face was utterly serious.

"I'm glad I could provide security for your peace of mind."

"Thank you."

Silence again, but it wasn't uncomfortable. He relaxed back against the couch. My eyes were drawn to his abs. Sigh...

"So, do you want to talk about Chad?"

I leveled a glance at him. "Seriously?"

He shrugged. "Sometimes it helps to talk. I knew him. Though it was briefly, we were in the same situation together."

I took a deep gulp of my wine and then a breath. "I was pregnant."

Cal stilled. "What?"

My laugh was a mixture of bitter and hysterical. "You told me it was the kiss of death, right? He was getting ready to come home, then I told him I was pregnant. It's my fault. He's dead because of me." My eyes burned with unshed tears.

"Oh my god, Em, no." Cal jumped off the couch and came over to me, taking a seat on the ottoman in front of my chair. "It was not your fault. I'm so sorry for what I said. I'm such an asshole." He grasped my free hand in his.

I couldn't help the tears that dripped down my face. "I was so sure we'd live happily ever after. He was coming home. We were going to have a baby. And then it all went to hell."

"Fuck," Cal muttered. He scooted closer, set my glass on the table, and took me in his arms. I settled against his chest and let the tears fall.

"I miscarried, a few weeks after the funeral," I whispered, "and I've grieved them both, but the thought that maybe I was part of why Chad didn't come home…it's tearing me apart."

Cal pulled me closer. "Em. It's not your fault. I'm a hundred percent certain that Chopper was thrilled to know he was going to be a dad and was coming home to you. It's war. Shit happens. It fucking sucks. I can't tell you enough how much it fucking sucks. And I'm so fucking sorry."

I forced my tears to dry up. Cal didn't deserve me crying on his shoulder. And what he said made sense…in my head. My heart was just more stubborn and refused to let go of the guilt.

"Thank you," I managed, pushing away slightly. "Sometimes I just mourn what might have been."

His eyes were clear and steady as he met my gaze. "Life doesn't ever end up how you'd planned or imagined it. Sometimes it's better, but mostly it's worse."

Sounded like a tried-and-true pessimist who'd been through some stuff. I reached out and grasped his hand.

"It doesn't have to be that way. I know things are hard right now, but you're a young, hot guy with a lot of skills. There will be women knocking down your door."

Cal's eyes narrowed and took on a predatory glint. "You think I'm hot?"

My face heated. "By anyone's measure, yes, you are. I'm not just being kind."

He reached out, his fingers barely brushing my cheek and jaw. "Am I allowed to say how beautiful you are?" His voice was barely above a whisper and his gaze was mesmerizing. He looked at me as though I was the most amazing thing he'd ever seen. I couldn't move and couldn't look away.

He leaned forward, his hand cupping behind my head and drawing me closer. His gaze dropped to my lips which caused the involuntary reaction of licking them. Cal pulled me into him, his mouth pressing against mine.

It was better than before. Knowing him, him knowing me, that made it so much better.

I allowed him to pull me onto his lap. His arm curved around my back and he deepened the kiss. He tasted like Cal mixed with the chardonnay I'd drank. My head spun and my heart sped up. I scissored my legs, trying to ease the sudden ache between them.

His hand crawled up my thigh, pushing aside my sleep T-shirt and settling on my bare back. I desperately wanted to straddle his lap as our kisses grew heated. He smelled so good. Not cologne, but just man and skin. He kissed me like he couldn't get enough. It sent my head spinning.

He pulled back and I tried to catch my breath.

"Why did you stop?" I whispered.

Cal shook his head. "The time's not right." He pressed a gentle kiss to my forehead.

I suddenly felt guilty. We'd been talking about Chad and then I fell into another man's arms. I squirmed to get off his lap and Cal must've sensed my discomfort because he stilled me.

"Hey, babe," he said softly, a hand beneath my chin tipping my eyes to his. "It's okay. You're so amazing. I'm glad I could be here for you. No worries. Go to bed. Sleep well. I'll protect you."

Oh wow, I wanted him so much just for that statement, and the look in his eyes that said he meant it. How was he even for real?

"Can I carry you to your room?" he asked.

"Um, no," I blurted, still feeling guilty. "I've got it. Sorry to bother you! See you in the morning!"

My uncomfortable gaity was as false as my hairdresser's lashes. I hopped off his lap and hightailed it out of there so fast, you'd think a dad on prom night was on my tail.

Burying myself under the covers and between my two bed hogs, I tried to reconcile all that had happened the last few days.

Wait. An awful thought crept into my head.

All of my troubles had started when I had met Cal. I'd never had any trouble with clients or stalkers before. Suddenly, I was a stalker Flavor Of The Month. And now I was offering Cal free lawyer services if he'd solve my case, not to mention letting him kiss me.

What if *he* was the reason for my case? Find a single female lawyer, make her feel threatened, then handily present yourself as the solution. Do a little research, a bit of Googling, and suddenly he knew my dead husband's name. Throw in some made-up tale that I'd never be able to verify and boom! We had a bond.

My blood went cold. He was guarding me in my house. But what if he was the enemy? As long as I did what he said, I guess he was on my side, but what if things didn't go the way he wanted? Why was I even thinking this? But I couldn't stop. The coincidence was just too much. Maybe I needed to find out who was my stalker on my own. Who did I trust?

No. I was just being paranoid. Surely I wasn't *that* bad a judge of character. He was ex-military, after all. They're supposed to be the best of the best. Worthy of immediate respect and trust.

But I also knew that desperate people did desperate things. I'd seen it all too often in my profession. No matter how many times I told myself I was being ridiculous, I just couldn't shake the thought.

What if I was completely wrong about Cal?

chapter ten

IT TOOK ME so long to get to sleep that I didn't wake until past mid-morning. Donny and Marie were gone and I had a moment of panic that they'd piddled on the floor. Marie held it but Donny just didn't care. Typical man. I pried my eyes open and crawled out of bed. I ran a brush through my hair and brushed my teeth, then grabbed my terry cloth robe and slid my feet into fuzzy slippers.

Downstairs was a hive of activity. Two men I didn't know were installing gadgets by the front door and the window in the front room. In the kitchen, I could overhear two men talking. One was Cal. He smiled when he saw me.

"What's going on?" I asked, confused at the presence of all these strangers in my house.

"Alarm company," he said. "Greg here is a buddy of mine and he agreed to come out this morning to install it for you."

The aforementioned Greg nodded and smiled, too. "Nice to meet you," he said. "Cal here picked out a good package for you, to cover all available entrances to the house. It's all wireless, so no drilling in your walls. Twenty-four seven monitoring. Three keypads: one by the front door, one by the garage door, and another in the master bedroom. Along with a key fob and, of course, we have an app that lets you monitor the cameras and arm the system."

I wasn't awake enough for all that information. "Cameras?" I asked weakly.

"You bet. One in the front and one in the back. You can view the footage yourself and it also records. No one's getting in here without you knowing, ma'am."

Oh. He'd just "ma'am"ed me. Was I now the terrified spinster living alone? I guess so. I sighed and headed for the kitchen, setting the eletric kettle to boil and dumping coffee grounds in the French press.

Cal and Greg went on talking and disappeared into the living room, I suppose to check on the installation. Donny and Marie both pattered over to me for their morning treats. Once I had my coffee in hand, I went outside on the deck to drink it.

It was a lovely morning, already warm, and the sun was bright in a cloudless sky. I watched the dogs sniff their way around the yard. Marie came and nosed my leg until I stretched out a fuzzy blanket for her to lay on. I always kept one out here because the cushions just weren't soft enough for the Spoiled Ones. She let out a huff of breath as her chubby frame settled down next to me, her chin on my thigh.

I was glad Cal had taken the initiative and gotten someone here so quickly to put in the alarm system. I remembered the doubts I'd had last night about trusting him. I was just being paranoid. After all, look at what had happened the past few days. If I was feeling paranoid, I certainly was allowed.

Remembering last night, I could feel my face get hot. I hated the feeling of regret, so I didn't indulge in it. We'd kissed. That was all. Nothing to do now but figure out how to move forward. I wondered if Cal would think there was something more between us, or the possibility of something. I didn't want to damage our professional relationship any more than I already had. And considering what he'd done for me, I'd better find a way for him to see his daughter, sooner rather than later.

I'd almost finished my coffee when Cal emerged from the house.

"Greg and his guys finished and left," he said, lowering himself onto the wicker chair opposite me. "He gave you the equipment at cost and the installation was free. I'll show you how to operate the system."

And then Cal would also know all about my security system, including the code I chose to arm and disarm it. The thought came unbidden. Uncomfortable, I pushed it away. "Why would he install for free?" I asked. "Especially on a Saturday?"

Cal shrugged. "A favor. He owed me one and had the time today, especially when I explained the urgency. He's a good guy." He handed me an invoice that was a fraction of what it probably should have been.

"Looks like it." My eyebrows rose at the total. I'd been expecting a hefty surcharge for a Saturday morning install. "You're sure this is right?"

"I'm sure."

Okay then. "Thank you."

"Not a problem."

We spent the next twenty minutes going through the system and setting up codes. I Armed and Disarmed, set for Stay and Away, downloaded the app, and did all the things. I had to admit, it made me feel safer.

Cal glanced at the watch on his wrist. It was almost archaic to see an actual watch nowadays. Everyone seemed to use their phones for the time.

"I need to get to work," he said.

"You have a job? And you work on the weekends?" I'd thought he was out of work.

The tips of his ears turned a bit red and he glanced away from me. "Just a manual labor thing at SS Tractor & Feed. Time and a half for weekends."

Somehow it struck me as endearing that he was embarrassed. "My dad drove a truck for a living when he was young," I said. "Any work is good work, especially if it involves getting a paycheck."

His lips tilted up slightly and I had the most absurd notion to give him a kiss goodbye, like a wife kissing her husband before sending him off to work. I played with the tie of my robe to disguise the urge.

"Well, thank you again. You can come to the office Monday and evaluate the security there. I'll let the other partners know what's going on and what you'll be doing."

"Absolutely."

He grabbed his keys from the table by the door and stuffed them into the pocket of his worn jeans. The sight of his hands made me think things. His fingers were thick. And long.

Emmy. Stop. You're staring.

I swallowed hard and gave him a nod. "Sure."

Cal hesitated for a moment, then gave me his own businesslike nod, and was out the door. A few moments later, I heard the engine of his truck rev, then fade as he drove away.

I let out my breath in a rush. Sex-starved Emmy would've really liked to have dragged him up to her bedroom and have her wicked way with him. Logical Emmy said be cautious and suspicious of everyone, including brand new people in her life—like Cal.

I needed help, and not the security kind. Pulling my cell out of my pocket, I texted to the group chat that had been going on for years.

Carly, Bridge—Emergency meeting. One o'clock at Havanna Grill.

Within moments I had confirmations from both of them. Excellent. I headed upstairs for a shower. My girls would help me work through this.

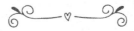

I was first at the restaurant, which didn't surprise me since I was also fifteen minutes early. My mind was churning and I desperately needed to get some of this off my chest. Carly and Bridget would have no problem giving me their opinions, which was usually a blessing but sometimes a curse.

The restaurant had the patio open, since the weather was gorgeous today, albeit hot, and sat me at a table with the umbrella raised. I'd worn a sleeveless dusky orange dress closer to a rust color than orange. It was just a shade darker than my hair. There was a slim belt and it even had pockets. I ordered a pinot grigio and drummed my fingernails on the tabletop, waiting impatiently.

Bridget was the first to arrive. Like me, she wore a sundress, only hers was a navy paisley with spaghetti straps and I immediately loved it. Platform wedges adorned her feet with peeping bright coral toes. She sat down with a huff, tossing her ebony hair, and I knew something was wrong.

"What is it?" I asked.

She frowned into her glass of water, eyes on the tablecloth. "Rick and I had a fight."

Oh no. Rick was the first man Bridget had gotten serious about in years. She'd married young, from a long history of family who'd married young, and that hadn't turned out well. They'd been divorced shortly after their first anniversary. Rick and she had been together now for almost two years.

"What happened?"

"The same," she sighed. "I had the audacity to talk about where we were going to spend Christmas this year. Then he started hemming and hawing and should we be talking about holidays at this stage of our relationship, yadda yadda yadda."

"But you've been together for quite a while." I was bewildered.

Bridget sighed. "I know. I wanted to take things slow at first, after the divorce, and he was good with that. But I'm over thirty. We've moved in together. I'm ready to settle down, pop out a couple munch-kins. It's been two years with Rick. And I'm over the whole 'we're partners' thing. I want a *husband*. My happily-ever-after, complete with a real honeymoon, diapers, PTA meetings, saving for retirement, and hideously overpriced trips to Disney World."

"They really are overpriced," I mumbled. Both Bridget and Carly knew my secret desire to eat and drink my way around Epcot during the annual International Flower and Garden festival. I desperately needed to see a Mickey Mouse topiary at some point in my life.

Just then, Carly showed up and dropped into the third out of the four chairs. The fourth held our purses and she added hers to the stack. She wore denim cutoff shorts and a breezy, peasant-style ivory blouse. Carly was tall, blonde, and had gorgeous, tanned legs up to there. Oversized sunglasses shaded her eyes.

"A Saturday lunch? We haven't done that in a while," she said, turning her gaze on me. "What's going on?"

"I don't think I'm the only one with a crisis today." I nodded toward the glum Bridget.

Bridget recounted her boyfriend woes, pausing only to give the waitress her drink order that duplicated mine. Carly opted for chardonnay. We all ordered the half-sammy, half-salad deal. I wanted the wedge with all the bleu cheese dressing ever but opted for the house with the vinaigrette instead. Over thirty metabolism sucked.

We did small talk until our food arrived, then Carly got down to business.

"So what are you going to do?" she asked Bridget. "Are you going to break up with him?"

Bridget gave a limp shrug. "No idea. But I'm hitting my line in the sand."

"Line in the sand?" I asked.

She glanced at me, then morosely picked at her house salad with Ranch. "The max time I'm going to waste on a man who's not going to commit." She sighed. "But the thought of being out there again, starting over with someone new…it sounds exhausting."

I agreed wholeheartedly but, "You don't want to stay with someone just because it's easier," I reminded her. She grimaced.

"Well, you called this meeting," Carly said, turning to me. "What's up?"

Taking a deep breath, I launched into lengthy explanation of what had happened, ending with the Barbie and the kissing Cal.

"…and now I think I'm having some doubts if he's legit. Or if he's the one doing these things," I finished. I took a bite of my BLT and chewed, watching Carly and Bridget mull over what I'd told them.

"First of all," Bridget began, "you should've called us sooner. A stalker is nothing to brush off. I agree with you. This guy sounds a little too convenient. I don't believe in coincidence."

"And he knew Chad?" Carly added. "It's just…a little too fortuitous, if you ask me."

"You should come stay with me and Rick," Bridget said. "I don't trust the alarm system he supposedly had installed."

"Totally agree."

Both my besties had gone into super-protective mode, which was incredibly sweet. Like two momma bears circling the wagons. Wait. That's mixing my metaphors.

"I'm giving him the benefit of the doubt," I said,

spearing lettuce with my fork. "I know you don't believe in coincidences or serendipity, but it really could be that. We shouldn't convict the guy until we know for sure. Innocent until proven guilty, remember?"

"You're too trusting," Bridget groused. "If I have to identify your body, I'm going to be seriously put out."

I turned to Carly. "How'd your date go the other night? The Angi's guy from Bumble?" A change of subject was always good.

She grimaced but didn't object to the change of subject. "We went to dinner, where he told me in no uncertain terms that I should pay for my own meal and that he thought expecting the man to pay was an antiquated notion, though sex on the first date was totally okay." She rolled her eyes and took a bite of her chicken salad sandwich.

"So what did you do?" Bridget asked.

Carly grinned as she chewed. "I ditched him out the back after dessert on my way to the ladies' room." She used air quotes for *ladies' room.*

Bridget held up her palm and they high-fived.

"Antiquated, my ass," Carly growled.

"Looks like we're all at square one for Clarice's wedding," I said. At this, Bridget grew somber once again.

"I'm going to have to break it off, aren't I," she said. It wasn't a question.

Just then, the waiter came by.

"We'll have the brownie sundae with extra whipped cream," I ordered. I held up three fingers. "With three spoons."

He grinned. "Got it."

The girls looked at me. I shrugged. "Thought we all could use a little comfort chocolate."

The brownie sundae was huge, and I had the feeling the waiter had been generous with the ice cream and hot fudge as well as the whipped cream. We devoured it in short order.

"Okay," I said once we'd all but licked the bowl clean, "Operation Clarice's Wedding. We need dates. It's only three weeks away."

"I can't imagine going with someone other than Rick." Bridget's eyes filled, alarming me. Bridget never cried. She hated crying.

"Are you going to be okay?" Carly asked. "You can come stay with me until he moves out, if you want."

Bridget blinked back the tears and took a deep, shuddering breath. "I might do that. It depends. I think he knows what's coming. It didn't end well this morning."

Impulsively, I leaned over and gave her a hug. Bridget wasn't much of a hugger, but she hugged me back.

"You'll get through it," I said quietly. "We're both here for you."

We each paid our check and left, exchanging hugs one more time. I wasn't any clearer on what I thought about Cal, but I knew that I wasn't going to assume the worst without proof. Though nothing said I shouldn't be cautious and perhaps not so trusting.

On my way home, I had an idea. I still had numbers for some of Chad's Marine buddies. Maybe one of them could confirm Cal's story. That would go a long way to making me feel better about the whole coincidence of his appearance in my life.

Disarming the alarm via the keypad took me twice, but it eventually stopped beeping and the light turned green. I took that as a good sign.

Donny and Marie were overjoyed to see me ("You've been gone like *forever!*") and once I'd settled them down with fresh treats, I sat cross-legged on the couch and began searching through the contacts on my phone.

Chad's closest friend in the Army was a guy named Oliver—Ollie for short. He'd stood beside me at the funeral and been a rock for me, even when I'd miscarried a week later. His wife had helped me recover, being a soft presence that was as steady as her husband's. By that time, my emotions were numb. I would have been more surprised had I *not* miscarried.

There he was. I stopped scrolling and pressed the Call button. In a moment, I could hear it ringing. After three rings, a woman answered. I assumed it was May, his wife.

"May?"

"Yes. Is this Emmy?"

I smiled. "Yes, it is. How are you?"

"I'm good! It's wonderful to hear from you. It's been a long time."

"It has. How are the kids?" Ollie and May had four kids, all under the age of seven. I didn't know how she did it, especially with a husband who was often deployed.

We chitchatted for a few minutes, catching up, until I got around to asking if Ollie happened to be home and not away.

"He is," she confirmed. "He retired from the Army

and now he works in real estate. It's nice because he can work from home so can help me a bit. Let me get him for you."

I was glad to hear he'd retired. He had a family to think about now. My heart squeezed itself into a tight little ball. This could've been Chad and me.

The thought was painful, but not the knifing pain it would've been five years ago.

"Emmy?" Ollie's deep voice rumbled on the line.

"Hey, Ollie. Yeah, it's me."

More chitchat, though less since Ollie wasn't much of a chitchat kind of guy.

"Hey, Ollie, I have this guy here who says he knew Chad. It seems like a really big coincidence, so I was just wondering if you might've known him, too." I relayed Cal's full name and his story about the second Battle of Fallujah. When I finished, I asked, "Does this ring any bells?"

Ollie was silent for a moment, and I assumed he was thinking, remembering. Finally, "Well," he said slowly, "I remember *a* guy. I don't know if I ever got his name. Part of a platoon got holed up with some of us and pinned down for a while until air support was deployed. This guy and Chopper were sharing smokes, but I was a little busy at the time. Don't remember much about what he looked like, either. We were pretty much all covered in dirt and blood."

I winced slightly.

"Sorry, Emmy," he continued. "Wish I could be more help."

Well. That was that. "That's okay. Thanks so much Ollie."

"You need to come down for a visit, Emmy. See

the kids. You work too much." He and May lived outside Baton Rouge.

"I'll wait until fall when it's cooler," I said. "Too hot there now. How you guys can stand it, I'll never know."

He just laughed. A few more words and we ended the call. Like I said, Ollie wasn't much for chitchat.

Cal's story was still unverified, though it *could* be true. I chewed my lip in uncertainty. What should I do? As far as I could see, there was nothing more I *could* do. So far, he hadn't done anything to hurt me…that I knew about. Ugh. I really hated being suspicious of Cal. It just didn't seem to fit his MO.

I needed a nap. That would make everything better. The stress and lack of sleep last night was wearing on me. It was a Saturday afternoon. I was allowed to indulge.

"C'mon, you two," I called to Donny and Marie. "Let's head upstairs."

A few minutes later, I was snuggling down under a blanket, bracketed by the twins. With a sigh, I drifted off.

"Hey, Cal."

I looked up. One of the few guys who'd also shown up for time and a half was standing nearby. I crawled my brain, trying to remember his name.

"Hey, Jeff. What's up?"

"I've got a girlfriend who's moving," he said, and I immediately knew where this was going. "I said I'd help her with the furniture, so she didn't have to hire a moving company. Think you and your truck could help me out after work for a couple of hours? I'll pay you fifty bucks."

I'd been anxious to maybe go check on Em, but fifty bucks would come in handy. Before I could stop the thought, visions drifted in my head of taking Em to dinner. A real date.

Like she'd want to date a broke loser, Cal.

The inner voice had a very good point.

"Yeah, sure." We got off at three. "Where does she live?"

"She's literally moving like six blocks, but the change in neighborhood is like night and day." He rattled off an address, then said, "You can just follow me."

"Sure thing."

I went back to shifting bags of feed, sweat soaking through my tank. Muscles strained. Free phyz, I thought grimly. Silver lining. My hands were sweating inside the heavy work gloves. At least it was shaded where I was unloading and stacking the feed. It could've been worse. The sun was relentlessly beating down now at midday. I idly wondered what Em was doing.

Last night drifted through my head and I let myself indulge in the memory of her on my lap, her arms twined around my neck, her breasts pressed against my chest. Her lips were so soft. Her taste so sweet.

My jeans were growing uncomfortably tight. I forced my thoughts away from Em's delicious body. Last thing I needed was a hard on at work.

I wouldn't be able to stay there tonight, not with the alarm system now installed. Damn. I told myself it was just because of the air conditioning. It had felt amazing. A welcome break from the oppressive heat in my apartment.

Nice, Cal, using a woman for her air conditioning. Classy.

She was fine. She was safe. The alarm system was state-of-the-art. I'd gone over all the ins and outs with her, the details and codes, where the cameras were, everything. If she was home, she'd set it to Stay. If she left, she'd set it to Away. Easy peasy. No one was getting into that place without that alarm screaming.

Somewhat reassured, I continued the backbreaking work. Time crawled by. Maybe I could just drop by Em's later tonight, just to check in. Surely, she wouldn't mind, right? Or would she think I was being smothering and overprotective?

I should leave her alone. She wasn't paying me to watch over her 24/7.

With some difficulty, I shoved thoughts of Em away. My mind drifted to Lisa. Lisa brought up a lot of emotions in me, most of them negative, but some positive. I tried not to look at the past through rose-colored glasses. We'd married too young. Regret, sadness, and resignation were all I felt now. We weren't in love any longer. Was there a deep, lingering affection? Yes, and there always would be.

The fact that she was the mother of my child wasn't going to change. We'd been happy once. Had pinned our futures on each other. It hadn't worked out the way either of us had hoped or planned. Perhaps once the divorce was finalized, we could be more civil, perhaps even friends. Eventually.

Lisa had found someone else to comfort her while I was gone and I wasn't going to fault her for that.

It sucked, but she hadn't been prepared or suited to be a military wife. She'd resented my devotion to my fellow soldiers. It was what it was. I couldn't change who I was any more than she could change who she was. At this point, I just wanted this over and to settle into whatever would be my new normal, especially with Amber.

Three o'clock finally rolled around and I followed Jeff in my truck to the northwest side of downtown, the warm breeze as I drove cooling the sweat on my skin. We pulled up to a two-story apartment building and parked around back. I didn't bother rolling up my windows. If someone wanted to steal my beat-up POS truck, they could have it.

Jeff's girlfriend was named Amy and while she was tall, she was as slender as a beanpole. Two other women were there helping pack. Amy introduced them as her friends. Other than that, it looked like it was just Jeff and me who'd be doing the heavy lifting.

Three hours later, we finished setting up her bed in the new apartment and my back ached. Her queen sized bed was one of those adjustable kind and it was the heaviest piece of furniture I'd ever lifted. Both Jeff and I had cussed blue streaks as we'd hauled it to and from the UHaul. Between that and my truck, we only had to make one trip from one apartment to the other.

Amy was sweet, though, and seemed very grateful for the help, as was Jeff. Amy handed us two bottles of beer that we cracked open outside as we leaned against my truck. I took a long, deep swallow. An ice-cold beer on a hot day. One of life's simple pleasures. Four long pulls and it was gone. I gave a deep sigh.

Jeff handed me a hundred-dollar bill. I glanced at him in surprise.

"You earned it," he said. "That fucker was a pain in the ass to move."

I knew he was referring to the bed and I snorted in agreement, taking the bill from him.

"Thanks, man."

Jeff grunted in acknowledgment, finishing his own beer and reaching for my empty bottle. "Yeah. See you Monday." With that, he headed to the new apartment which thankfully was on the ground floor.

I climbed into my truck, the door creaking as I slammed it closed. It was almost seven and I was starving, but a nagging worry about Em had me pointing my truck East toward Meridian.

I was almost at her house before I remembered what condition I was in—dirty, sweaty, and no doubt I probably stank. Fuck. Way to impress, Cal.

Just check on her and leave, no big deal. Five minutes, in and out.

After parking in the driveway, I headed to the front door and knocked, but not before I'd retrieved my automatic from the glove box. I expected to hear the yapping of the twin poof balls, but there was nothing. Immediately, I was on alert. Those noise machines were constantly barking at nothing. They wouldn't miss a knock on the door.

I tried the doorknob, and it turned easily in my hand. I pushed the door open, expecting to hear the beeping of the alarm, but there was silence. The cool air from the air conditioning wrapped around me.

All my spidey senses were tingling and I slowed my breathing, getting my panic under control and shoving it into the corner of my mind. Reaching around my back, I took out my gun and flicked off the safety before racking a round into the chamber as quietly as possible.

My steps were silent on the wood floor as I searched the first floor. There was nothing and no one. The house was still and quiet. I heard the A/C kick on outside. A neighbor's dog barked.

Carefully, I eased up the stairs, sticking close to the wall. If stairs are going to creak, it'll be in the middle, the weakest part. I held my gun with both hands and pointed it at the ceiling.

The door to Em's bedroom was closed but not latched. With one hand, I gently pushed it open.

The bed was made, but rumpled and empty. My blood ran cold. Em had been here but was gone. Had she gone into the office? I hadn't checked the garage for her car.

Just then, the door to the bathroom flew open. Acting on pure instinct, I jerked the gun down and pointed it at the open doorway.

chapter eleven

A MAN. A GUN. I screamed.
My piercing shriek made him wince and then my brain caught up. Cal. Not an intruder. Just Cal.

I stopped screaming and clutched the towel wrapped around me, breathing hard. Spots danced in front of my eyes and I fell into the nearby slipper chair. Resting my head in my hands, I took a moment to just breathe.

"Holy shit, Em, you startled me."

I glanced up. "Startled *you*? You damn near made me pee my pants. What are you doing here?"

He did something with the gun, then tucked it into the back of his jeans. "I was just checking on you after work. Your front door was unlocked, and the alarm wasn't set." His tone was accusatory.

A pinch of guilt bit at me. "I forgot," I said honestly. "I'm not used to having an alarm. I came home from the gym and took a nap." Donny and Marie had escaped the bathroom and were currently welcoming Cal in their usual fashion. Ollie's inability to identify Cal flashed through my mind. "I don't appreciate you just wandering through my home, armed." My tone had taken on an edge and I was acutely aware that I wore nothing but a towel. I pressed my knees together. No need to give him a peep show.

"I knocked. I figured the noise machines would hear me even if you didn't."

"They were in the bathroom with me and I was blow drying my hair," I explained, not that I needed to explain myself. *He* was the one standing in my bedroom looking like he'd been ridden hard and put away wet. I frowned. "Did you come straight from work?" It was after seven. Had he worked all this time? And in this heat?

"I helped a friend move after I got off," he said. "Then I thought I'd drop by for just a minute. Check on you."

"I didn't feel like being at home tonight," I said with a shrug. "Thought I'd dress up and go get a drink somewhere, maybe a place with some live music." Something to also get my mind off Cal and hey, maybe I'd meet someone. *And we all laughed and laughed…*

Cal looked vaguely uncomfortable, his gaze dropping as he shifted from one foot to another. "Have you had dinner yet?" he asked, shoving his hands into the pockets of his worn, dusty jeans. "Maybe we could grab a bite to eat. I'm pretty hungry. Been a while since lunch, you know. I mean, if you want to. You don't have to. You know, just a friend thing."

He glanced up, his eyes meeting mine. They were such a smoldering dark brown, framed by those lashes and dark brows. I was momentarily distracted.

"I know a place with some pretty good music on Saturday nights, if you're a fan of the nineties."

Hmm. What? Oh, yes. Dinner. I smiled. I couldn't help it. He seemed so adorably awkward, which was pleasantly unexpected. Where was the self-assured, cocky guy who'd taken me to bed?

"I'd just need to grab a quick shower and change first," he continued, glancing down at himself. "Should only take ten minutes. Sorry to come here looking like this." He grimaced.

"It's fine," I said, shaking my head as I stood. I noticed his gaze drift to my legs and crawl upwards. The towel wasn't very long. "I'd love to go to dinner. Just give me a minute to get dressed." I'd already done the hair and makeup thing.

He took a step back towards the door. "I'll be back in like forty minutes?"

"Wait, don't go. I'll just throw on some clothes and go with you. That's easier than you driving all the way back here. Just give me five minutes." I was already heading towards my closet.

"No!"

His sudden outburst had me spinning around, my eyebrows climbing. "No?"

I could swear the tips of his ears turned red.

"I…uh…I mean, my place isn't really picked up. I haven't had time to clean in a while."

I headed for the closet. "That's fine. I don't mind. Just give me a sec." Disappearing into the walk-in closet, I shut the door behind me, ending his protests. I rolled my eyes. He was a man. Did he think that I'd be expecting a designer crib and leather furniture? I snorted.

Five minutes later, true to my word, I stepped out of the expansive closet that was the size of a small-ish bathroom. My shoes took up one entire wall of shelves, and that didn't count the ones I kept in their boxes.

I'd slipped on a little denim skirt with a tight, pale-sunshine halter top that tied behind my neck and my waist, leaving my back mostly bare and dip-ping in a deep V between my breasts. I'd added a pair of wedge sandals, a chunky necklace, and gold bangle bracelets. A squirt of perfume and I was ready to go.

"My purse is downstairs," I said. He'd looked at me when I came out of the closet and I didn't think he'd blinked since. "Do you want to drive or should I follow you?" His eyes dropped to my chest and I was glad I'd worn the halter top—it showed off the girls. "Cal?"

He jerked his gaze to meet mine, looking decidedly guilty. "Yeah, sure."

I stared at him, waiting, then tried to clarify. "Does that mean you're driving?"

"Yeah, sure," he repeated, then turned on his heel and headed downstairs. I followed.

He wore big, heavy work boots, the kind with the steel toe. As we walked down the staircase, I won-dered how in the world he'd thought he could get the drop on someone with those shoes and so many creaky stairs.

"Don't you think someone would've heard you?" I asked. "Those shoes aren't exactly Cinderella slip-pers."

"I was quiet," he said simply.

Hmm.

I grabbed my purse and made sure to arm the alarm before closing and locking the door. Cal watched me do it. I turned to him. "See? Safety first!" I grinned but he didn't return the smile. I guess it was Too Soon.

I didn't have any problems hauling my ass into the seat this time, though it flitted through my mind to pretend so Cal would help me again. He might've gotten a glimpse of my white thong because as I said, the skirt was a short one. And maybe I didn't try super hard to prevent that.

He hurriedly grabbed a small Coleman cooler that was sitting on the floor and tossed it into the bed of the truck, then made sure all my limbs were in the truck before slamming the door shut. It creaked loudly, protesting on its hinges.

Cal took the gun from his jeans before climbing into the driver's seat. He reached over for the glovebox, his hand brushing the knee of my crossed legs as he did so, sending what felt like an electric shock through me. I moved away to give him more room.

"Sorry," he apologized, sliding the gun inside the space and closing the little door.

We drove in silence. The windows were down, and I didn't feel like yelling to make myself heard over the sound of the rushing wind. My hair was whipping around my face, so I grabbed it in a makeshift ponytail and held it, resting my elbow on the window frame of the door.

I took a deep breath. It smelled like summer. The heat of the day was fading slightly and the sun was slowly sinking, though sunset was still an hour away. It didn't bother me, the state of the truck Cal drove.

It suited him. And it had been ages since I'd driven with the windows down.

We pulled into the lot of an apartment building that had seen better days. I eased down to the broken asphalt, careful where I was putting my feet. I didn't want to twist an ankle. Someone was grilling and the delicious aroma filled the air. I could hear kids squealing and yelling from one of the tiny terraces that spotted the building's façade.

Cal rounded the truck and took my hand, surprising me. Without a word, he led me toward the concrete stairwell that was in the center of the building. We climbed two flights before following the hallway to the last door. Paint was peeling on the walls and the wrought iron banister was rusted. I heard a baby crying from somewhere and smelled cigarette smoke.

Cal dropped his hand to dig keys out of his pocket. After unlocking the door, he stepped aside, letting me enter first.

The stifling heat hit me after two steps. Although windows were open, no breeze stirred the limp curtains that had been pulled aside on their rods. I immediately began to sweat. Shit. There went my makeup.

I looked around. There was a futon in the main area with a faded cushion, a card table with two folding chairs, a small table that held a television, and that was it. Carpet covered the floor and I could see a few stains. The kitchen was relatively empty except for a coffee cup on the counter and some dishes in the drying rack.

Pasting a smile on my face, I turned to Cal, whose face was a blank mask.

"It's very…open," I said. There was an uncomfortable tightness in my chest that he was living like this. Divorce did indeed suck.

"Sorry for the heat," he said, ignoring my comment. "I don't leave the A/C on when I'm not here during the day."

I nodded. "Smart."

"Can I get you some water? A beer?"

"Beer would be good." Not my favorite, but a little grease for the wheels would be good.

He went to the small fridge and returned with two bottles. He twisted them open and handed one to me.

"Cheers." I clinked the neck of my bottle against his and took a swallow. The bitter taste of hops touched my tongue.

"I'll be really quick," he said.

He tipped up the bottle and drank it all down. My eyes were glued to his bare throat as he swallowed. He didn't stink, though he did smell like sweat. His arms were bare in the used-to-be-white tank and the muscles were enough to make my eyes widen in admiration. Veins stood out from his skin in a mouth-watering way.

Setting the empty bottle on the counter, he turned away and headed down a short hallway. As he walked, he reached over his shoulders and grabbed the shirt, pulling it up and over his head. The sight of his tanned, bare back had me craning my neck to watch as he walked through a doorway and disappeared from view. A door closed and I heard water running.

A gasp of air left me. I'd been holding my breath.

Well, if any man's body was worth swooning over, it was Cal's.

I nursed the beer as I sweat in the sweltering apartment. I knew why Cal left the A/C off. It was expensive. Money was tight for him at the moment. Sleeping must be a bitch in this heat. Indiana in the summertime was no joke, especially when you factored in the humidity.

Cal was as good as his word, emerging exactly ten minutes later in fresh jeans and a clean, black T-shirt. The cotton fit tight to his shoulders and chest, slightly loose at the waist. He'd carelessly tucked in the front, showing a thick black belt and silver buckle, while the back remained untucked. He'd swapped his work boots for a pair of what looked to be Western-style boots. His hair was still damp and was so thick and wavy, I immediately wanted to run my hands through it.

Okay. I had to stop. He was a client/employee now. It didn't matter that we'd slept together and that I kept replaying that night in my head. And our kisses. This was a Just Friends thing.

Right.

Cal grabbed his keys from the counter. "Ready?"

I nodded. I was more than ready to get out of the rather depressing—not to mention steaming hot—apartment. He brushed by me and I could smell a hint of cologne. It was a subtle, spicy scent and I smiled inwardly that he'd made the effort.

We were back in the truck and I turned to the window, letting the wind cool me as he drove. I lifted my hair again and sighed in relief as the breeze hit the back of my neck. I hated sweating after I'd fixed myself up. I wasn't exactly what you'd call the "out-doorsy" type.

"So where are we going?" I asked.

Cal glanced at me, noting how I was holding my hair. I let it drop, not wanting him to feel self-conscious about the lack of air conditioning in his truck.

"A bar and grill north of downtown," he answered. "It's a nice place, not a dive."

My brows raised. "I didn't think it would be." His gaze met mine and I gave him a little smile. "I trust you not to take me to a joint that regularly has to replace the furniture and mop blood off the floor."

That prompted a chuckle from him. "I've been in those places. Especially when soldiers need to blow off steam."

"Have you ever been in a bar fight?" I was curious. I wanted to know more about him, his life and past.

He nodded. "More times than I like to remember. It usually always starts the same way. Some drunk guy wants to take on a soldier. I've at time had to break up bar fights and other times had to win them. That always goes well." The sarcasm was thick in his voice.

"Did you ever get hurt?" I'd never known some-one who'd been in bar fights before. Chad had been a guy who seemed to get along with everyone, and everyone with him.

Cal nodded. "Sometimes. Nothing really bad. Broken nose. A broken finger or two. Once a knife wound from a guy who didn't want to play by the rules."

His tone had changed now, turned darker. I decided he probably didn't want to relive whatever he was thinking about, so I changed the subject. "Do you have family here in Indy?"

"I have three younger sisters," he said. "One lives in Indy, the other two moved away. One to St. Louis and another to Iowa."

"Iowa?" That seemed quite a departure from Indianapolis.

He shrugged. "She met some farmer in Ag School when she was in college and now she lives on a big spread near the middle of nowhere. She's happy, though, and I guess that's all that matters."

Three sisters and he the only boy. Wow. "And your parents?"

"My dad passed a few years back. Heart attack. My mom is still around and lives near where my sister lives here in Indy. She keeps an eye on Mom." He glanced at me. "What about you?"

"My folk are still alive and live between here and Bloomington," I answered. "They've been married almost forty years. Dad got into insurance when I was young and did that for a long time. Eventually, they bought some land and built their dream house. Now my mother pesters me on a regular basis that there are too many bedrooms, and wouldn't it be perfect to have grandkids stay there? They'd even put in a pool." I rolled my eyes.

"That's great," he said with what sounded like genuine appreciation. "You're an only child?"

"How did you know?" The wind blew my hair as I faced Cal and I used my fingers to comb strands away from my eyes. Good thing I'd gone for the messy just-rolled-out-of-bed look tonight.

His grin showed that damn dimple again. "Lucky guess."

I rolled my eyes. I knew all the things people said about only children. "I'm not a spoiled narcissist."

Cal's grin widened. "Only a spoiled narcissist would say that." He winked at me, and my pulse gave a little jump.

"Takes one to know one," I blustered. Great. What a comeback. Channeling my inner ten-year-old.

He just laughed.

I kept stealing glances at Cal underneath my lashes. I was entranced by his arms and hands. He grasped the wheel with his right hand, his left resting loosely from where his elbow was lodged on the rolled down window edge of the door. He was so tan. The black of his T-shirt contrasted nicely against his bronze skin. I was too fair to tan—I just burned then went straight back to pale.

I'd never been with a man so…big…before. Even Chad hadn't been cut like Cal was, though he'd been in shape. His frame just hadn't been as large and he'd been a couple of inches under six feet. Cal was at least six-three, maybe six-four. And his muscles looked carved rather than mere flesh.

My gaze caught again on his shoulders that had arched muscle between his neck and shoulder, which had always been a feature that made me weak in the knees. Tom Hardy had it, which may have been why I'd always been overly fond of movies that had at least one scene where he was shirtless.

I sighed a little inside as I watched Cal. I couldn't touch, but no one said I couldn't look.

Which reminded me. "Hey," I said. He glanced my way. "I forgot to ask what the tattoo was on your arm." I'd seen flashes of it but hadn't wanted to stare or hold his arm still to scrutinize it. I just knew it was about the size of my palm and that it wasn't easy to figure out with just a glimpse.

In answer, he reached over and pulled up the sleeve of his T-shirt so I could see.

"It's Amber's footprints from when she was born," he said.

I leaned over, getting a closer look. Indeed, it was two tiny baby footprints with Amber's name stylized above them, the date that I assumed was of her birth inked underneath.

"That is incredibly sweet," I said, leaning back. Cal let his sleeve drop and his eyes returned to the road.

"Best day of my life."

There was nothing to say in reply to that. I just stared at him for a moment or two longer, digesting all the information I was gleaning about the kind of man he was.

Finally, I tore my eyes away and looked out the window, though I was acutely aware of his palpable presence on the seat mere inches from me.

A few minutes later, we pulled in to a gravel parking lot of a low-slung building with clapboard siding. It looked like it should've been out in the Arizona desert somewhere, with its wooden shutters and neon beer signs in the window.

Both of us got out of the truck at the same time and Cal left the windows down. I almost said something but rethought it. It was his truck, after all.

"I know it doesn't look like much," Cal said, meeting me in front of the truck, "but the music is great, and they have the best wings in town."

"I'll take your word for it."

Cal again reached for my hand and I let him take it. The parking lot had loose rock and the last thing I wanted was to twist an ankle and end up on my ass. The beauty of a closet full of heels and a desk job: smooth floors and a chair.

Inside was cool with the air conditioning on full blast, and a woman who looked to be in her early twenties showed us to an empty booth along one wall. It was decorated in a western saloon style with an elevated stage in front and a long bar along one wall with comfortable-looking stools. There was a small dance floor surrounded by tables. Booths took up the wall where we were seated.

All the ladies serving tables were of similar age, all dressed in tiny black shorts and V-neck white T-shirts with the bar's name emblazoned on them. The place was about three-quarters full, and I was surprised we didn't have to wait for a table, especially a booth. Then we arrived at the booth and the explanation presented itself.

"Good to see you, Cal," the blonde hostess/server said with a smile, handing him a couple of menus. "I'll make sure Corinne is your server. I know she's your favorite." She winked at him, completely ignoring me. My eyebrows rose as she sashayed away. Her ass, barely clad in the denim, made me jealous.

We slid into the booth on opposite sides and Cal handed me one of the laminated menus.

"I'm kind of a regular," he said by way of explanation, looking slightly abashed. "Well, when I can."

"I got that," I replied, perusing the menu. They had eight different sauces for their bone-in wings. I realized that I was slightly jealous, which I had no right to be. It's not like Cal and I were a couple.

Despite the waitresses' attire, the place had a distinctly friendly, neighborhood-bar vibe. The patrons were couples and even a few families with kids. I could smell the food cooking and my stomach growled. The half-sammy and half-salad at lunch hadn't gone very far.

Wings, eh? Guess the house specialty was the way to go.

A waitress stopped by our table, and I looked up. I was taken aback. She was gorgeous. Tall and willowy, her chestnut hair was thick and braided into a French braid that lay across one shoulder. Her legs were long and showcased by the short shorts whereas her chest received the same treatment from the tight T-shirt. A nametag pinned to her shirt said *Corinne*. She smiled at Cal and it was mega-wattage.

"Hey, Cal," she said in a soft voice with a Southern lilt. "How ya been?"

Cal grinned back, his expression softening. "I'm good. Nice to see you again. How are the boys?"

"Terrors, as always."

Her voice was straight out of *Steel Magnolias* and I pressed my lips together, resolutely resuming my study of the menu, though I couldn't concentrate on a single word printed.

"Most of them are when they're six years old," Cal replied. "Just ask my mom."

They both laughed, then chatted a bit more before she finally asked, "Can I get ya'll something to drink?"

Cal ordered a beer. I hesitated for just a moment. I doubted the wine here would be that good and also that any drink over two ingredients would also be less than stellar. Not throwing shade, just adjusting expectations.

"I'll have a vodka soda with extra lime," I said. "Grey Goose."

"You bet." Corinne smiled and walked away.

"Do you know all the girls here?" I asked before I could help myself.

Cal looked momentarily surprised by my tone and I could've kicked myself. Then he smiled in a slow, sexy way that made butterflies dance in my stomach.

"Are you jealous?" His smile widened.

"Don't be ridiculous," I scoffed, again burying myself in the menu as though it were the Dead Sea Scrolls and I alone responsible for translating. My face was burning.

Cal just chuckled softly, which I resolutely ignored. Suddenly, the menu I held was flattened on the table by his hand.

"Corinne is married with twin boys," he said. "She had to bring them in to work one night because her sitter bailed and her husband was at work. So, I entertained them for a while, helped her out. They think I'm 'cool.'"

Of course they did. Hell, I thought Cal was cool.

His grin was what one would call "shit-eating." I wasn't jealous, damn it. Except maybe of Corinne's long legs.

I raised one eyebrow. "I'll have the wings with the sweet chili sauce," and handed him the menu. "With fries." Diet be damned, I wanted French fries. With all the ketchup ever.

Cal leaned back, relaxing against the fake leather of the booth. I resolutely kept my eyes on his face and didn't let them drift down to his chest.

"Got it," he said, still with the smirk on his face that was both infuriating and hot at the same time.

Corinne came back with the drinks and set them down in front of us along with a basket of rolls and butter. "Ya'll decide what you're havin'?" she drawled.

"Yes, we have," Cal answered, reaching for a roll. He gave her my order first, then ordered a double order of buffalo wings with a side of fries and another side of coleslaw. Corinne nodded, smiled and went on her way. I watched her go, enviously staring at her shapely legs.

"Tell me about your job," Cal said out of the blue, tearing a bite off his roll. I glanced at him in surprise.

"You want to hear about my job? I'm a lawyer. I'm sure you have better stories than I do." I crossed my legs underneath the table and settled back, taking a sip of my drink through the tiny cocktail straw.

He took a drink of his beer before answering, the frosted, glass mug somehow looking small in his grip. "I need to know what your clientele is like, what your typical day and week are like, so I can come up with the best way to keep you safe. And maybe find out the identity of your stalker."

Ah yes. My stalker. Ugh. I frowned. "I don't want to have a stalker." That may have bordered on a whine.

"I don't know anyone who does," he countered.

I sighed. "My clientele are what you'd expect. People going through one of the most difficult things a person *can* go through. They're emotional, sometimes angry, sometimes irrational. My job is to get them through the process as best I can and safeguard their interests, even when they can't or won't. I protect them from the worst of it, if they'll let me. Sometimes they're their own worst enemies. And more often than not, I'm their only ally."

Cal's expression was serious as he considered this. "I can see that," he said, taking another drink. "Are they usually satisfied with how things turn out?"

I shrugged. "I'd say three out of four are as satisfied as it's possible to be in these situations. The last one is someone who's never going to be happy because they didn't want the divorce in the first place."

"Are divorces all you handle?"

"They're the majority of my clients. I have occasional cases regarding custody or emancipation of a minor or something else."

"And this was the first time a client has ever attacked you?" His fingers idly drew patterns in the frost on the mug and my eye was briefly drawn to them.

"Um, yeah," I managed, forcing my gaze back to his. "We've never had any problem before. At the firm."

"And do the other partners know I'll be around and recommending what I think you need to make the place safer?"

I nodded. "I sent them both an email, explaining. They were supportive."

Corinne returned just then with two platters. She set one in front of me, and another that was nearly overflowing in front of Cal. The dueling aroma of

sauces filled the air. Before I could ask, she set a bottle
of ketchup on the table.

"Can I get ya'll anything else?"

I shook my head as Cal politely refused.

"Enjoy!" she said cheerfully, turning to another
table and picking up some empty glasses.

Cal picked up a drummy and took a bite. I watched
him briefly as he chewed.

No way was I going to eat with my hands and risk
getting sauce all over my face. I hated that. I'd used
a fork and knife many times to eat wings and that's
what I did now. I was pretty good at it.

I picked up my utensils and dug in.

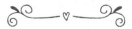

I watched Em delicately cut into the wing and put
the resulting bite into her mouth. I chewed a couple
fries as she cut more.

"Gotta say," I said after she'd stripped the wing
down to the bone, "I've never seen someone eat
wings with a knife and fork."

She didn't bother looking up as she started on the
next piece of chicken.

"I don't like eating with my hands. Too messy and
sticky."

I snorted. I couldn't help it. It was just such an…Em
thing to say. "You don't seem to mind some things
that are messy and sticky." Sexual innuendo? Check.

Her gaze flew to mine and her cheeks turned pink.
Even in the low lighting, I could see the flush. It was
adorable. As was her jealousy over Corinne. Nice to
know she was still thinking about us "that" way.

"I don't know what you're talking about," she said archly, attacking the chicken with a bit more vigor.

"Mmm," was my non-response. I went back to eating as well and we were both silent for a while. I was starving and the food disappeared quickly, bones discarded.

Finally, I was cleaning my fingers with the wipes Corinne had dropped on the table in little packages. She'd come back by and refilled our drinks. I was halfway through my second beer when I sat back from my empty plate with a sigh.

Em had done a decent job on her wings as well, even with the utensils. She was nibbling on a fry, then took a sip of her cocktail.

She looked amazing tonight. Her hair had that just-fucked look from how she'd tousled it and then the wind had added to the careless style. Her top showed off her breasts and flat stomach that made me want to touch the bared skin. And that skirt was doing wonders for her ass. I wondered if I could get her to walk ahead of me back to the truck.

Corinne dropped off the check and I picked it up just as Em reached for it. I looked at her.

"I invited you to dinner. It's on me." I tried to keep my tone even and not offended. I hadn't been able to buy a woman dinner in ages. It felt like part of my manhood was back, being able to take care of the tab. A woman with me isn't going to be paying for her own dinner.

"Sure, of course," she said, backtracking. I guess I hadn't quite been able to keep my tone even. "I was just…" Her voice trailed off and she cleared her

throat, then took another drink as she looked every-
where but at me.

I didn't want her to be embarrassed. "I appreciate
it, but I earned some extra cash today and I'd like to
spend it on you."

Em finally looked at me and her face softened, a
small smile curving her lips.

"That's very sweet," she said softly. "Thank you."

"It's my privilege."

She picked up her purse. "I'm just going to the
ladies' room." Scooting out of the booth, she passed
by towards hallway at the back of the bar.

I paid the tab, pocketing the change after leaving
Corinne a decent tip. She worked her ass off in this
place, which was currently packed. It was almost
nine-thirty and the crowd that wanted to dance and
drink was replacing the crowd that had wanted to eat.

The band that was going to play was warming up
in on stage. It was a cover band that was actually very
good. I hoped Em would like it.

Emmy returned and I stood, my gaze snagging
on her lips, which were freshly coated with a shiny
veneer of pink gloss. I had the insane urge to kiss it
off.

"The band is going to play," I said. "Want to stay
and watch?" I asked. "We can grab a spot by the bar."
Which would free up the table to turn for Corinne.

She took one last sip of her drink, finishing it off.
"You bet."

Em walked in front of me, and I appreciated the
view. Then we had to wade through a knot of people.
I took the opportunity to rest my hand on the bare

skin at the small of her back, which was soft to the touch.

Someone bumped into me and my connection to her was broken. The crowd quickly filled the space, widening the gap between us. I pushed through, catching sight of her as she turned around, looking for me.

Then I saw a man grab her arm and pull.

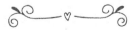

I tried to yank my arm out of the man's grip, but he had a tight hold and pulled me toward him. He was a few inches taller than me and burly, with a thick beard and moustache, and a formidable beer belly.

"Hey there," he said, smiling. I could smell the beer wafting from his breath. "Let me buy you a drink, beautiful."

"Ah, no thank you," I said politely, still trying to remove my arm from his grip. "I'm with someone."

"Aw c'mon," he persisted, taking a step toward the bar, tugging me along with him. I bumped into a few people as he dragged me through what had become a full crowd while Cal and I had eaten. "It's just one drink."

"Sorry. Sorry. Excuse me. Sorry." I was apologizing profusely to the folks the man was making me bump into.

Okay, enough was enough. The man finally stopped at the bar and waved to get the bartender's attention.

I sank my fingernails into the skin of his arm, bared by the black Harley-Davidson T-shirt he wore. I dug in and he yelped, abruptly letting me go. Immediately, I stepped back. Just then, Cal appeared next to me.

"She said no, dickhead." Cal wrapped a possessive arm around my waist and pulled me against his chest. The tension fled my body and I breathed a sigh of relief.

The guy looked at Cal and apparently was *not* so drunk that he couldn't assess the situation and make a wise choice.

"Hey, man, I was just being polite." He held up his hands in the universal gesture of surrender. "Didn't know she was with somebody."

Liar. I'd *told* him I was with someone. Whatever.

"I'm okay," I said to Cal, who moved us toward a just vacated stool at the bar a few stools down. This time, he kept a tight hold around my waist and people moved out of our way. Without a word, he picked me up and set me on the stool.

"But what about you?" I asked, surprised. But he just smiled.

"I don't mind standing. Nice view from up here."

He glanced down towards my chest and I reflexively looked down, too. Well. Yes, indeed, this particular blouse allowed for quite the view from overhead. Looking back up at him, I didn't bother trying to formulate a snappy comeback. I just winked.

His eyes darkened and took on a familiar look that I was beginning to recognize. An answering heat went through me. No nononono. Yes yeyesyesyes. Ugh. The angel and demon on my opposite shoulders were having a knock-down drag-out fight.

Deliberately breaking eye contact, I glanced around the bar, just people-watching. Cal ordered us another round as well as two waters. As I was taking in the crowd, I thought I saw a familiar face. I frowned, but then the person I'd thought I'd seen was swallowed in the crowd. No, it couldn't have been... I'd just been imagining it.

The band was bustling about the raised stage and taking their places. I suppose their warm-up was finished. I was looking forward to hearing live music. It had been a while. Idly, I wondered if Cal knew how to dance. I loved to dance, but finding a man who could actually do more than shuffle about a dance floor was harder than finding one who could explain what the color "salmon" was.

Cal stood behind me, one arm loosely wrapped around my midsection. I leaned against him and could feel the cotton of his shirt against the bare skin of my back.

The band launched into a nineties' tune and I quickly realized that they were pretty good. The music was too loud to talk over, so I didn't try. One of the bartenders set our drinks on the bar in front of us. Cal handed her a bill and must've said to keep the change because she smiled and hurried away.

I love cover bands, and just enjoyed the moment. I sipped at my drink and didn't try to move out of Cal's light embrace. More people came in and couples started dancing, quite a few doing the two-step to the country song the band was now playing. I watched, delighted, especially when they did spins and turns as they danced.

Cal took a drink of his water, which moved him even closer to me. Instead of dropping his arm, he slid the other one around my waist, his arms crossing in front of me in a snug grip. His palms rested against the bare skin of my abdomen and waist. I again marveled at the size and strength of his hands.

I'd had just enough booze to turn off my brain, which I decided wasn't a bad thing. The feel of Cal's hard body against me was enough to send a warm rush to places I shouldn't be thinking about.

Lightly, I crossed my arms, resting them on top of his. Skin against skin. It felt forbidden and secret and a tremor I couldn't control washed through me. I knew Cal felt it because his arms tightened.

We stood like that and I barely breathed. The band was playing, but I couldn't say what the song was. All of my attention was on Cal's touch and the nearness of his body. I could feel my pulse hammering, but I was determined to play it casual, as though this was not a Big Deal.

The room was shoulder to shoulder, and groups of people flanked us, also drinking and talking loudly so their friends could hear them. I moved slightly to pick up my cocktail and take another sip. Cal's arms loosened and his fingers brushed over my abdomen in a caress. I swallowed the cold liquid and set the glass back down before letting Cal draw me back against him once again.

The next song was one of those hair band ballads from the eighties—*Angel*, I recognized, by Aerosmith. The lead singer was really good, and I was enjoying the music when Cal lowered his head to my shoulder, gently nuzzling my neck.

I sucked in my breath, unconsciously tilting my head to accommodate him. People pressed in around us and with all the dancers on the floor, I could no longer see the band. It was warm and my skin was slightly damp with perspiration.

Cal inhaled deeply, one hand raising from my waist to move my hair aside. His lips brushed the skin of my neck in a featherlight touch. Gooseflesh erupted on my arms and my nipples tightened. I didn't move, afraid that if I did, he'd stop. I could feel the warmth of his breath and my eyes drifted shut.

The singer was belting out the lyrics to the song and other sounds faded into the background. His tongue touched my ear and my lips fell open so I could suck in more air that suddenly seemed in short supply. My fingers dug into his arm when he sucked the lobe of my ear into his mouth. I had the absurd, happy thought that I was glad I'd worn my diamond studs and not dangly earrings.

The flesh between my thighs ached and I was stunned at how easily he could arouse me. The chemistry between us was electric, had been since the moment he'd set foot in my house. I tried to remember all the reasons why having sex with Cal was a bad idea.

Nothing came to me at the moment.

His arms were around me again, pulling me tight against him. I could feel the hard press of his erection against the small of my back. The song changed. It seemed the band were big fans of the eighties as the next number was *You Shook Me All Night Long* by AC/DC.

The change in the crowd was nearly palpable, the energy ratcheting up a notch as they raucously sang along.

Cal's fingers crept inside the V-neck of my halter

top. My breath hitched when he touched my breast, bare underneath the fabric. I was thankful for his size, my lack of stature, and the crowd pressing in, which kept me hidden from casual view.

His thumb brushed my nipple, sending a pleasant shock through my nerve endings. He moved his hand further until he was cupping my breast. He squeezed the nipple, harder than I was used to, and I gasped at the sensation. All the while, he kept kissing and sucking the tender skin of my neck, which had always been extremely sensitive.

Somehow, the venue for this, being surrounded by music and people, added to the eroticism. The electric guitar and drums were vying with the lead singer and I felt the bass thumping through the floor into my body.

My hand left his arm and reached behind me, finding his denim-encased cock, straining at the zipper of his jeans. I traced its outline, squeezing and rubbing. He made a sound, low and male.

Abandoning my It's Not A Big Deal façade, I turned on the stool, wrapped my arms around his neck, and pulled his head down until our lips met.

chapter twelve

EM KISSED ME like she was on fire. I kissed her back just as hungrily. I wanted her so bad. My hands gripped her hips, pulling her against me. I ached to be inside her. Our tongues entwined and she tasted like vodka and Em. I couldn't get enough. I had to have her.

Pulling back, I broke the connection. She whimpered and the sound went straight to my cock. Her fingers were combing through my hair at the nape of my neck, her nails lightly scraping. I bit back a moan.

"Let's get out of here."

I didn't know if she could hear me over all the noise, but she didn't object when I firmly took her hand and led us to the nearest exit. We'd be at a different area of the parking lot than where my truck was, but I didn't care. I didn't feel like fighting my way to the front door.

In a moment, we were outside, and I took a deep breath of the clean air. It was still humid and hot, but the oppressive sun was gone, leaving behind the sultry heat of a summer night.

Glancing around, I saw that we were on the side of the building by the back corner. A few cars were parked nearby but no people. Perfect.

I turned and took Em, positioning her against the wall, deep in the shadows where the glow from the lights in the lot didn't penetrate. She looked up at me, her lips still moist from our kisses.

Em was the most sexually charged woman I'd ever encountered, and I wondered if it was just her, or if it was us. Together.

I closed down my thoughts and kissed her again, our mouths melding in mutual want and need. She clung to me like a damp cloth, molding her softness to my body. Her breasts pressed against my chest and my cock was straining against her stomach.

I had to touch her.

My arms were wrapped around her back but I freed one, sending it skating down her hip until I reached the edge of that little skirt she wore that had teased me all night. I dragged the fabric up her thigh until my fingers touched the her ass, exposed from the tiny white thong I'd had a tantalizing glimpse of earlier. I don't know if she even noticed, our kisses were so heated.

I slipped my hand between her legs from behind, easily moving aside the scrap of satin, and touched the warm heaven there. She was wet and so hot, it felt like she burned. Without even thinking, I slipped my middle finger between the moist slit and pushed inside her.

I think we both moaned then. She widened her stance, giving me better access, and I deepened the kiss as her attention was otherwise diverted.

I moved my finger slowly, feeling utter satisfaction that she grew even more wet. Rubbing her clit with every thrust, she soon tore her mouth from mine, panting. Her skirt was around her waist now. I didn't worry about anyone seeing. My body was big enough to hide her. She was little, but packed so much fire.

Adding a second finger made her moan louder and I captured her lips with mine, muffling the sound.

"Shh, baby," I whispered, moving my hand faster and with more intent. Her clit was hard now, and I could feel her body trembling. Nails dug into my shoulders, and I didn't mind, not one little bit.

"Come for me." I loved the feel of her, silken heat and so tight. I was so turned on, I thought I might come in my fucking jeans.

Liquid rushed against my hand as she buried her face in my chest, muffling the sound as she cried out. Her pussy was swollen and dripping. Holy shit. She was fucking awesome. So passionate and responsive. And I hadn't come in my jeans like a pimply-faced teenager. I was painfully hard, but I could deal with that later.

Em pulled back, her lips parted as she panted rushed breaths. Her gaze lifted to mine and time seemed to stand still. I couldn't breathe. My hand was still between her legs and the intimacy of the touch, my arm around her, her hands on my chest, and our eyes drinking each other in was a moment that I wanted to etch in my memory. It was then that I knew.

She was mine. Somehow, fate had brought us together—twice—and I didn't believe in coincidence. And I wasn't going to let her get away.

"Cal," she said, her voice rough, which was sexy as hell, "what are we doing?"

"Having a good time." I tugged her skirt back into place, then cupped her ass in my hands. Pulling her against me, she sucked in a breath.

She shook her head. "We shouldn't have done that. I'm your lawyer, not your...your..."

The sentence hung in the air, unfinished.

"Do you wanna be?" My voice was little more than a whisper. I brushed a hand across her cheek and cradled her delicate jaw as she looked up at me. Her hair slid over my fingers, stirred by a slight breeze.

I was captivated by her mouth, which looked so inviting, and my gaze was fixed on her lips. Her tongue darted out to wet her lips and I couldn't resist. Bending down, I pressed my mouth to hers. Our tongues danced together as she surrendered to my kiss. My hand slid from her jaw to the nape of her neck, my fingers buried in her lustrous hair.

It was heaven and torture at the same time. Her curves fit perfectly against me, just like I remembered. I could smell her perfume mixed with her own incredible scent. This was so much better than the Tinder hookup had been, because she meant so much more to me than the stranger she had been.

Suddenly, she broke the kiss, pushing me away. I obediently moved backward, not because she was strong enough to move me if I didn't want to, but because I didn't want her to feel as though I wasn't giving her a choice or space that she needed.

"I can't do this," she murmured, almost to herself. She rubbed a hand over her eyes, pushing her hair back from her face. "It's the alcohol. I shouldn't have drank tonight."

That stung. "Alcohol lowers inhibitions," I argued. "It doesn't make you feel things you don't already feel."

But she wasn't listening. She was digging in her purse and pulled out her cell.

"I'll get an Uber," she said, her voice shaking slightly. "I don't think you should take me home."

"No. Em—" Before I could think about it, I reached out and snatched the phone from her hand. "Please don't run. I promise I won't do anything. But I'll take you home."

I didn't want to go with him.

How had this even happened? I'd never been an exhibitionist...and yet I'd just had an orgasm. In a parking lot.

Holy shit.

Heat flooded my face, and I couldn't even look at Cal any longer. I tore my gaze away, mumbling, "Fine."

He handed me back my phone, which I slipped into my purse, then he took my hand and led me toward where we'd parked out front.

I glanced around. The lot was empty of people, thank goodness. I kept my head down and my eyes on the gravel as we walked. I didn't know how I was going to look Cal in the eye again.

My head was fuzzy from the drinks and my body was still humming. I shouldn't have finished off that last one. I wasn't going to blame the booze, but it certainly hadn't helped. And it was continuing to not help because I couldn't help but notice how tight his jeans were across his crotch and my palm itched to touch him.

Stop it stop it stop it. Cal was off-limits.

I was such a hypocrite.

We were back at his truck, and I reached for the door handle, only to be spun around.

"Don't regret it." Cal's voice was low and insistent. "You're beautiful. Amazing. Don't regret something I'll remember for the rest of my life."

He was looking at me the same way he'd looked at me just moments ago, as though I was something undefinable and exquisite. Butterflies in my stomach took flight.

I cleared my throat. "We can't do this," I said, matching his low tone. "I'm your lawyer. And in case you've forgotten, you're still married. When I asked you to protect me, I wasn't asking for this." I motioned between us.

"What we have isn't something that comes along every day," he insisted. "I'm not asking for an answer or commitment right now. I just don't want you to immediately dismiss it. Please."

He was hurting from the divorce and lonely. I got it. He wasn't seeing this—seeing me—clearly. His life was a bit of a dumpster fire right now and he was viewing me as the bucket of water that would put it out. I sighed inwardly.

"Okay," I acquiesced. "I'll think about it."

That seemed to mollify him and he helped me into the truck. In another moment, he was behind the wheel and firing up the engine. He pointed the truck toward my house.

I refused to think about what had happened. We just had incredible chemistry, more powerful than anything I'd ever felt with any man before. Even Chad. Chad had been comfortable and home to me. We'd known each other since middle school, been together since ninth grade. Being with him had been effortless.

Cal was *not* comfortable. He was an unknown quantity that enticed and intrigued me. I wanted to know everything about him, preferably while curled up naked and lying on top of him.

Ugh. I was leading him on, which was despicable. Even if there *could* be something between us, now was not the time. His divorce needed to be finalized and he had to settle into his new reality before a relationship could even be considered. Also, I had serious doubts about his sudden certainty that we should be together. Drowning people grabbed on to anyone who might rescue them, which condemned the rescuer to the same fate. The partners at the firm would have a serious problem with my sleeping with a client. And I wouldn't blame them.

We didn't speak the entire ride to my house. I couldn't help thinking of how he'd "taken care of" me, yet I was leaving him hanging, so to speak. I winced slightly. Not my usual way of doing things, but no way was I going to offer anything. That would only encourage him. He was a grown man. I was sure he knew how to take care of things himself.

An image popped into my head and I immediately scrubbed it away. I certainly didn't need to dwell on the particulars. I deliberately turned to look out the window as Cal navigated my neighborhood to my driveway. I was out of the truck as soon as the vehicle stopped.

"Wait," Cal called out, slamming his door shut. "I want to check out the house first."

"But I set the alarm."

"Still. Better safe than sorry."

That's when I saw the gun in his hand. I swallowed. Oh yeah. I had a stalker who thought I was a whore. Awesome.

After unlocking the door, I stepped inside and disarmed the alarm. Cal followed.

"Stay here. I'll check the house."

Obediently, I stayed. After kicking off my shoes I crouched to greet the twins, who were overjoyed at my reappearance. Donny flipped onto his back and I quicky rolled him back over. The last thing I wanted was to be sprayed with doggy potty.

After a few minutes, Cal returned. "It's clear," he said, shoving the gun into the waistband in the back of his jeans. The twins rushed to greet him, too.

"Okay, thank you." I stood uncertainly, suddenly nervous. Self-consciously, I smoothed my skirt down my thighs, remembering how it had been around my waist earlier. I averted my gaze away from Cal.

He stepped closer and tipped my chin upward until I was forced to look at him. The deep brown seemed to swallow me whole. His eyes were completely unfathomable.

"Tonight was amazing," he said, his voice rough and low. "*You're* amazing. Thank you." His palm cupped my jaw, the callouses on his hand were rough against my skin. I remembered how that hand had felt touching me and a shiver went through me.

Cal's gaze dropped to my lips, giving me a moment's warning, before he bent down and settled his mouth on mine.

It was a gentle, sweet kiss, full of unsaid things. His thumb brushed my cheek as his lips moved against mine. My head seemed to spin, the world losing focus until it was just him and me.

I wanted him, desperately, and it took all I had to keep my arms firmly at my sides, my hands curling into fists. I mentally cursed the situation that had thrown us into one another's sphere in such a way as this. If I'd only met him under different circumstances...

After what seemed like both forever and a mere moment, he broke off the kiss. I was breathing fast and Cal's lips curved into the faintest of smiles.

"Call me if you need anything," he said, taking a step back. His hand dropped from my face. "Anything at all."

He was out the door and gone before I could get my voice to work. In a moment, I heard the roar and rev of his truck's engine, which faded as he drove away.

In that moment, I didn't know if I should be grateful that we hadn't ended up in my bed, or incredibly sad.

Sunday passed without hearing from Em, which was frustrating. I picked up my cell at least a dozen

times to text her and put it down just as many times.
I wasn't going to make a nuisance of myself. I'd been
plain about what I wanted. She needed time.

I did hear from Amber, which shocked the hell out
of me. She was having a blast at Disney World and
I had to ignore the jealousy I felt that she was with
Lisa's parents instead of me. At least they'd had her
call, I reasoned. It could be worse.

Amber said she'd met Cinderella and Snow White
and that the teacups were her favorite ride. When she
topped that with the fact that grandpa had "tossed his
cookies" (a phrase I'd taught her) after the ride, I felt
positively joyful. Served him right.

They were staying at one of the resorts on the
property and were going to spend the afternoon
swimming before dinner. I reminded Amber to have
grandma put sunscreen on her and to wear her float-
ies, then she was gone. There was a pang of sadness,
but I tried to reason that she was having a wonderful
time and that she had a much different relationship
with Lisa's parents than I did. I was grateful that they
did actually dote on her, though I could have done
without them fighting for unfair custody.

That reminder soured my mood. At least a small
weather front had gone through Indy and the temperatures had cooled to the mid-eighties, making my
apartment much more tolerable. I was pretty acclimated to the heat by now after working outside all
day for weeks. There was even a slight breeze coming
through the open windows.

My cell rang as I was getting a frozen pizza out of
the oven. I leapt for it, hoping Em might be calling
after all. To my disappointment, it was just Shane.

"Hey," I answered, trying not to sound too bummed.

"Cal!" His exuberant greeting made me grimace. "I've been thinking about you. Meet me at Johnny's for a beer. I may have a client for you."

"Yeah, I decided not to go that route," I explained. "But I'll meet you for a beer." A cheap beer.

"Why not? Wait, never mind. You can tell me at Johnny's. See you in ten?"

"Make it twenty." I wanted to eat the pizza first.

"Will do."

He hung up and I dug in, tossing on a T-shirt as I ate. Twenty-three minutes later, I was walking in to Johnny's and spotted Shane sitting at the bar. I straddled the bar stool next to him.

"Hey, man," he greeted me with a smile. Motioning to the bartender, he signaled for another round. We waited until he'd set two bottles in front of us, then Shane turned to me.

"Why'd you decide not to do it?" he asked. "I had some lady calling me, all pissed off because she said you—" he glanced around before leaning closer and lowering his voice. "—had *issues*."

I rolled my eyes. "It wasn't that. It's just not my thing. Listen, I gave it the old college try, but it didn't work out." I took a pull on my beer.

"I get it. Honestly, I didn't really think you'd go for it, no matter the money." The bartender set a massive platter of loaded nachos in front of us along with two plates. "Have some," Shane offered, scooping some onto his plate.

I was more than happy to oblige, and we spent a few minutes munching. It wasn't nearly as good as

Em's cooking, but it was better than the rest of the shit I'd been eating lately.

"How's the divorce going?" Shane asked. "Dating anyone?"

I had the incredibly strong urge to tell him about Em.

"Divorce is going," I replied. "Got a new lawyer. A woman this time."

"Is she hot?" Shane asked around a mouthful of nachos.

"Actually, yeah. But that's not why I hired her. We're exchanging services—"

"You dog." Shane nudged me with an elbow, wearing a sly grin.

I refrained from rolling my eyes. "Not that. Get your head out of the gutter. She's got some stalker thing going on with zero security at her job. She's doing the divorce and I'm providing the security detail."

"Body work? You hate playing bodyguard."

"I hate it because it's defensive and reactive, not proactive. But she needs it and offered to do this deal, which I'd have been a fool to turn down."

Shane took another drink and eyed me. "You have the look," he said. "There's something going on with this woman."

"What are you talking about?" I blustered. "I don't have a look." I took another bite of nacho so I wouldn't have to say anything, but Shane wasn't deterred.

"I know you, Calamity," he said, dropping the nickname I'd gone by in the Army. "You have a thing for this woman. Does she know?"

With a sigh, I caved. Shane knew me too well. "Yeah, but I don't think she's taking me seriously, not with the divorce not finalized yet. And I'm technically both a client and an employee. Not an ideal situation."

"Man, you were over Lisa six months before you came back. She told you she was seeing someone else. Why you were surprised when she filed, I'll never know."

"I thought maybe she was just trying to make me jealous, make sure I didn't re-enlist." I stared glumly at the brown beer bottle, sweating on the bar. "She succeeded in the second one, but that was more due to Amber than Lisa's extramarital love life."

I remembered when Lisa had told me. I'd been taking my turn with the phone, sweat trickling down my back as I stood in a T-shirt, fatigues, and my combat boots, receiver held to my ear. I could still taste the dirt in my mouth from the never-ending sand and smell a hundred other men that had traipsed through the building. Her words had frozen inside me and I'd known my world was coming to a sharp corner that would cut me.

"If you ask me, you dodged a bullet." Shane shook his head. "She made you miserable, then used your daughter as a weapon. Not cool, Cal. If this woman can get you out of Lisa's clutches and make things right with Amber, I'm all for it."

When my thoughts turned back to Em and her face was in my mind's eye, my whole mood shifted—from sadness, anger, and mourning to hope, affection, and anticipation. When I thought of Em, I didn't dread tomorrow quite as much as I used to.

"Dude, she must be something," Shane said with a huff of laughter. "Your whole face just changed."

My ears grew hot, and I turned my attention back to the nachos, sliding another portion onto my plate. "Shut the fuck up, dickhead, and tell me about your latest customer."

Shane laughed out loud this time and slapped me on the back, then launched in to a tale about a woman named Kandi and how much of a pain in the ass she was, but that she paid well and was smoking hot.

It was late when I finally drove back to my apartment. Shane and I had put away four beers each along with the nachos and an order of chili cheese fries. I was pleasantly full and ready to hit the sack. We'd reminisced for a while about our deployment and some of the shit we'd gotten up to. We'd had to make our own entertainment over there because if we didn't laugh, it would have driven us insane. That time with the visiting general's quarters had been particularly hilarious…

I parked the truck and rolled up the windows. It might rain and I had no desire to sit in a puddle tomorrow.

It was after I'd unlocked the door and stepped inside that I saw it. Someone had shoved a folded piece of paper underneath the door and I'd nearly stepped on it. I picked it up and opened it.

I SAW

YOU CAN'T HAVE HER

The words were scrawled in all capital letters with a

black Sharpie. No punctuation, just the letters. It sent a chill through me. He saw. Saw what?

Oh.

Last night at the bar. I'd been so sure no one was around when we were outside. I was wrong.

My phone was in my hand and I was dialing without even thinking about it. Em's cell rang. And rang again. Four times before her sleepy voice came on the line.

"Hello? Cal?"

Relief flooded through me.

"Em—" I hesitated. I didn't want to scare her. I cleared my throat. "Just checking on you. Did you set the alarm?"

"What? Yeah. I did." She paused. "You waited until twelve-thirty to check on me? I was asleep, Cal. I have to work in the morning."

The reproach in her voice stung, but it was what it was. I'd had to make sure she was okay.

"Sorry about that. I'll let you sleep. See you in the morning."

"Yeah. Okay." Her tone was grumpy and she ended the call. I didn't blame her. I'd have been pissed, too.

I knew that the apartment building didn't have any security cameras, so there was nothing to go on for whomever had left the note. But I had to find this guy, then he would sorely regret threatening Em. And me.

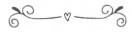

I briefly greeted Cal when he walked into my office Monday morning. I was still crabby about the late-night phone call. I knew I should appreciate his concern, but I had the alarm system now. No one was getting inside my house.

Cal settled into one of the chairs opposite to where I sat behind my desk. Today he was wearing jeans again and another T-shirt. "I'm going to assess the building for security issues and then I'll put together a recommended plan to address them."

"What about your other job?"

"I made arrangements for this morning," he replied. "I'll head there around noon and be back by six to see you home."

"You don't have to do that," I protested. "I can drive my car home."

"Until we get this place secure and more lighting in the parking lot along with cameras, I'll be here to see you home."

I could tell by his tone that this was on his Non-Negotiable list.

"Fine."

He reached over to my desk and took a blank legal pad and pen. "Can I use this?" At my nod, he leaned back, clicking the pen. "I need you to list every person who you come into contact with on a regular basis."

Oh, wow. "Why?"

"Whoever is stalking you is someone who knows you well, well enough to pass unnoticed and unremarkable. They know where you live and work. It's not a stranger. And while it's likely a man, I want the names of women, too."

I sighed. This was going to take a while. Pulling up

my calendar, I saw that I had thirty minutes until my next client. That would do.

I started listing names, pausing when Cal would interrupt me to ask questions about how I knew the person, how often I saw them, what kind of relationship we had, etcetera. By the time we were done, there were around twenty or so names on the list and it was almost time for my meeting.

"I'll need to use your computer tonight," he said. "I want to do some research on these names."

"That's fine." I'd noticed there was no computer at his place. "Just know that I'd vouch for each person on that list. I can't think of any reason why a single one of them would want to scare or hurt me."

Cal's gaze met mine, the look on his face grim. "You may think you know someone, the things they are and aren't capable of. But that's not true. You can never really know someone. Not ever."

I blanched at his frank assessment, which not only surprised but also saddened me. If he was saying such a thing, it meant that he'd lived it firsthand. I wondered if he was thinking of his soon to be ex-wife who'd cheated on him.

"Um, okay." I was clueless as to what to say next. Thankfully, I was saved by the buzz of the intercom. I pressed the button.

"Emmy, your next appointment is here," Karen said, her voice sounding tinny over the speaker.

"I'll be right out."

Cal stood as I did, replacing the pen into the holder on my desk. He kept the legal pad. I moved toward the door, but he stepped in front of me. I caught my breath, tipping my head back to look at him.

He was in my personal space, but I couldn't make myself step back. He smelled like soap and skin and Cal.

Leaning down, he kissed me. My eyes drifted shut and I kissed him back. I wanted to put my arms around him but didn't let myself. The only thing that touched was our lips.

His kiss was gentle yet intimate, his tongue touching me until I let him in. I desperately wanted to press against him as he deepened the kiss. Memories of last night and our one time together assailed me and my body hummed in anticipation.

After a long moment, he broke the connection, but stayed close.

"Have a good day." His throaty whisper said much more than his actual words. "I'll be back for you." He pressed a kiss to my forehead, then turned away.

The words were a promise I could feel. I watched as he left my office, leaving the door open behind him.

It took a few moments to gather my shattered composure, then I went to usher in my client, pushing all thoughts of Cal out of my head.

chapter thirteen

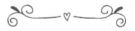

THE AFTERNOON PASSED too slowly as I slung one feed bag after another onto the loading dock. I'd stripped off my shirt since I was working in the sun and kept my sunglasses on. I was slick with sweat, but it felt good to be doing some manual labor today. I was frustrated that this stalker guy kept getting the best of me. I had to figure out who it was.

I'd memorized the names on Em's list as she'd given them to me, as well as all the other information about her relationship and ties to each. They ranged from a handful of judges who she saw on a regular basis to the guy who mowed her lawn to the teenager who walked the noisemakers while she was at work.

The plan for the office and parking lot was already in my head, I just needed to type it out and get a quote from Greg for equipment, installation, and monitoring. I'd do that tonight at Em's. Lisa had gotten the family laptop and I'd had no reason until now to need a computer for myself, not that I could afford one. A little embarrassing, having to use Em's equipment to do the job she'd assigned me, but there were worse things.

Despite my phone being noticeably silent this afternoon, I still worried about Em. She'd said she only had appointments at the office today and wouldn't be in court. That made me feel slightly better, but then again, she'd been attacked in her own office.

Which reminded me that I was going to have to do some training for Karen as well, since she was the first person any visitor would interact with when they walked in the door. She needed to know the right way to deal with someone who was angry, unreasonable, or threatening.

It was nearing quitting time when I heard my name. Glancing up, I saw the foreman motioning to me. Swiping my arm across my forehead to wipe away the sweat, I headed toward him.

"You have a visitor," he said gruffly. "A woman. She's in my office. And remember, you're on the clock."

I nodded, my thoughts already on my visitor. It had to be Em. I rushed toward the grimy room that served as the foreman's office, wondering what had happened and why she hadn't called me. When I opened the door, I saw why.

It wasn't Em. It was Lisa.

Panic struck. "Is Amber okay? What's wrong?" That had to be the reason she was here. Something had happened to Amber.

"Nothing is wrong," she hastened to say. "Amber is fine."

I closed my eyes as relief hit me. I nearly sagged, my knees suddenly weak. After a moment, I opened my eyes. Lisa was watching me, apprehension in her eyes and uncertainty written on her face. It was an expression I hadn't seen on her in a long time.

"Why are you here, Lisa? What do you want?" I couldn't imagine what it could be. I was already on the underdog end of this divorce and custody battle.

She hesitated, glancing away for a moment before again meeting my gaze. "I want us to go to couple's therapy."

My jaw nearly dropped and it took me a second—or three—to find my voice. "Couple's therapy? Why?" For the life of me, I couldn't think of a reason.

Lisa shifted nervously from one foot to the other. "I thought maybe it might help us, you know, work things out."

My brows climbed. "You mean reconcile?" She nodded. "Lisa, you've been seeing another man—sleeping with another man—for months. You told me in no uncertain terms that we were over. You *had me served* when I stepped off the plane. What in the world made you think I'd want to reconcile?" My voice had risen with my anger as I glared at her. "And you show up at my job for this?"

Lisa winced and my conscience twinged, not that it should. She deserved my anger and more.

She's also the mother of your child.

Damn it.

Suddenly, I felt exhausted. I rubbed a weary hand over my face and looked out the one grimy window into the room. A few men were busy on the warehouse floor and a forklift drove past. Neither of us spoke.

Finally, she said, "Cal, don't we owe it to Amber to try everything before we call it quits forever?"

Fuck. She was pulling the Amber card on me.

"Isn't she worth it?"

My jaw clenched in anger and I stared at her. The plaintive expression she wore didn't change. Apparently, she felt not a shred of guilt for using our daughter like this.

But what could I do? What would she tell Amber when she got older? That she'd tried to reconcile and I'd refused to attempt it?

"What brought this on?" I asked. "Did the doctor break up with you? Did he find another nurse he liked more?" The sarcasm was thick.

She shrugged. "I was just thinking about us," she said. "We had some good times. I know things have gotten really fucked up, but before we move on to other people, I thought we should try one more time."

Stepping toward me, she placed her hands on my shoulders, leaning into me. My hands came up automatically to rest on her hips as I repeated her words in my head. Then realization struck and I moved out of her reach.

"It's because of the woman, isn't it." It wasn't a question because I knew the answer. "The woman in the ER with me. You're jealous."

She laughed but it sounded forced. "Don't be ridiculous."

I shook my head. "We're not doing this, Lisa. You are not going to fuck with me."

"I'm not doing that," she protested.

"I don't believe you."

The plaintive look dropped from her face, her expression turning hard. "I don't think it's good for Amber if you're bringing around some other woman. I've informed my lawyer."

"I knew it." I didn't think Lisa still had the power to hurt me, but the tiny nugget of hope that had emerged was crushed into dust. My lips pressed into a thin line. The nail had been hammered into the It's Really Over coffin.

"I need to get back to work," I said, my voice flat. "I'll let my lawyer know about your visit."

"Don't threaten me." Her voice was angry now. Menacing.

"I'm not threatening you. It's just a statement of fact. Goodbye, Lisa." I turned and left the room. Lisa didn't say anything as I let the door swing shut behind me.

For the next thirty minutes, I tried not to dwell on Lisa's visit. Divorce sucked, I thought for the millionth time.

Deliberately, I turned my thoughts to Em. She represented a new chapter of my life. Lisa was the past. I had to move forward and let it go. We'd both made mistakes, but I couldn't change anything. There was too much bitterness, anger, and disillusionment between Lisa and me. She was moving on, despite her flash of jealousy. No doubt she'd regret the impulse that had brought her here today.

At quitting time, I pulled my shirt back on and fired up my truck to head to the firm. It was an indulgent treat to drive to and from work today rather than the run I usually did.

I found myself pleasantly anxious to see Em. She

was soft and kind, as opposed to the vicious cuts Lisa inflicted. Em wanted to see me, wanted *me*. After Lisa's rejection and affair with that doctor, being wanted was a balm to the wounds.

Abruptly, I stopped myself. I shouldn't compare Em and Lisa. That wasn't fair to Em. And no doubt at this point, she was telling herself that getting involved with a man going through a divorce was a really bad idea, that she was just the "rebound" girl.

Was she?

The little voice asked the question, which gave me pause, because I couldn't answer it. And that scared me.

There was a tap on my door, and I called out without looking up from what I was working on.

"Come in!"

The door swung open. I glanced up to see Cal walk in. My stomach did a flip and I swallowed hard, my mind immediately replaying the memory of Saturday night in my head.

Pushing those thoughts away, I cleared my throat just as the alarm on my phone went off. Ah. Six o'clock on the nose. I bet the Army had drilled promptness into him.

"What's the alarm for?" he asked, coming to stand in front of my desk.

I silenced the alarm, then started gathering up the papers and folders I'd been reviewing, sliding them into the suede bag I carried for just that purpose. "Donny and Marie get upset if I stay at work too long," I explained. "I set an alarm so time won't get away from me."

He nodded, his eyes studying me. A small smile curved his lips.

His jeans were dusty, but the T-shirt he wore was mostly clean, an incongruity, considering his job.

"How did you keep your shirt clean?" I asked, just wondering. I slipped on the heels I'd taken off and left under my desk, reaching down to adjust the straps around my ankle.

"I took it off."

Well. *That* was an image I didn't need to dwell on. Cal, shirtless and slick with sweat, his jeans slung low around his hips, showing off the carved muscles of his back and abdomen.

Clearing my throat, I stood, gathering my things and rounding the desk. Cal reached to take my satchel. I let him ease it from my shoulder, grabbing my Yeti to-go coffee cup.

"Ready," I said.

Cal followed me home and there were no incidents, which gave me a sigh of relief as I turned off the house alarm. Donny and Marie greeted us in the usual fashion. I noticed Cal was carrying a bundle of clothing.

"What's that for?" I asked.

"Oh, well I was hoping you'd let me take a shower and change into some clean things before I got to work."

He leaned down to pet the twins, who were ecstatic in their slavering devotion to this recurring visitor. This put him closer to me and I got a whiff of him.

My eyes drifted shut. I shouldn't be so turned on by the sleek smell of him, but there it was.

"Um, yeah, that's fine." I'd already forgotten what I was saying yes to. I forced my eyes open and moved away, slipping off my shoes. "There's a guest bath upstairs. Feel free to use that one. I'm going to go change."

I headed upstairs and Cal followed. I fancied I could feel his eyes on my ass with every step. Showing Cal the guest bath with fresh towels, I left him to it. In my bedroom, I changed into a pair of denim shorts and a vintage eighties' band T-shirt. After pulling my hair back into a ponytail, I went downstairs. As I passed the guest bath, I could hear the shower running. My imagination painted the picture of Cal naked and wet, water streaming down his body.

I sighed.

Downstairs, I let my babies outside then set up my laptop at the kitchen table. Once satisfied with that, I began pulling ingredients for dinner from the fridge. Cal seemed to like my cooking, so hopefully he would be a fan of my homemade spaghetti and meatballs.

I was shaping the meatballs and putting them in the casserole dish when Cal came downstairs. He was wearing a form-fitting dark blue T-shirt and jeans, bare feet. His hair was still wet and I could smell the faint aroma of the soap he'd used. I hadn't realized how sexy that scent was when I'd bought the gender-neutral body wash, or maybe it depended on who used it.

Tearing my eyes away from him, I resolutely focused on my task.

"The computer is over there," I said, motioning with my head towards the table, lit with dappled light from the window. As I spoke, Donny and Marie began scratching at the sliding glass door.

"I'll get it," Cal said. He let the twins inside and they ran over to me, smelling the raw meat I was working into generous-sized meatballs.

"Dinner?" he asked.

I nodded. "You like spaghetti and meatballs, I hope?"

"I have a feeling I'm going to love anything you make."

His smile warmed me and I returned it before he went to the table and took the seat in front of the computer. He began typing.

"Don't you need your list?" I asked with a frown.

"I memorized it."

Oh. Well, okay then.

We both worked in silence. I finished up the meatballs, added the sauce and cheese, then slid it into the oven. Getting out plates and utensils, I set them in front of the barstools along with napkins and glasses. Removing the container of dog food from the fridge, I put it in two bowls—each emblazoned with the appropriate name—I added some shredded cheese and zapped them in the microwave.

"You're heating up their dinner?"

I glanced over to where Cal was watching me, brows raised.

"Yeah, so?" My insolent and defensive reply made him grin and hold up his hands.

"All right, all right. Just asking for a friend."

That made me laugh as the microwave dinged.

The twins fell on their food as though I was blatantly starving them to death. I poured two glasses of iced tea and set one in front of him as I took another chair at the table and sat.

"Thanks," he murmured, his gaze fixed on the screen of the laptop.

We sat in companionable silence. It felt incredibly...domestic. And comfortable. And natural. The dogs were still licking their bowls, Marie's scooting across the floor. I'd put on a pot of water to boil the pasta and it was beginning to steam. The heady aroma of tomatoes and garlic was beginning to scent the kitchen.

Altogether a much too domestic scene for a woman looking for a more permanent relationship from a man who was in no way ready to jump from one fire into another.

Was that what I wanted from Cal? The first man I'd slept with since Chad? The only man I'd slept with *besides* Chad? Surely this was just an overreaction. My biological clock was ticking, that was all.

I couldn't imagine marrying again. I took a sip of my tea and tried to picture it. The white dress. The flowers and candles. Walking down the aisle. The vows.

'Til death us do part.

I hadn't realized that death would come so soon.

Surprisingly, tears didn't sting my eyes at the thought of Chad's death, so far from home. I was glad we'd had the time together that fate had allotted. Even knowing how it had ended, I still wouldn't have changed anything, even to avoid the heartbreak.

"Here's something," Cal said, interrupting the chain of thoughts going through my head.

"What is it?"

"This woman—Anita Bowes—she has a misdemeanor on her record for harassment of an ex-boyfriend."

"Anita is the secretary of one of my best friends," I said. Carly's promotion last year had included a new administrative assistant position. She'd hired Anita to fill that role and I'd developed a casual friendship with her since I went through her sometimes to make sure Carly had put brunch and other random things on her calendar. I'd spoken to her in person several times when I'd occasionally show up at Carly's office for an impromptu lunch. "She'd have zero motive for something like this, and I can't see her doing these things. It feels more like a man than woman."

Leaning over, I took a look at the screen of the laptop. My brows rose in surprise. "You're accessing the Indiana State's criminal database? How can you possibly do that?" I couldn't even do that and I was a registered member of the Bar.

Cal shrugged. "You make friends in the military and one of mine trusted me enough to give me access once. Looks like the account I use is still in there." He glanced over at me, then back to the screen. "It comes in helpful sometimes."

Huh. "Well, I don't think it's Anita. And it sounds like her ex was a girly-man she's better off without." Anita was even shorter than me, a bit on the curvier side, with blonde curly hair and an infectious grin. "To my knowledge, she's happily involved with a large animal veterinarian and spends her weekends with him, camping and riding horses."

Cal released a pent-up breath. "That's it then. I've been through the list and there's nothing that would wave a red flag for anyone. Everyone is boringly normal."

"Boringly normal sounds fantastic." My dry statement made his lips twitch.

Getting up, I put the noodles in the boiling water then buttered the garlic bread, adding it to the oven with the meatballs. Cal continued working, the only sound that of the keyboard's quiet clacking.

A few minutes later, I'd dished up dinner and refilled our glasses with the iced tea.

"Soup's on."

"Was just finishing," Cal replied, closing the open apps and shutting down the laptop. In a moment, he'd taken the barstool next to me and was eyeing his loaded plate with eyes that looked like he'd spotted a present on Christmas morning.

"This looks amazing," he said, placing the napkin I'd provided on his lap. "It's been ages since I've had homemade spaghetti and meatballs."

I cut a meatball into bite-size pieces. "Did Lisa cook for you?" I couldn't help that I was curious about their relationship. I told myself it was just to know his case better and not because I wanted to know what kind of woman she was that prompted a marriage proposal from Cal.

Cal shrugged, his mouth full of garlic bread. After a moment, he replied. "Sometimes. Being in the kitchen wasn't really her thing. I cooked occasionally. But we ate takeout a lot and frozen stuff. Nothing as awesome as this." He shoveled in a huge bite, his eyes closing in seeming bliss, which made me smile.

I ate a few bites, thinking. "Is there anything you think would be salvageable in your marriage?" At his questioning look, I added, "It's just that divorce is hard, especially on the kids, and this one also involves Lisa's parents who, as I understand, have a good relationship with Amber."

Cal wiped his mouth with the napkin and took a drink of tea before answering. "Funny you should say that. Lisa came by my work today."

"Oh?" That was good. Just a curious, one-word query, though the fact that my stomach tightened and my heart sped up didn't bode well for a dispassionate response.

He grimaced, winding more spaghetti around his fork. "Yeah. It was dumb, trying to convince me that we should give it another try, go see a therapist or something."

I cleared my throat uncomfortably before answering, my eyes on my plate and not on Cal. "What did you say?"

Cal made a disgusted noise. "I told her that wasn't going to happen, because I knew why she was there and it wasn't because she suddenly realized she loves me and doesn't want to throw away our marriage."

Finally, I lifted my gaze to find him watching me.

"Then why was she there?" I asked.

"Because she was jealous."

I frowned, confused. "Jealous? Jealous of what? I thought you weren't seeing anyone?"

"I'm not," he said frankly. "She was jealous of you."

I watched Em's face go from confused to surprised, her mouth falling open slightly. Finally, she spoke.

"Jealous of me? But…that's ridiculous. I'm your lawyer."

"She's always been very possessive," I said. "She saw you with me in the hospital. I doubt she knows you're my lawyer. She's let her parents handle all aspects of the divorce. Lisa never was one who got involved in the details of adulting."

I'd paid all the bills, even while deployed, and handled things like taxes and insurance and home maintenance. The most she could be bothered with was signing where I told her to sign. I was sure she was doing the same thing with her father.

"May I ask what brought you two together in the first place?"

I swung my gaze back to my nearly empty plate. Should I tell her the truth? She might look at me like I was a jerk, or worse.

"You don't have to say, if you don't want," she hastily added.

"She got pregnant," I said, my voice flat. "We had a fling on prom night. She got mad at her date for dancing with another girl. Even though I'd already graduated, I was there with a couple of buddies, crashing the prom. We'd both been drinking, and she caught my eye." I pushed some noodles around my plate. "I was young and dumb and I believed her when she said she was on birth control. A month later, she called me, told me the news."

I fell silent, finally daring to look at Em. Her face was carefully impassive.

"So you married her out of duty?" she asked.

I nodded. "It's how I was raised. Plus, she was carrying my kid. I wasn't going to be one of those dads who just sent a check every month." I dropped my fork onto my plate with a clatter. "Now, she's turning me into that despite everything." Even I could hear the bitterness in my voice.

It killed me, being away from Amber. I missed her every single day. My throat thickened at the thought of her, and I hastily took another drink of the iced tea.

"Cal, I'm going to fix this." Em rested her hand on my arm and I looked up, our eyes meeting. "Trust me. I'm good at what I do. I'm going to get proper custody for you and Amber. No matter what Lisa's father does."

The look on her face was dead serious and fuck me if I didn't actually believe her. A little spark of hope flared in my gut. Maybe I finally had someone on my side. I covered her hand with mine, still resting on my arm.

"Thank you." I meant it with everything I had. "Amber means everything to me. Although I hadn't planned on becoming a father that young, she's been the best thing to ever happen to me."

Em smiled. "I don't have a child, but I still understand. It was very gallant of you to marry her. Lots of men nowadays wouldn't. It's a bit antiquated, I suppose, shotgun weddings."

"I was raised to take responsibility for my actions. If some guy had gotten one of my sisters pregnant,

I'd expect him to do the right thing, if that's what she wanted."

I realized I was still touching her and removed my hand. Hers dropped as well. She took a bite of meatball and chewed, looking off into space. I resumed eating, too. Amber would be back soon. I'd see her then. And maybe some progress would've been made on the case.

"I have something to ask you," she said after a few moments. I'd cleared my plate and was wondering how rude it would be if I asked for seconds. "But I don't want you to feel obligated to say yes."

Hmm. Interesting. "Okay. What is it?"

"Well, it's just that I have a friend's wedding to go to next weekend, and I was wondering if you might come with me." She paused. "You know, as friends." She smiled a little and her cheeks turned rosy with a blush.

A wedding. Wasn't that one of those things you definitely weren't supposed to attend with a woman until you were engaged? I couldn't remember. My Miss Manners etiquette was more than a little rusty. Not that I cared what Miss Manners thought. My only hesitation was wondering if I had the right clothes to wear.

"I'd love to go," I said honestly, "but let me check my wardrobe situation first." Surely I had something I could wear. Lisa had done the bitch thing and given away ninety percent of my clothes to Goodwill.

"Sure. No problem." She smiled again, though it was a more practiced smile. "Would you like some more?"

"Yes, please." I eagerly handed over my plate and

her smile softened. She added another heaping pile to the plate and set it down in front of me.

I ate while she added dishes to the dishwasher and I watched. She was graceful in her movements, her face serene. When she turned away, I couldn't help but admire the way the denim of her shorts clung to her ass. Her legs looked pretty damn good, too, with her bare feet and hot pink-tinted toes.

She turned again toward the dishwasher and I averted my gaze back to my rapidly disappearing pile of spaghetti. A staple in Italian restaurants, there was still nothing like the homemade version, and Em's was fantastic.

"Two home-cooked meals in a week," I said. "And amazing meals at that. Thank you. You'll spoil me."

"It's not a problem. I enjoy cooking and it's much more rewarding to cook for two than for one." She added a glass to the dishwasher and closed it. "I was able to move up the hearing regarding temporary visitation during the divorce proceedings. It's tomorrow morning. I thought you should know."

Sudden tension made my hands close into fists. "So soon? Are you ready?"

Em raised one eyebrow at me as she reached for my empty plate. "Your confidence is astounding."

Her dry reply made me wince. "I'm sorry. It's just that at this point, I kind of view lawyers as a necessary evil, especially after the last one screwed me." And he still hadn't returned my last deposit.

"I get it. But lawyers are like everyone else. Some are good, some are bad. I'm one of the good ones."

"I'm counting on it."

After dinner, I typed up the security proposal for the firm while she sat at the other end of the table with a pile of manila folders in front of her. We worked in companionable silence and when I was finished, I printed and gave her the document, which she agreed to go over with the other partners. With no more excuses to stay, I closed the laptop and put my iced tea glass in the dishwasher.

"Thanks for following me home," she said, walking with me to the door. She had her hands in the back pockets of her cutoffs, which pulled her shoulders back. I tried not to stare at her breasts, wonderfully showcased with a worn-thin V-neck cotton T-shirt with a band logo printed on the front. Bon Jovi. She had good taste.

"Not a problem," I said, bending down to give the two dogs a pat each. They sat together, watching us curiously, tongues lolling.

Without any other way to prolong my exit, I opened the front door. It was after nine and the sky was dark, the heat milder without the sun's blaze. I turned back to say goodbye.

In the frame of the doorway, with her hair in a ponytail and her legs and feet bare, she looked every inch the sixteen-year-old sending her boyfriend home for the night before her daddy caught her up past curfew. I couldn't resist.

Leaning down, I pressed my lips to hers. She started in surprise, then kissed me back.

Her lips were soft and it was as though we just knew how to kiss one another. The now-familiar charge of electricity and attraction flared between us. I wrapped my arms around her, my hands on her ass, and pulled her against me. Up on her toes, she curled her arms around my neck.

We just kissed, and it was sweet and heavenly, as though we really were those teens ending a night of studying together and knowing we could do nothing more than kiss.

Pulling back, I pressed my lips to her brow, her cheek, the corner of her closed eye, before settling again on her lips one final time. When I pulled away and loosened my grip, she looked up at me, her green eyes brilliant.

"That was quite a kiss," she said, slightly out of breath.

I hid a satisfied smile. "I wanted to feature in your dreams tonight." My hands had drifted upward underneath her T-shirt and stroked the bare skin of her lower back. A shiver went through her.

"Aren't you smug," she said without heat.

"Some would call it confidence." I pressed one more kiss to her forehead. "See you in the morning, Em. Sweet dreams."

"Bye, Cal."

She stood at the doorway, watching me, until I fired up my pickup and drove away. In the rearview mirror, I saw the door close, the light shining from it slowly disappearing.

I thought of Em all the way home.

chapter fourteen

I WAS AT THE front of the courtroom, behind the desk and arranging the files I'd brought, when Cal showed up. He tugged lightly on my sleeve to get my attention. I looked up in surprise.

"You don't have to be here," I said. Maybe I hadn't made that clear last night. But he'd dressed nicely for court in the same shirt and tie he'd worn for our first appointment.

"I know. I want to be."

He'd probably had to take off work, which couldn't be good for his financial situation. Luckily, this wouldn't take long.

"Okay, well you can sit in the first row behind me, if you'd like."

Cal took his seat just as the opposing counsel arrived. It was someone I knew.

"Jill, good to see you," I greeted her, extending my hand, which she shook.

"Good to see you, too," she said with a smile. "It's been a while."

"You're in for Atwell?" I asked. She nodded.

"Junior partner there now," she replied. "Managing partners don't get involved in something as mundane as a visitation hearing." She rolled her eyes.

"Well, congratulations on junior partner." At as large a law firm as Atwell's, they were very choosy about who they promoted.

"Thanks. I worked my ass off for it, that's for sure." She unloaded some files onto her desk as we chatted, which was cut short by the entry of the judge. Ronnie, our bailiff today, called for everyone to rise and I hurried back to my place.

"Judge Madison Carter presiding." We all sat after the judge sat.

Ken-not-Kenny settled himself into the court reporter's chair and adjusted his machine. I noticed he studiously avoided looking at me, not that I blamed him. I'd tried to be nice in my rejection when he'd asked me out, but it was still a rejection, which sucked.

When I had seen that I'd pulled Judge Carter for the proceeding, I'd been thrilled. Judge Carter was a fair and impartial judge, which couldn't be said for all of them. The times I'd been before her, she'd ruled in my favor ninety percent of the time.

Ronnie announced the case and Jill and I introduced ourselves to the court. The hearing was quick and no-nonsense, just as I knew it would be. Each of us got one chance to speak and one opportunity for rebuttal.

"…gainfully employed and there is no compelling reason he should not be granted fifty/fifty visitation rights until the divorce is finalized," I finished.

"Plaintiff asserts that the father suffers from PTSD and is a danger to himself and others."

My eyebrows went up, surprised, and it seemed the judge was as well.

"That's quite an accusation," she said, eyeing Jill over the top of her glasses. "Do you have any proof?"

Jill gathered some papers. "I have two sworn affidavits from my client and her father, the child's grandfather, attesting to the father's behavior that coincides with the classic symptoms of PTSD."

"Defendant was not provided these affidavits," I asserted.

"Evidence is provided to refute the claim of no compelling reason," Jill asserted.

"The court will accept the affidavits." The judge gestured to Ronnie who took the papers and handed them to her. Jill handed me copies, which I quickly skimmed.

"We object to these affidavits," I said. "PTSD is a medical condition that requires an expert's diagnosis. The court cannot justify withholding visitation on hearsay."

"Sustained. Visitation granted at a fifty/fifty split until the divorce and conditions of custody are settled by counsel." The bang of the gavel signified the ruling was final.

I let out a breath. I didn't appreciate the curveball, but I'd won. All was fair in love and war.

Jill smiled and we shook hands again. "Have a good one."

"You, too."

I know it always seemed weird to others, but none of this was personal for the lawyers. It was just another day on the job and there were lots of other clients whom we represented. If we allowed it to become personal, we couldn't effectively do our jobs. So, I remained cordial and friendly to opposing counsel at all times. You never knew when you'd have to ask a favor or call one in.

"Thank you so much." Cal grabbed me into a bear hug that squeezed the breath from my lungs.

"You're welcome," I managed, patting him lightly on the back. He released me and I sucked in a breath.

"When will I get to see her?"

I put the files back into my portfolio. "As soon as she returns. I'll send a revised visitation schedule to the other side before then to hash out the details." I wasn't envisioning any issues with this. "Then we can get down to brass tacks and finish up the divorce proceedings."

Cal's elation faded and he pushed his fingers through his hair. "Yeah. I really want to be done with this. I don't want it to drag out any more than it has."

I'd dealt with too many clients who'd felt the exact same way not to know how he was feeling. It was almost like the phases people go through with grief. It seemed that Cal had entered the final phase: Acceptance.

"The division of assets is pretty straightforward," I replied, "barring any requests for alimony or child support. Though if you're splitting custody fifty/fifty, that should nullify requests for either."

"And the fact that she makes more money than I do."

Cal's words were bitter and I didn't blame him. It was disgraceful that he could serve his country for so long and yet be unable to find anything better than a manual labor job that paid by the hour. Not that it was a bad job, it was just that Cal was qualified for so much more.

"Did you get the security plan approved?" he asked as I started down the aisle toward the doors. He fell into step with me and I felt his hand settle lightly on the small of my back. I decided to ignore it rather than make a scene moving it away from me.

I nodded. "Yes. Your guy can start next week." After the attack in my office, it hadn't taken much for the senior partners to agree to the level of security Cal had proposed. They weren't stupid. They were more aware than most of the ramifications of a lawsuit should something happen again.

"Good."

We reached the parking lot without further discussion, and I headed for my car. "Shouldn't you be at work?" I asked as Cal still followed me.

"I told my boss I had this going on this morning. I can stick around for a while."

Hmm.

We reached my car and I pressed the fob, unlocking the doors, then I turned. "You need to get back to work," I said quietly. "I know things are tight. You need the money."

His face flushed bright red and he glanced away, sliding a pair of mirrored sunglasses on to hide his eyes.

My breath caught slightly. Cal was so incredibly good-looking. I hadn't allowed myself to fully appreciate this formally attired version of him while in the courtroom, sure that everyone would be able to see the electricity between us. But he was downright gorgeous, a melt-your-knees masculine. I had thought he'd been unbearably sexy in his work clothes that left his muscled arms bare and jeans clinging to his thighs, his skin slick with sweat.

I'd been wrong.

Cal was rapidly becoming a constant presence in my mind as I toyed with the possibility that what we had might turn into something more. And was that what I wanted? A real relationship and not just toe-curling sex? I didn't know because I couldn't entertain the possibility while we had this professional entanglement. Even more incentive to get this divorce fast-tracked.

"Did you finish the paperwork?" I asked, fishing my sunglasses out of my purse and sliding them on. The sun was approaching its zenith and the summer day promised to be clear and sweltering.

"Yeah, let me grab it."

I waited while he crossed a couple of rows to his truck. The asphalt reflected waves of heat while I watched him cross the lot. He returned with a sheaf of papers and I felt sweat gather at the back of my neck underneath my hair.

"Here's everything," he said, handing the stack to me. "She got rid of almost everything when she moved out, just left enough to stage the house to sell. I'd like some of that furniture and half of the proceeds from the sale of the house. That's it."

Glancing through the papers, I nodded. "I'll draft the settlement agreement today and send it to you." Oh wait. Crap. He didn't have a computer. "Or you can come by for a paper copy," I added. I could tell his expression was grim, even with his eyes hidden by sunglasses.

"Yeah. I'll drop by at closing time and get it, follow you home again."

"You don't have to do that," I protested.

His lips twisted in a humorless smile. "Consider it self-serving. It would be a total pain in the ass for me to find yet another lawyer if something happened to you."

I was startled into a little laugh at that. A true, albeit cynical, statement.

There was silence for a moment. Cal shoved his hands in his pockets and glanced away from me, his lips pressed in a thin line. Impulsively, I reached out and grasped his arm.

"I know this is hard," I said. "It is for everyone, regardless of the circumstances. But it'll be okay. You'll get through it and move on."

Cal didn't say anything for a moment and I just stood there, waiting. Finally, he spoke.

"It's just that I didn't think this would happen to me, you know?" His words were quiet, edged with a sadness that tore at me. "Despite the circumstances, I meant my vows. I thought we'd raise a family. Go to T-ball games and gymnastics, dance classes and teacher conferences. Vacations to the beach and Disney World. Christmases and birthdays." He paused. "I thought we'd grow old together."

My heart ached for him. "I know," I said softly. "I thought that, too."

He focused on me again. "Christ," he huffed, his face chagrined. "I'm sorry, Em. I didn't mean to—"

"It's fine," I interrupted. I gave his arm a squeeze then let go. "Let's focus on moving forward, okay?"

"Yeah, you're right. I'll, um, see you this evening."

I got in my car and he watched me drive away.

Back at the office, the afternoon flew by with barely a nod to my lunch hour. I was proofing a brief on the computer when my phone's intercom buzzed.

"Emmy," Karen's voice was urgent, "there's a woman—"

My door burst open.

"—here to see you," she finished somewhat lamely.

"Got it, Karen. Thank you."

A woman stood in my doorway. Of average height, she was older—perhaps mid-sixties—and very thin, almost austerely so. Impeccably dressed, her silver hair was pulled back tightly into a bun and she carried what I could see was a designer purse on one arm. Diamonds flashed on her fingers and there was a wide silver bracelet on her wrist. She wore a well-tailored skirt and matching jacket in a charcoal gray with what seemed, given the severe expression on her face, a frivolous pink scarf around her neck.

"May I help you?" I had my suspicions as to who this was, but I'd wait for her to confirm.

Without a word, she walked in and settled into a chair opposite my desk, taking her time to perch on the edge, her back ramrod straight.

"That man is not getting another moment with my granddaughter."

Ah. Just as I thought. I'd half expected this. "Mrs. Atwell, I presume?"

"You presume correctly. And as I said, that man isn't getting Amber."

Lovely. "Well, Mrs. Atwell, that's not how the law works. And 'that man' is her father."

"He left her and my daughter to go run around

in the sand in some godawful foreign country. He couldn't be bothered to stay home and be a husband and father."

Run around in the sand? I could feel my blood rising and I deliberately kept my voice calm as I replied. "I believe it's called *going to war*, Mrs. Atwell, and we're very lucky that men like Cal do it. Now I can appreciate the level of emotion you have invested in your granddaughter," I continued, not letting her interrupt when I could see she wanted to argue the point, "but the law is the law. Mr. Mackenzie has been honorably discharged and will be residing here in Indianapolis. There's no reason Amber can't have the best of both worlds and see her father, mother, and her grandparents, equally."

"But—"

"And isn't that what we want?" I asked. "In a divorce, the children often get overlooked. But not in this case. We want what's best for the child. What's best for Amber. Wouldn't you agree?"

I had her and she knew it. Her eyes narrowed and her thin lips pressed together. She'd be a pretty woman if she wasn't quite so thin and didn't seem so...dour.

Gracefully, she got to her feet. "This isn't over."

I stood as well, leaning forward with my palms on my desk. "Oh, I assure you. It is."

Without a word, she left.

Well.

Despite my win today for Amber, I was still in a foul mood. The heat and blazing sun didn't help, though I should be used to it by now. I slung feed bags and dwelled on what I'd said to Em about Lisa and me. It was all true, but just when I'd thought I'd come to grips with the fact that my marriage was over, something came along to blindside me.

It wasn't that I wanted to be with Lisa again. I didn't. She and I were no longer compatible—much less in love—and there was too much pain and hurt to go back to what we were. It was the loss of the dream I'd had—the vision of love and family—that was what I was mourning. The lost innocence of the man I used to be. Most of that innocence had been wiped away during my first deployment, but I'd held on to the dream of happily-ever-after once I came home. Now that had faded away, too, in the face of life's hard knocks.

My only bright spot had been meeting Em. Was fate handing me a gift? Or another heartache wrapped in shiny paper? I didn't know the answer to that question. What I *did* know was that I looked forward to seeing her, talking to her, whenever I got the opportunity.

But I had to find that stalker.

It would be just like duplicitous fate to show a possible future, only to yank it from me in the worst way imaginable.

I couldn't let anything happen to Em, not least because I was growing increasingly attached to her. The woman was incredible. Gorgeous, passionate, clever, smart, funny. Not to mention an excellent cook. Her home was welcoming and peaceful. She was confident and successful. Em was the whole package. And for some reason, she seemed to like me, of all people. She could have her choice of men. But she'd asked me to go to the wedding with her. Yeah, just as friends, but after Saturday night, I had faith in my ability to make her change her mind about that.

My phone buzzed midway through the afternoon and I took a moment to wipe the sweat off my forehead with my arm before digging in my pocket. Glancing at the screen, I grinned and hit the button.

"Mac, my man! How's it going?"

Mac was a British soldier I'd served under while in Afghanistan working with NATO. He was funny, charismatic, wicked smart, and deadly. A born leader of men. We'd kept in touch after we'd left the service, though I'd been surprised that he hadn't again re-enlisted. I suppose every man can reach his limit for entering combat, over and over, year after year, deployment after deployment.

"Calamity, you bloody bastard, I'm brilliant," he answered good-naturedly. "You still digging ditches?"

That had been my first brief job when I'd gotten out. I'd shared with Mac a little of my frustration with finding employment.

"Not digging ditches, but damn close." The grime on my skin and shirt irritated me. I'd thought once I got out, I'd finally be done with the endless dirt and sweat and sand of the Middle East. All that was currently missing was the damn sand.

"I've got a proposition for you," he said.

Leaning against the wall, I hiked up one foot, resting my steel-toed boot on the stack of feed bags. It felt good to take a break.

"What's that?"

"About a year ago, I started a private security company," he explained. "We provide security for private firms and businesses that send people over there for projects and infrastructure building."

I knew what "over there" meant. Iraq. Syria. Afghanistan. Turkey. Israel. Lebanon. Jordan.

"And?" I prompted.

"And I need employees that know what the fuck they're doing," he finished bluntly.

Going back… I couldn't fathom it. While I'd loved the brotherhood of the service, I was done with being deployed.

"Hey, man, thanks a lot for thinking of me, but—"

"Don't say no just yet," Mac interrupted. "It's not like the Army. We have state-of-the-art equipment, body armor, transport, and facilities. You'd be housed and fed well and have a regular rotation of time stateside. It's not combat. You'd just be keeping people safe from the bad guys."

That certainly sounded better than the Army, but—

"…and the salary starts at two-fifty a year. Plus benefits and year-end bonus."

Fuck.

That was a quarter of a million bucks a year. Even before taxes, that was a nice payday. I didn't speak, my thoughts spinning. I could provide a good life for Amber with that kind of money, save for her college. I could live in something other than a shitty apartment.

I'd *be* something, *have* something to offer Em.

Pushing the thought aside, I refocused on what Mac was saying.

"Don't answer me today," he said. "Think on it. Give me a call in a few days. We're based out of Charlotte, North Carolina, but you don't have to live there. I don't give a fuck where you live. So just let it simmer and marinate. You have any questions, you ring me up, any time, night or day."

"All right, Mac. I'll think about it."

We ended the call and I shoved the phone back into my pocket. Men don't do small talk. I went back to work, my mind digesting what he'd said and wondering if I wanted to take on that kind of position.

Private security in that part of the world was just as dangerous as being in the service, probably more so, because you didn't have the power and might of the US military to back you up. All you had to have your back were the guys with you.

I was glad to climb into my truck at quitting time and head to Em's office, deliberately setting aside thoughts of Mac and his job offer and instead focusing on her. It had been cool today, watching her in action. I thought a courtroom was one of the most intimidating places in civilian life. But she'd seemed right at home, relaxed even. Ironically, it had been a huge turn on—something she probably wouldn't want to know.

My lips curved into a smile just imagining how that conversation would go.

Soon, I was pulling in at her work and parked next to her car. I gave the tires a cursory inspection as I passed by, but they looked okay. Since there was still about ten minutes until the office closed, I did a quick recon of the immediate area. I found nothing and no one, which was a good thing, though a part of me wished this guy would make another move. Another move would be another clue and with another move also came the possibility he'd make a mistake.

Inside, Karen was packing up and smiled a welcome as she waved me back to see Em. I rapped lightly on the door frame, peering through the open door. She was focused on her computer monitor and tapping away on the keyboard. At my knock, she glanced up. If I'd been expecting a warm greeting or smile, I was out of luck.

"Hey," she said with a quick glance at me before returning to her work. "I'm just finishing up."

"No worries." Stepping inside her office, I decided to peruse some of the bookshelves while I waited. Books lined the shelves, but also lots of personal effects. The various knick-knacks had intrigued me at a passing glance when I'd first seen them, and I welcomed the chance to inspect them more closely.

Interspersed with the knick-knacks were little wooden signs with phrases painted on them. *I'll Always Have Hope* was one. *Love is a 4-Letter Word* was another. I cracked a grin. It seemed there was a cynic to balance out the eternal optimist.

There were several awards from various law organizations, and I carefully read the inscriptions. A framed photo of a grinning Em with a man who looked like someone I vaguely recognized…maybe an actor? A White House Christmas ornament. An empty wine bottle, the label in what I assumed was French. An elaborate wooden spoon that must've been about six inches long and a couple of inches wide—I wondered at the story behind that one. A beautifully ornate and delicate teacup and saucer. It seemed Em was a bit of a magpie, collecting little things to remind her of events and people in her past.

I wondered if anything relating to me would some-day be up on a shelf in here, and would that be a Good Thing or a Bad Thing? Good as in she remembered me fondly? Or bad in that I was part of the past? Gone but remembered.

"Ready."

Em's declaration interrupted my reverie. I turned as she was sliding her laptop into its case and slinging the strap of her bag onto her shoulder.

"Here. I can carry that." I took the satchel from her, leaving Em with just her purse.

She followed me out to the parking lot, but the silence seemed tense between us. After she unlocked the car, I put her things in the back seat.

"I'll follow you home," I said, but she only nodded, avoiding my gaze.

I puzzled over it as I followed her taillights to her house. Absently, I noticed the sky darkening. Looked like we were in for a summer storm. I hadn't listened to the weather all day and flipped on the radio. At least *it* still worked.

"*...front moving in from the west and expected to move through the downtown area in roughly thirty minutes. The entire area is under a tornado watch and residents are urged to seek shelter until the watch expires. Conditions expected include high winds, driving rain, hail, and flash flooding. Again, we have a storm front moving in—*"

I turned off the radio. I'd grown up with storms and tornado watches. If you lived in the Midwest, it was just a part of life. But I made a mental note to mention it to Em when we arrived. She'd need to get in the basement along with the noisemakers.

Em pulled into her garage and by the time she'd closed the door and gone through the house, I was waiting at the front door. She opened the glass door to speak to me, standing in the opening to hold it open.

"Thanks again," she said. "I appreciate it." She handed me a manila folder with papers inside. "Here's the proposed settlement. Let me know if you have any questions. Once you approve, I'll send the final version over to opposing counsel."

She seemed remarkably businesslike, which felt strange. I expected her to open the door wider and invite me inside, but she didn't. Unsure what to do, I shifted my weight from one foot to another, shoving my free hand into the pocket of my jeans.

"Listen, Cal, we should talk."

I froze at those words. Nothing in the history of ever had something good followed those words. But before she could say anything more, a nearby siren went off. I glanced in that direction.

"That's the tornado siren," I said, shifting into action mode. The military had honed the ability to compartmentalize. Put everything not related to your immediate survival into a box and shut the lid. Prioritize what was going to get you through the next few minutes, then do it. My gaze flew back to Em, who looked frightened.

"Inside," I said, yanking open the door and stepping over the threshold. Luckily, both furballs were at my feet. Reaching down, I grabbed them both and deposited one in Em's arms. "Basement." Taking her elbow, I half led, half dragged her to the basement door. In a moment, we were downstairs. I placed her farthest away from the one ground-level window and sat her down.

"Where's your flashlight?" I asked, handing her the squirming bundle of fluff I was carrying.

Em's eyes were wide, her face pale as she responded, "Upstairs. Top drawer to the right of the fridge."

I took the stairs two at a time, finding a heavy, working flashlight in the drawer she'd specified. I also grabbed a blanket from her couch in case of glass. Although I took a moment to look around the kitchen, I didn't find a radio. After grabbing two bottles of water from the refrigerator, I was back downstairs.

"Cover up with this," I said, draping the blanket over her, then handing her a bottle of water. The blanket would shield her from flying glass. I sat down beside her, listening to the wind rage outside. It had picked up exponentially in just the past few minutes.

The good thing, no doubt the only good thing, about tornadoes was that they were over pretty damn fast. It suddenly got very quiet and Em sighed in relief, making as if to stand. Grabbing her arm, I pulled her back down.

"There's a reason they say quiet before the storm."

The wind began again, this time in even more earnest, screaming outside like a freight train. I was fervently glad Em's house was made of brick. Just then, I noticed her hands shaking. The dogs crowded around her, one was trembling and the other was panting, the whites of its eyes showing.

Sliding an arm behind her back, I pulled her in

close, wrapping both arms around her and resting my chin on the top of her head.

"It's okay," I said softly. "It's going to be okay. You'll be fine." I could feel fine tremors shaking her body.

"You don't know that." Her voice was too small.

"I'm not going to let anything happen to you." I tightened my grip on her.

Glass broke upstairs and she started, jerking in my arms. More glass and thuds of things hitting the floor. It felt like forever but had to only have been maybe two minutes or so, then the quiet was peaceful and not a prelude. This time when Em went to move off my lap, I let her.

I could hear a soft rain falling and I got to my feet, holding out a hand to help Em to hers. The spoiled eating-machines had already forgotten the recent almost-disaster and happily followed Em toward the stairs.

"Me first," I said, taking her elbow and slowing her down. "Just in case there's anything against the door."

As though I'd been prescient, the door took me nearly breaking it down before we got through it, a kitchen chair being the culprit. When I saw the house, I took a breath. It could've been worse. The walls and roof were intact. Everything else could be fixed or replaced.

Emmy gasped at the mess. Glass littered the floor along with overturned chairs and the kitchen table, the bowl of lemons that had been centered on it now scattered.

"Oh my god," she whispered.

"It's okay," I reassured her, wrapping an arm around

her shoulders. "It's just cosmetic. We're all safe and this can be cleaned up with a little elbow grease."

Em looked up at me, her eyes brilliant green with unshed tears. "You're right," she managed. "I should be grateful. It could've been much, much worse." She suddenly stepped close and hugged me, her arms around my waist.

"Thank you," she said. "You kept me safe. I hadn't even paid attention to what was going on."

I took a moment to appreciate Em in my arms, holding her close. Who said Mother Nature didn't play favorites?

We spent the next hour or so cleaning up the place. I put up some temporary plastic sheeting she had in her garage over the handful of broken windows. After I took the fifth and final trash bag to the bin, I looked at Emmy.

"I should probably head home," I said.

Em released a breath. "Oh crap, I nearly forgot." Her stricken face looked up at me. "Your place. We need to go check and make sure it's okay." She grabbed her purse and locked the front door.

"Well, let's go," she said, motioning me out through the garage.

Okay, fine. If she wanted a trip to my POS apartment, who was I to argue?

It took longer than usual to make our way across town, Em following close behind my truck. There were downed power lines and tree limbs littering the streets. Emergency vehicles sounded distant sirens and I grew more concerned as the damage seemed to increase with each passing block.

My worst fears were confirmed when I had to

pull off the road because the debris closest to my apartment was too thick to get through. The skyline which the building should have occupied was clear. I turned off the engine of the truck and got out, staring in shock.

"Oh no," Em breathed, suddenly standing beside me. "Cal…oh my god."

Numb, I got out of the truck, taking in the damage and people walking around. Emergency vehicles were already there, and I saw someone being loaded into an ambulance. A television crew was setting up, the anchor searching for the optimal place to stand.

I barely noticed when Em stepped up next to me and took my hand.

"Cal, it'll be okay."

I didn't respond, still processing what my eyes were telling me.

"Cal…Cal!"

Em's insistent voice calling my name finally penetrated and I did the compartmentalize thing again.

"Yeah. Yeah." I turned to her. "It'll be okay." Though I no longer had a home or possessions or literally anything but the clothes on my back, I repeated the phrase inside my head.

"I have to go help," I said, giving her hand a squeeze before letting go. "See if there are any people trapped under the rubble."

"I'll help, too," she replied. Our gazes met in mutual understanding.

"The debris isn't stable. It's dangerous."

Em gave me a look. "Then I'll be careful."

We went our separate ways for a couple of hours. I dug through debris with other volunteers, searching for anyone who needed help. We found a Hispanic woman and her dog. Luckily, she'd suffered nothing more than a cut to her head. An elderly man had a broken clavicle bone, and a little girl was bruised and scraped. In the end, everyone who'd been in the building had been accounted for, one way or another.

Em was leaning against the back of my truck when I arrived. She looked as tired as I felt.

"Let's get you home," I said. "I'll follow you."

She didn't argue, just climbed into her car. I fired up the truck engine and in a short while, I was parked in her driveway as she pulled into the garage. Without thinking, I got out of the truck and met her in the still open garage. She leaned against her car, arms crossed.

"Where will you stay?" she asked.

I hadn't processed that far. I figured I was still in shock. Maybe this would be the straw that figurately broke my back.

"Um, I don't know. A motel, I guess." A cheap one, and not for long. I didn't have the money for that.

"You can stay here."

Wait. What?

"What are you talking about?"

She looked up at me in some surprise. "What do you mean?"

"I'm not staying here." No way would I be able to keep my hands off her if I stayed in the same house. And she'd sent plenty of signals that she didn't want that kind of relationship with me. At least right now.

"Of course you are," she replied, "You saved me. Now I save you."

I didn't have to. I could actually go to my sister's place in Indy, now that I thought about it. She wouldn't turn me away. But she also had a husband and two small children. I'd be on the couch, which was fine, but I'd also be in the way.

The feelings of disaster and desolation that I'd been avoiding hit me with the force of a Peterbilt. My breath left me in a rush. But just as quickly—the signs of a survivor—I grasped the lifeline I'd been handed.

"Okay." I followed her to the door.

chapter fifteen

CAL. IN MY house. Living with me. For the fore-seeable future.

What had I done?

"I'm sure you'll be more comfortable in a room than on the sofa," I said, leading him up the stairs. I opened the door to the guest bedroom. "There are fresh linens on the bed and the mattress is brand new, used barely a half a dozen times." Turning, I added, "I'm going to change and make dinner. I'll yell when it's ready."

Within a moment, I'd gone into my room and closed the door, leaning back against it with a relieved sigh.

I'd had no other choice, I argued with myself. Where was the man to go? I had a huge house that was mostly empty. It would've been selfish and cruel to make him go to some kind of shelter for those whose homes had been destroyed. And after tonight, there was no way I was going to tell him about the visit from his soon-to-be ex-mother-in-law today.

All I had to do was treat him like any other friend whom I'd invited into my home. Be friendly and hospitable. Besides, I was gone at work for most of the day anyway. He'd have the run of the place. Hey, maybe I could get rid of the dog-walker...

Forcing myself to stop second-guessing, I changed into my favorite at-home summer comfy clothes: my denim cutoffs and a worn, soft T-shirt. My lounge pants were a close second, but it was too hot outside. Though the A/C kept the inside cool, it was a mind-game thing.

Opening the fridge, I surveyed the contents. There would be someone to cook for from now on, at least for a while. That perked me up. Too often, I settled for a sandwich or salad rather than cooking, because it was just me to feed. Even with the meal service I ordered for those cook-at-home things, a lot of times the protein went into the freezer. But not tonight. It was late, but I was starving and I was sure Cal was, too. In these circumstances, I'd probably just pop in a frozen pizza, but I thought Cal had had probably enough of those. I didn't mind cooking.

Taking out some pork cutlets, I set about peeling potatoes and breading the pork. Flipping on the television in the sitting area, I turned it to the news. Not that I was really listening. I just wanted the noise. Living alone had its benefits...and drawbacks.

The cool wood floor felt good on my bare feet and I dodged the twins as I made more trips to and from the fridge and pantry. The potatoes were boiling and the pork was frying, the asparagus ready to pop in the oven, when Cal appeared. He'd showered but put on the same clothes. I was abruptly reminded of his lack of possessions. I'd have to fix that, but not tonight. Tomorrow.

"Dinner will be done in a few," I said, taking out two plates and some cutlery from the cupboard. We ate mostly in silence, though Cal was quick to express his enthusiasm for my cooking. I tried not to preen under his appreciation. Afterwards, I loaded the dishwasher while he finished wiping down the bar top.

"Well," I said, once all the things were done and I'd set out my coffee service for in the morning. "I don't know about you, but I'm exhausted."

Cal absently nodded, his gaze landing somewhere over my shoulder and seeing something far away. I couldn't imagine losing everything I owned in one fell swoop. The poor guy must feel like the hits just kept on coming.

Now to put my houseguest to bed.

"C'mon," I said, heading for the stairs. He obediently followed.

I stopped at the door to his bedroom, feeling as unsure as he looked. This would work. It would be fine. Again, what else was I to do? I wasn't heartless, and Cal had come to be someone I was fond of.

"Goodnight," I said. "I'll see you in the morning."

"Goodnight," he replied, seemingly automatic.

I figured he was probably still processing what had happened and still in shock. I hoped he could sleep tonight. I didn't know if I would, and I was right.

The next morning, I called in to work, and given the wreckage the tornado had unleashed on Indy, half the staff wasn't in either. I was in the kitchen finishing up cooking a breakfast with eggs and bacon and all the trimmings when Cal appeared. He looked surprised to see me.

"You're still here," he said. "I thought you'd be at work by now."

I took a sip of my coffee, plucking the crispy bacon off its sheet pan with a pair of tongs with my other hand. "Took the day off," I explained. "The office is practically closed anyway with what happened." I set a loaded plate in front of where he'd sat at the bar just as the toaster popped up. "Hope you're hungry."

"Yeah, I am." He was solemn, and I didn't blame him.

I buttered the toast and set two slices on his plate, then fixed myself a plate. "Coffee?"

"That would be great, thank you." He surveyed his plate for a moment, then waited until I'd set a cup of black coffee by his plate and took the stool next to him. Only then did he dig in.

We were quiet as we ate and I was thinking. What I wanted to do might be difficult. Cal had his pride, after all. I'd just have to make it sound self-serving. I waited until we'd finished and cleaned up before announcing my intentions.

"Time to go shopping."

Cal frowned at me, pausing as he was folding a dish towel to set by the sink. "Shopping?"

"Yeah. You need some clothes and stuff." Moving forward. Don't dwell.

"Em, I can't," he said, shaking his head. My heart hurt at the defeat on his face. "I don't have—"

"Stop." I interrupted him, knowing what was coming next. "You need things and it's fine. We're in this together. Besides, you need a new suit for Saturday. I'm being self-serving in my altruism. It'll be a tax write-off, I'm sure. My accountant will handle it." Doubtful.

Without giving him a chance to argue, I slipped on some shoes and grabbed my purse, looking at him expectantly.

"Let's go."

His expression said he was going to fight me on it, so I gave him a look that said it would be best if he didn't. A moment passed and I raised my eyebrows. His lips thinned, but he grabbed his keys. The military in him. Practicality overcame pride. He needed clothes, period.

"Fine. But I'll drive."

I stepped in front of him on his way to the front door. "Okay. But we take my car." I liked air-conditioning when it was ninety-five degrees outside. Sue me. I handed him my car keys, which he took without comment.

I realized Cal expected me to go to the mall, but I had a better idea. There was a very exclusive men's apparel store I knew. So exclusive, they didn't even have a sign. If you knew, you knew. And I did.

"What's this?" Cal asked as I directed him to park in a small lot in front of a nondescript building.

"A place you need."

Cal opened the shop's door for me and the salesman, René, spotted me.

"Emerson!" he called out, a wide grin spreading on his face. "It's been too long."

René insisted on calling me by my full proper

name, despite my repeated attempts to have him call me Emmy.

I shook his hand, greeting him with pleasure. Over sixty, his head was bald and shone in the low light, his charcoal skin a bit more leathery than the last time I'd seen him, but his suit was exceptionally tailored right down to the elaborately folded pocket square. His cufflinks shone and his shoes gleamed.

"So good to see you," I enthused, then gestured to Cal. "I have a new employee who needs outfitted with everything."

"Everything?" René questioned.

"From the skin out. Including denim and cotton along with a nice suit or two." I leaned forward, adding conspiratorially, "I'm taking him to a wedding as my guest."

"Ooooh." He drew the word out, brows raised. "I will take care of him, ma chérie." René liked to pretend he was French, and I'd never disabused him of the notion.

Taking my seat in a nearby velvet-covered chair, I took on my *Pretty Woman* designated role while Cal was dragged into a dressing room. Two young, male assistants trailed eagerly after him, both with armfuls of clothes.

It was nearly three hours later when Cal finally had enough. Honestly, I thought he'd have caved sooner. I set aside the paperback I'd been reading.

"Make it stop," he pleaded, his eyes the very picture of helpless distress. He held a tie in one hand, a shoe in the other, and was dressed in button-fly jeans that weren't done up all the way…and that was all. I swallowed. Hard.

Clearing my throat and averting my eyes, I asked, "Did René finish getting you everything you need?"

"I don't *need* all of this," he protested, gesturing behind him toward the dressing room. "I just need a couple changes of clothes."

Rolling my eyes, I huffed a "Please." Fixing him with a glare, I said, "You need some clothes and shoes, Cal. It's not a big deal. Good lord, you've just lost everything! I am more than happy to help you out."

He answered with a mirror of my glare, plus interest. Suddenly, he leaned over, bracing his hands on the arms of my chair, his face inches from mine.

"Or was this just your way to see me without clothes?" He came two inches closer, his lips close enough to mine that I could almost feel his touch. "I would've done that for free." His whisper sent a shiver through me. But before I could respond, he'd disappeared into the back.

It took longer than what felt comfortable to regain control of my breathing. For someone who'd lost the only home he had while going through a divorce and custody battle, he appeared to be rolling with it exceedingly well. Better than he'd looked last night. I supposed it was the military in him.

He wanted to drive again and I didn't mind. I allowed him to open the door for me and I slid inside. With a feminine intuition, I felt that he needed to have control over something. I didn't blame him. I had no idea how I'd feel if I'd suddenly lost everything I owned in one fell swoop, but odds were I'd be in worse shape than he was. At least, that which I could see.

Now I directed him now to the mall where I

dragged him through Bath & Body Works for men's body wash and lotion. He was very anti men's body wash, so I had to choose the scent for him, which I totally didn't mind. Then it was to Target for more toiletries and anything else I could think of. Then to a sportswear store for workout clothes and good tennis shoes. He'd been wearing his work boots, so that was one thing that didn't need replacing. And all the while, he protested, getting vehement until I had to give him a frustrated "Shush!"

"I love to shop and this gives me an excuse," I insisted, tossing sport socks into the cart. "Are these the right kind?" They had all kinds of heights and thickness and whatevers.

"They're fine." He sounded like a petulant child and I rolled my eyes.

We continued.

By the time I was satisfied and Cal well and truly disgruntled (at least he carried all the bags), I was starving. We'd skipped lunch.

"A greasy fast-food burger sounds awesome," I mused as Cal was pulling out of the parking lot.

"I can do that."

His voice was upbeat, which caught my attention. Hey, if he wanted to buy me a whopper, that would be fine with me.

So that's what we did. I wanted fresh, hot fries and to not eat in my car, so we went inside. I knew I'd smell like grease when we left, but whatever.

Cal was polishing off his second double cheese-burger and I was plowing through my chocolate shake before we said much.

"I'll pay you back," he said out of the blue.

I looked up, surprised. I'd told Reneé to put everything on my account, in no small part because I didn't want Cal to know how much it had cost. Nothing in the shop had price tags. If you could afford to shop there, you didn't need to ask the prices. I sincerely doubted Cal could guess the amount.

I hadn't minded spending the money. I made a very nice living and really didn't spend much. I didn't take lavish vacations or buy myself expensive jewelry. My salary was socked away into savings, retirement, and my investment accounts. Lucky for me, the stock market had had a good few years.

"Okay."

He nodded, as though that had been settled. I shrugged inwardly. It felt nice to buy someone something. I only had my parents, a few friends, and some co-workers that I bought gifts for at Christmas. No siblings, nieces, or nephews. Not even fake nieces and nephews since neither Carly nor Bridget had kids either.

The drive home elapsed quicker than I thought since I found myself nodding off, my tummy packed to the brim, and we were pulling into my garage as I let out a huge yawn.

He had clothes now. He'd been fed. He had a bed to sleep in and roof over his head.

Good lord, I was thinking of him like he was one of my dogs.

We met at the door into the house.

"So," he said with a rueful smile. "What happens now?"

I took a breath. "Now, we go our separate ways. Same as last night. Me to my room and you to yours."

Best to keep reiterating that distinction. For him *and* for me. No room and board *with* benefits. Damn it.

"Are you sure?"

His words sent a shiver through me. I arranged my face into a mask of indifference.

"Quite."

I left him to his own devices and went into the house. Cal carried his new possessions inside, making several trips, and passing me as he headed into his bedroom. I felt a pang of remorse for rejecting him, which only intensified as the evening wore on and he didn't emerge from his room for even a "good-night." Not that I cared.

Right.

I wondered if he was feeling as right-as-rain as he'd seemed this afternoon, or if he was just putting on a show for my benefit. Nobody likes a Debbie Downer, right?

Trying to pretend it was none of my business *how* Cal was feeling and coping, I removed my makeup and got ready for bed, prolonging the time when I would usually be crawling under the covers. Worry for Cal ate at me in spite of myself.

Finally, I couldn't put it off any longer and got into bed, Donny and Marie settling in to their usual places. Yet, I stared at the ceiling, unable to sleep. Again.

For some reason that I couldn't put into words, I got up. The clock said it was the wee hours of the morning. I tiptoed down the hall to Cal's room, easing open the door. Donny and Marie had decided not to follow me, being too comfortable in their own spots.

My eyes were adjusted to the darkness and I saw him

lying in the bed on his back, one arm bent behind his head. His chest was bare, the sheet down around his hips, and I automatically admired the view. Then his head turned toward me, but he didn't speak.

Moving aside the sheet, I climbed into the bed beside him, cuddling under his arm and resting my head on his chest with a sigh. I slid one leg over his and realized he was wearing boxers, so not naked. Damn.

His arm closed tightly around me, holding me close. Sometimes…you just needed to hold and be held.

I fell into a deep sleep.

Saturday arrived, the day of our pseudo-date to the wedding. Cal looked…mouthwatering.

The suit he wore fit him like a glove, his freshly shaven jaw and still damp hair made him look as though he should be modeling rather than…well, anything else.

Self-consciously, I smoothed the fabric of my skirt. I'd chosen a vintage-style dress with off-the-shoulder sleeves, a fitted bodice, and a skirt that flared to hit right above my knees. It was made of a diaphonous floral material that had a silk underslip. I wore a pair of lavender heels that I was particularly fond of.

We didn't say much before or during the wedding. Clarice looked radiant. There was a minor snafu in that one of her bridesmaids fainted during the ceremony, but she was immediately helped by two men who seemed very solicitous of her care.

The reception was lovely, if a little warm being as

it was held outside. But the tents with lovely glowing strands of lights and the dance floor were beautiful. Cal had discarded his suit jacket and loosened his tie, undoing the top two buttons of his shirt and rolling up the sleeves. I didn't blame him. I was fervently glad that I hadn't worn hose, though my lack of a tan had prompted my vanity. Fortunately, good sense won out. And a good tanning lotion.

"May I have this dance?"

I looked up in surprise. I'd been picking at the remaining wedding cake on my plate, lost in my thoughts, when Cal spoke.

The music was a tune back from my high school days, and thoughts of swaying on the gymnasium floor with my hands on a boy's shoulders came back to me. Here's to laying to rest old memories.

"Of course." I smiled at Cal and stood. In a moment, he'd swept me onto the dance floor.

I was shocked but tried not to show it. He knew how to dance. I was in his arms, following his lead, the scent of him making me want to close my eyes and drift away on a fantasy.

We danced a few more times, including to one of the best dance songs ever, in my opinion—*Uptown Funk*. Cal spun me and swung me and made me laugh in delight. He was an excellent lead—why was I not surprised—and I found myself marveling at how perfectly in tune (ha ha–pun intended) we were with each other.

We ate cake and sipped champagne, and he made me get onto the dance floor for the bouquet toss (I didn't catch it, but I also didn't try very hard). Carly and Bridget had come to the wedding together but had left directly after the ceremony. Bridget was upset about Rick, and Carly had appointed herself as Comforter-In-Chief for the evening. They'd glanced at Cal as they'd waved goodbye but hadn't pressed for introductions. I thought they were curious to meet him, but Bridget was wrapped in her own misery and Carly was playing matchmaker for me, as usual. Carly was ever the romantic.

The sky grew darker and not just with evening. Clouds were moving in. Cal took my hand just as a few fat, heavy drops fell. I swiped the back of my hand across my cheek, wiping away the wetness.

We were still a ways from the car when the heavens opened up. I gasped as the cold torrent hit me, soaking right through my dress.

"Sorry, Em. This will be quicker."

With only that warning, I was swept off my feet into Cal's arms. He doubled his pace as the rain fell, revelers squealing and shouting on either side of us as they also raced to their cars. Cal slid a bit in the mud, but never slacked in his speed or his hold on me.

We arrived at the car and he set me on my feet with a laugh, turning his face up to the heavens and closing his eyes.

"It's like a benediction," he said, so quietly that I almost didn't hear him.

I didn't know what to say. "Do you need one?" I asked.

His gaze fixed on mine. "You tell me."

I had no answer for that, and he drove us home in silence. I'd had a brief moment of indecision about where the night would be headed, but he was all friend-zoning/roommate-zoning me when we arrived. And as usual, we went to our separate rooms.

"Goodnight, Em," I heard him call softly to me as he entered his bedroom.

I paused at my door, glancing back. "'Night, Cal."

Dear lord, what were we now? The Walton family?? *'Goodnight, John-Boy.'* Ugh.

I'd never gone back to his bed since that one night, and we'd never spoken about it. Maybe we should've, but it was past time for it now.

With an internal sigh, I did all the things and climbed under the covers, Donny and Marie the only warm bodies with me in my bed.

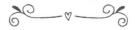

Weeks passed and we fell into a routine. Cal was usually up and gone before I'd set foot in the kitchen for my coffee. He showed up every day to escort me home from the office. I cooked. He cleaned. We went our separate ways for the evening. I would've liked to spend time with him, just watching a movie or something, but we didn't and he didn't ask.

I ended up having a TV delivered for his room, meeting the delivery on my lunch while Cal was at work. He thanked me later that evening. I told him that I thought he needed something to do while he was in there other than stare at the wall, and if my tone was a bit less than gracious, oh well.

And no more was said or done about the sexual tension between us. It was the silent but very present elephant in the room that we both ignored. I think we both knew that the timing was just too bad for there to be anything serious between us.

It had been a welcome help to have him here. He was handy around the house, fixing little things that I either hadn't been able to fix or hadn't been able to find someone to fix for me. He seeded the lawn and mowed, telling me to cancel my service for the time being because he said he enjoyed yard work. So every weekend he cut the grass and edged around the walkways and driveway. He trimmed the bushes and made sure to empty and take out the trash every week. He'd even power-washed my patio and deck, then stained the deck again. Two coats.

One Sunday afternoon, I found him underneath my car in the garage, changing the oil and then checking the tire pressure. He'd also gone to the store and gotten things to put in the walls of the garage to hang and arrange the various tools I'd bought over the years that I'd rather haphazardly stuffed in various corners.

It was ridiculous, but it made me feel looked after—cared for—in a way I hadn't been since Chad was alive. And I returned the favor by quietly making him lunch for work every evening. At first, he'd protested, saying I didn't have to do that. But I just ignored him. He couldn't live on fast food every day. And he brought home the Tupperware nearly licked clean if it was leftovers; an empty lunchbox cooler if it had been sandwiches.

I'd completely lost interest in trying to online date. It was too much work and too demoralizing. I deleted all the dating apps from my phone without any qualms.

I knew I was settling in to a dangerous place, emotionally. Cal and I weren't dating. He wasn't "my" guy. We were roommates, not lovers who lived together. He'd move out eventually, and then I'd be in for heartbreak. But it was easier to just push aside those thoughts à la Scarlett O'Hara, *I'll think about that tomorrow.* I enjoyed each day as it came and didn't think about the What Ifs and If Onlys.

Cal's divorce proceeded apace, on schedule without any issues, which was a welcome surprise. I'd thought I'd hear again from the oh-so-charming Mrs. Atwell, but nothing. Cal regularly saw Amber and was noticeably more cheerful on the days preceding a visit, and more glum after one was finished.

Such was divorce. Everyone suffered.

It seemed his soon-to-be ex was as ready for things to be over as he was, since there were no further delays in the paperwork. I'd expected more of a fight from the in-laws, but they'd agreed to the visitation schedule I'd offered. It had only taken my pushing back a few times against what were unreasonable demands, and they'd acquiesced. I thought perhaps it had to do with the fact that I wasn't a big-name attorney in this town with political aspirations which Atwell could hold over my head. I was just a family law attorney who was happy in my little niche of the world and the law.

Tonight, I reached for my satchel after finishing dinner. I'd cooked a simple meal tonight—a home-style version of a one-pan recipe. Cal was finishing up his second helping.

"Here is the final settlement and divorce agreement," I said, handing him the papers and a pen. "All you have to do is sign."

Cal went still. I hated this part. The final nail in the coffin, so to speak. Even after everything, it was hard to come to terms with the fact that a signature on a piece of paper had the power to sever the tie made in love and vows and *'til death do us part.*

But he took it and swiftly signed, handing the papers back to me. "Is that all?" He stood, gathered our empty plates and headed to the sink.

"Yes, that's all." I rose as well and laid a hand on his arm. "Cal. I'm sorry."

"It's not like this is unexpected," he said, not acknowledging my touch. He moved away, putting the rinsed plates into the dishwasher, and I tried not to read anything into it. "I wanted to thank you for being so hospitable to me. I've been able to save enough to move out to another place."

My heart stuttered in my chest, which was dumb. This wasn't unexpected. He'd been bound to find another place to stay eventually, and if the thought of him being gone—of being alone again—bothered me? Well, it was my problem, wasn't it. Not his.

"Of course," I agreed, deliberately keeping my voice even. "It was the least I could do."

"I'll move out this weekend."

This weekend? Wow. That was…so soon. I grasped the edge of the counter to steady myself as I grew lightheaded. Panic nibbled at me, and I hesitated, then made my mouth move, putting words out there that would leave me vulnerable, but I had to say them.

"You don't have to, you know," I blurted, talking to

his back as he started scrubbing the pan I'd used. "I have this big house and it's empty most of the time. We could work something out. It might be cheaper for you. Or if you want to exchange services, I mean you've been mowing and doing things around the house, which I really appreciate. Saved me a ton of money on hiring people to come do them. Like my bathroom sink that you unclogged? I'd have had to call a plumber, you know, so that was a huge—"

"Em."

He'd turned off the water and was facing me. I hadn't even noticed. At some point, my gaze had shifted to look over his shoulder beyond him. I had a death grip on the counter's edge.

"—favor," I continued. "And I hate having to get my oil changed, you know. Well, you probably don't know, but I do. And there's just about a hundred other—"

"Em!"

This time his hands had closed on my arms, his voice breaking through to me. I looked at him, startled.

"What?" My voice was smaller than I was accustomed to hearing it.

His lips curved into a sad little smile that made my heart hurt. "You know I can't stay," he said softly, reaching up from his grip on my arm to tuck my hair behind an ear. His fingers lingered a moment, lightly touching the sensitive skin. "It wouldn't be fair to you. I'm a walking red flag, remember? Just divorced. Crappy job. Got a kid. You deserve so much better. And you'll find it. I promise. You'll find it."

My eyes were wide and my breaths came too fast

and shallow. I reached for some dignity, and it was a long reach by this point. My face felt hot.

"Absolutely. You're right." I forced a smile that felt like trying to make concrete crack. "Well. I'm just going to get some laundry done. Need anything washed?" I could feel tears threatening and hurried to disguise it by fussing with the placemats on the table, aligning them just so.

"No. I don't."

The words were flat and I didn't look at him as I nodded, adjusting the chairs so they were perfectly square with the placemats.

"Okay, then," I said brightly. "I'll fix your lunch in a bit and leave it in the fridge, like usual." Though my days of making him lunch were now numbered in the single digits. I didn't look at him as I headed out of the kitchen, calling back, "Have a good night." He didn't reply.

And that was all we said about it. Until Saturday morning.

I woke up early, my stomach churning. Cal would be leaving today. I'd have no further reason to be in touch with him, and he no doubt would want to leave behind anything that reminded him of the divorce, which included me. This was it. I'd made him his last dinner and last lunch. He'd followed me home from work yesterday for the last time.

We hadn't said much at dinner, both of us being rather quiet, an almost somber mood hovering over the table. Small talk. That was it. September was just days away and there had been brief periods of cooler weather in Indy this past week. The weather. That was what we'd been reduced to discussing. I'd barely been able to eat more than a few bites of the meal I'd made, which had been the same dish I'd first made for him, so many weeks ago when summer had first begun. I wondered if he remembered. If so, he didn't mention it. I wasn't sure if I should have been glad or disappointed.

Just then, my stomach sent a signal that had me hurtling into my bathroom, heaving into the toilet. I had nothing in my stomach to throw up, so I was just retching, which was awful in and of itself. The tile was cold and hard on my bare knees, and I was shaking. So engrossed was I in how horrible I felt, I completely missed Cal's entrance into the bathroom until he pulled my hair back from my face.

By now, it was finally passing and I slumped to the side, exhausted. A cool washcloth was pressed to my forehead, and I grasped it, wiping my mouth. My hands were visibly trembling.

"You're sick," Cal announced, a little anti-climactic.

"No shit," I rasped.

"C'mon, let's get you to bed."

I was too weak to resist as he led me and tucked me in under the covers. The twins could sense my distress and crowded around me, whining.

"I'll get you some ice chips," he said. "You must be dehydrated."

"No, I'm fine. Don't—" but he was already gone.

I must have dozed, because the next thing I knew was a cold thing against my lips. Obediently, I opened my mouth and the chips of ice slid inside.

Cal fed me the ice until I wasn't thirsty anymore. I sighed and turned onto my side. My stomach felt better, and I told him so.

"I'm okay, but thank you," I said, sitting up. It was mid-morning now and I felt right as rain. So weird.

Then it hit me.

"Oh god. Oh no."

I vaulted from the bed and ran into the bathroom, closing and locking the door behind me. I dug into the cabinets underneath my sink, finally finding what I sought.

"Em. Let me in. What's going on? Are you okay?"

Cal's words fell on deaf ears as I did the due diligence, then I waited. He eventually fell silent, and I watched my phone for the timer to go off. When it finally did, I couldn't move. It took me another two minutes to reach out and look at the pregnancy test.

When I opened the door, Cal was sitting on the floor next to it. He looked up and hurriedly got to his feet. By the look in his eyes as they met mine, I could tell he already knew.

"I...I don't know what to do." Silently, I handed him the stick. I had to vocalize it. To make it real.

"I'm pregnant."

The silence was so heavy and thick, I thought of all those times I'd read in a book about how it could be cut by a knife. Now I knew what that meant. How it felt.

To my utter shock, Cal's face broke into a beaming smile.

"Oh my god," he said, his voice not that steady. "This is...amazing. Incredible. Oh my god."

He pulled me into his arms, his obvious joy infectious. I couldn't help but smile, too.

"We have to plan," he said, pulling away. He took my hand and tugged me to sit on the bed. "We can get married at the courthouse. We need to go to the doctor. Have you been to the doctor? And a nursery. We'll need a nursery. And you'll need to cut back on your hours. I can take up the slack. I have a friend who's asked me to join his…company."

I didn't want to analyze that pause before he'd said "company."

His rapidfire words were like a douse of cold water. "Stop." My voice was loud and it served to shut him up. "My life isn't yours to arrange."

Cal looked momentarily speechless, which he overcame in record speed.

"It's not just your life. It's ours. It's the baby's."

"And you think you know best what we should do for the baby?"

"I know what it needs. Which is a family." He took my hands in his. "I know the timing isn't great. But it is what it is. And I want to be with you." He paused. "Emerson. Will you marry me?"

I went utterly still.

As proposals go, it was decent. He wasn't on a knee, but I didn't want to quibble. And he'd said nothing about love. But I had more to think about than myself. I had to think about the baby. A baby who would grow up much better in a household with a mother and father, so all the statistics said.

And to be a wife again—to have for real all that I'd been pretending to have these past few weeks, to see the prospect of being a mom on the horizon—I couldn't have said no even if I'd wanted to.

"Yes," I said, my decision made. "Yes, Cal. I'll marry you."

Cal's exuberance was infectious, and his crushing hug made me smile. It would be okay. It just had to be.

Sunday brunch started normally. Bridget was glum because Rick had finally moved out. They'd tried to tough it out in the weeks since the big blowup, but today her eyes were red-rimmed. I wanted to ask about how she was doing, but Bridget didn't like to appear weak. Still, I couldn't help myself.

"So, did he say where he was staying?" I asked weakly. Carly shot me a look as she bit into a piece of bacon.

Bridget sniffed, not looking up from her Belgian waffle loaded with chocolate sauce and whipped cream, something she never usually would have ordered. But I couldn't blame her. It looked much better than my egg-white omelet. Thank goodness we were eating at a time past my morning sickness, which had come again this morning. I didn't like it, but it was a reminder that I had a life growing inside me again. And this time would be different than the last.

The thought of the last time made me uncomfortable, so I pushed it away.

I hadn't told them, Bridget and Carly. It wasn't something you announced over text. I was going to tell them in person. Today. I just…hadn't yet.

"He's staying with a friend," she answered, before flagging down the waiter and asking for a side of the chocolate sauce.

Carly and I looked at each other and an awkward silence descended.

"Um, are you…sure…that it's over?" Carly asked once the waiter had dropped off the side, taking up my slack.

Bridget poured the additional chocolate sauce over the waffle and ate a gigantic bite before answering.

"Yeah." Her voice was thick, and she blinked rapidly, then lifted her tear-filled eyes to ours. "I couldn't do that anymore and I told him so. I said this is what I want. Commitment. Marriage. Family. And he said well, I don't. And that was that." She ate another chocolate-soaked bite through her tears.

Reaching across the table, I squeezed her hand. Carly did the same, so we were all connected.

"We're here for you," I said quietly. "Just like you both were there for me when Chad was killed."

Bridget smiled weakly. "Thank you. I'll be okay. This is just my mourning period."

"Which you absolutely need," Carly said, emphatic. "It's healthy."

Sitting back in our chairs, we resumed eating. I took a few listless bites and knew it was time. I took a deep breath and set down my fork.

"I'm pregnant."

The blurted words had quite the effect. Carly and Bridget jerked their gazes to me in unison, wide-eyed. There was a pregnant pause—hardy har har.

"Excuse me?" Bridget asked.

"You're pregnant?" Carly's query was quick on Bridget's heels.

I nodded. "Yeah. It's Cal's. I guess now I know why they say that no birth control is one hundred percent effective." A weak laugh bubbled from my throat and quickly died.

"What are you going to do?"

"Congratulations!"

They spoke at the same time, Carly's effusiveness warring with Bridget's no-nonsense.

I addressed Bridget first. "I'm keeping it." Then Carly. "Cal asked me to marry him…and I said yes."

Twice in as many minutes that I'd stunned my two best friends.

Carly appeared to be at a loss for words. Bridget found her tongue first, her eyes narrowing.

"Are you doing this because you think you won't get another chance to marry and have kids?"

Well. That was certainly direct. But that's who Bridget was. She didn't beat around the bush.

I took another deep breath. "It's not that. But I don't want to terminate the pregnancy. I make a good living. I can support a baby by myself if necessary. So first, yes, I want to keep it. Second, Cal is a good man. I've gotten to know him since he's been staying with me. We haven't slept together again—not since that first time—but we have chemistry."

Neither of them had been very thrilled that I'd invited Cal to come live with me until he could get back on his feet, but we were all grown women. They let me know what they thought and had left it at that.

"Is he still working at the warehouse?" Bridget's tone said she was not impressed. I stiffened.

"Yes." Bridget's gaze swung to Carly's, her lips pressed together. "He's a hard worker," I defended him. "It's not his fault that he hasn't been able to find other work."

"Maybe you should think about a prenup," Carly interjected, seeking to ease the growing tension between myself and Bridget.

I hesitated. The thought had crossed my mind, which had immediately made me feel guilty.

"Maybe."

"Do you love him?"

Carly's question was typical of her, ever the romantic.

"I could." It was as honest as I could be. I wasn't in love with Cal. We were good roommates so far. We had explosive chemistry in bed. But how did you get from here to there when there's suddenly a baby thrown in the mix? And oh, by the way, can you sign this prenup? Ugh.

"Well, I'm glad for you that you're having a baby," Bridget said, precisely cutting another bite of the waffle with her fork. "And a prenup will protect you. As for all the romantic bullshit…" She dismissed it with a wave of her bite of waffle before stuffing it in her mouth.

"When are you getting married?" Carly asked while Bridget was chewing.

"I don't know," I said. "Probably soon. I don't want to be a cliché redneck shotgun wedding with the pregnant bride, waddling down the aisle."

"Are you getting married in a church? Have you told your mom?" It seems the floodgates had opened for Carly's questions. She waited for my answers, wide-eyed, and barely looked at the bite of pancake burrito she forked into her mouth.

I shook my head. "I did the whole white wedding with all the trimmings once. I don't need to do it again." Not to mention that I was still coming to terms with the idea of impending marriage and motherhood. "Probably just at the courthouse, I guess. And I told Mom yesterday."

"What did she say?" Bridget this time.

"Are you kidding? She was ecstatic. You know how much she's been wanting grandkids. She's already buying toys." And demanding to meet Cal. I hadn't yet told her that he was ex-military. I wasn't sure how she'd feel about me marrying yet another military man.

"Do we get to come?" Carly looked slightly anxious at asking this question, as though she weren't sure of my answer.

"You're kidding, right? I'm just trying to figure out the Maid of Honor thing."

"No," said Bridget, emphatic. "I'm sorry, Emmy, but the thought of actually being in a wedding right now..." Her voice trailed off and her eyes grew slightly bright before she blinked rapidly and cleared her throat.

"I'll do it!" Carly's enthusiasm made me smile. She loved weddings.

"Then it's settled," I said. "Though I thought maybe you'd both like to come over for dinner Saturday and officially meet him."

"Yes!" Carly jumped on that, beaming at me.

"What can we bring?"

Which is how I ended up feeling more nervous than I thought I would that following Saturday as I slid a casserole dish of manicotti into the oven. It wasn't just about my two best friends meeting Cal, but them meeting my *future husband*.

We'd braved brunch with my parents this morning. My dad and Cal had immediately hit it off, talking about—you guessed it—sports. The fact that Cal was ex-military and now a blue-collar worker were bonus points in his favor. By the time my mom and I finished our lattes and French toast and the men had finished their third cups of black coffee and omelets with sides of bacon, they were the best of friends.

As for my mom, she beamed the entire time, quizzing me on if I'd gotten a dress yet and if I'd ordered a bouquet, quickly offering to order the flowers despite my protests. Not to my surprise, she overruled my objection to a church wedding, somehow finding a small chapel that I reluctantly agreed would be perfect.

"Every bride needs a bouquet," she tsked, waving her manicured hand. "And flowers work wonderfully as decorations. I'm happy to help."

She'd gone on to say she'd spoken to a company who could set up tables in the chapel's garden, with tablecloths and chair covers. "And the weather looks like it will be lovely, though that could change. Do you have a preference for catering or shall I look into it?"

"You can, Mom." The less I had to do with the details, the better, in my opinion.

"Have you chosen Carly and Bridget as your bridesmaids?"

I saw my opening for a diversion and took it, shamelessly throwing Bridget and Rick's breakup out there as carrion fodder as to why she didn't want to be a bridesmaid. Thus, we spent the rest of the outing engaging in gossip about them, for which I ruthlessly repressed all guilt. It was survival of the fittest when confronted with a wedding-and-grandchild-minded mother.

"I'm so excited for you, dear." She pulled me into the tightest hug we'd had in a long time.

"Thanks, Mom." My throat was a bit thick and grew even more so when my dad hugged me. He just wasn't a big hugger.

"I want you to be happy." His gruff whisper in my ear was nearly my undoing—my emotions had been on a hair-trigger the past few days—but I held it together. I didn't want Cal to see some blubbery, red-nosed mess of his future wife.

Wife.

I couldn't help the joy those words brought even with my self-imposed caution.

I hadn't mentioned the prenup either. That would be an awkward conversation, so I was putting it off. But putting off that conversation also put off deciding on a date and this baby was only going to get bigger.

But will it?

I shoved the thought away. Again. I wasn't going to lose this baby. The last time had been an aberration. I'd just gone through a severe emotional trauma. This baby would be just fine. It would be born healthy at nine months, and we'd bring it home from the hospital in perfect health.

The same doubts and fears kept plaguing me and every time they shoved their way to the front of my brain, I had trouble breathing.

My hands shook slightly, and I forced a deep breath. Tonight, I'd decided that a nice big plate of carb-heavy comfort food and some red wine for dinner with my friends would put Cal in a relaxed, sleepy mood. Then maybe I could just kind of slide the pre-nup into casual conversation once they'd gone.

The doorbell rang and I took off my apron and headed for the foyer, but Cal was already there.

He'd dressed in one of the nicer shirts I'd gotten him, and I took a split second to admire how he looked.

Designer jeans that fit him perfectly, slung low round his hips and hugging his incredible ass and thighs. A pair of leather, lace-up mahogany dress shoes and a deep blue dress shirt with thin pinstripes. He'd rolled back the sleeves a couple of times and I noticed he had two buttons undone in the front. He saw me and smiled.

My libido went into overdrive, which seemed to happen a lot lately. He was just So. Damn. Hot. And he should've looked like a ridiculous pimp with the shirt buttons undone that much, but he carried it off, and carried it off very well, indeed.

I'd paused and now shook myself back into motion and smiled back, joining him at the door.

"Ready?" I asked.

"Out of the frying pan…" He lifted one eyebrow, his lips quirked in that wicked way that made my heart stutter.

"Into the fire."

He pulled open the door.

chapter sixteen

TWO WOMEN STOOD on the front porch, avidly eyeing me. They were both very attractive and I could imagine the three of them together were a knockout punch for any man. A willowy, ethereal-looking blonde akin to a fairytale princess, a toned brunette who looked like she could give Angelina Jolie a run for the money, cheekbones and pouty lips included, and Em, the petite, fiery redhead with curves to make a man's mouth water. No man stood a chance.

"Cal, this is Bridget," Em motioned to the brunette, who shook my hand, her grip firm, her face unsmiling. "And Carly." The blonde gave me a bright, sincere smile that reached her eyes and I realized she was one of those rare women—like Em—who had no idea of how beautiful she was. To my surprise, she bypassed my outstretched hand and hugged me.

"It's so wonderful to meet you," she enthused, her voice a melodious soprano in contrast to Em's sexy alto. "I can't tell you how happy we are that Emmy and you found each other. And we're going to be aunts!"

Carly's unabashed warmth and clear affection for Em had me liking her immediately. My return hug was genuine. As she stepped back, my attention turned to Bridget, who'd entered the house along with Carly and was chatting with Em, ignoring me entirely.

Ah. I saw the lay of the land. It was the friendship version of Good Cop/Bad Cop, though I didn't think they were putting on an act. Obviously, Bridget was the cynic of the group, Carly was the optimist, and Em the realist.

Bridget linked her arm through Em's and they began walking toward the kitchen, still talking. I followed, Carly falling into step beside me.

"Do you have other children?" she asked.

"I do." I was a bit surprised Em hadn't already told them this, but perhaps she had and Carly just wanted to hear my version. "I have a daughter from my previous marriage. Her name is Amber." I went on to give her the brief rundown of her age and which school she went to, before adding, "She lives with her mom and her parents most of the time, but I get to see her every other weekend. Em worked out a better schedule in the divorce settlement, so that'll take effect soon."

I couldn't watch Amber during the day in the summer since I worked all day, but once school started, she'd be with me every other week. I couldn't wait.

"Was your divorce amicable?"

That question took me aback, then I realized that

Em couldn't discuss my divorce with her friends, since I was also her client as well as her fiancé.

"Amicable enough." My answer was deliberately vague. I didn't want to discuss my divorce. That chapter of my life was closed. Time to start a new one.

By then, we'd reached the kitchen. Carly and Bridget had obviously been here many times because they took seats at the kitchen table, which Em had already set.

"Would you open the wine?" she asked, pulling a large bowl of green salad from the fridge.

I uncorked the bottle, then got the casserole dish out of the oven and let Em fuss over the salad dressings and garlic bread. In a few minutes, we were all sitting down to dinner.

"This looks amazing, Emmy," Bridget said, dishing some manicotti onto her plate.

I couldn't disagree. I'd been fantastically spoiled by Em's cooking the past few weeks. She cooked and I cleaned. We'd fallen into a comfortable routine and in the week since I was supposed to move out—the day Em had discovered she was pregnant—I'd modified my schedule. Before, I'd taken pains to make sure I wasn't intruding on her space, making sure to leave the house very early and just show up at her work to follow her home every day. I hadn't texted or called while she was working. We'd been roommates only, she'd made that clear, and I hadn't wanted to press her for anything more.

But this week, I'd hung around to help her with the morning sickness, taking her some dry toast and tea when she could keep something down. I'd followed her to work, called to check on her during the day, and followed her home at night.

We'd had no more incidents from the stalker, but I didn't know if that meant that he'd moved on or was just biding his time. I didn't like that it wasn't resolved, and that fact nestled in the back of my brain, never going away, so I didn't forget about it, nor did I let myself relax into complacency. There was too much at stake should he get by me.

Bridget and Carly swung into girl talk with Em about the wedding and I tuned out as I ate, my thoughts drifting to all that had happened in such a short amount of time.

Em had spoken with the other two partners in the firm about her condition and after their congratulations, they'd had no problem agreeing to more flexibility in her hours. They'd even agreed she could work from home a couple days a week, which would make me feel loads better. Em behind locked and armed doors sounded pretty damn good.

The security at the firm had been finished a few weeks ago and I spent several hours every week testing it and checking the cameras and what they recorded. I didn't see any blind spots outside the building. They'd done a good job.

I'd told my mom the news over the phone, and she'd been ecstatic at the thought of another grandchild, though not quite so much at the prospect of the ink barely dry on my divorce papers before marrying another woman.

"Callan," my mom always called me by my full name, "are you sure you really want to do this? Honey, it's common to rebound from a divorce. But you don't usually marry your rebound. You just sleep with them."

"Mom!" Seriously. My mother didn't believe in tactfulness anymore. She said she was too old to worry about such things.

"I'm just calling it how I see it. I understand that she's going to have your child, but that doesn't mean you need to tie your life to hers. You already tried that once and look how that turned out."

Ouch. "I want to," I'd retorted, a bit defensively. Do we ever grow out of regressing to fifteen when our moms call us out on our bullshit? Lowering my voice a notch and taking a deep breath, I said, "I want a family, Mom. A wife to come home to and another baby to hold." I paused. "I guess I want another chance."

And I suppose that's how I saw Em and me and the baby. My second chance, served up to me on a silver platter. If I blew this, somehow I doubted I'd get a third shot.

"Have you told Lisa?"

My mom's question had the effect of thrown cold water. I was chilled all over and anxiety gnawed at me as I tried to imagine how that conversation would go.

"Not yet. But I will."

"Has Amber met Emmy?"

Add to my To Do list. "Not yet." I felt like a broken record. "She's with me next weekend, not this one." Em had taken great pains to make sure she was scarce on the weekends when I had Amber, giving us privacy in her home, and even one of the unused bedrooms for Amber to use as her own.

The day she'd told me about the bedroom for Amber, I'd been shocked.

"*C'mon,*" *she said with a smile, motioning up the stairs. We'd just finished cleaning up dinner, some kind of grilled pork chop thing with a sauce had turned me into a complete glutton.*

"*What is it?*"

"*I have something I want to show you.*"

I obediently followed her up the stairs. She stopped in front of one of the closed doors to the two other bedrooms. Her smile was bright as she looked at me before opening the door, pushing it wide.

My mouth fell open. Before, the room had been a nice but generic bedroom with a double bed, chest of drawers, and a nightstand. It was now a little girl's paradise.

The bedding had all been swapped out for soft lavender linens etched with tiny white flowers. The walls were now painted in wide stripes of alternating lavender and white. A white canopy draped the bed with little twinkle lights stretched along the top. A child-size vanity with mirror sat in the corner, the seat topped with a puffed purple cushion. Stuffed animals were scattered here and there around the room—on the bed, on shelves in a new bookcase filled with kid books, and even a hippo in a pink tutu sitting in the window.

My vision turned blurry, and I had to clear my throat before I could speak.

"*Em…I can't believe you did this. She's going to love it.*"

Em's smile grew even wider. "*I'm so glad, Cal. I thought she could use a little TLC, too.*"

And I'd been right. Amber had squealed when she saw the room, dropping the naked Barbie she carried (I never could figure out why she always took off the clothes) and rushing to climb the little stairs Em had bought so she could climb on to the high bed.

"Daddy! I love this place!"

The whole house had been a revelation for her, including Thing #1 and Thing #2, who'd immediately began jumping up on her so they could lick her face. I'd tried to shoo them away, but Amber had laughed and tried to hug one of them, so I let it be.

"I'm glad you like it, snuggle bunny."

It had taken a while before we'd left that day. Amber needed to explore every nook and cranny of her room. When she'd opened the closet, I'd gotten another surprise.

"New clothes!"

Amber had decided she liked the hippo better than the Barbie, so that was what she now had tucked under her arm as she surveyed the clothes on the hangers. The bar the hangers were on had been lowered so Amber could reach them. Shoes were neatly lined up on a slanted rack on the floor, everything from little white sandals to colorful tennis shoes and black patent Mary Janes. I was stunned all over again. Em's generosity was humbling.

When I didn't immediately answer, Amber twisted to look at me.

"They're mine, right Daddy?"

Her innocent question yanked me out of my stunned amazement. I made my feet move, landing next to her at the closet. Reaching out, I moved the hangars, surveying the clothes.

"Of course they are," I answered absently. Em had gotten some of everything, for every season, all arranged according to type and color. Rompers, casual T-shirts and nicer shirts, dresses and shorts and skirts and even jackets and coats and a snowsuit.

On a hunch, I went to the chest and pulled open a drawer. Little underthings filled the drawers. Undies, socks, tights, and two entire drawers full of pajamas. I sat down heavily on the floor, eyeing the contents of the bottom drawer. Amber was peering over my shoulder, her mouth drawn into an O of amazement, her eyes wide. Reaching around me, she grabbed out a pink satin gown with a ruffled hem and a rainbow unicorn printed on it.

"Look, Daddy! Can I wear it?"

"Sure, sweetie. After your bath tonight, we'll make sure you wear it to bed." I got to my feet, unsure how to feel about all of this. The room itself had been an amazing gift, but now all these clothes... My pride stung. Did Em think I couldn't provide for my own daughter? "Let's go get that pizza and ice cream, okay?"

Amber had abandoned the nightgown and had taken off her Velcro sandals and was sprawled on the floor, busy shoving her toes into a pair of tennis shoes with soles that had flashing lights. I took a pair of socks from the drawer.

"Hold on, sweetie. It'll be easier with some socks."

A couple of minutes later, Amber was stomping around the room, eyes glued to her shoes as they lit up with every step she took. A giggle burst from her and I couldn't help smiling. Was there anything more precious than the sound of your child's laughter?

Fuck my pride. Amber was thrilled and happy. I'd just have to find a way to pay Em back.

Reaching down, I swung Amber up in my arms. "How does pepperoni sound?"

Amber's hands rested on my shoulders as she looked at me, grinning. "Extra cheese?"

"All the cheese ever, snuggle bunny."

Amber had loved Em and they'd taken to each other like cinnamon to applesauce. She had been thrilled when I told her, over our ice cream sundaes, that we were getting married. Lisa hadn't been quite so thrilled, but it was what it was.

"Cal? Are you okay?"

Em's words dragged me back to the present and I realized all three of them were looking at me oddly.

"I'm sorry," I apologized with a smile. "Was just thinking. What did I miss?"

"Bridget asked if you're still job searching."

I glanced at Bridget, my smile turning stiff. "Not at the moment. I've actually taken another job that will start in a couple of weeks."

This wasn't something I'd yet told Em. A week ago, I'd thought we were going our separate ways since I'd have no reason to see her anymore. I'd called Mac right after the tornado and told him what had happened, that I needed some time to get the divorce finalized and get my shit together.

But I told him I'd take the job.

He'd readily agreed to a start date that was now three weeks from Monday. My first assignment was going to be a four-month tour in Izmir, Turkey. It was a relatively calm location to ease me back into the swing of things, which I appreciated.

"What other job?" Em asked.

I turned to Em. "I was going to tell you. An old Army buddy of mine has a firm that provides security for companies that do business in areas that could have…" How to put this so she wouldn't worry? "…a measure of unrest. He called right before the tornado and offered me a position."

Her brows had flown up and her eyes were wide in surprise. "Security? A measure of unrest? Cal, that sounds dangerous."

I smiled a little, reaching out to take her hand which rested on the table. I noticed she'd cleaned her plate, which made me feel good. I wanted her to take care of herself and her health. After all, she was growing a new human.

"It's mainly a deterrent. Bad guys see us there and think twice about doing something stupid. And the job has a good salary and benefits. You'll be able to take more time off work, if you want, to be with the baby."

Em' frown just grew deeper. "I don't want you to take a job that will put you in danger just because it'll be for more money."

"It's my job, and privilege, to take care of you and our child," I said in what I hoped was a reasonable voice. Em's mood swings could go from hot to cold to horny to sub-zero within the span of sixty seconds. I didn't want her to get upset. "I want you to be happy, and if being with the baby makes you happy, then you should be able to do that."

I must've said just the right words because instead of flying into a rage at what some women might call chauvinism, her eyes grew bright with tears. She squeezed my hand.

"That's very sweet of you, but I can't let you do that."

Now it was my turn to be surprised. "Excuse me?"

"Yeah, so, we'll just get going," Carly interrupted, standing as she gathered up the empty plates. "It was so nice to meet you, Cal."

Bridget stood, too, taking their glasses and following Carly to where she'd deposited the dishes in the sink.

"You're leaving already?" Em asked, following them toward the foyer.

"I have church in the morning," Carly explained, picking up her purse.

"And it looks like you two have some things to discuss," Bridget added, one eyebrow raised as she looked at me, then Em. "What color dresses should we buy, Emmy?"

Em looked a bit dazed, but murmured, "Summer colors. Pastels. You pick."

"Got it." Bridget opened the door and stepped out. Carly cast one last smile at me, then Em, before following her.

"Have a good night," she called over her shoulder as her heels clacked on the sidewalk's pavement.

"Bye," Em called back.

In another moment, they'd both gotten into a car parked in Em's driveway, which started and backed out before zipping away up the street.

"Well, that was abrupt," she said, sounding somewhat disgruntled and crossing her arms over her chest.

"I'm sure you'll hear their verdict soon enough."

"Verdict?"

"If I passed the Best Friends Test." I winked, sliding my arm around her waist. She nestled her back against my chest as if it was the most natural thing in the world. And it felt good. So good, in fact, that I circled my other arm around her and rested my chin on top of her head.

"Did *you* like *them?*" she asked.

I turned her to face me but kept my arms around her. She lifted her hands and rested them on my shoulders. Her eyes were the clear, brilliant green of spring grass, and made my breath hitch in my chest.

"You're so beautiful," I murmured, trying to memorize every inch of her face. Reaching up, I took a lock of her mahogany hair in my fingers. It was like silk, almost as soft as her skin.

Em's cheeks turned pink. "You must hate them if you're trying that hard to change the subject."

I huffed a laugh. "They seemed nice."

"Hmm. Very generic of you." She focused on the buttons on my shirt, fiddling with the top one.

"Somehow I'm sure I'll be seeing more of them." Leaning down, I couldn't resist pressing my lips to her forehead. My eyes slipped closed, and I inhaled the scent of her, tinged slightly with her perfume.

The mother of my child. A second chance. Another little human I'd helped bring into the world. Maybe this time, I could get it right.

"So what's this about a new job?"

Cal dropped his arms from around me and I immediately felt the loss. But there was something more important we had to discuss.

"It's a good position," he said, his expression shuttering. I was familiar with the look. It said, *Questions will only get you half the answers you want.* "Better than anything else I'd get."

"But you'll be gone."

"Just for a few months, then back stateside. I'll be here when you're in the eighth month. I've already told Mac about the baby, and he's agreed to give me six weeks of PTO after the baby's born."

Cal would be gone for four months. He'd be in danger. And there was a baby on the way. Just like Chad.

Suddenly, I couldn't breathe and my heart began racing. I gasped for air and my vision grew dark. I reached out, fisting Cal's shirt in my hand.

"Em, what's wrong? What is it?"

Cal's anxious voice filled my ears, but I couldn't speak. I was breathing now, but much too fast. I couldn't let go of his shirt even when my hands began tingling and when I could no longer feel them. My fingers wouldn't unbend.

"Panic…attack," I gasped.

Without saying a word, Cal swept me up in his arms and rushed into the living room, carefully laying me down on the sofa.

"Just breathe," he said, the calmness in his voice belying the anxiety in his eyes. "In through your nose, out through your mouth. Watch me. Breathe when I do."

He was kneeling on the floor next to me, one hand stroking my hair back from my face and the other covering my fist still clutching his shirt.

A panic attack is hard to describe. You can't understand what's happening, your heart and breath rate are skyrocketing, and your skin is clammy with sweat.

You can't see your way through. It feels like the walls are closing in.

"In…" He took a deep breath through his nose. "Out." He blew out the air. Then repeated it. I tried to follow along, concentrating only on breathing, not thinking about anything else.

Just breathe.

After a few minutes of Cal patiently breathing along with me, I could feel my hands again and the darkness at the edges of my vision had cleared. I slowly unclenched my fist, letting go of his shirt, now wrinkled where I had grasped it.

"I'm sorry," I managed, utterly mortified.

"It's fine." He lifted my outstretched legs and sat down, resting my legs on top of his thighs. I'd worn a little sundress this evening and Cal slid his palm up and down my thigh, over my knee, and back up again. "Do you often get panic attacks?"

I lowered my lids so I didn't have to look at him. "Sometimes. But not for a while." I hesitated. "But that was the worst." So far.

"Because of what happened to Chad."

It wasn't a question, so I didn't bother answering.

"Em, look at me."

Reluctantly, I lifted my eyes to his.

"I'm not Chad. And I'm not going to war. I'll be doing a job with other highly qualified people in a location that's ninety-nine percent safe. I swear to you. For something to happen there, it would almost take an act of God." Cal's gaze didn't waver. I studied him. He believed what he was saying.

"I want to meet him," I said.

He frowned. "Meet who?"

"Whoever you're going to be working for. I want to meet him, know the man in charge of sending you over there and where you'll be sent." I couldn't explain it, but I had to see him. I wanted him to meet me, to know that I was pregnant with Cal's child. There was this irrational hope inside that said if I did that—if I made him put a face and person to my name—he'd take especial care of Cal.

"Okay, that's fine. We can do that." Cal's voice was smoothly calm again, his hand not ceasing stroking my skin, which is when I realized that I'd started breathing faster. I deliberately slowed my breathing and forced my body to relax. "I'll call him."

It was silent for a few minutes as I focused on breathing slowly and deeply. Cal didn't say anything, but it wasn't uncomfortable. I liked him touching me. His palm was work-roughened against my much softer skin, which felt amazing. I concentrated on that.

"Where are you going again? And when?" My voice broke the quiet and I was glad I sounded normal. For the most part.

Cal didn't look at me as he answered. "Izmir, Turkey."

I sat up. "Turkey?" I squeaked. "Turkey isn't safe!"

"Relax," he said, putting a hand on my shoulder and gently pushing me back down onto the couch. "It is. There's a NATO installation there that we'll use as our home base."

"And when you're not at home base?" Without realizing, I'd taken his hand in mine and was gripping it.

"Then we'll have each other's backs and be armed

to the teeth." He squeezed my knee. "I'm good at what I do, Em. And this job pays two-fifty a year. You'll be able to cut back on your hours, and I'll be back for six weeks at a time."

I could tell that there was no way I'd be able to talk him out of this. He'd been handed a job that would give him his pride and dignity back, and heaven help the woman who stood between a man and his pride.

"Can we at least say that it's on a trial basis and we can revisit the issue if it's not working out for either of us?" Being a lawyer, I knew the fine art of not only choosing your battles, but compromise.

"Absolutely."

I smiled. I'd live to fight another day. We'd just have to see what the costs versus benefits of this new job were.

Easing upward and swinging my legs off Cal's lap, I heaved a sigh. "I'd better go clean up the kitchen and get things ready for morning." I liked to put out my things for my coffee before I went to bed—choose which coffee beans I wanted, which mug I'd use (I had a collection of mismatched mugs I'd collected and been given), fill the kettle with water, etc. Although I couldn't eat first thing in the morning, my coffee went down just fine.

"I'll do it," he said. "You just go upstairs and get ready for bed. You've been cooking all afternoon. I'll clean up and set out your coffee."

Looking at him, I raised my brows. "Much more of this pampering and I'll be spoiled."

"As you deserve to be."

Cal stood, pulling me to my feet as well. As I turned to head upstairs, he lightly smacked me on the butt.

I squeaked in surprise, scooting forward out of his reach.

"What was that for?" It had literally been years since I'd been smacked on the butt.

He just shrugged, grinning. "Just an excuse to touch your ass."

I decided to take a chance, after all, we *were* getting married. "If you hurry, I might let you touch more than just my ass."

His response was immediate. "Give me five minutes."

I laughed as he rushed toward the kitchen. Water was running and there was the clang of pots and pans as I climbed the stairs.

My nerves jangled. I wasn't yet showing, so that was good for choosing what to wear, but this would be the first time we'd actually been together—like *together* together—since the one-night stand that had started this whole thing. What if it wasn't as good? What if *I* wasn't as good?

Ugh. I couldn't think like that and the clock was ticking. I needed to hurry.

Turning off all the lights, I lit two candles (a wonderful sage and sandalwood scent). A girl looks her best in dim lighting, dontcha know? I grabbed my mountain of throw pillows from the bed and turned down the quilt, blanket, and sheet. Stepping back, I surveyed it. Yes, it looked inviting, and the candles had those wood wicks so they were making soft crackling sounds. Next, the closet.

I surveyed the lingerie hanging on their padded hangers before finally choosing a little slip of a satin gown that was a deep hunter green. I'd bought it because I thought it matched my eyes and contrasted nicely with my hair. Hurrying into the bathroom, I jumped in the shower and did a quick wash of the pertinent areas. I chose unscented lotion because I wanted my perfume to be the only scent on me. The lingerie still fit (for now) and I ran a brush through my hair, which still had waves from when I'd curled it earlier today. Underwear or no underwear?

No underwear.

A brief touchup of my makeup and I was ready.

I stepped out of the bedroom and was startled to see Cal standing there, leaning against the wall. He'd taken his shirt off and his arms were crossed. I was momentarily distracted by the bulging muscles of his biceps and shoulders. Then I noticed the top button of his jeans was undone. Mmmm. Yes, please.

"I was told ass-touching was on the choose-your-own-adventure list," he said, one side of his lips tipping up in a knowing smirk. The look in his eyes made my heart beat faster.

What he said registered and I gave a little laugh. I liked that he could make me laugh and my nerves calmed.

Sashaying towards him, I said, "Show me yours and I'll show you mine." I stopped right in front of him, tipping my head back so I could see his eyes. He felt so much larger than me, so much stronger. It was a huge turn-on.

I was close enough to feel the heat radiating from his body and I wanted to touch him, but I didn't. If he wanted me, he'd have to make the first move. I'd already given the invitation.

The deep chocolate of his eyes was warm, and it

felt as though I could get lost in their depths. He was gazing at me with an intensity that made me shiver, and I couldn't look away.

His hand shot out and grabbed my arm, pulling me against him. Our bodies met and it felt electric. I'd wanted him for weeks now and had to just look and not touch.

Cal wrapped his arms around me and his mouth came down on mine in a fierce kiss. My arms went around his neck, my hold on him tight.

He tasted so good, just as I remembered. His tongue slid against mine, his lips soft, the kiss relentless, until I was gasping. Cal's hands slid under my gown to cup my ass, his mouth sliding from mine to my jaw and neck. My eyes slid shut and I tipped my head to give him further access, and it felt like surrender.

His passion was overwhelming. I could feel the hard length of him through his jeans pressing against my abdomen. He squeezed my ass, pressing me upward until I was on my toes. The blood flow started heading south and wetness pooled between my legs. I could feel myself getting—that horrendous word—*moist*.

I was never quiet during sex and tonight was no exception. My breath was coming in pants as he sucked and kissed my neck, trailing down to my collar bone and the top edge of the deep V of the gown. His tongue was warm and wet against my skin and I wished the stupid gown was off so I could feel his skin against mine.

As though he could read my mind, Cal slid the satin up, his palms against the skin of my sides. I let go of him and put my arms up so he could pull it off me, but he paused ever so briefly at my breasts, his thumbs taking a moment to brush my nipples in a caress that made me moan. Then the gown was off and tossed aside. Without a word, Cal dropped to his knees, startling my eyes open.

He gripped my ass again, settling his mouth against the apex of my thighs. His tongue darted out, deftly stroking the slit that concealed me from him. I sucked in a ragged breath. He teased me, his tongue delving inside until he touched my swollen clit. My nails dug into his shoulders and my eyes again slammed shut.

Cal pushed my thighs apart, widening my stance. His thumbs pressed against my flesh, baring me to his gaze.

"So beautiful," he murmured.

I had no time to react to the unexpected compliment because his mouth was on me in a most determined way that I strongly encouraged. Cal was very good at this and my body remembered his touch, climaxing within just a couple of minutes of his devout attention to detail.

I thought he was done and we'd move on, but he scooped me up and the next thing I knew, he'd deposited me on the bed and was situated between my thighs. His tongue found my sensitive clit as he pushed two fingers inside me.

Oh. Oh wow.

Cal fucked me with his fingers, his tongue stroking and licking me. I was lost in sensation. My thighs were spread shamelessly wide and my fingers were buried in his hair. Inside me, his fingers curved, pressing against something that caused an immediate reaction from me. My breath caught and held. I was utterly captivated by the stroke of his fingers and tongue in two places.

The orgasm started where his tongue was licking me and radiated outward. I didn't breathe. It rolled through me until my toes curled. I felt the rush of hot liquid between my thighs and I let out a sound somewhere between a cry and a scream. The tremors inside me didn't abate. I heard Cal moan softly. His fingers slid out, but his tongue was still stroking my clit, very lightly. The touch made my orgasm after-shocks keep going. It was too much and I tried to push him away, but he didn't move, his tongue relent-less. The warm wetness rushed out of me again and I cried out in pleasure, completely at his mercy. Only after that orgasm had finally abated did he take his mouth from me.

My body felt on fire and despite the multiple orgasms, I wanted him with a desperation that was purely carnal. He was on his knees, his hands braced next to me, one on each side. I leaned up and wrapped my arms around his neck, tugging him down and kissing him just as he entered me.

I moaned into his mouth and wrapped my legs around his waist. He pressed me back into the pil-lows, kissing me with an urgency that sent a wave of want through me.

The last and only time we'd been together, he'd turned me over, which I hadn't minded. It wasn't my favorite position, but I knew men liked it. This time, he seemed pretty darn happy with the good old fashioned missionary style. And I had no complaints either. I squeezed inside like those Kegels you're sup-posed to do, and he moaned.

"Damn, Em, you're so wet."

Cal's lips moved against mine as he whispered to me. I didn't speak, my mind utterly silent as I focused solely on him and the sensations of him moving inside me and his body pressed against me. My hips lifted to meet his in a steady rhythm. My eyes were closed and I inhaled the scent of his skin, damp with sweat.

His arms tightened around me, overlapping as he clutched me to him. His hips moved faster until I could no longer keep up. It felt amazing. He'd been kissing me, but now tore his mouth away, breathing heavily. My whole body was trembling against his in the aftermath.

I felt yet another orgasm coming over me, taking me by surprise. His cock was sliding against me in just the right spot, hard and fast, and my nails scraped his back as I came, my back arching upward.

Cal cried out, thrusting hard and deep into me, his breaths ragged as he stilled. His body jerked slightly and I moaned, the sensation of his cock releasing inside me something I could feel as he came.

Cal's arms gave out and he rested on top of me, his head on my shoulder. His chest heaved as he tried to catch his breath.

"Oh fuck, Em," he gasped. "That was incredible. I think we came at the same time."

Ah. That's what that had been. "It was amazing." I stroked his back, reveling in the feel of his weight on top of me. It had been nice not having a condom, too. I wasn't a fan.

After a few moments, Cal withdrew and turned onto his back, his arm that was curved around my back pulling me with him until I was settled against his side, my head resting on his shoulder and my arm across his chest.

"I hope I wasn't too enthusiastic," he said dryly. "It's been a while since we were last together."

I was glad to hear that he hadn't seen anyone on the side, even for a one-night stand. He could've, after all. But I was glad that he hadn't.

"We have fantastic chemistry, Em," he said, his hand stroking my skin. "I love touching you. Watching you come. You're gorgeous."

Good to know I didn't look ridiculous, which was how I usually felt afterwords, given my vocal performance. I didn't know what to say, so I just pressed a kiss to his chest.

He squeezed me, then began to sit up. I frowned, confused.

"Are you not sleeping in here with me?" Surely, he wouldn't go back to his bedroom?

"Of course I am. Just give me a minute." With that, he disappeared down the hall, only to return a moment later, holding something. In the dark, I couldn't see what it was until he'd come closer. It was a gun.

"What are you doing with that?" I squeaked, my eyebrows climbing up my forehead.

"You still have a stalker, remember?" Reaching down, he tucked it somewhere under the bed, maybe beneath the mattress? "I'm always armed. It's been in my room since I've been here. Better safe than sorry."

I wasn't sure how I felt about that, but I suppose if someone were to break in, Cal was right. And unlike me, he knew how to actually use a gun.

Settling back into bed, he pulled me into his arms. "Now, where were we?"

With a sigh, I allowed myself to be cuddled against him, and exhausted after our...endeavors...I dropped off to sleep.

chapter seventeen

WHAT KIND OF cake do you want?"
I glanced up. Em stood in the doorway to her closet. She was working on and off this week and taking next week off. Today, she was going with her mother, to order a cake and flowers.

I shrugged. "It only comes in like white or chocolate, right? I like them both, so you decide."

The look she gave me said I was a moron.

"What?" It was cake. I didn't care what flavor it was but didn't want to say the words *I don't care* because that would be rude and insensitive. And the last thing I wanted to be to my pregnant fiancée was insensitive. That tended to have nasty consequences which may or may not include my sleeping on the couch.

"Cake comes in many flavors but yes, those are the two most common for a wedding. But it will be in layers so we have to choose the flavor between the layers and the flavor of the icing." Em said it patiently, like she was explaining math to a six-year-old.

I walked over to her and lightly grasped her upper arms.

"Sweetheart, you get whatever tastes the best to you. I don't like coconut. Everything else is fair game. I'm a man. I'll eat almost anything." Leaning down, I pressed a light kiss to her lips before murmuring, "Odds are I won't even notice what I'm eating because I'll be fantasizing about getting you out of your dress."

I kissed her again, a deep kiss this time, and when I pulled back, her pupils had dilated and she was breathing harder. She had the same effect on me. My jeans were now uncomfortably tight in a sensitive place.

"Got it," she whispered, her gaze drifting from my eyes to my mouth.

"Don't look at me like that or you'll be late to meet your mother," I admonished, releasing her.

She heaved a put-upon sigh and returned to looking through her clothes before pulling out a yellow sundress on a hanger.

"What will you be doing today?" she asked.

"I need to meet with my landlord. He's having open hours today with the insurance guys. They're supposed to be handling the settlement payouts from the tornado." It had taken weeks, which hadn't surprised me one bit. Insurance companies rarely lined up in a hurry to give you money.

"You'll go by to see René about your tux, right? He knows the one I like."

Ugh. The penguin suit. A necessary evil. "Absolutely. That's on the agenda." As was the ring, which I didn't want to say anything about. "So are we supposed to meet with this preacher or whatever he is?" The chapel came with a built-in priest. Who knew?

"No. He sent an email about the ceremony and I just opted for the traditional things as far as vows and such. That okay?" She held the dress against her front, checking the waist and length.

"Sounds good to me."

"Mom is insisting we have the reception outside in the chapel's garden, which I think is a good idea," she continued, glancing up at me. "It's been such a mild and wet August, the lawn is gorgeous and there were flowers blooming. They even said they'd put little twinkle lights in the gazebo with the dance floor, you know, like *Twilight*."

I stopped lacing up my boots and looked at her. "What is it about me that leads you to believe that I've *ever* seen *Twilight*." It wasn't a question, and it was dry as dust.

Em laughed out loud, a tinkle of bright sound that made me smile.

"My apologies," she said, still grinning. "I didn't mean to insult your manhood. Let's just say it'll be pretty and leave it at that."

"Done."

I gave her one more kiss before I left and promised to let the kiddos outside to pee when I got back. Then I was suffering through the fitting and measuring with René, who didn't appreciate my sense of humor in the least. The shoes were surprisingly comfortable, for dress shoes, and I said so.

"That's because they're handmade Italian leather," he informed me. "They're not something you can get at the Wal-Mart." His disdain for said chain was obvious and I hid a smile. Not to mention that he'd added a "the" before the name.

"Speaking of which," I began, glancing in the full-length mirror. Hey, I didn't look so bad in this. I straightened the cuffs of my shirt, tugging them further from the tuxedo jacket's sleeve. René had put real cufflinks in them, and not the usual kind you get when you rented a tux. But larger ones that were silver and heavy. "When do I have to get this baby back to you?"

He was running a fancy wooden lint brush across my shoulders and back, but he paused, his gaze landing on mine in the mirror. "Back to me?"

"Yeah. Usually they give you forty-eight hours, right? Do you do that? Or does it need to be returned sooner?"

His eyebrows climbed so far up, I thought he might grow hair again on his bald head. Tipping his chin down, he stared at me over the tops of his glasses.

"This is not a *rental*," he said, his tone suggesting such a thing was vile and disgusting. "This is yours. Take very good care of it. A man always needs a gorgeous tuxedo in his wardrobe."

I stopped, stunned. "It's mine?"

"Of course." He continued brushing lint I couldn't see from the jacket. "And since it was a rush, I'm glad to see it fit so well from the measurements we had, though the fabric around your upper arms is a bit too tight for my liking. I'll have Marie let it out just a tad."

I tuned out after the *Of course*. Em was buying this for me? And it was custom tailored for me?

"Um, hey, René, so like…how much does something like this cost?" Plus the shoes. Holy crap, did I even want to know? But René just *tsk*ed at me.

"One doesn't discuss money in public," he briskly informed me. "It's *vulgar*."

Alrighty then. I'd just have to Google it.

After I'd dressed in my jeans and polo shirt—again, things Em had bought me at this very store—and was lacing up my boots, I thought of another question.

"Hey, René," I said as he was arranging the parts of the tux on multiple hangers. "Where would you go to get an engagement ring and wedding band for Em? I mean, Emerson." Who better to ask than him? He'd know the kinds of places Em would like a ring from.

René didn't even bother turning around as he buttoned the shirt. "Tiffany's, of course."

Of course.

Which was how I found myself sitting in my truck, parked outside the Tiffany's near the mall on the north side of Indy.

I knew less than nothing about jewelry, but I did know that Tiffany's was expensive. But I still had to at least look. I knew that Em would go nuts for one of those little blue boxes. I'd gotten a decent check from the insurance payout this morning before I'd gone to see René. Surely they'd have something for the amount I'd received.

No, they did not. At least, not in the engagement ring section. And I didn't think Em wanted an engagement pair of silver earrings (gemstone available for an extra fee).

I rubbed my palm across my face. Even with the money I'd managed to save the past few weeks from my job, I'd only end up with a ring where you'd need a microscope to see the diamond. The blue box would be more valuable.

Glancing at the entrance to the mall, I considered. I knew what I had could buy me a decent ring at one of the chain jewelry stores inside. But I wanted more for Em. She deserved the best. She'd quite literally been my savior the past few weeks, generously bringing me into her home and getting me clothes and feeding me. Now she was unexpectedly having my child. And for some reason, had agreed to marry me so we could raise the child together.

I really wanted to get her a Tiffany ring. Which was when I had the idea to call Mac. Buoyed by this new prospect, I punched a button my my cell.

"Hey, Mac. Thanks for taking my call."

"Absolutely. I'm thrilled you're coming on," he said. "Solves one of my biggest headaches."

I hesitated, hating to have to ask, but also having no choice. "I was wondering, I know I don't start for a couple more weeks yet, but I was wondering if I could have an advance on my salary." I paused. "I need to buy a ring, man." My pride was hurting, but it would hurt more if I had nothing to put on Em's finger when we said *I do*, which was now just five days away.

We'd decided a few days ago that we'd do a small ceremony at a historical local chapel that had been built in 1894. Well, Em's mom had found the place and it sounded fine to us. It had wooden pews, stained glass, cultivated gardens, and only held seventy-five people. Since it was so small, it had apparently been easy to schedule, even this late in the game. So Saturday evening at five o'clock, Em and I would say our vows to each other. We'd have a week together before I left for Turkey for four months.

"Shite, Cal, didn't I tell you that you get a signing bonus?"

My brows flew up in surprise. I scrambled for what to say.

"Mac, I don't need—" I began, but he didn't let me finish.

"Told you this job had perks. Send me your bank info—routing and account numbers, you know the drill—and I'll have it sent over today."

"Thanks, Mac." It wasn't much, but it was sincere. He had to know what it cost me to ask and, as ever, was gracious to me.

"No thanks necessary," he said. "Just business. When you fly out, there will be a car to pick you up at the airport when you get here. It'll all be in the email."

"Got it. And hey, I have one more favor to ask."

"Sure. What is it?"

I paused, hesitating, then said, "I thought maybe, if you wanted to, you might be my Best Man."

The silence made me wince. Maybe I'd overstepped.

"Cal, that's fantastic. I'd be honored. I'll make my flight arrangements out and fly back with you."

"Thanks, Mac. That means a lot to me."

"You're welcome. I'll text you."

Now, I sat in the parking lot, repeatedly checking my phone for an email from my bank confirming the deposit of the signing bonus. Mac hadn't said how much it would be, so I had my fingers crossed that it would be enough to get a respectable ring for Em from the place René had said she'd like the most.

I was impatiently drumming my fingers on the
steering wheel, listening to Toby Keith singing about
red Solo cups on the radio, when my phone dinged.
Grabbing it, I thumbed through to my email. Yes. It
was from Mac's company—Down Range Security.
Opening it, I was momentarily stunned. I read it
again. Then yet again.

The "signing bonus" Mac had sent was seventy-five
thousand dollars.

Holy shit.

My throat thickened and I cleared it. Twice. Swallowed hard. Well. Okay then. Time to shop.

I'd had the foresight to bring one of Em's rings
from her jewelry box (which I was stunned to learn
was an actual piece of furniture that stood four feet
tall and had several drawers and two side cabinets)
which the salesman used to size the ring I finally
chose—which took me quite a while to pick, and
that didn't include the time it took to pick the diamond (size, shape, clarity—I'd been overwhelmed).

Taking the little blue bag from him—he looked
quite pleased at the sale, probably worked off com-
mission—I headed for my truck, nervously glancing
around. I wished I had my gun on me. I had never
in my life spent so much money on something that
didn't also include four wheels.

On the way back to Em's house—I guess it would
be partly mine after the wedding?—I spontaneously
decided that I should make a production of it. Pulling into the parking lot of the best butcher shop in
the city, despite its locale in one of the worst areas, I
headed inside after pocketing the ring. No way was I

leaving that in the truck. I'd even stuffed the bag and box into the glove compartment.

The butcher shop was cold, as always, with the same aroma in the air it always had. I wasn't sure if it was just the meat or maybe blood, too, but it wasn't unpleasant. It was just how it smelled. I stopped in front of the glass display case, surveying the contents. I realized that I had absolutely no idea what cut of steak Em preferred.

"Cal, it's been a while."

I glanced up. Saul, the owner, greeted me from behind the counter. He was the third generation to run this butcher shop and the seventh generation to be a butcher. To say he knew his meat was an understatement. Italian by descent but Midwestern by accent, he was in his sixties and showed every year on his face. Perpetually sounding exhausted by it all, he still had more energy than a four-year-old boy with ADD. He just hid it well.

"Yeah, I know. Been a little busy." And short on funds to purchase luxuries like meat from an actual butcher. "Tornado took out my apartment building."

That bit of news served to startle Saul, which you could see by the fractional widening of his rheumy eyes.

"Sorry to hear that. Glad you're okay, though."

"Yeah, no casualties, fortunately. Just wiped out what little I owned. Divorce is final now." He'd known about that after I'd gotten back. I'd stopped in to buy myself my own coming home dinner.

"Am I glad to hear that?"

I grinned. "Yeah. I'm trading up, Saul. Getting married this coming weekend to an amazing woman. Just got the ring today and thought I'd surprise her with a nice dinner. So of course I came here."

His lips curved ever so slightly under his thick moustache. "Then you came to the right place. What's she like?"

I thought. "Well, she's gorgeous, first. Smart. Funny. Tiny little thing. And she has the cutest little laugh. I swear, I can just hear it and—"

"I meant, what *cut* does she like," Saul interrupted, rolling his eyes.

"Oh. Oh yeah. Right. Of course." I felt like an idiot and cleared my throat, my eyes down again as I looked through the case filled with stacks of red meat. "Honestly, Saul, I have no idea. It hasn't come up." I shrugged helplessly. "What do you suggest?"

"I'm gonna give you two cuts for her and one for you," he said. "I'll be right back." After disappearing through the swinging door into the back of the shop, he returned a minute or two later. I'd been surveying the stacks of vegetables on kebobs. They'd work as a side. Then just shove a couple potatoes in the oven and I'd be golden.

"Here," he said from the counter by the register, setting down a tall stack of meat on white butcher paper. "Two tomahawk steaks. And if you overcook them, I swear to God they will tell me and I will hunt you down." I grinned. "And this," he continued, picking up a steak about three inches tall and round, with about a four-inch diameter. "A filet. Women like 'em. No idea why. They have no flavor."

He leaned closer, glancing around to see if anyone was listening. There were two other customers—a man and a woman, not together—and they were both browsing the aisles where Saul kept his marinades and sauces.

"Now, if she picks the filet," he said to me in a stage-whisper, "she's not gonna do that thing you like in bed." He paused, his lips curving into the closest thing I'd ever seen to a grin on his face. "But if she picks the tomahawk? You better be hydrated, cause she's gonna wring you dry."

Laughter burst from me at the unexpected advice and Saul chuffed a laugh, too. After wrapping up all the steaks, I reached for my wallet.

"What's the damage?"

But Saul waved me off. "No charge. Consider it a wedding gift." He winked.

Saul had smiled, laughed, and winked at me all in the same day. The world must be coming to an end.

I argued with him briefly, but he wasn't having any of it, and just ended up walking away without a word to help another customer. Now *that* was the Saul I knew.

Seeing another employee, I got him to sell me the kebobs I wanted before leaving. Once back in the truck, I locked the doors and carefully replaced the ring into its pretty blue box, though I had a hell of a time fixing the white bow. I had no idea why I was so paranoid about the ring. Paranoid and anxious and… nervous.

There was no reason for me to be nervous. She'd already said yes.

And yet…I was.

Shoving those feelings way down, I started the truck and drove out of the lot. Only another couple stops to go.

My ears were nearly ringing after listening to my mom all day. She'd gone on and on about Cal and how much Dad liked him. How happy she was that I'd found such a good man and that they'd be getting another grandbaby.

We'd gone over the flowers and tasted cake until I was stuffed. Since we were going simple, I'd wanted summer flowers that were colorful and aromatic. No roses. I'd had an antipathy for roses ever since Chad's passing. We decided on a dark chocolate cake with a raspberry filling and cream cheese icing. It was wonderfully decadent.

I closed the door to the garage and slipped out of my heels, nearly groaning in relief. My toes curled on the cool hardwood floor and I sighed. The best part of the day was finding my dress.

Originally, I hadn't planned on buying a fancy dress, but my mom had convinced me to go by the best bridal boutique in the city "just in case." Since she was driving, I didn't have much choice.

It had been patently obvious from the start that she'd called ahead. A lovely woman named Rose had met us with champagne for my mom and sparkling cider for me. I sent a look to my mom, who blithely ignored it.

"Let's see how it looks," she called from outside the dressing room. This was the fifth dress I'd put on and I couldn't move, mesmerized by my reflection in the full-length mirror.

"It's lovely on you," Rose said, fussing with the chapel-length train.

"Um, yeah. I like it." An understatement.

Stepping outside the room, my mom caught sight of me. She gasped and set aside her champagne flute. "Emerson, oh my goodness, it's absolutely perfect." Her eyes were wet which made mine start watering. Pregnancy hormones again? Check.

She'd bought the dress instantly, and I couldn't argue against it. The lure of happiness was too strong. Cal had immediately stepped up to the challenge. Which was what he did. What a man like him did.

It wasn't because he loved me.

Circumstances had thrown us together and now worked to keep us together. Not because he wanted to be with me. But because he had to. Just like he'd done with Lisa.

It was on that rather discouraging note that I entered the house, immediately confused by the lack of lights and the scent of grilled meat. Setting aside my shoes, I padded into the kitchen. I assumed Donny and Marie would be rushing to greet me, but they were MIA. When I walked into the kitchen, I saw why.

Slavering at his feet were my two traitors, begging for scraps from the mountain of sizzling meat on a tray.

"Mommy's home!" He headed for me, tray in hand, and kissed me. "You just have to tell me what kind of meat you want and dinner will be ready."

Feeling cheeky, I cupped the bulge in his jeans. "I prefer this kind of meat."

"Yes, please," he murmured, brushing his lips against my cheek. "These are for you."

Somehow, he brandished a bouquet of flowers. Not roses. They smelled wonderful.

We sat down to eat and it was fabulous. It took my mind off the things still bothering me about all of this. Cal had asked me what cut of meat I preferred and I'd selected one of the two tomahawk steaks on the platter. It was cooked perfectly. I was ravenous and ended up eating almost the whole thing.

We chatted a little during dinner and I kept it light. I didn't want to bring up his upcoming job and trip right now. It had been a really great day. I'd save that conversation for tomorrow. He'd entertained me by telling me about his trip to René's and to the butcher shop, making me laugh.

Afterwards, we sat outside on the deck, the evening descending and watching Donny and Marie wander about the yard. I curled my legs up onto the loveseat and leaned my head against his shoulder. Cal slowly rocked the slider back and forth.

"I need to trim those hedges before I leave," Cal absently said, taking another sip of the wine he'd had with dinner. I'd allowed myself one six-ounce glass, then switched to iced tea. He'd gone to the trouble of getting the wine and making the tea, saying you had to have a bit of red wine with red meat.

"Don't tell my mother," I'd warned him.

His talk of leaving made me stiffen slightly and I sat up, taking a swallow of my tea. The ice had melted in the summer heat so it was more just colored water now.

"What?" He looked at me in concern. "Are you all right? Do you feel okay?"

"I'm just still really on the fence about this new job of yours." There. I'd said it.

He took my hand. "I thought we'd agreed on a trial run."

"I know, it's just...it's making me anxious, thinking about you leaving. I'm pregnant, will have a fiancé and husband who'll be with me for barely a couple of weeks, then you'll be gone and I'll be alone." Lots of fears in that sentence, and I had deliberately not mentioned my fear of something happening to him, which would leave me a pregnant widow. Again.

"You won't be alone," he said. "Your mom and dad are here. Your friends are here. And you'll be *forced* to spend time with my mother." He added the last in a light, teasing way, but it didn't make me smile.

I turned to look at him. "It's not the same and you know it."

Cal just looked me for a minute, his gaze serious.

"I have something for you," he said. "I'll be right back."

With that abrupt change of subject, he got up and went inside. I had no idea what was going on and I rubbed a tired hand across my face, my heart heavy despite the lovely day.

In a moment, Cal had returned, startling me. He moved so quietly, despite his size. Without a word, he knelt on one knee in front of me. A hand was behind his back and now he brought out something and held it out for me.

My breath caught in my chest and my eyes widened in shock.

A blue box. An unmistakably blue box that came from only one place on the planet.

Tiffany's.

"Cal. Oh my god, what did you do?" My voice was a mere whisper.

"Open it," he insisted. His smile was wide but tentative, as if he wasn't sure of my reaction.

We hadn't discussed rings. I knew things were tight for him and I was getting him one of those titanium rings that were indestructible, considering where he'd be going and what he'd be doing. This was a complete surprise.

I took the box and tears lingered in my eyes. I had no idea what he'd done to buy a ring from the best jeweler on the planet, and I wasn't going to ask.

Carefully, prolonging the moment, I tugged at the white bow, which looked a little lopsided. Not that I cared. I lifted the lid and stared at the velvet box inside. Tipping the box, the velvet one fell out into my hand. I set aside the bow and box, knowing that this kind of moment for a woman was once in a lifetime. Well, I hoped it would be.

I lifted the lid and again, couldn't breathe.

Inside was a platinum ring with a center diamond, surrounded by two rings of smaller diamonds. It was not round, but square with rounded edges. And it wasn't small. It was gorgeous and I had a hard time believing it. Even in the dwindling light, it sparkled.

I stared for several moments, just taking it in.

"Do you like it?" Cal's voice was anxious.

Looking up at him, I was surprised again. How could he think I wouldn't like it? I'd be a fool not to.

"Cal. I love it. It's the most beautiful thing I've ever seen."

The anxiety left his face and his smile was wide. Taking the box from me, he removed the ring and lifted my left hand.

"I can't wait to marry you," he said, sliding the ring onto my finger. It fit perfectly. Why was I not surprised at that?

He leaned forward and kissed me, a sweet, lovely kiss.

That night we made love, and I didn't bring up his job again.

"Mac agreed to come to the wedding," Cal said the next morning as I was nibbling on some toast. Today hadn't been as bad and I'd gotten ready for work, but I still treated my stomach like a temperamental toddler.

He was sitting beside me at the kitchen table, having coffee while I sipped decaf tea. I missed coffee. Sigh.

"I asked him to be my Best Man," he continued. "Two birds. One stone. Is that okay?"

"Oh, yeah, sure. I didn't realize you wanted a Best Man." I didn't know if I'd want to thank Mac or strangle him. Cal had told me that a generous signing bonus had been responsible for the lovely ring that I spent way too much time staring at on my finger.

"Well, I thought since Carly is your Maid of Honor, I should have someone, too."

"Well, good. I'm glad you have someone." Even if I might strangle the Best Man at some point.

"And Amber is going to look adorable in that little dress you picked out," he continued.

"My mom wants to do a dinner for the reception," I said, changing the subject. Cal frowned.

"How much is that going to cost us?"

I shrugged. I'd given up on reigning in my mother. I had other things to worry about. 'Nothing. Mom and Dad want to pick up the tab. I'm going to let them." I took a few more nibbles. Almost had the whole piece down now without any nausea making me regret it. "Do you care what the menu is?"

"I'm not a huge fan of fish, but it's your call."

The mere thought of fish had me setting down the rest of my toast and taking a large drink of tea. My stomach hadn't liked the thought of the smell and texture of fish.

"No fish," I agreed.

"What are you doing today?" I asked. I was heading back to work and had a court appearance this morning.

Cal hesitated before answering. "Mac sent over some things I need to review." He rushed on. "Then I'm taking Amber go-carting. Probably ice cream will be involved."

"I'm glad to hear Lisa's parents are being reasonable."

After the initial clash, they'd been models of cooperation. So long as they had fifty-fifty visitation, which Cal hadn't argued with. I assumed Lisa would be sharing in that visitation, though she seemed pretty wrapped up in her new relationship. Whatever.

Not my monkeys, not my circus. Though I was looking forward to spending more time with Amber. She was a sweet little girl.

"Thanks to you." He leaned over and kissed my forehead. "Ready to go?"

"Yeah, just let me get my things."

Cal now insisted on driving me to and from work, explaining that while we hadn't heard anything from the stalker in months, that didn't mean he could let up his guard.

"I'm going to hire Greg's company to actively monitor your video feeds while I'm gone," he casually dropped while we were on our way.

"Excuse me? I already have a stalker." I was half-kidding.

"It'll make me feel better."

Well, I couldn't argue with that, so I let it go. "Okay," I said with a shrug. "If you think it's best." He was worried about me. It was nice to have someone worry about me like that.

He glanced over at me as he drove, and a visceral part of my mind took note of how gorgeous he was. He'd dressed in a T-shirt that hugged his arms and shoulders, with jeans that clung to his ass. He rested one wrist on top of the steering wheel and his hair was thick. He'd already informed me that he'd have to get it cut very short, which I'd not been happy about.

He dropped me off with a long kiss goodbye, that had my fingernails curling around the back of his neck. He smelled incredible. I finally pulled away in disappointment.

"Better go," I said. "Have fun with Amber."

"Have fun in court." He winked.

There was a spring in my step as I walked inside and I couldn't resist stopping to show Karen my ring. She properly *oohed* and *aahed* while I preened. Then it was a complete blur of work all morning until I was rushing across the street at eleven-thirty to be in court. I arrived breathless.

"You're late," the judge said, his irritation obvious. He was a new appointee and we hadn't established a relationship yet.

"My apologies, Your Honor." I hurriedly set my things on the plaintiff side and nodded at opposing counsel, a lawyer named Janice Craft whom I'd gone up against several times. We'd even had a few business lunches. She was a good attorney and she sent me a quick smile.

Glancing around the courtroom, I saw that Ronnie, the bailiff, was present and the court reporter was the Ken-not-Kenny who'd asked me out so long ago. He'd been in several of my court cases since then, but hadn't ever again addressed me, just went about doing his job.

This case was again one of those that I wished I hadn't bothered going to law school for, and since I didn't know the judge, this would be a rough one. And probably embarrassing. Janice probably felt the exact same way.

I represented the wife of a nasty divorce from her husband of sixteen years. They had no children, thank goodness, but the husband was very wealthy. She'd caught him cheating on her and she was a tad...vindictive. Not that I blamed her.

"Your Honor," Janice began, standing. "My client

requests that the doorknobs, drawer pulls, and cabinet knobs all be returned to his home which the plaintiff has removed. Every single door, cabinet, and drawer in the entire home has had its hardware removed."

The judge's eyebrows climbed, but he said nothing.

I stood. "Your Honor," I said. "My client does not admit to doing such a thing. However, if she had, the home is currently still her property as well, and after the defendant left her prized koi fish—valued at approximately $100,000—on the front porch to die, she may have felt a small retribution was in order. And we'd like to add the value of those koi into the divorce settlement."

Okay, so the husband was a tad vindictive, too. Though I had to give them both props for creativity. The house was over six thousand square feet. That was a *lot* of doorknobs, drawer pulls and cabinet knobs. I had no idea how long it had taken her, and I hadn't asked.

The judge closed his eyes for a moment, and I didn't blame him. Ken-not-Kenny even smothered a snicker.

"Those koi were joint property and it was an accident—"

"How in the world could fish on the porch be an accident?" The judge interrupted.

I kinda wanted to know the answer to that, too. There had been six fish and they hadn't been small. My client had cried for days, and I'd had to play therapist—a role relatively common for a divorce attorney.

Janice cleared her throat and glanced down, her cheeks reddening. I felt for her.

"The killing of the koi also represented an emotional loss to my client," I added. In for a penny, in for a pound. "Knowing that they died in such a cruel and inhumane fashion—"

The judge cut me off, too.

"I've heard enough. Counselor, what do you propose?"

He was talking to me.

I cleared my throat. "Your Honor, we're proposing the hundred thousand in actual loss with an additional two hundred thousand in punitive damages, all added into the already agreed upon settlement."

"What about my knobs?" The husband had shot to his feet, red in the face and livid. He was a short, portly man, balding, wearing an ill-fitting suit. My client was a statuesque blonde who was in her fifties and had clearly kept herself in prime condition. Why he'd want to cheat on her was beyond me, much less how he'd found someone to cheat on her *with*. Well...I guess he had money, so...

The judge banged his gavel. "Keep your client in check, counselor."

Janice spoke in a hushed whisper to the husband who finally sat back down. I struggled to suppress a grin. I didn't see what was so special about the knobs—he could afford to replace them—but maybe it was the principle of the thing? Who knew?

"I'm ordering an additional amount totaling two hundred thousand added to the settlement," the judge said. He raised an eyebrow. "We'll split the difference over the...knobs."

I could tell by the dryness of his tone that this case had probably made him regret going to law school, too.

He banged his gavel and that was that. I congratu-
lated my client—it was more than I'd thought we'd
get—then turned to Janice. Her client had already
stormed out of the courtroom.

It was lunch and the judge was about to depart, so
I took my time gathering my things before I walked
over to her.

"Worth the student loans?" I asked, joking. Janice
just gave a wry laugh.

"Another day in paradise."

"We need to do lunch again sometime," I said,
then added. "I have some news." I couldn't keep the
shit-eating grin from my face.

She glanced up from packing away her papers.
"What news?"

I didn't answer, just held up my left hand. She
gasped.

"Oh my god, you're getting married!" She grabbed
my hand. "And look at that rock. Wow. That's gotta
be Tiffany's."

"Yep."

Janice laughed and gave me a tight hug. "Congratulations, Emmy. I'm so happy for you." Pulling
back, she added, "And yes, we definitely need to have
lunch. I want to hear all about it. Call me, okay?"

After a promise to call, she headed down the aisle
and I turned to follow, only to be nearly startled
out of my wits. Ken-not-Kenny was standing right
behind me, his face stricken.

"You're getting married?"

He was a bit too close, and I instinctively stepped
back. "Um, yeah, Ken." I nearly bit my tongue when

I wanted to say *Kenny.* "Next weekend." I forced a stiff smile.

"Oh."

He sounded crestfallen and I immediately felt bad. But what was I supposed to say?

"Well, uh, congratulations, I guess."

"Thank you." The words came automatically. Then we just sort of awkwardly stood there. Finally, I said, "Well. I need to go. Have a good afternoon."

He just nodded and walked back to his desk, pulling out a small lunchbox from underneath and sitting down to eat. I wondered if he did that every day, ate by himself in an empty courtroom. Maybe he was afraid he'd miss the opening of the afternoon session?

Pushing aside the weirdness that was Ken-not-Kenny, I headed back to the office. I still had a stack of work to do before Cal came to pick me up.

At that thought, I smiled. I was marrying a good man—a gorgeous, gentle, hard-working man—in just a few days. I'd be a bride and wife and mother. And I was going to focus on the good this week, even if it killed me. Even if it felt like the past was repeating itself—for him *and* for me.

Friday. Finally. I'd had to work up until the last minute and then had an urgent call from one of my clients and then this and then that and ended up having to call Cal to tell him I had to work late.

"You do realize it's our wedding eve," he said, teasing.

"I know, I know, but I'm going to be off so I'm try-

ing to tie up some loose ends so no one bothers us."
I paused. "I hope you'll be keeping me busy doing
other things." My own teasing. Part of my head was
just trying to wrap itself around the fact that I was
getting married tomorrow.

"Yeah, sure. I really think that we need to orga-
nize the garage. I bought some stuff that will hang
tools on the walls, you know. They even have these
little shape outlines so you can figure out what goes
where."

I laughed. "Jerk."

"Yep." He laughed, too. "Okay, so gimme a time. I
do need to run by the auto store. I want to change
the oil in your car. It's about due."

Change the oil in my car. He was going to do that
for me. It seemed utterly ridiculous, but my eyes
stung. I cleared my throat.

"Another hour?" If I worked fast and didn't answer
any after-hours phone calls.

"Gotcha."

We hung up and I got to work.

I was so involved in the brief I was typing—I don't
know how much time had passed—when I heard the
soft chime of the alarm system in the hallway that
always sounded when the front door opened. Shit.
That must be Cal. And I wasn't quite done. Well, he
wouldn't mind giving me another fifteen minutes or
so.

I felt more than saw him in the doorway and I kept
my eyes on the screen, typing furiously.

"Almost done," I said. "Just like another fifteen
maybe? That okay?"

No answer. It took me a moment to realize he

hadn't spoken. I glanced up, then promptly stopped breathing.

It was Ken-not-Kenny. And he stood in my office, dressed...in a tuxedo that looked to be from the seventies. It was powder blue with black trim, a black bowtie (poorly tied), and one of those ruffled vest things. There was even a white rose tucked into the lapel.

I gaped. His hair had been slicked back with some kind of gel or oil. It shone in the fluorescent lighting. In his hands, he carried a small bouquet of matching roses...and a pistol. A pistol that looked as though it, too, had been made in the seventies. It had a long barrel and an ivory-inlaid grip. His hand shook slightly, which set off the remaining alarm bells that hadn't yet started ringing.

"Ken—,"-ny, I finished in my head but managed not to say. "Um, what...what are you doing here?" My voice sounded too weak. "And, um, why are you dressed like that?" My fingers were frozen over the keyboard. I didn't dare say anything about the gun, but that's where my gaze was.

"You're not marrying that guy," he said, his voice shaking as much as his hand. "You're marrying me."

Oh, dear lord. *Kenny* was my stalker? But...how? I wouldn't have thought in a million years that he had it in him.

"It was you?" I asked. "You broke into my house? Slashed my tires? Left that awful Barbie?"

"You were supposed to be scared and let me comfort you. Take you out. You were supposed to love me." He seemed near tears and despite everything, I felt a twinge of pity. Then I thought of the unborn life inside me that he was also threatening...then not so much.

"That's not how it works, Ken," I said, able to keep my voice calm due to years of dealing with emotional, erratic clients. "How could you do those things to me? I thought we were friends."

Perhaps some psychological manipulation would help the situation, cause him to give me the gun. Slowly, I sat back in my chair and set my feet flat on the floor. My chair had wheels. If need be, I could push it left or right and perhaps throw off his aim should things go...awry. I felt a hysterical laugh bubbling up at the word choice in my head and swallowed it down.

"I didn't *want* to do those things. I don't think those things about you. You're perfect and good and you help people." He was whining now, and the areas underneath his armpits were growing dark with sweat. Great. This was bad. This was very bad.

"I do help people, Ken, and I've always been nice to you. You don't want to hurt me."

"These are for you." He eased forward just enough to be able to awkwardly toss the roses onto my desk. I didn't try to catch them, just remained where I was. "They're white."

Duh. No shit. I could see that.

My mouth was dry and my heart was racing, but I was also furious. How dare he? How dare he break into my home, try to scare me (and succeeding), and now threaten me and my baby? My hands curled into fists, freshly manicured nails biting into my palms. I wanted to take that gun and beat him over the head with it.

"How thoughtful of you," I managed, forcing my lips into a smile. "Did you bring a ring, too?"

He looked momentarily perplexed. "A what?"

"A ring," I said, as though it were obvious. "If I'm going to marry you, you have to give me a ring. Did you bring one?" If I could just stall for time, Cal would get here and take this sonofabitch down.

"Um, I, well, I don't have the money—"

"Because without a ring, it's not legal, you know."

"What?"

"Yeah. It's an Indiana state law. That's why all married people have to wear rings in public." Bullshit bullshit bullshit. But whatever. I was doing the talking and he wasn't, that's all that mattered. "And we'd have to get a license first. You have to wait three days from when you apply for a license before you can get married."

Kenny just stared at me, mouth slightly open. His hand had stopped shaking and the gun barrel drooped slightly, which I saw as a Good Thing.

"And I'll need a dress," I continued, babbling away. I slid a sideway glance at the lower right corner of my computer screen. It had been an hour. And Cal was nothing if not punctual. Thank you, Army.

Then I remembered. The door. The alarm. It would chime when he opened it. Kenny would hear it.

Oh God.

The slight ease I had felt when I saw the time evaporated. Kenny would hear and would know it was Cal coming to get me. No doubt he'd been watching us come and go this past week. He knew my car wasn't in the lot.

Kenny's eyes narrowed and the gun righted itself, pointing straight at me.

"He's coming, isn't he." It wasn't a question. "I saw your light on, saw you were working late, and took my chance. But he's coming." Kenny smiled. It wasn't a nice smile, and it sent a chill down my spine. "He won't even know I'm here when he walks in."

I felt like I couldn't breathe. Cal would be walking straight into a trap.

As though our mention of it had made it reality, the chime sounded. I started at the sound, my gaze flying to the doorway behind Kenny, then back to him.

"Make a sound and I'll shoot you," he said softly. His hand was rock steady now. He moved to the side of the doorway opposite the direction from which Cal would come down the hallway.

If it was just me, I wouldn't care. I'd scream my lungs out. But it wasn't just me. The baby needed me. And I knew Cal would choose my saving our baby over him in a second.

Helpless tears filled my eyes and I had never hated anyone so much as I hated Kenny in that moment. And the moment stretched and stretched...and stretched. I kept waiting for Cal to appear, to hear his footsteps in the hallway. But there was nothing.

Kenny seemed to be confused as well, his weight shifting from one foot to another. He had on some cheap, white dress shoes that squeaked slightly. A moronic psychopath with absurdly bad fashion taste. At least I should've deserved a stalker that knew vintage tuxedos were not a good look.

We waited. I barely breathed. My whole body was

bathed in a cold sweat and I trembled slightly. Adrenaline. My hands were still in fists and I made myself
open them and take deep breaths. The last thing I
needed was to hyperventilate.

I could tell that Kenny was getting impatient. His
face was locked in a grimace as he focused on the
empty doorway.

Suddenly, there was a blur as Cal swept past the
door, tossing something inside. It hit the floor and
rolled toward us.

"Duck!"

Cal's call out hit my ears and my brain worked
faster than Kenny's, who just stood there, staring at
the small, metal object. In a flash, I was down, underneath my desk, instinctively covering my ears and
squeezing my eyes shut.

The noise was so loud, my ears rang, despite my
covering them. I made myself as small as I could,
drawing my knees to my chest. I felt more than heard
something hit the floor on the other side of the desk,
then a muffled sound like a gunshot. It was hard to
tell since my hearing was so impaired. Another gunshot. Then nothing.

I didn't move. Did Kenny manage to shoot Cal?
What if he was injured? Should I get up and see?

Before I could decide, Cal was there, crouching by
me and reaching to pull me out from underneath the
desk.

"It's okay now," he said. I could understand him.
My hearing was returning. "You're safe."

I flung myself into his arms, knocking him back on
his ass. I didn't care. I was sobbing and curled up on

his lap, my arms in a stranglehold around his neck. He held me close and kept talking in my ear, telling me it was okay, over and over, until I finally believed him.

chapter eighteen

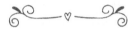

THE WEDDING DAY arrived and I paced the small room they'd assigned me within the chapel. Last night hadn't exactly been ideal for a wedding eve. After Em had calmed down, I'd called 911 and done all the things when the police had arrived. Em hadn't left my side, her hand holding mine in a vice grip.

Kenny was in the hospital under guard, recovering from a gunshot wound to the abdomen. When I'd arrived, I'd seen him on the video feed that I automatically checked when I came to pick up Em every day. My blood had run cold when I saw him in her office, gun trained on her as she sat behind her desk. I'd thrown a flashbang into the office, hoping Em would heed my call to duck. It wouldn't hurt her if she didn't, but it would be slightly less unpleasant if she did.

As designed, the flashbang went off, startling and disorienting Kenny enough for me to get in and take him down. He'd instinctively pulled the trigger, but the gun hadn't been aimed at anything in particular and the bullet went wide. Mine had not.

I hadn't particularly cared if he lived or died, but Em insisted on calling 911 and the paramedics had stabilized him. The cops had come and taken copies of the video feed which clearly showed Kenny threatening Em.

After all was said and done and I'd brought Em home, she'd been remarkably calm. Serene, even. I'd asked her if she was okay.

"Actually, I feel good, knowing the answer to who the stalker was and that I don't have to worry anymore. I feel bad about Kenny. I didn't want him to be hurt."

"He'll be okay, then he'll go to jail." My bullet hadn't killed him, and I was a little disappointed it hadn't.

We'd gone upstairs and gone to bed like any other night, and if Em had cuddled a bit closer than usual, I hadn't minded.

Yet today, as I paced, I couldn't help memories that assailed me of when I'd married Lisa...and how terribly that had ended.

But it wasn't going to be that way with Em. She was different. *We* were different.

And yet...

I shoved a hand through my hair and went back to pacing.

A sharp knock on the door, and I stopped mid-step. The door swung open and a man I knew very well strode in.

"Mac." I grinned, letting out a breath. Relief flooded me. Another man I could actually relate to.

Shane was great and all (though he hadn't exactly been effusive in his congratulations when I'd told him), but Mac was a different kind of man. He was someone I greatly respected. A man of honor and intelligence. I couldn't have chosen better.

Mac grinned back, a dimple in his cheek, his teeth white against his tanned skin.

"Congratulations, Cal," he said, clasping my hand in a firm grip.

"Thank you for doing this," I replied, shaking his hand. He'd even brought his own tuxedo. I was glad I'd chosen him to stand up with me at my second— and hopefully last—wedding.

Where had that pessimistic thought come from?

"It's my honor. And I've met your bride." He cocked an eyebrow. "Quite the looker. Though I'm not sure I'm her favorite person."

"She's not thrilled with the new job." I briefly explained about Chopper, his deployment, Em's pregnancy, and Chopper's death. "She fears the past repeating itself."

Mac's face had turned grim as I spoke. "Don't we all."

Neither of us were strangers to the horrors of war and we shared a look between us that said more than words possibly could. We'd both lost buddies and seen life-altering injuries. Some of those memories, I never wanted to think or talk about ever again.

"You're not going to be anywhere terribly dangerous, this time out," Mac said. "The company that hired us just wants an added layer of protection. Better safe than sorry."

"I'm not worried." The only thing I was worried

about was leaving Em by herself. I resumed pacing while Mac settled himself into a distinctly uncomfortable-looking chair with a wooden-spindle back and a pad on the seat that looked paper-thin.

I needed to talk, and I knew *Mac* knew I needed to talk, but he didn't say anything. He just waited. He was good like that. Patient.

After a few more laps, I opened my mouth and the words fell out. "You know, Lisa and I had to get married. She got pregnant. It was the right thing to do."

"Yeah." Mac's response was noncommittal and nonjudgmental. And he waited some more.

"Em's not the only one who feels like the past is repeating itself." There. I'd said it. Something I'd barely even allowed myself to think, much less voice aloud.

"Yeah." This time Mac's reply held a bit of a sigh. Again. He was very British. Understated. Understanding, not judgmental. After a moment, he said, "You know, you don't have to get married right now, Cal. It's not nineteen-fifty anymore. You've only known this woman a few months, correct? You can wait, give it some time."

But I was already shaking my head. "That's not me, man. She's having my kid. And I care about her. A lot."

"Care." Mac snorted a bit. "Don't bend over backwards there, mate. Do you love her or not? Because we're talking the rest of your life here. I know you hated getting that fucking divorce and I sure as hell know you don't want another one. So shit or get off the pot."

His tone had turned hard and commanding, which

pushed me over the fence I'd been sitting on. I stopped pacing and stood in front of him.

"I'm marrying her. And it's going to last this time. Because she deserves it." I'd do everything in my power to make Em happy.

"You deserve it, too," Mac insisted. "And I seriously doubt she'd want you to marry her out of obligation. Women tend to not like that sort of thing."

"We're good together. We'll figure it out." I felt a new resolve this time when I said it. Em and I were both grown adults. Lisa and I had been too young and immature. Em knew what she was getting into, and I'd promised her this job would be on a trial basis.

"Here." I handed him the matching wedding band I'd purchased when I'd gotten Em's engagement ring. Mac tucked it into the inside pocket of his jacket.

Just then, there was a polite knock on the door before the preacher poked his head in. He smiled.

"It's time."

Taking a deep breath, I left the room, Mac in tow. We followed the preacher to the doorway leading to the front of the church by the altar and took our places.

The preacher stood to my right, exuding peace, a small smile on his face. He was on the shorter side—maybe five-ten—and looked to be in his mid-sixties with a sparse head of gray hair and kind eyes.

The aroma of flowers filled the small chapel. Em's mom had hired someone to decorate and they'd done really well, adorning the end of each pew with a bouquet that cascaded in a waterfall all the way to the floor. The place looked pretty and sunlight filtered in through the stained glass windows. Two candelabras flanked the altar, the candles flickering.

There were a couple dozen people there—people from Em's work, her friends and her parents. My mom and sister were there, too. My mother looked radiant, her smile wide when she caught my eye. We'd foregone the whole processional other than Amber, Carly, and Em herself. Our parents hadn't minded. They'd already done the thing once.

Again, I was struck that this was the second time around. Was I making the right decision?

My palms were sweating. That hadn't happened since I was a teenager. The tux's bow tie felt like a noose and I slipped a finger in between the collar and my neck, tugging a little. I swallowed. My throat was dry.

A pianist began playing. I didn't recognize the song. It wasn't a traditional wedding processional song. It struck me that Em was probably fighting her own feelings of doubt and déjà vu.

The doors to the chapel opened simultaneously and Amber stepped into view. I smiled and felt my body relax at the sight of her. Em had somehow gotten her a dress that fit perfectly, the color a sweet cream. Her hair was curled around her shoulders and a crown made of tiny flowers sat atop her head. She carried a basket and when she saw me, she grinned.

"Daddy!"

Everyone heard her and soft laughter echoed in the chapel. A woman appeared behind Amber and whispered in her ear. Amber's face took on a determined expression and she set about walking down the aisle, scattering more of the tiny flowers that were in her hair. I didn't know what they were, just that they were white and looked delicate.

When she got to the end of the aisle, she grinned at me again, then went to sit in the front pew with my mom and sister, settling in between them.

Carly was next, looking elegant in a gown the color of the ocean in the tropics, more green than blue, and the long skirt swirled around her legs, slightly transparent. She carried a bouquet of flowers that matched those decorating the pews. Her smile was serene and her walk steady.

The tune on the piano changed slightly, becoming more...majestic was the only word I could think of to describe it. The doors to the chapel opened again and I forgot to breathe.

Em stood there, dressed in a gown that took her from beautiful straight into enchanted princess.

It wasn't white, but more the color of champagne. It was sleeveless, baring her shoulders and with a neckline that dipped between her breasts, showing a hint of her lovely cleavage without being tacky. Although it didn't have sleeves, it did, they were just made of some kind of see-through material and started at her upper arms and went to her wrists, with elaborate lace adorning the tops and wrists.

The fabric clung to her curves to mid-thigh, before flaring out into the skirt and short train. The train looked to be made of the same champagne fabric, but that transparent stuff with more lace around the edges.

Her gorgeous red hair had been left down and lay in waves over one shoulder. The same flowers that had been in Amber's hair were fastened in hers. The contrast of the deep mahogany of her hair against the champagne color of the dress was striking. She didn't look like a blushing bride. She looked...like the very epitome of a classy, elegant, voluptuous woman.

And she was mine.

Doubts fled and I only had eyes for her.

Em had decided she wanted to give herself away rather than having her father walk her down the aisle, and that spoke volumes about the woman I was marrying. She was confident in and of herself, and that was a helluva turn-on.

Every step seemed to be in slow motion and it felt like an eternity before she finally stood beside me. Our gazes met and I saw just a flicker of doubt in hers which, oddly enough, made me feel better. She was my bride. It was my job to reassure her. Her smile had turned tentative.

The piano tune was wrapping up and I stepped closer to her so she'd be able to hear me speak but no one else could.

"You are the most beautiful thing I've ever seen."

Her smile turned real and I saw her shoulders relax. The green of her eyes was a deep emerald and they sparkled in the fading sunlight, the candles' glow making her skin look like cream.

"You clean up pretty well yourself."

I grinned at her teasing and winked. To my surprise and delight, her cheeks blushed, and I was utterly charmed.

The rest of the ceremony was a blur, with vague impressions of repeating vows and sliding a ring onto her slim finger. I hoped she liked the matching band. She seemed to. She'd gotten me a ring as well, which was black and silver, though I bet they were both titanium, judging by the light weight.

Everything went by in a blur until I heard the words, "You may kiss your bride."

You know, that's a lot of pressure on a man. The kiss. It has to be memorable. Like a first kiss. This would be the first kiss to start the rest of our life together.

I pulled Em toward me and bent her over one arm, the other curved around her back. And I kissed her.

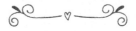

I would remember Cal's kiss for the rest of my life. I knew that immediately. As I would always remember the way he looked at me when I'd walked down the aisle, as though Christmas had arrived early. He'd given me the confidence to take each step toward him, when I was quaking on the inside. Memories of Chad had assailed me prior to the ceremony, but they finally felt put to rest, and Cal had done that.

Doubt had plagued me this week. I'd never thought I'd fall into the category of "had to get married because I got knocked up." And honestly, it wasn't as though I *had* to marry Cal. We had something special between us, even if our relationship hadn't exactly been conventional so far.

We did all the things. Greeted the guests—I was gratified to see so many of my work colleagues there, even a judge or two as well as Ronnie the bailiff—threw the bouquet, had dinner, then cut the cake (Cal decided he really liked the choice I'd made for the flavor). We mingled with the guests as white uniform clad servers moved through the crowd, carrying trays of champagne flutes. The aroma of the chapel's hydrangeas hung heavy in the air and the twinkly lights on the gazebo looked enchanting as the sunlight faded.

My mother had hired a deejay—though she'd sniffed in disdain at not having proper musicians for the dancing, but I'd insisted on keeping at least that part simple—and he played classical music during dinner. Then it was time for our first dance.

I hadn't known what song to choose. Had no clue. So I'd gone with just a generic love song that the deejay had suggested. My mom caught my eye and nodded, signaling it was time. I turned to Cal.

"Ready to dance?"

His eyes were soft as he gazed at me. He'd impressed me tonight, easily melding into conversation with people he didn't know and charming them. I could tell he was liked by those I'd introduced him to, even the austere judges. The partners already knew him, of course, from his work at the firm. And Cal had always kept a touch on me. His hand on my elbow, or my lower back, taking my hand...never more than an arm's length away.

I felt cherished and protected. It was a wonderful, warm feeling that I hadn't had in a very long time.

"Isn't that my line?" he teased. He was holding my hand, his thumb lightly caressing my knuckles and brushing across my engagement ring and now wedding band as well. "Is the gazebo appropriately *Twilight*-ish?" He tugged me a bit closer and those milling around us discreetly gave us space, talking and laughing as they sipped champagne.

I laughed. "Yes, actually, it is. And sorry. My mother is giving the The Look."

"Well, I wouldn't want to tick off my new mother-in-law." I was close enough now that he rested his other hand on the curve of my waist and gazed down at me, his lips curved in a smile that made my breath catch. "Mrs. Mackenzie, may I have this dance?"

I liked the sound of that. I raised an eyebrow in pretend aloofness. "Yes, you may."

His soft laugh wrapped around me as he led me to the large gazebo. It was almost an exact replica from the movie and I could see that it was probably a big attraction to have a wedding at this chapel (the cost hadn't exactly been cheap). It was very romantic.

Cal assisted me up the stairs to the empty dance floor and the twinkly lights were perfect. Mom had made sure that the same floral theme from inside the chapel had been used to decorate the gazebo as well. She'd chosen wisely, the flowers' aroma drifting around us.

Once we were in the center, Cal drew me into his arms. "I hope you don't mind, but I changed the song," he said.

My eyebrows flew upward. "Really?" What could he possibly have chosen?

"Really."

The beginning of a piano playing came over the speakers and it took me a few moments to recognize the song. Cal was turning us slowly on the dance floor, swaying slightly. My left hand was in his right and his other hand rested on my lower back, He held me close as he led the dance, gazing down at me with a look in his eye that I could only describe as...

adoring. I met his eyes and it felt as though we were the only people in the entire world. The lyrics of the song drifted over me.

Just another love song from a simple man
I been searching for some chords underneath these hands
So I can try to tell you I love you

My breath caught. He'd chosen this song. Did he mean it? Did Cal love me? Did I love him? But Cal's eyes were unreadable.

I am yours
Now and always
Wouldn't dream to be anything more
You take my breath away every night
Still can't believe it when you say you're mine and
I am yours, I am yours, I am yours

My eyes filled, touched beyond words that Cal had chosen a song for us, and one that was so beautifully romantic and vulnerable. Despite my trying to blink them back, one tear escaped and slid down my cheek. Cal let go of my hand and brushed it away, then placed a kiss to my cheek where it had fallen without saying a word.

The dance was over too soon and the deejay launched into another tune where Carly, Mac, and my parents joined us on the dance floor. Then Cal danced with his mom while I danced with my dad and the time flew by.

The reception was over in a few hours after that and the guests gradually departed. His mom and sister both hugged me tightly and I saw my dad give Cal a hearty handshake and clap on the back. My mom allowed him to give her a peck on the cheek and then it was just myself, Cal, and the catering staff cleaning up. We'd elected not to do the whole going away thing since we'd decided to delay our honeymoon indefinitely out of necessity.

"Well," I said, staring at the retreating taillights of my parents' car, "I guess that's done." I wasn't sure what else to say. I felt unaccountably awkward, which was strange. We'd been together, obviously. We'd been living together for weeks. Yet I found myself feeling shy, an emotion I hadn't experienced in a long time.

Cal's hand reached for mine, interlacing our fingers. "So it is."

He tugged gently and I moved closer, tipping my head back to look up at him. I gave in to my urge to press against him, resting my hands on his shoulders.

He smelled good. Cologne with the scent of his skin, damp with some sweat due to the heat and humidity. It was still technically summer in Indiana, though the weather had smiled on us today with milder temperatures.

"How are you feeling?" he asked, his fingers lightly sweeping my cheek. I knew he didn't mean physically.

I thought about it. I'd had doubts, but they were quiet now, smothered underneath a blanket of contentment. Cal was my husband. He would take care of both myself and our baby.

"I'm good," I said with a smile. "I'm happy."

That must have been the right thing to say because his face lit up with a wide smile. Without warning, he swept me up in his arms, making me squeal then laugh. I hooked an arm around his neck. "How did you know my feet were hurting from these shoes?"

"I'm thoughtful like that."

He carried me to where I'd parked earlier today when I'd arrived. Mac had driven Cal in his rental. Setting my feet on the ground, he dug in his pocket for the keys, then unlocked and opened the door. I eased into the passenger seat, Cal helping me make sure my dress was all inside before shutting the door. In a moment, he was climbing behind the wheel. He started the car.

And we went home. *Our* home.

chapter nineteen

CAL LEFT AT five in the morning nine days later. We'd had the week and one weekend before he'd had to leave. I dreaded his leaving with every breath I took.

We didn't talk about it and pretended it wasn't happening. Instead, we closed ourselves off from the world and spent every moment together. We made love, cooked and ate—sometimes at the table, sometimes in bed—made love some more. The television was never turned on. Phones were turned off.

We christened nearly every room in the house—including the kitchen counter, which I'd never look at the same way again—but I drew the line in my formal sitting room. Grandma's quilt lay over that particular couch and it seemed sacrilegious.

The night before Cal left, I lay in his arms afterwards, unable to sleep. It seemed he felt the same because he lightly stroked my back as I lay draped naked across his chest, my head on his shoulder. He stared at the dark ceiling. Closing my eyes, I savored the rise and fall of his chest.

Neither of us had said the words. *I love you.* The song had been lovely and had meant a lot to me, but it wasn't enough for me to say it first. I was self-aware enough to know that I was afraid. If I took that final step, would I jinx it? Would I lose him? What if he'd done all of this out of a sense of duty and he just really liked me a lot? His life had changed drastically in the past several months. I knew military men could roll with change better than most, but it had been a lot.

The clock downstairs tolled the hour. Three in the morning. He'd have to get up in an hour or so. Shower and shave. Finish packing. He hadn't packed much. I imagined that he wouldn't need many civilian clothes, that Mac would outfit him in his kit once he was deployed.

At the word—*deployed*—my breath caught and I felt my heart begin to speed up. The beginnings of a panic attack. I'd learned to recognize the signs and deliberately took a deep breath, holding it, then releasing. Just breathe. After a minute or two, my heartrate eased.

Somehow, Cal must've known. His other arm came around to enclose me in an embrace. I felt his lips brush the top of my head.

"It'll be okay," he whispered. "Get some sleep."

And I tried to believe him.

Leaving Em was one of the hardest things I've ever had to do. I'd said goodbye to Amber Saturday when she'd spent the night. She'd be there with Em every

couple of weeks, which I was grateful for. I wanted
her to know she was just as much mine and Em's as
the baby would be. And she was so excited to see Em's
tummy rounding ever so slightly. I let Em address her
questions on how the baby would grow and "come
out." I'd decided that was an excellent time to grab a
beer from the fridge.

Zipping up the carryon suitcase, I glanced at Em,
who was perched on the edge of the bed, watching
me. Her expression was carefully blank but she held
herself as though any sudden movement might break
her. A sharp pain struck my chest. I was the one hurting her by leaving, and yet...I had to provide for my
family, and this was the only way I knew how.

"It's about that time," I said quietly. She nodded.

"I could've driven you to the airport."

I shook my head. "It's too early and Mac's sending
a car anyway. But thanks."

Her eyes were on the suitcase and my gut twisted.
There was nothing more I could say or do to make
this any easier. Without a word, I carried the suitcase
downstairs, Em trailing behind me.

The morning sickness had passed, which was good.
That would make me worry slightly less about not
being there to help her. My mom had agreed that
she'd be glad to pop in every week and check on Em,
see how she was doing.

Disarming the alarm, I opened the front door and
glanced outside. Sure enough, a black car sat idling in
the driveway. It was still an hour until sunrise.

I'd done this before, left home for deployment. But
it felt different this time. Em and I had forged a bond

that pulled at me in a way that went deep. I wouldn't be back until she was eight months pregnant. I hated that I'd miss so much.

"It's time."

She didn't cry. Her face was pale. She just stood there in her emerald silk robe and bare feet, pink toes gripping the floor just like they had what seemed a lifetime ago. Who knew that a swipe on Tinder would end up like this? If I had known, would I do it again?

Em nodded. "I know." Walking forward, she pressed against me and I folder her in my arms. I closed my eyes, memorizing the feel of her. She was so tiny, and I could feel the bump of her belly. My chest tightened and I had to swallow. I had to be strong for her. Reassure her.

Partings were a bitch.

I squeezed hard, pressed a kiss to the top of her head. She looked up at me and I kissed her. A long, sweet kiss that said a lot of things. Things I hadn't been able to bring myself to put into words. Actions spoke louder, right?

When we parted, her eyes were bright, but still no tears fell. She forced a thin smile.

"You'll text when you land?"

I did my own forced smile, brushing her hair back and tucking a lock behind her ear. "Of course. I'll be at headquarters for a week before I head over to Turkey."

Reluctantly, I picked up the suitcase and headed out the door. The driver popped out and took the suitcase from me, despite my objections, stuffing it into the trunk. I got into the passenger seat, not bothering to climb into the back seat. I wasn't some government dick that needed to be chauffeured.

Em stood in the doorway, silhouetted against the light behind her, looking too small and vulnerable. I didn't look away, didn't even blink, as we backed out of the driveway. And she stood there until I could no longer see her.

I made it to the bathroom just in time.

Slumping on the chill tile, I shakily flushed the toilet, stomach rolling. It had been a minute since I'd thrown up in the morning, though I didn't think this time was due to morning sickness.

It had taken all I had to watch Cal walk out the door and not cry and beg him to stay. But I knew he felt he had to do this, had to be the provider, for his own self-worth and self-esteem as a man. I couldn't take that from him. It was his choice. But that didn't mean I had to like it.

I got up and rearranged my robe, taking a deep breath. I could do this. I was into my fourth month. The second trimester was supposed to be the easiest. And Cal would be back for most of the last and the birth. I was just being a wimp. What's four months? Chad had been deployed for a year at a time, if not more.

It was after five. I didn't have to be at work until nine, but I didn't really feel like sitting around, staring at the walls. Nor did I feel like climbing back into my now empty bed.

On auto-pilot, I disrobed and stepped into the shower, doing all the things. It was only when I was towel-drying my hair and caught sight of my baby bump that the tears came.

"Your Honor, the dog was first purchased by my client. She should get custody."

"The dog has bonded with my client, Your Honor," Jack Donner, the opposing counsel argued.

I heaved an internal sigh. The two had been fighting about the dog for twenty minutes, having to bring it before the judge since they couldn't come to an agreement. Not that I blamed them. I'd fight tooth and nail for Donny and Marie, too.

"Let's set up visitation," the judge suggested.

"My client is adamantly opposed to sharing the dog, Your Honor," Jack replied.

The judge's tone turned from conciliatory to firm. "It's my ruling, like it or not. Counsel, set up a fifty-fifty visitation schedule between your clients." He banged his gavel and that was that.

I conferred with my client for a moment before she departed, not happy but not unhappy either. At least the judge hadn't gone the Solomon split-the-baby route.

Stretching, I tried to ease the kinks in my back. I was thirty-two weeks pregnant and felt every one of those weeks. I was counting down the days until Cal returned. I missed him with a deep ache that wouldn't ease. He called as often as he could, but the time difference was a problem. And talking on the phone or Facetiming was great, but it wasn't the same.

I was also worried about him returning, self-conscious as I was. My body looked a lot different than it had four months ago. Bridget and Carly said I was lucky—I just looked like I'd swallowed a beach ball and hadn't gained weight anywhere else. But I didn't see it that way. To me, my face looked puffy and my ankles and fingers were swollen.

At least it was no longer a hundred degrees. It was much more comfortable to be pregnant in the chill of an Indiana winter than the heat and humidity of late summer. Christmas was days away and I'd had a neighborhood kid come help me drag out boxes of decorations and put up my fake tree. I'd tried a real tree once. Never again.

Therefore, the house looked very festive. I'd bought the nursery furniture and the store even put it together for me for an extra fee. No problem. I had no wish to add *Can assemble crib* to my resumé. I'd chosen a theme of powder blue and a pale yellow. Even if it was a girl, I'd never liked pink and wasn't about to start now. Little ducks and geese were part of the theme, too. I could've hired a decorator but wanted to do it myself.

The furniture was an off-white and the drawers were filled with little onesies and tiny socks. The closet had a handful of outfits on tiny hangers. Things were very real. I still sometimes had nightmares about Kenny, but they'd gradually gotten fewer and further between.

Cal had texted me when he'd boarded the plane for Indy, but it was snowing outside and I had no idea if the flight had been delayed. It might still be on the tarmac in North Carolina for all I knew.

I'd had no idea what to get Cal for Christmas, so just kind of went generic with some shirts and jeans that I thought would make his ass look even more awesome. Have I mentioned how pregnancy hormones are a thing? I couldn't wait to get my hands on Cal, so long as he wasn't utterly turned off by my "basketball," which had the tendency to be very active after I'd decided it was time to go to bed. Of course. Already keeping me from sleeping. I smiled a little to myself.

Heartburn was also an issue, along with the fact that the little one liked to succumb to hiccups every night, which kept me awake. And it looked like tonight was no exception, I thought, as my stomach jumped a little. Weirdest feeling ever, by the way.

I tried all my previous methods of stopping the hiccups. Walking through my bedroom, I jiggled my belly, hoping the baby would be jostled out of his hiccup attack, which shook my entire body about every thirty seconds. A nagging pain began pushing at me, centering in my back, but it couldn't be labor. My due date wasn't yet. I refused to think it was labor. Probably just those early labor pains they warn you about in the books. And I'd read *all* the books. Twice.

Suddenly, I heard the house alarm beep, signaling that someone had entered. I stopped mid-stride. Cal? Was he home? Then the beeps sounded again, telling me that the alarm had been disarmed.

Excitement flooded me and I headed for the stairs, eager to greet him. Then another pain hit, creeping around my belly and down my inner thighs. Ouch.

Cal stepped into the room and I smiled in spite of the cramping pain, my arms reaching out for him. In a moment, he'd swept me up off my feet in a hug that wrapped all around me.

"You're home," I said, stating the obvious. My face hurt from smiling so wide. The relief and joy I felt at seeing him was something I hadn't felt in a very long time.

"I am." He kissed me for a long time, which I reveled in, until another pain hit and I gasped. He pulled back in alarm. "What's wrong?"

"Um, I think I'm going into labor," I said, somewhat breathless. The pain had been sharp, but passed quickly. "Well, like early labor. I'm not due for a few weeks yet."

"Okay. Let's do this."

With his help, we got my shoes on and just put a robe on over my flannel jammies (sexy was not what I'd been going for) and headed down the stairs, pausing by the front door as he reached for the car keys hanging on the wall. Cal wasted no time hustling me into the car.

Another contraction and I felt wetness between my legs. I grew lightheaded with terror.

Pushing my hand down in my pajamas, I felt where it was wet and pulled my hand back out.

There was blood on my fingers.

"Oh god," I breathed. "Cal. I'm bleeding."

Then everything went dark.

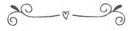

Barely had the words left Em's mouth before she was slumped against the door, out cold.

Blood. Not good. I drove faster.

I had time to think while I drove, and I realized something. Something very important.

I loved Em.

I didn't love her because she carried my child. I just loved *her*. I couldn't say when it had happened. It just had. And now it felt like my life was on the line in the seat next to me.

Slamming the brakes in front of the ER entrance, I shoved the car into park and got Em out of her seat.

"Help! Please help!"

One look from the nurses on duty and I was swarmed. They led me to a curtained exam room and I laid Em down on the bed. A man appeared in a white coat and another nurse brought in a machine to check her vitals. I explained the best I could what Em had told me.

A nurse had begun removing Em's clothes while another had brought heated blankets to cover her. The doctor called for a sonogram machine. I breathed a sigh of relief. He was going to check the baby. His stethoscope pressed against Em's chest, then her belly.

I wanted to stay with Em, but they made me go to the waiting room until they'd finished examing her and she was stabilized. The nurse promised me she'd come get me the moment the doctor said it was okay.

The ER waiting room was full of worried relatives and overworked staff trying to answer questions the best they could. I paced, unable to sit still. Time slowed to a crawl. It only involved my avid pacing from wall to wall. Then I belatedly realized that pacing was affecting others in a negative way, judging by the nervous sidelong glances directed toward me. So, I sat. I watched whatever show was playing on the requisite television in the corner. Kids who were bored with waiting pestered their parents for change to put in the vending machines for snacks.

I stopped bothering the nurses after several times of inquiring. They had better things to do and I knew they'd let me know if Em's status changed.

All of that was very well and good theoretically, but when it was your very life...not so much.

I hadn't been in a hospital before. Not like this. A broken elbow when I was twelve didn't compare to an ER with nurses and doctors and machines all around me, hyper-aware of what appeared to be hypothermia and the fact that I was pregnant.

Quite the attention-getter. Cringe.

But I was grateful, for the baby's sake. I could feel the baby and could sense that everything was all right. I'm not sure how I knew. A mom thing? But I could just tell. And yet I couldn't stop the hand I kept protectively over my swollen abdomen.

The labor pains that had been so intense earlier had abated. The doctor said it was most likely just premature labor. If that was premature labor, what would on-time labor be like?

"Fetus heartbeat is steady at 125."

I was distracted from my thoughts as I heard the words while they slid the sonogram over the cold gel on my belly. A blood pressure monitor had already been attached to my arm and two needles into my forearm, one to take blood and the other to input fluids. I was a hard stick, as they'd found out every time I've given blood. I tried to tell them, but the nurses didn't believe me. Until they had to get the special ultrasound machine to find the veins.

I decided I really hated hospitals, despite the wonderful nurses (who were truly angels on Earth).

Once the vitals were done and the sonogram confirmed the baby was bouncing around just fine and all the needles ever, I was left alone. My nausea had passed and I was now ravenous. With puppy dog eyes, I begged one of those lovely nurses for crackers and some water. I ate the crackers one nibble at a time.

After a while—during which I desperately wished I'd never been brought to the hospital—a nurse popped her head in the curtained room.

"I have a visitor for you," she said with a small smile.

Cal moved past the curtain into the room. Relief rolled through me as he pulled me into a hug. I clung to him as tightly as I could.

"Are you really here?" I whispered. His arrival had been overshadowed by everything else.

"Yes," he replied, pressing a kiss to my forehead. "It's all okay now."

"How'd you get back here?" My voice was thick as tears threatened, but I blinked them back. "I thought visitors weren't allowed."

"I have my ways."

"Slept with the nurse?"

"We have a second date on Saturday."

I couldn't stop my huff of laughter. Something that

was indefinable: when someone "got" you. Cal "got" me. Letting him go, I settled back against the bed.

"It's okay," he murmured, his hand gripping mine. He smoothed my hair back from my face, tucking some behind my ear. "It's all going to be okay. I'm here. And I'm so fucking sorry."

"It wasn't your fault. It just happened." Which was true. And his presence, after so long an absence, broke my resolve, and I began to cry. I didn't want to think. I just needed to feel. And the pressure inside my chest that had been building for months…it finally eased. And I sobbed. And he held me. His constant stream of apologies and reassurances were a beautiful serenade in my ear.

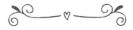

It took several hours to be discharged and all the things and by then, my back was aching. I had a heating pad at home that helped, but it had been a while since I'd gotten to use it. I got dressed again, wincing as I pulled on my flannel shirt and buttoned it up. Back was not happy with the time spent on the very uncomfortable ER bed. My arm hurt from where the IV had been.

Wow. Really hated hospitals. Wasn't thrilled at being pregnant either at the moment.

Since I'd be back here in a few weeks, I supposed I should get used to it. Though the very idea of labor and delivery terrified me. But it wasn't as though I could avoid it. The baby was coming whether I was afraid or not.

"Here, let me help."

Cal was there, doing the thankless job of helping me put on my underwear, pants, and shoes. It was humbling. And deeply affecting. Such a task was very sweet of him, and it took a bit of doing on my part to allow it to be done. My pride might have interfered if my need hadn't been so great. Bending over was beyond me at the moment and it wasn't as though I could see my feet.

We didn't speak much as he ushered me to the car, helped me inside, and then headed home.

The ultrasound had been a relief to see, the tiny human inside with its tiny feet and hands curled into fists. My distraction of Cal being gone all these weeks and my working long hours had served to keep at bay the utter panic of being responsible for a tiny human. To be the mom. A mom. Me.

My breathing hitched and I felt my heart racing. I couldn't get my breath. My hand reached out blindly, finding Cal's warm palm.

"It's okay. I'm here."

To not be alone in this. To have him here. The relief and comfort was like a warm blanket.

Cal helped me into the house and to my bedroom. I felt like a fat cow that could only waddle around. The least sexiest thing ever. But I just needed someone to help right now, because I'd been through a lot. A. Lot. Even walking to my bed felt beyond me.

"Are you thirsty?" he asked, pulling a blanket over me as I settled back into the pillows with a sigh of relief. The pillows eased the pain in my back.

I nodded. "Yes. Please."

"I'll be right back."

The water had ice, thank goodness, because room

temp water was just too European, even for an Anglophile like myself. I'd once asked for ice in a British pub, and they'd given me three cubes. Three. Cubes. And looked at me with that you're-such-an-American look while they were at it. Judgy much?

My head was clearer when he returned. And I had to ask.

"Are you leaving again?" The words felt torn from me.

His eyes met mine, and I saw naked honesty on his face.

"No. I'm not leaving you again. I shouldn't have left in the first place. I should've been here with you. And I'm so sorry."

I looked at him. "I understand. I really do. But I can't do this alone. I'm afraid, too, Cal."

"Don't be. You won't be alone. I'm here now."

"And why should I trust you? That you'll really be there when I need you?"

He took a moment to think before he spoke.

"Because I've realized that I need you. I'm a man, Em. Sometimes I need to be hit over the head."

"Need me?" I wanted more. I wanted all of it.

Cal sat next to me on the bed and took my hand in his.

"Em. I love you. I should've said it months ago. But I was afraid. It felt like the past was repeating itself, and I didn't want to go through the pain of losing you. And I knew if I wasn't around, it might be easier when you did leave."

I tried to follow his train of thought and emotion. "Why would I leave?"

"I had nothing to offer you, Em." The pain on his

face hurt to see. "Broke. Divorced with a kid. Everything I own destroyed. Not even a decent job to provide for you and the baby."

My heart hurt. I squeezed his hand. "I never needed any of that. I just need you." I paused, then smiled. "I love you, Cal. And I want our life together. I married you for a reason and it wasn't because of the baby."

Leaning forward, he kissed me, and it felt like he'd finally come home.

epilogue

YEAH. THE REAL labor was *way* worse than the premature labor.

"You're at a four," the doctor said, draping the sheet back over my bare legs. The nurse helped me back into a more comfortable position. "I'll send in the anesthesiologist for the epidural."

"Oh, heavens to Besty, yes," I breathed. My forehead was bathed in sweat. Cal gently mopped my face with a cool washcloth. I wasn't going for any gold stars or medals. An epidural sounded like the Best Thing Ever after being in labor for nine hours already, six of those in the hospital and three at home.

Thank goodness Cal worked from home now. Mac had changed his position within Down Range Security and he'd never be deployed again. Occasional trips to headquarters in Charlotte, but that was all. I could live with that. And I had Mac to thank for it. Damn it. I wasn't super fond of him, regardless of what he'd done for us.

Cal didn't talk much, which I was grateful for. I

couldn't concentrate on talking right now. All I could think about was resting between contractions. Labor had started around midnight, so I'd already been tired and now I was utterly exhausted. The doctor said my labor was progressing well, but it felt like it was taking forever.

"I guess he doesn't want to move out yet." I managed a wan smile for Cal, whose smile back was tender.

"You're so sure it's a boy, are you?" he asked, teasing. "Maybe I should have you pick some lottery numbers for us."

I huffed a laugh, then another pain hit and my eyes slammed shut. I kept my lips firmly pressed tight, not wanting to make noise. Cal looked as though he was already in pain vicariously every time a contraction came and I absurdly didn't want to cause him more distress. Though, honestly, this was all his fault.

Okay, that was the contraction talking.

The anesthesiologist took her sweet time getting there and I saw Cal's face whiten when she took out the needle. I didn't care how big it was so long as it brought me relief. (The thought hit me and I had to add a "That's what she said" in my head.) I gripped Cal's hand tight as the needle went into my spine, the pain paling in comparison to the contractions I was going through. I was almost at a five by now, halfway home.

Laying back on the bed, the relief was almost immediate. Blessed numbness. And with the numbness came a return of my personality. With the absence of pain, I felt nearly downright cheery, though tired. Cal looked as relieved as I felt. It was hard to see your loved ones in pain, even for something as benign as childbirth.

"I still like the name Mark," I said, reaching for the small Styrofoam cup of ice chips on the table by the bed. They'd allowed me these, but no water.

"And I like Christina," he countered, grabbing the cup and handing it to me.

"I told you, it's a boy." I didn't know why I was so certain, I just was. Not that I'd be disappointed if it was a girl. Just so long as it was healthy and all that. Ten fingers, ten toes. One heart, two lungs. And all the rest.

After another hour where we batted names back and forth and talked about nothing much in particular and I'd only dilated a half a centimeter, I made Cal go get something to eat. He had to be as tired and hungry as I was.

"And not hospital food," I insisted. We were close to a lot of nice restaurants. "Even if it's takeout, get a decent breakfast. I think there's a First Watch close by." I loved breakfast so was slightly jealous that he'd get one and I wouldn't. Sigh.

We argued for a moment, but hey, I was the one giving birth so I got my way by default and he reluctantly left, promising to be back in less than thirty minutes.

"I'm not going to have the baby in thirty minutes, Cal." I rolled my eyes. He ignored me, pressing a kiss to my lips, and left.

It was while he was gone that my folks showed up along with his mom and sister. They came one on top of each other. Cal must've called them once it had gotten to be a decent hour as opposed to the middle of the night. I was a bit overwhelmed and was glad I had the epidural so I was coherent enough to talk to them. When Cal returned—exactly thirty minutes later—I gave him a death glare and he looked properly sheepish. After herding everyone to the waiting room, he came back to where I lay on the bed.

"I didn't want you to be alone," was his excuse.

"So you sicced the whole family on me?" Seriously.

"Sorry." He looked like a little boy caught with his hand in the cookie jar. All he needed was to dig the toe of his sneaker into the dirt to finish off the image. Probably deliberate, the sneak. But it worked.

I reached for his hand and gave it a squeeze. "It's okay. A warning would've been nice, that's all."

Although I couldn't feel the actual pain, I *could* feel the tightening of the muscles in my back and stomach when a contraction would hit. Cal watched the contraction monitor printout, transfixed, showing me the increased intensity and frequency. Time passed. The nurses as well as the doctor routinely checked on me. More time passed.

"You're almost there," the doctor pronounced in the late afternoon. He turned to the nurses and began issuing instructions.

I felt a flash of nerves. The doctor had turned down the epidural medication a couple of hours ago and I could feel the edge of the pains now, which wasn't great. But the Big Event was here and as much as I wanted to meet the little guy, I was a teensy bit scared. Okay, maybe more than a teensy bit.

Glancing at Cal, our gazes met. He seemed to read my mind because he smiled and gave my hand a reassuring squeeze.

"I'm here."

Those simple words, like before, were like a balm and my nervousness eased. Nurses were bustling around me as the bottom half of the bed was removed and the oh-so-wonderful stirrups lifted into place. The doctor was talking to the head nurse in charge of me when I felt it.

"Oh my god," I breathed. "I have to push."

It was a feeling unlike anything I'd ever felt before. Something that went deep into the lizard part of my brain and had been around since the dawn of mankind. The baby was coming.

And wow, did I push. Everything faded into the background, even Cal, while I struggled to move this baby out of my uterus. I was really *really* ready to have my body back to myself, thank-you-very-much.

"I see the head," the doctor proclaimed.

I felt slightly disgruntled at his glee and wanted to growl at him, but another urge to push overtook me, yielding the head. I made a sound then. Not sure what it sounded like, but I was no longer concerned with staying quiet.

The shoulders were no picnic, but then the rest was a breeze. I collapsed back against the bed, drenched in sweat and panting.

"It's a boy!"

I sent a tired but gloating grin at Cal as the squalling of our baby filled the room. In a moment, the doctor had cut the cord (after first asking Cal, who'd turned a bit green and refused) and set the baby on my stomach while he dealt with the placenta.

The feelings that flooded me were indescribable. Immediate, overwhelming love as I took in our son's scrunched up face, still covered in white stuff. Cal was at my shoulder and gently stroked his wet head. It was a kind of love I'd never felt before. I suddenly understood all those moms who, when I'd told them I really wasn't a kid person, had looked at me and simply said, "You will when it's your own."

"He's beautiful," I murmured, my eyes filling with tears.

"Yes, he is." Cal's soft reply made me cry more.

We only had a couple of minutes with him before he was confiscated by the nurses and put under some kind of warming lamp while they cleaned him up. I'd had to have an episiotomy and the doctor spent more time stitching me up than he had delivering the baby. I grimaced, not looking forward to that particular area healing over the next few weeks.

It took a while, but eventually we were left with our swaddled baby, our nurses promising to return shortly to check on us. Cal and I took turns holding him. The baby slept, obviously worn out from the move.

"Mark," I said.

"Mark Christopher," Cal replied.

I looked at him and smiled. "Done."

Thus was Mark Christopher Mackenzie born.

We took him home two days later and began our own version of happily-ever-after, which sometimes included disagreements and Cal sleeping on the couch, but also included a happiness and contentment I'd never before known.

And I had Tinder, of all things, to thank.

THE END

sneak peek!

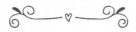

Keep reading for a sneak peek at
Book Two in the Love Online series.

YOU HAVE A MATCH

prologue

I WAS HALFWAY THROUGH my second piece of wedding cake, absently watching Cal and Emmy spin about the dance floor. She looked radiantly happy, her face wreathed in smiles and her eyes only for Cal. And Cal seemed to have eyes only for her, though he was much harder to read. I assumed that was either just how he was or how he'd been trained.

I was happy for Emmy. She was my best friend and of course I was happy for her. She deserved all the happiness life had to offer and more. And I would be an "aunt," which I was looking forward to. A baby to spoil sounded great, even if it wouldn't be mine.

Bridget sat next to me at the table, watery-eyed and sniffling. I didn't blame her. I knew she'd really thought that Rick was The One. Now she'd found out she'd wasted two years of her life on him, only to have him run for the hills when she insisted on determining their future, which she was entitled to do. He'd always seemed like a good guy to me and had treated Bridget well, but obviously I'd been wrong.

Men sucked.

That guy, Mac, caught my eye as I took a sip of champagne. Cal's Best Man, former commander and current boss, he was just slightly taller than me, though admittedly I was on the tallish side for a woman at five-nine. He was probably about five-eleven, but definitely didn't break six foot. He was wide—his shoulders broad and corded with muscle, all the way down his arms. I could feel the unyielding flesh under the tuxedo as we'd walked down the aisle and then later did the requisite bridal party dance with Cal and Emmy. He had a square jaw that looked as though it would hurt you more than it hurt him if you took a swing at him. Deep set eyes that were a dusky blue-gray and yielded nothing of what he was thinking had stared back at me during our dance.

His smile had come easily and he'd been polite, friendly, and even chivalrous. He'd complimented my dress and said I looked "lovely." I'd sent a casual glance at his left hand and hadn't seen a wedding band or, worse, a pale ring from where a band had been removed. I'd seen a few of those before, which had never been a good sign.

Mac had finished chatting with Cal and had come to take his assigned seat next to me. I was immediately self-conscious, my hand going to smooth my hair before I could stop myself. The things a single woman does to appear attractive to the opposite sex. Sigh.

"Gorgeous ceremony and reception," he commented to me.

It wasn't a question so I didn't offer more than a nod and murmur of agreement. I could feel in my bones that I was incredibly attracted to this man and the last thing I needed was another impossible relationship. Honestly, I should just throw in the towel and become the requisite Cat Lady of the neighborhood. But that would require me getting rid of my dog, Honest Abe, my GoldenDoodle that ate my furniture on a regular basis, then puked for good measure. But he loved me.

Another sigh.

"It looks a bit like rain," Mac said. "Smells like it, too."

That caught my attention.

"Smells?" I asked.

"Of course," he replied, his accent thick. And way too alluring. Damn it. "I've been in the desert too long to not smell rain when it's coming."

Alrighty then.

I wasn't like Emmy. I hadn't been married to a military man and had no idea what to say or how to even relate to Mac. Reaching for my conversational skills, which were actually pretty impressive, I replied to him.

"Why were you in a desert?"

"Deployed. But I'm home now. Have my own business. Based out of Charlotte, but I'm setting up a post here in Indy. Think I'll be here for a few weeks."

A few weeks. Was that a hint? If so, count me out. I'd done enough of the short-term flings.

"You'll like it here," I answered noncommittally. "Indy is a wonderful city."

"It might be."

His answer had me glancing his way, eyebrows raised. He met my gaze and smiled. I mentally cursed. He was everything I should avoid...yet wanted to have. The accent alone...sheesh. Could I be more American right now? I mentally rolled my eyes.

"May I drive you home?" he asked. "It looks like they are wrapping things up."

And indeed, Cal and Emmy looked like they wanted nothing more than to go home together and rip each other's clothes off.

"I can call an Uber," I replied. I knew I'd be drinking tonight so had planned ahead and not driven.

"Please. I'd like to be a gentleman and assist you home. You'd be doing my own hubris a favor."

Okay. Well. A girl could only withstand so much. And the sight of Emmy's happiness had led to a sadness that felt like emptiness inside. A handsome man wanted to drive me home? Yes, please.

"Thank you," I said, gathering my clutch purse and getting to my feet. The diaphanous skirt swirled about my legs as the breeze picked up. "I'd appreciate it."

Mac offered his arm and I linked mine through his. He walked us to his car, going slowly and taking small steps, which I appreciated. I had on heels and the rocky driveway was unforgiving if I should take a misstep.

Without a word, he remotely unlocked a black sedan and opened the passenger door for me. I sat on the seat, pressing my knees together before swinging my legs into the car. Not doing a Britney, thank-you-very-much. Manners and etiquette are a thing and I was devout.

Part of me was tired. Mentally. Emotionally. And what would be expected of me when he pulled up to my house? Would I have to invite him in? Yet part of me was resolutely hopeful. That life still had more to offer me. Damn it. And my optimistic nature. When would I learn?

I gave Mac my address and he typed it into his phone, then we were off. We didn't converse, but the silence was comfortable. Not oppressive.

He pulled into my driveway and before I could protest, was out his door and rounding the front of the car to mine.

I stepped out the same way I'd slid in, my clutch purse under my arm and the skirt swirling about my legs. The wind had picked up even more.

Mac offered me his arm and again, I took it. He escorted me to my front door.

I lived in a historical house built in the early 1900's in the English Tudor cottage style. Bridget said it looked like a hobbit lived there. It had three bedrooms, two baths, and a secluded fenced-in back yard with cultivated flower beds and an herb garden. Mosquitoes loved me, so I had to coat myself in repellent before tending to the gardens, but it was worth it. Like Emmy, I loved to cook and the fresh herbs were a pleasure for me.

"Thank you for the ride home," I said, stopping at my front door. I had a fob and had already disarmed the alarm system and lock. Oh, the wonders of modern technology.

"You're very welcome," he replied, politely halting in front of me.

Damn but he looked good. I wanted to throw caution to the wind and invite him in. But where would that lead? Exactly nowhere.

"May I see you again?"

His question took me aback. A man who actually wanted a date and not just a hook-up? Did they even still exist?

"Carly?"

That jerked me out of my surprise. "Yes, Mac. I'd like that." What was I saying?

He smiled. "Excellent." Gesturing to the door, he said, "I'd like to wait until you're safely inside, if you don't mind."

"Um, yeah, of course. I mean, yes. Thank you." My babbling made my cheeks heat in a blush. I was a grown, professional woman. Why was I suddenly reduced to a star-struck teen?

"May I have your number?"

He produced a pen and one of his business cards, handing them to me. I scrawled my phone number onto the back, still wondering what the hell I was thinking.

Mac smiled as I returned the items, sliding them into the pocket inside the lapel of his jacket.

Taking my hand, he pressed a kiss to my knuckles. "Enchanted to meet you, Carly."

My lady parts tingled which was a good and bad thing. I realized my jaw was agape and shut my mouth with a snap.

"Nice to meet you, too, Mac."

His smile turned a bit knowing—which was even more of a turn-on—and he turned to leave. I watched him walk to the car and get in, which was a near religious experience. The man was a woman's wet dream.

I didn't go in the house until he'd pulled out of the driveway and I'd lost sight of his taillights.

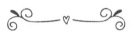

Printed in Great Britain
by Amazon

47104257R00215